### *The Star Walker*

The pack was waiting.

Kurtellicot took another step. He seemed to have found a path.

He could smell leather and fur. He saw—

Wonders!

Stars beyond counting . . . and walking among them were the gods: the founts of life, the taskmasters, the caregivers. They had lifted him up and set him on the path of light.

And yet, he saw something else. For beyond the gods there was something else, something greater, a power to whom even the gods bent low. . . .

# Face of the Enemy

RICHARD FAWKES

*An Imprint of* HarperCollins*Publishers*

EOS
*An Imprint of* HarperCollins*Publishers*
10 East 53rd Street
New York, New York 10022-5299

Copyright © 1999 by Richard Fawkes
Cover illustration © 1999 by Richard Rossiter
ISBN: 0-06-105795-9
**www.eosbooks.com**

First Eos paperback printing: October 2001
First HarperPrism paperback printing: July 1999

Eos Trademark Reg. U.S. Pat. Off. and in Other Countries, Marca Registrada, Hecho en U.S.A.
HarperCollins® is a trademark of HarperCollins Publishers Inc.

Printed in the U.S.A.

10  9  8  7  6  5  4

*To B.K.B.,*
*companion and brother in arms*

# PROLOGUE

**2307**
**IDL DEFENSE SECTOR 33—STATUS RED**
**CASSUELLS HOME**

Grammanhatay shivered. Despite his fur, despite the closely packed bodies of his fellows, he was cold. He pulled his robe closer around him. Here in the dark heart of the *quantaraden* the scent of the pack was strong; it should have been reassuring. It was not.

The gray-furs of the pack had come to him, asking why those who came from beyond the sky wanted him? He did not know. Though he had dwelt among the strangers, he did not know their minds. Huddled with the others, seeking reassurance in his pack-mates' touch, he thought that the gray-furs should have known that he would have no answers. Were *they* not the Wise Ones Who Led? Should not *they* have the answers?

Now his pack-mates keened their fear. The *quantaraden* buzzed with their voices, the deeper notes of the males mixing with those of the high-voiced bearing-mothers. Grammanhatay's voice was joined with the pack's. He was afraid, too.

Once, he had laughed at the pack's fear of the strangers and their strange machines. Strangeness, he had told them, was no threat. He had believed it, then. He would believe it still, had not the ones dressed like the midnight heavens come. Grammanhatay knew their kind. They were a hunter pack. Nightskyers, the gray-furs named them. Soldiers was the name that they called themselves. Grammanhatay knew better. Wreckers, ravagers, stalkers, and despoilers they were. They brought danger wherever they went.

He no longer laughed. Now he was as fearful as any pup, because the pack's outrunners had come home with the word that the Nightskyers wanted Grammanhatay, that they hunted *him*. Their intent was unknown, possibly unknowable.

He shivered in the dark, certain that the pack could not protect him from the Nightskyers.

Soon after the outrunners had brought their warning, the gray-furs had gathered around Grammanhatay, forming their communing pack, asking Grammanhatay why the Nightskyers sought him.

How could he know? He was not of their Nightskyers' pack! Who could know the minds of another pack's hunters?

The leaders questioned him until the setting sun sent long shadows sprawling across the *quan*'s dry clay walls. Though speaking of his life among the strangers made Grammanhatay uncomfortable, he answered as best he could. Just as evening finished its climb up the arroyo's wall, an outrunner came. "They are taking away all the Trademakers and the Questioners," he said.

Could that be true? This was not Nightskyer territory. They had no rights here. How could they take anything? Their desire to take Grammanhatay had been outrageous enough. Now this! What could the others have done to rouse the ire of the Nightskyers?

Grammanhatay had lived among a group of Questioners until they had all died. There were other Questioners abroad in the wide plains beyond the pack's canyon, but

Grammanhatay had never sought them. Their world was not his world anymore; he was done with that life. The pack was home and safety and love.

But would it be, now that the Nightskyers sought him?

"The Nightskyers will come," he told the pack. "They have eyes keener than any hunter's, and they can sniff out what they cannot see. They will find me."

"Our hunters know the land," Shessone the Bright-Eyed, grayest of the gray-furs, said with pride. "They will hide you."

"It will do no good," Grammanhatay said forlornly.

He told them how the Nightskyers would find him. The gray-furs looked at Grammanhatay suspiciously. The bearing-mothers clustered together and made the sign against evil, as if his scent had turned strange.

"I am of the pack," Grammanhatay insisted.

The gray-furs withdrew and conferred. At last they came back. Shessone, leader of the leaders, rubbed his muzzle against Grammanhatay's cheeks.

"You are of the pack," Shessone said.

The bearing-mothers gathered around him. Grammanhatay felt safe again. He was of the pack! The pack was home and safety and love.

IDLS *Resplendent* was an *Honorable*-class cruiser, 732 meters from the probe tips of her forward weapon array to the rims of her main thruster exhaust nozzles. She was not the largest ship in the Interstellar Defense League's space force, but she was far from the smallest. She was the lead ship of Sector 33's Fringe Squadron, and Colonel Christoph Stone was pleased to be her master.

For the moment, *Resplendent*'s bridge remained lit for normal operations. Cool, blue light in the range preferred by the predominantly Eridani crew lit the space. From his commander's couch Stone could oversee each and every one of the staff officers working diligently at their stations. Chatter was minimal, less than would be expected for normal operations, but this was no normal operation. There was tension—no doubt of it—but it wasn't cutting into professional efficiency. Though Stone expected no less of his select crew, he was pleased. *Resplendent* and her crew were not meant for the nursemaiding required by their mission's first phase. But orders were orders, and soldiers obeyed them. And he had good soldiers under his command.

Most of the main viewer was filled with the variegated brown arc of a planet, bright with reflected sunlight against the midnight of space. The Mercantile Union had named this planet Cassuells Home, after its indigenous intelligent species, and had invited scientists from nearly every star nation to come and study the natives. The Mercantile Union was only a memory now, shattered by the Remor invaders; but League scientists were among those who had come to Cassuells Home. Their reports had convinced MilForce Intelligence that the Cassuells were connected to the Remor enemy. Intel had convinced Strategic Command and StratCom had dispatched the Fringe Squadron to deal with the situation.

Had it only been four years since the enemy had first appeared? Stone knew too well that it was so. He had been sitting in a café in Marionberg on Rift's Verge when he'd heard the initial report of first contact. Who didn't remember where they were that day?

Janette Nichelle, a celebrated reporter of the Interstellar News Service, had been in the Nova Europa system on vacation when a huge, silent ship appeared out of hyperspace near the system's jump station. She had wangled her way aboard the vessel sent to investigate and had been broadcasting one of her famous "on-the-spot" commentaries when the enemy attacked. Stone still was chilled by the way her breathy excitement had turned to stark fear. Like so many others, he had been filled with dread when Nichelle's broadcast was abruptly flooded by jamming static and all communication lost.

The repetitive drone of the enemy's commo channel blanketing static had given the enemy their name: Remor. It was the closest to communication humankind had gotten with their new foe. Until recently, no one even knew what sort of life-form these implacably hostile aliens were.

The Remor laid waste to the Nova Europa system. They went on to do the same to the second settled system they entered. And the third. The pattern remained the same: no communication, no warning, no negotiation, and no mercy—just combat, death, and destruction. The Remor destroyed all the Humans that they came across, blotting the heavens with a swath of implacable death.

Humankind had been unable to stop them and had done little to slow them down. Across the stars, people had pleaded and prayed for something to be done. The Interstellar Defense League had been formed, but so far the IDL's forces had not been able to do much to hurt the enemy. The action here on Cassuells Home was going to change that. The League's strategists intended that the Remor be hurt here.

But first the squadron was tasked with the evacuation of all Human personnel.

"Commander." It was Warrant Officer Consaweo, at the long-range scan station. "We're getting a magnetic disturbance in the shadow of the seventh planet."

Stone felt a cold sweat break out on his brow. "A Remor emergence?"

"I'm not sure. There's a lot of interference from the planet."

"Make sure, Officer Consaweo. We're not going to jump at shadows." If it was a Remor emergence, it was confirmation of what StratCom believed about the Cassuells. The Fringe Squadron could be facing deadly problems. Stone didn't intend to have his command caught with their pants down. He swiveled to face Communications. "Officer Kent, put the squadron on alert."

"Will do, Commander."

Back around to Ground Operations. "Status on the ground teams, Lieutenant Chee?"

Chee's answer was ready. "Three shuttles en route to orbit, sir. Another two loading. We've got collection teams inbound to the landing site with most of the remaining civilians."

"Most?"

"All on-planet personnel accounted for except one, Commander. The assigned team is having trouble locating him. He didn't respond to the recall and he is apparently refusing to answer any commo calls. The Mercantile Union rep is recommending that we forget about him."

"Who is this allegedly forgettable person, Lieutenant Chee?"

Chee referred to her screen. "Professor Kurt Ellicot, sir. An socioxenologist." The ground operations officer's expression turned sour. "He's a Concordat citizen, sir."

The Serenten Concordat was one of the largest star nations, and not yet a part of the Interstellar Defense League. IDL Command wanted good relations with the Concordat. The representative of the ravaged Mercantile Union might be able to forget this professor, but Stone didn't have a similar option. The Concordat wouldn't be happy with the League if League forces abandoned one of their citizens, and if the Concordat was unhappy with the League, StratCom would be unhappy with Stone. Strat-

Com's unhappiness was something a career officer avoided whenever possible.

Consaweo interrupted Stone's thoughts. "Commander, computer gives a seventy-prob that the magdist is a Remor emergence."

Too high a probability to ignore. Yet they hadn't picked up any drive signatures. So far there were no enemy ships inbound on their position. How long would that last? Stone felt the first subtle poundings of a headache start at the back of his skull. If there were Remor ships out there, they *would* attack. The squadron would be pressed to finish the evacuation, possibly prevented from accomplishing its mission. That was unacceptable. The operation had to be accelerated. "Lieutenant Chee, I want Ellicot found and brought in. Now."

Chee looked unhappy. "He is reported to be traveling the outback with a group of indigs. He'll be hard to lo—"

"Hard, Lieutenant Chee? I don't recall asking for a difficulty assessment. Have our people inform Professor Ellicot that the only traveling he's authorized to do is with us, out of this system."

Stone wasn't about to leave anyone to the Remor's nonexistent mercy. Not even a Concordat socioxenologist.

Missiles buzzed around Anders Seaborg. Most shattered on the buff sandstone boulders sheltering his troops, but some found targets. Not that it mattered.

Anders plucked out a flint-tipped arrow from the mesh-shielded elbow-joint of his hardsuit. The arrows couldn't hurt him, not even when they found one of his suit's weak points, as this one had. Arrows! *Saint Sebastian, come out of retirement and preserve me!* He tossed the flimsy missile away.

He sent a pulse burst at the archers. The energy packets

shattered splinters off the rocks above. Several troopers followed his example. The fusillade drove the hostiles back. Anders's mikes picked up their yips of pain. Some had been wounded. Good—they'd keep their heads down for a while now. He could review the situation undisturbed.

The hostiles were a tribe of the indigenous bipeds. Four years of fighting the faceless Remor enemy made it hard to accept these indigs as relatives of the technic enemy who had obliterated more than a dozen Human colonies.

The Cassuell indigs were smaller than Humans, were tool-users, and built warrenlike adobe structures. They were something close to mammalian, but they certainly weren't human. Humans didn't have furry pelts, twitching black noses on pointed snouts, or the Cassuells' god-awful stink. When the reports had talked about the Cassuells' reliance on scent, Anders had not imagined their stink. Being close to one without a breather made him want to puke.

Command didn't say how exterminating a bunch of Stone-Age savages was supposed to hurt the star system–ravaging Remor fleets, but it wasn't Anders's job to question strategy. The enemy was the enemy, and the Remor had shown no mercy to Human colonies. Why should humans show mercy to Remor colonists?

Command wanted to minimize trouble with the indigs until all the Humans were evacuated, so blowing this indig settlement to hell and gone wasn't yet an option.

"No grenades," he said, reminding Milano. The man was swapping out his pulse generator for a grenade launcher. Not for the first time Anders wished his platoon was all Eridani veterans like himself. An Eridani wouldn't jeopardize the mission to satisfy personal desires. Anders had slipped badly enough in firing at the indigs.

Milano wasn't listening. Anders laid his hand over

Milano's and prevented the man from finishing what he was doing. "I said, no grenades."

"Let me shred 'em, Lieutenant," Milano begged. "For Queen."

Milano and Queen had come to MilForce from the Lancastrian Commonalty. Anders understood Milano's desire to have revenge for his comrade. He felt it himself—Queen had been under Anders's command, Queen's death was his responsibility. But the mission orders stood, and that was something Anders understood better than Milano; Lancastrians, like a lot of the troops belonging to some of the other League partners, lacked proper discipline.

"Do I have to repeat myself?"

"But they killed Queen," Milano whined.

"And, by St. Michael, they'll pay for it. But not yet. Switch back to your pulse generator."

As Milano reluctantly obeyed, Anders looked to where Queen lay, crushed by the ton or so of rock that the indigs had tumbled on him from above. The dust of his fall was still settling. There was no need to check on him; Anders's command display showed him all he needed to know. Queen's locator glowed red: the trooper was dead. It might have been the fall, or maybe one of the rocks had pierced the carapace, but one thing was clear: Queen's hardsuit hadn't been tough enough to save him.

Anders stared up at the *quan* nestled in its gash in the cliff face and at the natural bulwark that shielded the indig village. Queen's fate likely awaited anyone attempting to scale the near-vertical cliff, but climbing wasn't the only way that Anders's platoon could get at the indig settlement. When he'd thought that they had surprise on their side, a sneaky climb up to the settlement had seemed the best option. Now the noisy approach had become the most reasonable course. Lifters could put his men on top of the mesa. From there, they could rappel down and swing into the cleft where the Cassuells had wedged their adobe warren, reaching the *quan* without a dangerous climb made more dangerous by the hostiles' rock slides. Rocks didn't roll *up*.

Linking to battalion, he made his request and got an answer he didn't like. All of the landing force's lifters were occupied; he'd have to wait his turn. The delay would blow away his timetable, along with any hope of a good efficiency rating on the mission. *No*, he realized, *any hope of a good rating had died along with Queen*.

He sent two men to scout along the base of the mesa for a trail that might offer a way to the top. It was a long shot, but better than just waiting until the lifter arrived. Things were fairly quiet. Without the squad making a push for the *quan*, the indigs conserved their supply of rocks. Every couple of minutes an indig would pop up to send an arrow or two down at them. Milano would return fire, but as long as the trooper stuck with pulse bursts, Anders didn't object. The quarry wasn't likely to be one of the archers and nobody was going to cry over a few flashed hostiles.

"Brass alert," Sergeant Fiske announced on the platoon's channel.

As the warning finished, Anders picked up the sound of a blower coming up the draw. A library query offered a ninety-prob that the blower was a GLT Mark-8 Armored Scout Car in IDL service. Curious. Fiske had said that there was incoming brass and scout blowers weren't the usual transport for brass.

The racket echoed off the steep rock walls, alerting all but the deaf and the dead that it was coming. Anders had left the platoon's vehicles two klicks back to preserve the surprise of their approach. There was no more need for surprise, but Anders was annoyed that the brass in the approaching blower hadn't checked on the tactical situation. A sensible officer would have linked in before roaring his way into an operation. This guy was probably some goff of a self-important data-servant who just couldn't be bothered walking. To St. Michael's sorrow there were enough of them in the service.

Anders moved down to meet the blower, wanting to make sure that the machine stopped out of sight of the indig archers. The goff was probably using his own driver, and a back-range driver couldn't be counted on to be bright enough to pick a sheltered parking spot. Getting an officer sniped by hostiles wasn't going to improve Anders's rating any.

Anders's suspicion that the visitor was a goff of the first water started to solidify to conviction when the blower skidded to a halt and a hardsuited figure vaulted over the coaming of the Mark-8's crew basket. In contrast to the tawny ochre of the platoon's hardsuits, the newcomer's was set to parade colors: deep spacer blue, with silver trim highlighting selected plates. The scheme was real impressive on a parade ground, but here in the field the dark, unnatural color made the goff a target, a typical ship trooper's mistake. If the hostiles had been armed with serious weapons, the goff would have been a statistic by now.

Anders looked closer to see who this fool was. Although the suit's shiny surface was already dulled by dust, the rank and name flashes showed clear. The newcomer was Major Ersch, an Intelligence and Reconnaissance specialist. And the nationality bar proclaimed him Eridani.

Drawing himself to attention, Anders saluted while he reevaluated. Ersch was attached to Commander Stone's staff and the Stone Man didn't take on goffs. Scuttlebutt said that the major was nobody's fool. The no-brain approach didn't fit.

"What's the problem, Lieutenant?" Ersch barked as he stomped up.

"The indigs are holed up in a settlement wedged into the cliff face and they have the only access route blocked, sir. I've already lost one man trying to use that approach."

"That approach is the *only* access?"

"I've put in a call for a lifter to take us up to the top of the mesa. Once the platoon's up there, we can rappel down and—"

"How long?"

"Battalion C and C said thirty minutes before they can send a bird out this way. Another twenty to—"

"Too long," Ersch snapped. "The situation's changed. *Resplendent* reports Remor ships entering the system three AUs out."

Three astronomical units might as well be an infinite distance to a slogger, but IDL starships could cross the distance in a matter of hours. Remor ships could do it faster. The situation surely had changed. It would take at least three hours to gather the search teams and lift all of the landing force to *Resplendent*'s orbit.

The major tilted his head back to look at the cliffside settlement. "These *are* the indigs Ellicot was seen with?"

Ersch had his mind on Anders's mission, which was where Anders's own mind should have been. "Their tribal markings match, sir."

"Then we force passage and get our man."

Which meant a frontal assault. Facing the Cassuells in an open field wasn't a problem, but this *quan* was effectively a fortress. Its position let the indigs use rocks and gravity as weapons. Queen had proven that those weapons *could* stop a slogger in a hardsuit. The hostiles surely had more rocks ready for any climbers attempting to reach the settlement.

"I'll take point, sir," Anders said. According to MilForce

doctrine, a platoon's officer was not expected to lead a single-file assault. But Anders was Eridani, and Eridani didn't *send* men into death's parlor, they *led* them.

Ersch was Eridani, too. Their eyes met and Ersch nodded, understanding. Vaulting back into the Mark-8's crew basket, he swung the heavy pulse gun around. "Pick me a spot, Lieutenant. I'll cover your climb."

Grit shifted down from the ceiling as the *quantaraden* shuddered under another blast from the Nightskyers' heavy weapon. Between the deafening crashes, Grammanhatay could hear the hunters shouting as they valiantly, vainly, tried to defend the *quan*. Bows and arrows could not prevail against lightning.

The Nightskyers were coming for Grammanhatay because they wanted the Questioner. They didn't realize that they were too late. The Questioner was gone. They didn't understand.

Closing the shutter, Shessone turned from the window slit. The thin wood did little to shut out the cries of the dying. The gray-fur's voice was sad. "The hunters have failed. The Nightskyers have entered the *quan*."

No one had really expected any other result. It would not be much longer now.

The pack huddled close together, seeking comfort from each other's warmth. All that stood between them and the strangers was a makeshift brace against the *quantaraden's* door. The end would not be long in coming.

Anders burst through the door, weapon ready, but there were no indig warriors clustered to meet him. Light streamed past him, spilling onto the stamped-earth floor. The hovel was occupied, but only by twenty or so gray-furred oldsters.

The Cassuells recoiled from him, shielding their eyes against the glare. Against the back wall they huddled together, squirming around each other, intertwining bodies and limbs until it was hard to tell one from another. The indigs crowded together whenever they got excited. They also yowled. These were yowling to wake the dead.

Anders realized with a start that one voice stood out among the howling. "We cry for help, but are not heard," it said. Anglic words, spoken by a human voice. It could only be Ellicot. Anders caught a glimpse of pale, naked skin among the jumble of gray-furred bodies. Anders opened his link. "Major, I've found him."

"Get him the hell out of there," Ersch responded.

Anders waded into the pile of indigs. He felt Cassuell fists and claws and even teeth turned against his hardsuit. To no effect, of course.

"Professor Ellicot, you've got to come along with us now," Anders said.

The flash of flesh disappeared under writhing fur. Anders ordered his team to rally on him, telling off Milano and Wilson to keep a watch. It took all of them to get Ellicot separated from the natives, who, having finally realized that they had lost the fight, retreated and huddled together. But when two troopers finally hauled Ellicot out, Anders wasn't sure that what they had secured was human after all. A man, yes, but human?

The wild-eyed Ellicot was draped in the pelt of a Cassuell. The skin from dead Cassuell's head was draped over Ellicot's head like a hood and tied beneath his chin by a thong. Other thongs secured the pelt's paws to his wrists. The legs were wrapped around Ellicot's waist and the paws tied together at the claws. The fur hung on the begrimed socioxenologist like a ratty cloak. The only other things he wore were Cassuell bangles, beads, and fetishes. Some he wore under the pelt, others over it as though they belonged to the dead Cassuell. It was a grotesque sight.

"What have they done to you, man?" Anders asked.

Ellicot hissed and gobbled at him—indig jabber.

Appalled, Anders ordered his men to take Ellicot down to the blowers. As they dragged their captive to the center of the room, one of the furred indigs left the huddle. The Cassuell, battered and bleeding, limped to Anders and drew itself up. Its speech was halting, and blurred by a buzzing accent, but its words were Anglic.

"He not wants to going," the indig oldster said. "He Cassuell now. Grammanhatay. Our brother."

Anders couldn't believe what he was hearing. "Your *brother*? By St. Michael, he's not even your *species*!"

Looking at the pelt-draped Ellicot, Anders wasn't entirely sure that the man belonged to *his* species.

Ellicot spoke. "The Nightskyers don't understand, Shessone."

"To them speak, Grammanhatay," the indig said. "To them make understanding."

Ellicot's face contorted. He seemed confused, frustrated, and angry all at once. Anders was willing to listen. He *wanted* to understand how a human could wrap himself in a dead alien's skin.

Ellicot was still struggling with himself when Major Ersch's dark hardsuit appeared in the entranceway.

"What the hell's the hold up?" he snapped. "Get a move on here. The lifter's leaving in five. You don't want to be here when *Resplendent* downloads."

Anders didn't. Neither did the troopers. They tugged on Ellicot's arms to get him moving. The man snarled and started to struggle, kicking and clawing at the men holding him.

"You can't do this!" he screeched.

The troopers hesitated. Forcing civilians wasn't a normal part of the job.

"I don't belong to you!" Finally accepting that he wasn't going to break free, Ellicot slumped, weeping. "You have no authority."

Ersch's featureless visor turned to Ellicot. "War makes authority."

At the major's nod, the troopers hustled Ellicot out of the hovel. Anders followed, keeping a cautious eye on the indigs. But they made no move. Maybe their honor had been satisfied by their earlier defense of their "brother," or maybe they were just being smart.

"Inform *Resplendent* that we are away."

Major Ersch's words echoed across the bridge, saying what Stone needed to hear. He gave the necessary orders.

He settled back in his command couch and called for images from the monitors that his troops had placed on-planet. A montage of peaceful scenes cascaded across the viewer. Isolating the monitor nearest the indig settlement where the last evacuee had been secured, he set the viewer to display that image only. The fluffy white clouds blackened and roiled as the terawatt lasers punched through them. He saw the Cassuell village start to burn. The League's first blow was falling against the resources of the enemy. He'd seen enough; he killed the monitor.

The eradication strategy was difficult to square with Eridani honor, but orders were orders. There was honor in following orders.

"As soon as the shuttle's aboard, we boost for the jump point. Evasive track, Lieutenant Waters."

The con officer looked dismayed at Stone's order to run from the inferior force. "Aren't we going to take on the Remor ships, sir?"

He was not about to censure Waters for questioning him, especially not when he wanted to fight just as badly.

"We were sent here to do a job." Beneath them, Cassuells Home burned under *Resplendent*'s lasers. Soon missiles would be diving into the atmosphere. They *were* taking the war to the enemy. He just wished it could be open, honorable warfare. But soldiers did the jobs they were told to do. "The job's not done till we return with our passengers. Right now, we have no business engaging enemy forces."

He didn't like turning his back on a live enemy force, especially an enemy force he could beat. But Eridani followed orders.

"We are not prohibited from defending ourselves, however. Should any of the Remor ships try to intercept, flash them."

# 2317

## Part I

# Circumambient Attraction

## 1

**PAN-STELLAR COMBINE**
**CANESSA SYSTEM**

Sitting huddled over his command console aboard PSCS *Byrd*, Ken Konoye figured himself for the most luckless man in the Pan-Stellar Combine. Every time he reran the sim the answer came out the same. By all rights the probe should have returned by now.

The changes they'd made to the Serrie-built BIN–6100 probe's physical parameters couldn't be the problem. Nothing they'd done should have made a difference. Sure, the 6100 was designed for courier work rather than scientific exploration, but it was a damned *military* design. It was *supposed* to have redundancies. It was *supposed* to have a seventy-eight percent probability of returning from a war zone. So where was it?

God, it couldn't have landed in a war zone, could it?

That was a possibility that didn't bear thinking on. The Remor couldn't have penetrated *that* deep into Human space. If they had, *surely*, he would have heard. There had to be another answer. So why wasn't he finding it?

According to the sims, there were *no* problems. The probe should be sitting a hundred kilometers off *Byrd*'s starboard-ventral bow. Only it wasn't there.

This was crazy! Worse, it was *wrong*! He knew his figures were good. The PSC Survey Office had approved them. He checked the computations himself a dozen times on the trip out here. Winnie had checked them, too. The numbers were on. They were!

So where was his probe? After all, this hole was an all or nothing translator; the probe went, having achieved a safe translation, or it didn't go. It wasn't sitting out there, so it must have made translation.

So why hadn't it come back? Where was it?

He tried more sims, going so far as to input variations in the amount of local interstellar dust. He got the same answer, the same *damned* wrong answer. Vexed, he stared at his screens and willed them to show the probe's return, to be right, but nothing changed.

Maybe the probe had picked up some hull ionization. He started another sim.

"Captain?"

Jane Van Der Noogt's voice tugged at Konoye. He wanted to get an answer, not give one. Hell, this sim was turning out like all the others. He might as well answer. He returned his attention to the bridge of the PSCS *Byrd*.

The *Byrd* was a typical ship of the Combine Survey Office: a dispersed-structure vessel, all modules and pods and arrays. Officially she was commissioned as part of the Pan-Stellar Combine fleet, but she wasn't really a military ship. For that matter the PSC fleet wasn't a military fleet, but a hodgepodge affair of armed merchant and scientific vessels. Commerce was what interested the cartels who controlled the Combine's Governing Committee. The Survey Office existed to make sure that there would always be new ports for Combine traders.

Though Jane Van Der Noogt held the shipboard rank of executive officer, she didn't look the part. She wore an unadorned military-style jumpsuit that made her more like an overaged student than the eminent researcher she was. She scorned the badges of rank—not her style, she said—

although she said nothing of *his* wearing the marks of his captaincy. Of course his rank, and hers, were only temporary, just the Combine's way of doing business. Putting entrepreneurs and scientists in charge of ships was the sort of arrangement that other star nations often ridiculed, but it worked for the Combine. After all, interest held in the ship's mission was more important than spacefaring experience, especially when you had computers that could fly the ship better than most humans.

Jane was exec because she was a part of Konoye's research team, and she'd worked nearly as hard as he had on getting this survey up and running. Now Konoye saw a familiar look drawing out Jane's horsy face into a long frown. Clearly she had been trying to get his attention for some time while he was focused on the sims.

"I said that we've got the second probe configured," she said, with just a hint of her usual exasperation. She must be as worried as he was about the first probe's fate. She started reeling off the list of modifications.

He didn't listen. The backup BIN–6100 was supposed to have been unnecessary. He'd only taken it aboard to satisfy overly-cautious Combine regulations requiring redundancy on all remote systems. He had resented it when the Committee factor had reminded him of the regulation when examining Konoye's manifest. He had resented it even more when the factor had refused to authorize the use of any of the Committee's funding to acquire the damned thing. The second probe had cost Konoye all of his savings. When it went out, more than just the mission's success would be riding on it.

"—disaster waiting to happen. Gerry's programmed it to do an immediate download into the main system memory, just in case, to safeguard the data."

"But it's got hardened systems, military systems. It shouldn't—"

"You weren't listening, were you? I was talking about the damned, jury-rigged stellar cartog system, not the whole damned probe. Jesus, Ken! Where the hell is your brain?"

"Sorry. I'm just worried."

"As if no one else is? You're not the only investor."

"I know that." It was just— "You don't think it—the first probe, I mean—you don't think it was deliberately destroyed, do you?"

"What? Why would anyone do such a thing? Everybody aboard knows what it means if we chart the route."

"I didn't mean sabotage." He didn't really want to put voice to his fears, afraid that somehow that might make them happen, but he wanted someone to tell him that he was wrong. "I meant the Remor."

"Don't be ridiculous, Ken. Their ships haven't been seen within a hundred light-years of this sector. In fourteen years the Remor haven't ever bothered Combine space. I hardly think that they're starting now."

"You're right, of course." It really did have to be a technical problem. It did, *really*. And technical problems could be fixed. Murphy had been given his propitiatory sacrifice. Now it was time for things to go right. "Well, no money to be made wasting time. I want to make sure this probe comes home. Let's take whatever time we need, because we'll be wasting a lot more than time if we don't get it back."

"We've covered all the bases," Jane said, mouth quirking in irritation.

He knew that she didn't like it when her competency was questioned, however obliquely, but more than her ego was at stake here. So he reminded her. "We *all* thought that before we launched the first one. We were wrong then. We might be wrong now. Let's just take a last look before we toss our last probe down a rat hole."

That "last look" took a week of conferences, recalibrations, arguments, sims, refitting, more arguments, more sims, adjustments, and more sims until everyone, *everyone*—Konoye made sure of that, on record—was satisfied that they had covered every conceivable contingency. Still, Konoye watched nervously as his second—and last—expensive BIN–6100 ignited its thrusters and accelerated toward the jump point until, with the flare of translation, it was gone.

## SERENTEN CONCORDAT
## SOMMERSET SYSTEM

Knowing that he was dealing with a computer-generated reality didn't make the sensations feel any less real to Kurt Ellicot.

The dirt under his feet was moist and springy. The scent of the coramaranth blossoming at the forest edge almost overpowered the rank odor of the Mremm gathered around him. Unknown songbirds lilted a chorus from the trees and the Mremm chattered every time their chieftain responded to Kurt's questions or statements. The rich, dark taste of the local coffee-equivalent lingered on his tongue even as its aroma wafted from still-steaming palaver cups. A breeze cooled him in the few spots exposed by the voluminous native *shugana* he wore. His skin itched where the wool rubbed against it.

He didn't have to endure the itch, and not just because it could be programmed out. He didn't need to be wearing the Mremm *shugana*, his doctor said so. But his doctor also said that the sim needed to be as real as possible. If these computer Mremm had been real, and he had really been studying them, then he would have been wearing the *shugana*. Hence he wore the *shugana* here. The moccasin principle was one of the basic tenets of socioxenology; as expounded by his great-grandfather's seminal treatise on the subject, it stated that the least one could do in trying to understand an alien species was to wear their clothes. Many socioxenologists went further. Far further.

He had.

But that had been long ago. Long ago, when he had been a working socioxenologist. When he'd been sane.

He wasn't quite sane anymore, or so the doctors said. They had hopes for him, and plans to bring him back into the fold. Hence, the computer-generated world where his virtual self met with computer-generated Mremm.

The Mremm weren't bad for unreal aliens. They had customs that appeared to have developed logically from their putative history. They had a religion, simple and animistic, full of references to native wildlife, lifestyles, and to vaguely remembered "historical" events. They had individual personalities and interacted with each other when Kurt wasn't around, resulting in changes that he couldn't anticipate. They were, in short, complex, and quite convincing—if you didn't know any better. However, Kurt did know better. These "aliens" had been built by a Human mind. There was nothing in their heads that was not put there by a Human. Doctor Nellis had accused him of not being up to the challenge. Had the Mremm been real, the doctor might have been right, not because of Kurt's lack of ability but rather because of his lack of desire. He was very tired.

Yet despite Doctor Nellis's accusation, there was no challenge here. It was the non-Human that had always drawn him, the strange, the unfamiliar. But this? This was no mystery that he cared to solve. There were plenty of people who sought to understand the Human heart. Kurt Ellicot wasn't one of them. He knew that he hadn't a prayer of knowing anything about the human heart.

Clarise told him so almost daily.

He wasn't talking to Clarise now. Now he was dickering with the local Mremm chieftain, who had just said something. The Mremm chieftain looked at him expectantly. Kurt wasn't fooled. He knew that it was Doctor Nellis behind that face. Kurt excused his inattention, claiming a misunderstanding of the language, and asked the chief to repeat himself. He played the game.

What better word than "game" was there for what he was doing? The only thing for him to do was to give the textbook response. That was easy enough—he had written a textbook on the subject.

He went through the motions, just like he went through them with Clarise and the kids.

It hadn't always been that way. At least that's what he thought, even though Clarise told him otherwise. She told him that the happy times he remembered were a lie. She said there had never been a time he hadn't just gone through the motions, put up a façade. They'd had some spectacular fights when he'd disagreed, but he didn't argue that point with her anymore.

Sometimes, when she'd had a good day, she'd accept his façade. She wouldn't complain or accuse. Things would be the way he remembered. He liked those days, and wanted more of them, but he wouldn't get them if he failed to satisfy Doctor Nellis.

The dickering went smoothly. The Mremm chieftain was pleased with Kurt. To show him honor, the Mremm offered to induct Kurt into the tribe. Kurt couldn't refuse without wrecking the trust he'd worked to build. He didn't refuse. The rituals surrounding the induction were imaginative, equal parts of physical and mental mortification. Kurt bore the trials with serenity. The Mremm hailed the new member of their tribe, but Kurt remained apart. Not being a Mremm, how could he not?

He retired to his dome shelter and lay down on the cot. He was asleep in a moment, waking almost at once, but not in the dome. He lay on a medical couch in his doctor's office; where he had been all along.

He consulted his watch. Five hours had elapsed since the start of the virtuality session. His memories told him that he'd spent eleven standard months on the Mremm homeworld. Therapeutic virtuality could provide tremendous apparent time compression, far more than legal, commercial sims. Following the doctor's orders, he breathed slowly and steadily as she removed the drug taps.

"There," she said as she finished. "All flushed out. Feeling okay?"

"Fine, Doctor."

"Good. That was a very positive session, Kurt."

"Thank you, Doctor."

"No, no. Don't thank me. You're the one doing the work here." She beamed at him. " Keep it up and I think you'll get a positive report on your spring review. Your progress has been very good."

"I'm glad to hear that, Doctor."

"Are you finding the Mremm more of a challenge than the Yanellocyx?"

The Yanellocyx were real aliens, but Kurt wasn't allowed to interact with them, just with their Human-programmed and Human-directed computer simulations.

"The Mremm are intriguing."

Doctor Nellis smiled, nodding in satisfaction.

He'd given the right answer. Her right answer. But the Mremm were not the answer for him. He needed real aliens if he was to prove that he had overcome the weakness he'd succumbed to on Cassuells Home. Early in his therapy, Kurt had tried to explain to Doctor Nellis the difference between real and simulated aliens. He had been only just coming back to humanity in those days, and he hadn't done a very good job of explaining anything. By the time Kurt felt capable of tackling the subject again, they were well along in Doctor Nellis's program. She'd already begun saying that he was making progress, and he hadn't wanted to jeopardize that perception. Progress meant release from the "cure's" constraints on his life.

He knew the difference between real aliens and any of the virtual ones that Doctor Nellis conjured for him. There could be no mistaking the two. Not for him. He'd lived among the Cassuells. The computer's aliens weren't Cassuells, and at their fundamental core there was no way that they could ever be anything like the Cassuells. There were many reasons that was so, not the least of which was that there were no Cassuells anymore. They were all dead, all the packs. From pups to gray-furs—dead. Even the Unassailable, the leaders—dead. Even Shessone the Bright-Eyed had proved assailable in the end. His bones were ashes, tossed without prayer onto the wind, leaving his soul doomed to a packless life in the afterworld. Dead. All dead. Even Grammanhatay was dead.

Sometimes Kurt felt as though he were dead, too.

He smiled at Doctor Nellis and shook her hand. No, no, he wouldn't forget his next appointment. Yes, yes, he was looking forward to it, too. Yes, another step on the road to recovery.

How could he not look forward to another step on the road to recovery?

## IDL DEFENSE SECTOR 32—STATUS ORANGE
## GRENWOLD SYSTEM

"Well, Lieutenant, what do you make of it?" Commander Bunin's voice was clipped, strained.

Lieutenant Anders Seaborg guessed that the commander wasn't getting the answers he wanted from either the Grenwold planetary authorities or his own staff. Lieutenant Colonel Pinzón and most of IDLS *Shaka's* ground troops had been left on security duty in the Nos System, making Seaborg, commander of the last platoon remaining aboard *Shaka*, senior ground forces officer. That made it his responsibility to advise Commander Bunin on matters concerning planetary surfaces. It wasn't a responsibility for which Seaborg felt ready. He was just a slogger, a jumped-up hardsuit trooper. Why did this have to devolve on him?

No matter why, it had. He was Eridani, and he would do his duty.

Grenwold was a backwater system. It didn't even have a transit point station, just the jump point stabilizers and the buoy. *Shaka's* jaunt into the isolated system was supposed to be a milk run, keeping *Shaka* busy while Pinzón and the troops did what had to be done. No one had been expecting any problems in Grenwold. Expectations to the contrary, they'd found one.

When *Shaka* arrived, the buoy's data showed light intrasystem traffic. Perfectly ordinary and expected. What was not expected was that *Shaka's* sensors had picked up a dozen more tracks than Grenwold ATC had logged. Commander Bunin had immediately raised a yellow alert, put *Shaka* on silent running, and held a senior staff meeting, which Anders as commander of ground forces had attended. He hadn't had to do anything at that meeting but listen.

He learned that a tight-beam query to Grenwold planetary authorities had confirmed the buoy's data. According to them, there were no bogies. Commander Bunin chose to believe his own ship's sensors. Hence the alert and *Shaka's* continued, wary approach. Commander Bunin was the cautious type.

Grenwold's answer could have been an honest one. The system wasn't rich and was well behind the tech curve in lots of areas, including electronics. They might not know about the bogies. On the other hand, the extra bogies could be illicit traffic, and Grenwold ATC might know more about them than they were willing to tell a MilForce ship. Smuggling was a well-known activity almost everywhere Humanity went, and dealing with smuggling was a part of the Interstellar Defense League's mission only when planetary authorities requested aid. Since no aid had been requested, Commander Bunin might have dismissed the whole matter had it not been for one other factor. While awaiting Grenwold's response, *Shaka* had intercepted one brief burst of howling commo static, the sort that MilForce troopers throughout space associated with Remor activity; the yellow alert had gone to orange.

Commander Bunin had ordered the immediate launch of the stealth drones. The Grenwold authorities were informed that *Shaka* was making minor repairs before continuing onward. In fact, one of *Shaka*'s decoys sat and simulated a ship keeping station while *Shaka* herself made a stealthy approach to the planet. While inbound, the commander was doing everything possible to figure out what was going on. Now, with the first returns from the K29-S OSDs in orbit the problem had only grown more mysterious.

Looking at the indistinct images, which were the best the fully stealthed drones could provide, Anders was puzzled. "It doesn't make much sense, sir."

"We're in agreement there, son." Bunin scowled. "Give me your best guess."

Feeling sweat pricking through his skin, Seaborg studied the screen. The data coming from the surveillance drones just weren't good enough. The flickering pics were nearly unidentifiable. Unfortunately, they were in no position to make mistakes. In hopes of dredging up something to place what he was seeing in context, Anders asked, "What does Grenwold say about it, sir?"

"We haven't asked them yet. I'm looking to develop independent evaluations, and I am waiting for yours, Lieutenant."

Seaborg wished that he had one to give.

The K29s were more than adequate for their normal job of updating battlefield intelligence, but now they were being asked to do the job of standard reconnaissance satellites *and* do it while going undetected. If the stealth suite were stepped down, they could transmit better images, but the drones would be easier for potential hostiles to detect. He understood the need to take no unnecessary risks at this stage, but he still wished that he had something better from which to make an evaluation. As things were, he'd only be guessing.

Grenwold had three major continents. The largest, dubbed Woldnos by the founding colonists, straddled the equator and stretched nearly across a full hemisphere. Despite the fact that Woldnos was supposed to be uncolonized, someone was there and doing something. But what? It looked like massive landforming activity, but some of the usual signs were missing. For one thing, they weren't getting any heat plumes such as one would expect from the heavy machinery necessary for major landforming, even assuming that the Grenwolders had such things, which they supposedly didn't. What in hell was going on?

"I wish Captain Rodzinski and his engineers were here. They'd know."

"I wish Rod were here, too, son. But we have to play with the cards God dealt us. Tell me what you think. Are the Remor here, or not?"

So far they had seen no sign of Remor ships, but *Shaka's* sensors weren't capable of sweeping the entire system. There had been no more commo intercepts. Except for the unusual activity on Grenwold's surface and the extra intrasystem tracks, nothing was out of place. If the Remor were here, they weren't mounting one of their usual invasions. And if they weren't here, what *was* going on?

The enemy was MilForce's principal concern. If the Remor had come here, StratCom needed to know. Unfortunately, with MilForce stretched in their desperate defense of Human space, the consequences of a false alarm could be disastrous, but the repercussions of ignoring a Remor presence could be even worse.

"Lieutenant?"

"Sorry, sir." He'd been letting his mind wander and the only reason he wasn't sorrier still was the commander's obvious tolerance for a junior officer thrown in the deep end. "I don't think we're going to get the answers we need from orbit unless we run into an enemy ship."

"Something none of us would care to do." The commander leaned back in his chair. "Well, son, do you have a recommendation?"

"A ground recon will get us what we want, sir. I'd like to use the full platoon in dispersed detachments. We'll cover more ground faster that way."

"You can guarantee me an answer?"

"If there are Remor down there, sir, I guarantee I'll recognize them."

Bunin nodded. "We'll be near enough to launch shuttles in two days. I want minimal exposure to the Grenwold ATC net and any possible enemy perimeter scanners, so we'll insert you over the north pole and shape a descent over the supposedly unpopulated high latitudes of the northeast continent—Inthos, I believe it's called. Once your task group is down, you can cross to Woldnos without significant over-water travel. Recon the outlying disturbances on Woldnos and, if you encounter the enemy, do not engage. Get me my answers, Lieutenant."

Seaborg saluted. "Will do, sir."

There would be a lot of planning in the next two days. Seaborg was glad. It would keep him from brooding about what they might find on Grenwold.

# 2

## PAN-STELLAR COMBINE
## CANESSA SYSTEM

As he swam up the spinal access tube, Ken Konoye could tell that the bridge of PSCS *Byrd* was quieter than usual even for night watch. The regular watch had been let off so that the command staff could use the compartment for a private conference. He grasped the swing bar, scissoring his body to orient his feet toward the command deck. Swinging in, he imparted torque as he released the grab bar and corkscrewed himself into the compartment.

A huge holotank, ringed by the command staff's six control stations, dominated the bridge. The captain's couch commanded the most elaborate of the stations, directly facing the wall plotting screen. Opposite the captain's was the executive officer's only slightly less elaborate post. Jane Van Der Noogt raised her eyes from her main screen as Konoye spun from the access tube and landed lightly on the deck. She shook her head slightly in amused disdain for his showy entrance.

Konoye didn't mind. He was used to her belittling his occasional display of athletic prowess. Dropping cleanly and landing lightly on the command deck with its .7G effective gravity was nothing compared to the sort of things he'd done when he was in competition, but that had been over two decades ago. It wasn't as though anyone but Jane had noticed their captain's arrival.

*No different than when I showed up in the lab*. He supposed that he shouldn't complain about a team that was involved in its work.

Like Jane, most of the senior officers had been with Konoye at the university, working on the research that had led to discovery of the hypothetical jump route. The Combine rewarded the entrepreneurial spirit, wherever it arose. The Combine also preferred cold hard facts over theory, and its rewards only went to those who translated the theoretical into the practical. Thus, by law, it didn't matter who *said* the jump route was there, it only mattered who *proved* it was there. Thus, one set of discoverers could go down in the history books while a completely separate set went down in the accounting books.

The Combine's system had garnered much jeering from other star nations, but the Combine was too practical to let the system turn into the fool's circus it had the potential to be. No vessel spaced out without a qualified person as operations chief. That person effectively *ran* the ship and provided a wealth of practical experience to leaven— which was to say, correct—any questionable—stupid— decisions a novice captain or officer might make. Aboard *Byrd* the Survey Office had filled that slot with the estimable Master Mathieu Hoppe, a laconic twenty year veteran of the spaceways.

The others were all bright enough to qualify for their new jobs, having scored well on the certification tests after their mandatory week-long orientation courses, but they were even more inexperienced in command than Konoye. He, at least, had "commanded" a deanship.

As Konoye slid into the captain's couch, he surveyed the familiar faces.

Winnie Prasad held the survey officer's chair. Konoye could see from the reflections on her pale skin that she was running a private sim on her station's screen. Nothing unusual there; Winnie spent as little time out of her hyperspatial theory banks as she could. Konoye, as always, forgave her distraction; if not for her work, none of them would be here.

In the purser's chair to the right of the captain's, Lily Chu watched Winnie work, a hint of a tolerant smile lighting her face. Despite the long-legged, china-doll looks that led people to dismiss her intelligence, Lily was a brilliant hyperspatial engineer and just about the only person able to translate some of Winnie's more esoteric concepts into terms that the rest of the team could understand. Despite Lily's interest in getting rich, she wasn't really qualified for the purser's position, and she made no secret of it, but that was fine. This mission didn't really need a purser—though law required one—but it did need a good hyperspatial engineer, and Lily had *that* aptitude aplenty.

On the other side of the tank sat Chiang-shan Lawson. He'd been chief of Konoye's graduate assistants and now was the ship's communications chief. Given the young man's penchant for talking, the assignment seemed a perfect match. Even now, employing his usual extravagant hand gestures, Chiang-shan was chatting with Master Hoppe. The merchant spacer leaned back in his couch, smiling politely, although Konoye noted that Master Hoppe's eyes spent more time on his console than on his conversation partner.

They were a small staff for a small ship, but, he hoped, well suited to dealing with what the second probe found. He rapped on his console to get their attention. "All right, Jane. Let's see what our baby bird brought home for us."

The tank lit up with a starfield. Heads came up, but Konoye barely noticed. The display grabbed all of his attention. It didn't look familiar. He'd studied sims of the starscape around Ursa. He knew what it should look like, and he wasn't seeing what he expected.

"Computer, rotate field."

Konoye stared hard, looking for familiar arrangements among the dots of light. Nothing was quite the way he expected it. By all rights they should be staring at near-Earth stars, but they weren't. The probe hadn't exited the hyperspatial tunnel where he had predicted. If they hadn't enhanced the astrogation package, they wouldn't be looking at this data now. Much good that did. They'd failed. Unless . . .

"Maybe it's a pinhole."

"Let's hope that's all it is," Jane drawled.

"It's got to be."

None of the team looked convinced.

Well, Konoye wasn't convinced either. There was no guarantee that they were dealing with a pinhole. Indisputably, the probe hadn't made it to the jump path's predicted end. It *was* possible that the calculations were wrong, and the path didn't end where predicted. No! The universe couldn't be so cruel—there *had* to be a pinhole! Somewhere along the length of the jump route there must be a tiny break in the wall between the hyperspatial tube and real space, a leak sufficient to interrupt the passage of anything traveling along it and return the traveler to real space. That *had* to be what they were dealing with. Such phenomena were not unknown; other jump routes had turned out to have interim steps. But it wasn't what Konoye had expected. It sure as hell wasn't what he wanted.

It wasn't what the heads of the sponsoring cartels wanted, either. They wanted a new, shorter route to near-Earth space, a fast trip to the heart of galactic civilization, something they expected Konoye to deliver. The cartels had spent a lot, and they wanted a solid return on their investments.

Konoye didn't want to tell them he wasn't going to deliver. Disappointing the Committee—even when it wasn't your fault—was the sort of thing that sank careers.

Mathieu Hoppe cleared his throat. "If you all be excusing me, I'm not being an astrogation whiz. I understand that the stellar parallax be telling you bad news, but the data doesn't be meaning a lot to me. If the terminus be not at Ursa, where be it?"

"The astrogation package data is just coming up." Jane consulted her screen. "It says we're dealing with an unnamed system, Master Hoppe. SSCS grid reference is 12.-49.6. The description is 'astronomically logged' and nothing else."

"At least it's Earthwards," Lily said.

"Uncharted, you say? No claims? No claims at all?" Chiang-shan asked.

Jane nodded. "Data bank says no."

"Let's file," Chiang-shan suggested. "Let's file claim right away."

Jane threw him a withering glare. "Don't jump so fast. The probe wasn't equipped to search. It could have missed all kinds of signals. All we've got is negative data."

"We'll all have a negative bank balance if we don't get something out of this," Lily exclaimed. Winnie nodded in agreement. "If the system is unclaimed, even if it isn't the route we were looking for, it's still a route. A new jump route to a new system is worth *something*, if only the mining rights."

"Working out of Canessa?" Hoppe looked incredulous. "They be doing some work in the belt out here, but the system hasn't got the infrastructure to be handling a jump-distant operation. Not that they wouldn't be willing, mind. But you be talking some heavy up-front investing and a lot of time before mining's commercial."

"You don't know that," Chiang-shan protested. "For all we know, the system's got an asteroid belt full of heavy metal rocks. Just scoop 'em up and pump 'em out and to hell with infrastructure."

"You be dreaming, kid," Hoppe drawled.

"And you're—"

"Done," Konoye cut him off. Chiang-shan snapped his mouth shut and glared at Konoye through slitted eyes, but the important thing was that he shut up. The boy was bright, but he had too little common sense. The way Chiang-shan's temper was flaring, he was likely to insult Hoppe and that just wasn't good business. Worse, an annoyed and uncooperative Hoppe might ruin the plan that was beginning to form in Konoye's mind.

"I know that look," Jane said. "You're planning something."

"I am *planning* to inform the Committee of our findings."

"Findings? We don't have any findings yet. All we've got is raw data. Just what are you going to tell them?"

"We will tell them we've got a pinhole."

"We don't know that."

"We don't know we don't," he snapped back. There were times that Jane wouldn't agree that a vorhound had teeth until after the beast had bitten her. "You want to register a dissenting opinion?"

Jane looked doubtful. If she did register a dissenting opinion, and Konoye was right, she'd lose credibility with the cartels. Bailing out on Konoye now would demonstrate a lack of loyalty that a future employer would look upon with justified suspicion. Of course, if he was wrong, she would be in a position to save her own career while his went down in flames. He'd rather that she worked with him than against him.

"Look, if we follow the H-tube and get *Byrd* situated on the other end, the ship's instruments should be able to gather us the data we need to show that this new system is just a stop-over."

"Or that it's a dead end," Jane said.

"Or that it's a dead end. But either way, we'll *know*. Just sitting here, we can only *guess*. Come on, people. We've got to send word to the Committee in any case. If we tell them we're following up on a pinhole, we stay in the game. Tell them that all we've got is a new route to nowhere special, and they'll reassign the exploration to a regular Survey Office crew. Then if it turns out that our new system *is* a stop-over, we lose the discovery rights. And the prize money. And the royalties."

Konoye smiled inwardly to see that *that* had hit home with all of them, even Jane.

"Problem." Hoppe frowned. "We don't be authorized to take *Byrd* through the H-tube."

"I don't see the problem. According to the mission statement, we aren't authorized to take *Byrd* through to Ursa without confirmed authorization. No mention is made of jumping to stop-overs."

"Specious, Ken." Jane frowned. "We didn't predict any stop-overs."

"But the possibility existed," Lily said. "Right, Winnie?"

"Always possible," Winnie agreed.

"So they should have known we might have to." Lily looked over to Hoppe. "*Byrd*'s got a transit point stabilization array aboard, doesn't she?"

"Standard equipment," Hoppe replied. "But it be *emergency* equipment. I don't be thinking its presence constitutes expectation of a stop-over on this mission."

Konoye wished Hoppe wasn't such a ship-board lawyer. "But you do believe that we are authorized to use the ship's equipment as necessary to complete the mission, don't you, Master Hoppe?"

"Ah," Hoppe said with a grin. "I be seeing where this be going. All right, Professor Konoye. Yes, I agree that it be within the captain's right to order the use of any and all ship's equipment in fulfillment of the ship's mission. You be, of course, aware that a review board might be finding such usage 'unnecessary and illegal.' "

He was. But then, he was ruined anyway if they failed out here. "I understand my responsibilities, Master Hoppe."

"It does seem to be within the letter of the law," Lily said. "I think we can get away with it."

"The Committee only follows the letter when it is in their favor," Jane pointed out.

Ken spread his hands wide. "We'll just have to make sure that backing us *is* in their favor."

"Winnie and I are for it," Lilly said.

"Me, too," Chiang-shan said.

"Master Hoppe?" Konoye asked.

"As the captain orders, Professor Konoye."

A safe answer for him. That only left one. He looked to Jane, but she wouldn't meet his eyes.

"The stars will wait, Ken. Why can't we just wait for the Committee to authorize?"

"The Committee wants a fast return. Do you want them to reassign this search?" He gave her his best you-know-I'm-right smile. "Once we prove the route, they'll say that we took the right action. The value of a short route to the inner systems is just too high to let someone else get there first. We're here. We can do it. We *have* to do it."

"I hope you do as good a job convincing them as you've done on yourself."

"Have I let you down yet?"

"All right," she said, but she still didn't meet his eyes. "No dissent. But no assent, either. Log me as protesting the propriety of the captain's actions."

"Hedging your bets, Jane?" Chiang-shan asked.

"Doing what I have to do, C.S."

Chiang-shan sat back and smiled arrogantly. "Oh, well, I understand. In fact, I understand that the IDL is always looking for good astrospecialists."

Konoye came right down on him. "Don't even joke about working for those mart killers."

"I was just—"

"You were just showing how young and ignorant you can be. This discussion is closed. I'll have the message ready to dump to the Committee in an hour. Master Hoppe, when will we be ready to make the jump?"

"An hour will be fine, Captain."

"An hour it is. I expect everyone at command stations for this jump. You, too, Jane. Protest notwithstanding."

"I never said I didn't want to go, Ken."

Konoye considered throttling her. She could be such a bitch sometimes.

## SERENTEN CONCORDAT
## SOMMERSET SYSTEM

Kurt was fighting, struggling to escape the unyielding grip of the League troopers. He wouldn't let them take him away. He wouldn't! He was helpless, held in the iron grip. But he fought: furiously, viciously, vainly. He was still struggling when he awoke. He was gripped, all right, gripped by the tangling folds of his sheets.

He'd thought that he'd finished with the dreams. He hadn't had one in months.

Had he been screaming again? His throat was raw enough.

He should have expected a nightmare, though. In yesterday's session Doctor Nellis had set him to dealing with the Cassuells. The poor, dead Cassuells. He had maintained his calm through the session, earning the doctor's praise, but that had only been because he knew that the whole thing had been a lie. The Cassuells were dead.

But in his heart he'd known he'd see them again. In his dreams.

He didn't want to dream anymore.

Forcing his eyes open, he stared at the ceiling. Gray light filtered through the blinds. It was early morning, too early to get up, but he knew from experience that he was done with sleep for the night.

He raised his head to see if he had disturbed Clarise. Her side of the bed was empty, so he must have; it was far too early for her to be up and about. Turning his head, he looked toward the bathroom door. It was open and the room beyond dark. Not there. She must have retreated to the couch downstairs to escape his thrashing.

He felt bad about that. She shouldn't have to pay the price of his nightmares. It was enough that he paid.

The last time that Doctor Nellis had used the Cassuells, almost a year ago, the dreams had tormented him for weeks. It had been a terrible time. He'd felt guilty knowing that he was disturbing Clarise. She had fought with him a lot during those weeks. More and more, as her tolerance had slipped. She wasn't responsible, of course. It was the lack of sleep. He understood that. He couldn't blame her.

But they had stuck it out, hadn't they?

He'd often thought that perhaps he shouldn't have listened to Doctor Nellis. She had insisted that Kurt's life be "as normal as possible." Would separate beds have been so abnormal? Clarise didn't think so. Clarise, at least, would have gotten proper sleep. A normal life—Lord knew that he wanted a normal life. Clarise wanted it, too; she told him often enough.

But now, if the dreams really were starting again, a normal life looked very far away.

He heaved himself out of bed, hating the dreams. *The dreams are only a symptom*, Doctor Nellis would say. Fine; he'd hate the Leaguers, then. They were the ones who'd given him the dreams. They were the ones who'd killed his old life.

He showered, more to scrub away the psychic residue of his dreams than to cleanse his body of the sour sweat he'd generated. The pounding heat of the water relaxed his muscles and, in a small part, his mind as well.

*The past is past*, Doctor Nellis would say. *We must put it behind us and look to the future.*

He decided to look for Clarise. He tugged on a robe and padded downstairs, still toweling his hair. He abandoned the apology he was working out when he saw that she wasn't on the couch. It was still early for her to have left the house. The light flooding out from the kitchen suggested where she might be, but he gave up that hope almost immediately, for no sound came from there. He went in anyway and found it in disarray. The disorder didn't seem to be the usual clutter of a hectic morning rush. Before he could sort out what made it different, the memo light blinking on the screen snagged his attention.

Concern caught in his throat. Something must have come up to call her away. The kids? Her mother? He hit the PLAY button. No light came to the screen, just Clarise's voice.

"Kurt, I—"

A pause. He knew now that his fantasies of a normal life's problems were simply fantasies. The towel slipped unheeded to the floor as he listened to her words.

"Look, I keep telling myself that it's not your fault, that you're not responsible, but it's just gotten too much. I can't take it anymore. I'm sorry."

Another pause, then the screen came to life; but the woman who appeared there wasn't Clarise. He'd never seen this immaculately coiffured, business-suited young woman before. The word RECORDED blinked in the upper left-hand corner of the screen.

"Good morning, Mr. Ellicot," the woman said. "My name is Holly Bolton. I'm with Houseman, Hart, Jellicoe, and Associates, and our firm has been retained by your wife. It is my duty to inform you that she has filed for and received a preliminary custodial separation order conjoined with a no-contact restraint. You will, of course, be expected to comply with the court order unless and until it is rescinded as an outcome of the divorce proceedings. I would be most happy to begin discussions with your attor—"

Kurt cut off the screen.

He couldn't blame Clarise. She'd done what she felt she had to do. Understandable, really. Who in her right mind lived with a nightmare-haunted failure?

# 3

As the stars burst into glory around them, *Byrd* shuddered, metal groaning. The bridge illumination flickered as a brief whiff of ozone was smothered by a lingering soapy odor. Whatever had shorted wasn't going to start a serious fire.

"Sorry," Winnie mumbled from the hyper-navigation station. "Blind transitions can be such a bitch."

The sort of bitches that killed ships, Konoye thought. But *Byrd* seemed to have held together. He glanced over to Hoppe and was relieved to see that the spacer didn't look concerned. When Konoye asked for the ship's status, Hoppe's eyes never left his panels.

"She's gone through worse, Captain," he said. "All systems be operational, though we best be forming some repair crews as soon as convenient."

"See to it as soon as we secure from transition, Master Hoppe. Whatever you need." The repairs would delay the research, but they had to be made. Konoye was risking enough without adding charges of neglect. He tapped his command board and the *transit complete* bell rang throughout the ship. "Jane, find us the best place to locate the beacon. Winnie, get the arrays unfolded. I want to find that transit connection as soon as we can."

"If it's there," Jane reminded him.

Konoye didn't want to believe that it might not be there, but he knew that it was a possibility. Hyperspatial tubes were no respecters of true distance, and that was their strength. They allowed Human ships to cross light-years of distance in negligible time spans. But they only went where they went, and that was their weakness. Spacefaring Humanity remained tied to discrete linkages between systems, point to very specific point.

Of course the "very specific point" of a transit entry was actually a considerable volume of space, a sphere that could be light-minutes across. Established transit points were ringed with stabilizer beacons that helped to damp the quantum fluctuations accompanying transition. Had there been a beacon set up in this system, *Byrd* would have had a smoother arrival, with little likelihood of accumulating the damage she had taken. Stabilizing the transit point—for their departure if for nothing else—was a high priority.

Even higher on Konoye's list was finding the entry point to the rest of the hyperspatial route to Ursa. Some jump routes were actually a series of transits, a chain of hyperspatial tubes whose ends lay in close, real-space proximity. *Close* in a galactic sense, anyway—the real space leg in such a route could take days of travel to cover.

The transition point for the next leg of the sought-after route to Ursa was out there. It *had* to be! But there was a lot of space to search to find the connection. A lot of real space meant a lot of time. God grant that it wasn't on the opposite side of the system, like the Hoffreter link in the Cygnus-Wayfarer Station passage. He wished that he could devote all of his team's effort to the search, but other tasks needed to be done if he was to cover his butt.

Their initial scan data was already refining the probe's picture of the system on his console screen. The planets had been barely hinted at in the probe data, but that had been enough to raise his hopes. Planets almost certainly meant that there would be *something* in the system of interest to the Combine. As the information piled up, it was clear that the planets were real, and his gamble *had* paid off. A new, *useful* system for the Combine was a coup, even if a small one compared to the goal they had set out to achieve.

*There!* Spectrum reads from the fourth planet were showing water vapor. Vindication and relief brought a grin to his face.

"Jane?"

"Ken," she sounded irritated, "at least let me finish one job before you give me another one."

"Pass off the beacon work to Chiang-shan. He needs the practice. I've got something more interesting for you."

"It's busywork," Chiang-shan complained.

"It's all busywork," Jane said. "It's your busywork now."

Chiang-shan turned to Konoye. His voice had a whiny note. "I've got enough to do. I've got emissions scans still to run."

"That's right, you do. And you'll do them, too, without griping," Konoye told him. "Concentrate on the fourth planet."

"The fourth? Why that one?" Jane came around to look at Konoye's console. "What have you got?"

"A possible habitable."

To his delight, she looked incredulous. "No. We can't be that lucky."

"Maybe we can." He chuckled. "We're too far out to get more than the gross parameters. I want you to take a shuttle in and see what's really there."

"If this system has got a habitable biosphere, you've saved your ass."

Hoppe appeared at Jane's shoulders and looked over the data. Clearly he'd been listening to them as well as to the reports of his repair crews. Just as clearly he approved of what he saw on Konoye's screen. "The crew of *Prince Henry* retired rich after they found Lonesome, and that be just on standard service royalties."

"Let's not get ahead of ourselves," Konoye cautioned.

"Prelim does look good," Jane admitted. "But you're right, there's too much we don't know. But what's the rush? Your first message won't reach the Committee for a month or so."

"Doesn't matter," Konoye said with a dismissive wave. "I'd like to get this out on a messenger as soon as the transit point is stabilized."

Jane nodded knowingly. "Before they make any rash decisions, such as hoisting your ass for exceeding your authority?"

"The idea has crossed my mind."

"I thought so. Well, you'll need data to back you up. If Master Hoppe will gather me a crew, I'll get down there."

"Thanks, Jane."

"Don't thank me yet. If this doesn't pan out, you may still be facing a less than pleasant interview with the Committee."

Jane hated time-lagged communication even more than Konoye did, so he knew that he wouldn't be hearing much from her until her ship came back into minimal delay range at least. He didn't worry about it. Despite her official protest, maybe even because of it, he still trusted her.

Twenty-seven hours later, as Konoye was readying for sleep, she checked in. Tersely she reported everything nominal. Konoye simply sent an acknowledgment and went to bed.

A few hours later, Chiang-shan was buzzing him.

"We just got something in from Jane, Ken." Before Konoye could start bawling out Chiang-shan for waking him, Chiang-shan started reading the message. "She says: 'Returning soonest. Prepare laser comm link for five seconds out. Course follows.' That's all."

"That's it?"

"Uh-huh. Just that. You want me to—"

"Just acknowledge. And set up the link. Jane isn't going to talk until she's ready."

He was waiting on the bridge when Jane's ship rippled into range. Frustrated worrying about Jane's unorthodox behavior had kept him from getting back to sleep. After two hours of trying, he'd dressed and gone up to the bridge to wait. And to worry, which left him snappish by the time his captain's console lit with the comm link.

"What the hell is this all about, Jane?"

Seconds snailed by while he waited for his words to crawl out to her and her reply to crawl back.

"I put atmospheric drones down and Four was looking good. I'd guess a seven or eight on the Carson scale. But we might have a problem, Ken. We spotted some geometric regularities—"

"Buildings?"

She continued to speak as his interruption sped toward her "—on the day side that are unlikely to be natural. We're going to have to take— What?" She cursed at his breaking the comm protocol. "Maybe they are buildings. I don't know. It's hard to be sure what we're looking at. The vegetation's pretty dense. But given that the night side's as black as space, and that we didn't get any communications emissions or read any significant atmospheric pollutants, my guess would be we've got a dead civilization here."

Not impossible. Rare as habitable planets were, planets with civilizations were rarer still. Occasionally, survey ships found a so-called lost colony, the remains of a forgotten off-shoot of Humanity's first Diaspora. In most cases the colony had failed utterly after being isolated by the disastrous Parkinson Virus which had sent so many starships into oblivion; in some few cases the colonists had survived, usually with a severely reduced technological base. But Jane hadn't said that she thought it was a lost colony.

"Maybe it's not technic," he suggested.

Ten seconds later he got his answer. "Pre-technics don't get out of their gravity well. Our radar picked up reflections in orbit around Four's moon. Looks like debris, mostly. It all reads dead."

He hoped so. But if there were things orbiting the moon . . . "What about in orbit around the planet?"

"A scrap here and there. Orbital stability would be considerably less. That'll help us narrow down when the locals were active."

So maybe it was a dead lost colony, after all, which would be fine by Konoye since a dead colony wouldn't end their claim to the system. In fact, it might enhance the revenues. "The archaeologists will have a field day."

"The xeno-archaeologists, Ken. Spectral readings on a scrap we recovered from orbit suggest that we're not dealing with Human metallurgy. I want to get it into *Byrd*'s lab and do a more thorough study."

Aliens! So that was what had gotten Jane weirded! Konoye knew of less than a dozen intelligent alien species in all of Human-controlled space. One of them—thanks to the mart bastards of the Interstellar Defense League—was extinct. Only four of the remaining species had achieved space flight before they were discovered, and only two of those, the Mimaks and the Remor, had achieved interstellar technology. The Mimaks were members of the Pan-Stellar Combine. The Remor were implacable foes of humankind, who had yet—thank God—to seriously trouble the Combine. This system was too far from the Mimaks' worlds to belong to them, and if the Remor were here, Konoye wouldn't be worrying about what was on any of the system's planets; he'd be hauling butt for home and screaming for help. So whatever alien species had lifted itself out of its home gravity well here was dead. But dead aliens were safe aliens, and might be even better than safe.

"Ken?"

"Just thinking about what you've told me, Jane. I think you were wise in scrapping the landing. There's a potential gold mine down on Four. We don't want to get slapped with any contamination liens. If the planet's pristine when the xeno-archies get here, we'll all be better off. Make your best time back here. I'll be waiting for you in the lab."

"Understood. See you soon."

As soon as Jane signed off, Konoye turned to the communications station. "C.S., bundle Jane's transmissions with my packet and get that messenger off as soon as you're done."

## IDL DEFENSE SECTOR 32-ORANGE
## GRENWOLD SYSTEM

"All vessels, this is *Shaka* control. We've got a bogey emerging from behind the third moon."

The shuttle flight commander acknowledged with a blip.

Anders Seaborg had been almost dozing, exhausted by two solid days of preparation, but he shocked fully awake at the message from *Shaka*. He cursed himself as fatigue and unfamiliarity combined to cost him seconds while he got the feed from *Shaka* onto the main screen. His haste was unwarranted, or at least unrewarded. The bogey was out of visual range and the telemetry didn't mean anything to him. But the commander of the shuttle flight understood such things.

"Captain Metzler?"

"Yes, Lieutenant Seaborg?" Technically the shuttles were part of Task Group Seaborg, but the task group didn't officially activate until they reached Grenwold's atmosphere. Captain Metzler's voice contained just enough annoyance to demonstrate that he knew both facts and was not looking forward to being under the command of a junior officer, and a slogger at that; but he kept it civil. "What can I do for you?"

"What's happening?"

"*Shaka's* just picked up an unidentified ship on vector for Grenwold."

"Remor?"

"Too soon to tell. Whoever it is, they're not on intercept to *Shaka* or us. Either they don't know we're here, or they don't care."

Lying doggo as she was, *Shaka* was all but invisible, but even a slogger like Anders knew that the accelerating shuttles carrying his taskforce would be easily visible to the oncoming ship. If this bogey was hostile, the shuttles would be fat targets. Of course *Shaka* would avenge them, but Anders and his troops would still be dead.

"Should we abort the landing?" he asked.

"I've got no signal from *Shaka* to do so. As far as I'm concerned, we're still committed."

"Understood, Captain. Keep me informed, please."

"Will do, Lieutenant."

Anders switched his commo to the platoon frequency. Precautions were in order. "This is Seaborg. Seal up and strap down."

With their hardsuits sealed, the troops would at least have a chance should their shuttles be holed—assuming the shuttles weren't totally destroyed, the most likely result of a hit from any serious ordinance. Like his troops, Anders knew that there was nothing they could do but wait and pray while their lives were in the hands of the shuttle jocks. He sealed his suit, secured the acceleration straps, and settled in to wait. He said a prayer to St. Dismas, too.

After an eternity, word came, and it was bad.

Captain Metzler announced, "Bogey is a bandit. Repeat, bogey is a bandit."

The shuttle flight commander shifted the feed on one of Seaborg's repeater screens, giving him a view of the bandit. The incoming ship's silhouette looked like some unholy cross between a squid and a spider. He knew it at once: a Remor interface striker. Intel had codenamed its class *Thunder*, but he didn't need to name it to know it was dangerous. On Kuo's World, he had seen one of its kind come streaking down out of orbit to annihilate an entire company of troopers before their shuttles had finished shedding reentry heat.

A rivulet of sweat trickled down Seaborg's brow, and he felt his suit's coolers kick in. They would be easy meat for the *Thunder* if it decided it wanted them. Without the shield of the cruiser, the shuttles' only hope of survival was to go unnoticed.

Tense minutes crawled by. Anders watched the magnified image of the *Thunder* the way that a bird supposedly watched the reptile hunting it. The sinister shape grew no larger, but that was only the illusion of image compensation; the *Thunder* got closer to them every second. The tracking telemetry confirmed it. Still, unless—

"Bandit shifting course." Metzler sounded apprehensive.

And well he ought to be. If the *Thunder* was—

"Bandit on intercept vector! Intercept in thirty minutes. Outer edge of enemy attack envelope in five."

Five minutes till their death knell started to toll.

Anders stared at the telemetry on his repeater screens. How did commanders stand this waiting and watching as the inevitable played out? It was easier down with the grunts where you couldn't see what was coming.

"*Shaka*'s powering up," Metzler reported.

"Why now?" Anders asked.

"Bunin must have been hoping the bandit would ignore us. When the bandit turned for us, that was a lost hope. He's going to try to draw the fight toward *Shaka* and away from us."

The match-up of *Shaka* against the *Thunder* shouldn't have been a bad one for the Humans—had Shaka been active and ready. The cruiser had more armor and more point defense than the entire shuttle flight combined, and more than enough firepower to punch very big holes in a *Thunder*-class striker. But by lying quiet, *Shaka* had sacrificed mobility. Now she'd wallow until she could build some speed. *Shaka*'s attempt at stealth meant she wasn't ready for battle. Her weapon systems would be powering up, but would they be ready soon enough to save her?

"Bandit's seen her," Metzler reported. "Damn, that bastard's quick on the uptake. He didn't waste any time shifting course toward *Shaka*. Intercept in— Damn, they're launching!"

Anders saw the new tracks on the screen: a trio of missiles headed for *Shaka*. The cruiser responded with a ragged salvo, a half-dozen missiles, as she changed heading.

But *Shaka* was slow.

"Bandit's launching again," Metzler announced.

"What about the first flight?"

"Still incoming. Watch the tactical display. *Shaka*'s point defense should be just—there!"

A red blip vanished from the tactical. Two remained, falling in on the blue central image: *Shaka*. Blue and red merged, flared. Anders didn't need to hear Metzler's curse to know *Shaka* had just taken serious damage. The glare on the screen died down, revealing *Shaka*'s image, still there and still moving and accelerating.

Three more red blips stalked her. Behind them came the *Thunder*, closing range rapidly.

"Beams! The bastard's firing!"

Anders didn't know how Metzler knew. He was sure the information was there on his screens, but he just couldn't recognize it.

"*Shaka*'s hit!"

But not killed. Anders watched as the red blips of the enemy's second missile flight winked out, caught by the cruiser's point defense.

Human missiles didn't have the acceleration to match Remor birds. *Shaka*'s missiles were just reaching Remor intercept range.

The bandit ignored two of *Shaka*'s missiles; the pair tracked wide of their target, obviously having failed to lock on. The *Thunder*'s defenses flashed two of the rest, but the last two bore in. A final barrage claimed one more, but the surviving missile detonated, energizing a focused fire-fall of laser energy. Something aboard the enemy vessel exploded, and it transformed into an expanding sphere of wreckage.

The beams that had been ravaging *Shaka* died with the Remor ship. There were cheers on all the commo channels. Anders heard them over his own jubilant shouting.

The battle, brief as it was, would not go unnoticed. Task Group Seaborg's covert reconnaissance mission had become redundant. Anders signaled *Shaka* for new orders.

He got no response.

Anders got Metzler to feed him data on *Shaka's* wounds. The cruiser had taken a pounding. On the optical monitor, a brief red glow flashed as a compartment in *Shaka's* habitat ring exploded and vented its contents into the void. The glittering sparkle of flash-frozen liquids lent a bizarre holiday look to the expanding cloud of debris.

Anders sent again, and this time his commo screen lit, showing a harried face. It took Anders a moment to recognize *Shaka's* chief of engineering under the soot and grime. "*Shaka* to Task Group Seaborg. This is Captain Ryan," the engineer said.

"I want to speak to Colonel Bunin."

"You can't. He's dead. At least I think he is. We've lost commo to the bridge and have fire fore and aft of it. *Shaka* comp says I'm in charge, God help me. What do you want?"

"I want to know what happens now."

"So do I." If Ryan hadn't been a MilForce officer, Anders would have said there was an edge of hysteria in her voice. "You got a suggestion? Make it."

"I'd say we got Colonel Bunin's answer. Recommend shuttles return to *Shaka*. We got hands you can use for damage control."

"I'd love those hands, Lieutenant, but I don't think coming back here is a good idea just now. We've got three more bogeys on screen and at least one is a bandit and bigger than the *Thunder* we just took out."

Three more? The new bogeys didn't register on the shuttle's inferior sensor suites. Normally the shuttles' data was supplemented by a feed from the mother ship. "I don't see your bandit, Captain."

"Telemetry relay is down, like half the systems onboard. The bandit's out there all right, and his vector puts him in range about the time you'd make it home. The other bogeys are lining up behind him; I make them as bandits, too. You'd be coming in through fireworks."

Three to one were tough but not impossible odds for a healthy MilForce cruiser, but *Shaka* was far from healthy. "If you didn't have to worry about us, could you take them?"

"I don't know. If only the Colonel were—" Ryan's face clouded and she licked her lips nervously. "I don't think so."

No doubt Ryan was an excellent engineer, but she didn't seem ready for the job ahead of her. If *Shaka* faced the bandits under her command, the result was likely to be bad. Captain Ryan seemed to need to have the obvious pointed out.

"You've still got engines, yes?"

Ryan laughed nervously. "Oh yes. *My* command's fine. Not a scratch on anything aft of hab ring."

Missing the fact that her command was *Shaka* now, not just engineering, she proved unreadiness. Ready or not, she had a job to do. "All right, then. Forget about us for now. We'll continue down to the planet and establish a forward base. *Shaka*'s yours now and she needs to get out of here. Run like hell and get word to StratCom."

Her eyes lit at the plan. Anders saw that she wanted to get away as badly as he did. But she didn't jump right on it. "I can't desert you."

Her loyalty was commendable, but duty came first. "You have to. This is not a situation for pointless heroics. StratCom needs to know about the Remor here in the Grenwold System far more than it needs a platoon of sloggers and the shuttles they flew in on."

"There has to be another way. I could jury-rig a missile as a message torp and—"

"How long to make the rig?"

"Huh? Um, I'd say about an hour."

"Check your intercept time. Have you got an hour?"

Her eyes swiveled about, checking her screens. Forlornly she replied, "No."

"Exactly. *Shaka* has to go. She's the fastest way to get the word out. Right?"

Ryan nodded.

"Look, we'll be fine." Could she tell that he was lying?

"Are you sure?"

"Sure," he said, trying to sound certain. "Once Captain Metzler drops us, we'll be on the ground where we belong. Couldn't ask for more. You just make sure you come back and get us later."

Ryan drew in a deep breath. Some resolution finally seemed to take hold. "I will," she said.

"I know you will." Anders prayed to St. Michael that it would be so. "And, Captain Ryan, don't forget to bring the cavalry with you. Now goose your engines and get gone before the enemy moves to cut you off from the jump point. Task Group Seaborg out."

"Good luck, Seaborg. *Shaka* out."

Anders nodded silently. Luck was something they'd both need.

# 4

## IDL DEFENSE SECTOR 32-ORANGE
## TARSUS STATION

Christoph Stone sat and watched the newsfeed. The Serenten Concordat's Minister of State was making another speech denouncing "the expansionist policies" of the Interstellar Defense League and urging the unaligned worlds to reject membership in the League. Stone was angered. Didn't those people understand what was going on?

Much as he wanted to, it was not Stone's place to tell the minister where he could put his sanctimonious, wrongheaded opinions. He wished that peebs of the PoliState Bureau were better at their jobs of squashing the crap that got tossed at the League so often. Sector commanders like Stone had enough trouble with the enemy without having to worry about hostile fools behind their backs, but so far the peebs hadn't shut down any wrong-headed talk. Unfortunately the Remor didn't open conquered systems for sight-seeing tours. A short visit to someplace like Caledonia or Kuo's World ought to convince the anti-League yahoos of the need and necessity of the war underway.

The minister railed on, decrying the IDL's "predatory and presumptuous division of Human space." Trust the minister to distort the facts and attribute malicious motives to anything ordered by the League's Strategic Command. Yes, StratCom had divided Human space into wedges of galactic space centered on old Sol; smooth military operations required defined sectors of authority. But Command did not arrogate to itself authority over all systems in those sectors, only over member states. Despite an open offer of League membership, only a fraction of Humanity's governments had accepted. Most of the League's members were fringe systems, the small associations and the unaligned systems of the sectors' outer arcs—the ones most threatened by the Remor invasion. The inner systems liked to think themselves safe, and they wanted to believe that they didn't need the League and its MilForce. Often—as the Serenten Minister was doing now—their politicians and rulers called the Remor threat exaggerated. Some even went so far as to call it an invention of "imperialistic IDL leaders who wished to bring all of Humanity under their sway."

Idiots!

The Remor were as real a threat as Humanity had ever faced! The sectors of Stone's wardship might be only Orange code, but the bordering Sector 33 was Red code, a hot sector with active Remor incursions in progress. Just because the last confirmed Remor activity in his sectors had been dealt with more than seven years ago was no reason to assume that they were safe. No sector that had ever seen Remor activity was truly safe. The Remor could return as they had in Sector 35—after an absence of years. That was why the wardship of an Orange-code sector was given to an experienced combat officer like Stone, a command he'd held for seven years.

Seven years could be a long time. People could forget about the battles, and the sacrifices, and the danger. They could forget about the commanders who had led the single successful campaign against the enemy. Some things they could remember: all the wrong parts like Cassuells Home.

While Stone had been campaigning, he'd been insulated from the reaction to what he'd ordered there, but after the campaign had been won, the voices of the ignorant public had risen again. Some had actually demanded he be tried for war crimes! What matter the battles won and the sacrifices made? With the enemy vanquished, it was no longer a time for military necessity; it had been time to clean house.

Strategic Command knew that they hadn't won the war. They knew that cashiering their only victorious commander was not military wisdom. Yet it was not political wisdom for them to retain him. His victories had kept him from being thrown to the wolves. Still, he'd been shunted aside, pushed away from the commands he'd desired and promoted to sector commander. It wasn't a soldier's billet. Sector Command had rank and privileges, but he was being forced to live in a bureaucrat's world. And why? Because he'd made a hard call, and some armchair strategists and bleeding-heart fools thought they knew better.

Morons!

Still, assignment to his wardship had gotten him out of the public eye and allowed him to survive the public's selective amnesia. "Keep your head lower than your butt till it blows over," his old friend General Wahlberg had told him, and he had. Talk of war crime trials faded, but by then MilForce had forgotten him. When the Remor launched a new assault, he was not called to battle. When he had swallowed his pride and asked for a command, he had been told that they all were filled. An old friend whispered a word in his ear: "politics." StratCom hadn't needed the embarrassment of the "Casual Slaughterer." Telling himself that StratCom knew what it was doing, he waited.

And while he waited, he did his job like a good soldier.

Unfortunately, a sector commander's busy job wasn't the work he wanted to be doing. He knew that a lot of shortsighted junior officers envied his wardship post. They looked forward to the end of war with the Remor and saw a wardship command as a sure stepping-stone to post-war power. But there was a war to be fought first. Afterwards—if there was an afterwards—what was left of Humanity would likely look up to those who had commanded the forces of their salvation. Those politically hopeful junior officers needed to understand that the war came first!

Few of the MilForce troops in his sectors, and fewer of the officers, had actually been in contact with the enemy. They had yet to experience the onslaught of the implacable Remor, see their troops and ships wither under the devastating Remor weapons, or bear bitter witness to the casual and callous exterminations the Remor performed wherever they found Humans. Unlike Stone, most deluded themselves into believing that they were dealing with something less than a genocidal war.

How could they be so stupid? So blind?

Humanity was fighting a war for survival. Considerations of what might come afterwards must be held off. Humanity could not afford to divert resources from the struggle, especially not to advance self-serving daydreams of political power. Bad as the officers were, the politicians were worse!

Imbeciles!

He cut the newsfeed, silencing the Serenten minister to whom he had long ago stopped listening. He was disgusted with himself. All this brooding, accomplishing nothing— he needed to be doing something.

The operations deck was the nerve center of Tarsus Station and, as usual, it was abustle with activity. Stone felt better as soon as he walked through the hatch. Things were happening here. Work was getting done. He headed for the main holotank, where sector status was constantly updated, but before he'd gotten halfway there his intel officer Chip Hollister intercepted him.

"Courier boat just came in from our Sol-ward neighbors, Commander."

Something new from the Pan-Stellar Combine? Unlikely. "The Pansies still protesting how we saved their asses in Sector 31?"

Sector 31 held few adherents to the Interstellar Defense League and its wardship had been combined with that of Sector 32. Though a Yellow sector with no reported enemy activity, it had been the site of the most recent action Stone's forces had seen when the petty potentate of a two-system empire had gotten greedy and tried to snatch the Thorpe Agrell System from the Pan-Stellar Combine, judging quite rightly that the Pansies wouldn't stand up to her, even to defend the useful Thorpe Agrell transit junction. But she hadn't counted on Stone taking an interest. Her mistake. Stone had jumped on the trouble-makers with both feet. Citing his IDL-mandated authority to enforce the peace in his sector, his forces had squashed the invasion fleet and taken the war home to the warmonger. The new government had aligned with the League, and the survivors of the potentate's fleet now ran picket duty, watching the fringes for Remor.

Initially the Pan-Stellar Combine had been grateful, but their gratitude had vanished even before construction was finished on the waystation Stone established in the Thorpe Agrell System. He didn't care if the Pansies didn't believe him when he told them he had no designs on their colony world. The IDL had come to Thorpe Agrell and the IDL was staying. He needed the access route to some of the more isolated IDL worlds of Sector 31. Ensuring the safety of Sector 31's League worlds was Stone's responsibility.

When he'd told the Pansies that they'd have to get used to their new neighbors, they'd howled. They were howling still.

Knowing the situation as well or better than Stone did, Chip grinned. "Of course they're protesting, sir, it's their nature. But that's the old news."

"So what's the new news, Chip?"

"A Pansie survey team has opened a route to a new system in arc 12 of Sector 29. Konoye's team."

"Arc 12?" That was barely inside the boundary of Humankind's expansion during the first Diaspora. "I thought Konoye was prospecting for a route to the inner systems."

"He was. Still says he's going to make the connection, too, but for now the Pansies are a little distracted. An early report out of the new system says that they've got indications of life on the fourth planet. The Pansies are laying claim, of course. They haven't got a name for the place, but they've already posted affiliate status for the system."

"So they've got themselves more indigs to sell beads and trinkets to, do they?"

"The situation may not be so simple, sir. Our agents in the Combine's Marketing Directorate have provided us with the raw data from Konoye's first survey. I think you'll want to take a look. They're reporting objects in orbit."

"A technic civilization?"

"It would seem that they were at one point. The Pansies think they've got aliens who made it to local space and fell back, which since their estimate of the artifacts' age puts them much older than Humanity's expansion in that area, makes sense."

A fallen species? Why not? Humanity itself had almost lost the stars. But what if it were something else? "Humans aren't the only ones who can lose colonies."

"That's what I was thinking, sir."

They retired to Stone's office and dumped the purloined data into his holotank. Most of the material concentrated on the planet and the enormous structures visible from space. There was nothing on the reported aliens themselves. The Pansies had decided to ease back and do some observation, once they had realized what they had. Damned unusually bright for them.

Stone ran through the material a second time, more slowly. He ignored the pics of constructs on the planet's surface. Decayed buildings were decayed buildings. He scanned the pics of the material in orbit around the planet. Reaching orbit was a greater feat than just about anything done within the gravity well, and what a species elected to put into space told a lot about it. Most of the pics displayed unidentifiable junk. The pics of the material orbiting the planet's moon were even more informative, removing his doubts that some of the debris had once been armed. Physics demanded certain configurations for certain weapons, configurations that Stone's professional eye saw at once. Then he saw something that chilled him to his soul.

"Forward this to StratCom. Fastest courier."

But Stone didn't need to wait for the intelligence service's analysis to know what had been uncovered. The octahedral shape displayed in the holotank was burned in his memory. Despite the low resolution of the image, Stone knew it for what it was.

"You see this?" he asked, highlighting and expanding the image for Hollister.

"Yes, sir." Chip sounded puzzled.

"Look familiar?"

"I don't— Wait. It's not. It couldn't be!" he exclaimed as recognition lit his features.

"The Pansies would hardly be faking such a thing."

"Dear God, I wish I could think of a reason why they might."

The object looked remarkably like one that Stone had seen in the Cassuells Home System. That object had been a Remor device, possibly a buoy or beacon. What could this thing be but another one of those damned devices?

"Chip, we need to know a lot more about the Pansies' new system. I want an outline for a probe mission on my screen in six hours. Bring Ersch in and anyone else you think necessary, but keep it small for the moment. I don't want anyone panicking if word gets out before we can confirm. If that thing is what I'm afraid it is, we're looking at a lot of trouble."

## SERENTEN CONCORDAT
## SOMMERSET SYSTEM

"Congratulations, Kurt."

Kurt barely heard Doctor Nellis's words as she handed him his identicard. The garish red *limited rights* band no longer slashed across the card's face like a bloody wound. He savored the pristine look of the card. This was the final certification that he had returned from the brink. Once more, Kurt Ellicot was a sound, stable, and employable member of Concordat citizenry.

"Doctor, I don't know how to thank you."

"Whatever form you choose will be acceptable. Would you like to try the card?"

Kurt nodded and she slid a reader across her desk toward him. He fumbled his first attempt to insert the card. What was there to be nervous about? He was certified normal. He managed his second attempt, and the basic data screen came up. As he thumbprinted to confirm his identity, a blue header popped up. His hand froze. What was that all about? Blue headers were *not* normal on the cards of ordinary citizens.

Doctor Nellis noticed his halt, turned the reader's screen so she could see it, and frowned. "That's a legal dispute flag."

"What does it mean, Doctor?"

"Let's find out, shall we?" She screened the sanitarium's legal department and was immediately connected to Mr. Rafael Teng, one of the senior staff lawyers. It turned out he had been waiting for Doctor Nellis's call.

"Is Mr. Ellicot there?" he asked.

"Right here," Doctor Nellis replied as she adjusted the screen's pickup to include him.

"What is the problem, Mr. Teng?"

"Well, Mr. Ellicot, at this stage I'd rather call it a situation rather than a problem. We're looking at a suit from Ms. Ellicot alleging that Doctor Nellis's recovery declaration is biased and premature. Her attorney—Bolton I think the name is, yes, Holly Bolton—is suggesting collusion between the doctor and yourself, Mr. Ellicot. Anyway, Ms. Bolton says that her firm is in possession of certain tapes that will prove a prejudicial relationship between the doctor and Mr. Ellicot."

"What sort of tapes, Harry?" Doctor Nellis's eyes were narrowed dangerously.

"Therapy tapes. I'm sure you can guess which ones."

Kurt could guess, too. More than once Doctor Nellis's virtuality persona had conducted virtual sex with Kurt. Such sexual unions were occasionally demanded of ethnologists in the field, and Doctor Nellis had needed to test Kurt's reactions to such situations. Such doings were natural aspects of some of the "alien cultures" which Kurt had studied. It had been nothing more than role-playing, as unreal as the "aliens" themselves.

Doctor Nellis's tapes were supposed to be confidential, but early in Kurt's treatment Clarise had been named party to the confidentiality. It had seemed wise, a way to let Kurt's wife understand something of what he was going through. Clarise had viewed some of the early sessions, but as far as Kurt knew she had soon stopped.

"This is absurd!" Doctor Nellis was obviously incensed. "There has never been anything other than a legitimate doctor-patient relationship between Kurt and me. Anyone who says otherwise is looking to catch some legal trouble themselves."

"Calm down, Ginny," Mr. Teng advised. "You're jumping the gun. I don't think this is directed at you. I think we're looking at a ploy here."

"To reinstate the no-contact order against me?"

"Quite likely, Mr. Ellicot."

"I don't care who the target is," Doctor Nellis exclaimed. "It's *my* reputation and professional competency that this woman is slandering! She's got no case."

"I wouldn't be so sure of that. *Tumlu v. Tumlu* in 2108 offers them a solid entrance on intent of infidelity being synonymous with action regarding martial contracts with exclusivity clauses. Tie that with a firm body of case law upholding the principle that there are no virtual emotions, and we're looking at strong suspicion of infidelity by intent and that could be enough to sway a jaundiced judge."

Doctor Nellis fumed. "She had no right to her so-called evidence. It'll be thrown out."

"I don't think so. I checked this morning and Ms. Ellicot remains on the access list for Mr. Ellicot's tapes. She had legal access."

"It's marital privilege," Doctor Nellis countered.

"Nice try. Shared confidences are admissible in a marital contract dispute."

"We'll fight it, Harry," Doctor Nellis vowed.

"It'll get ugly," Mr. Teng warned.

"Doctor," Kurt said quietly, "there's no need for anything to get ugly, and no need to fight anything. Whether Clarise is right or not isn't the issue. She is only dragging you in as a way to get what she wants. What she wants is me out of her life and out of the childrens' lives. It's her choice. We should honor it."

Doctor Nellis sat back in her chair and frowned. On the screen Mr. Teng patiently waited. Kurt let them think about what he had just offered by implication; uncontested, Clarise's legal maneuvering would bar Kurt from ordinary citizenship. The doctor was the first to speak.

"What about you, Kurt? You can't want this."

"Want it? No. Stand it? I think so. I've survived worse." He shrugged. "It's time to look to the future."

"Kurt, I don't know what to say. Your reaction to this proves that I'm right and she's wrong. You don't deserve what this woman is trying to do to you. I don't think it's fair."

"Fairness isn't at issue here, Doctor. Viewpoints are. Are you afraid that I can't handle it?"

"No. Not at all. I wouldn't have signed your release documents if I hadn't thought you'd made a complete recovery."

"Thank you, Doctor." He turned to the screen. "Mr. Teng, I'd be obliged if you would see that my wife gets what she wants with as little damage to Doctor Nellis as possible. I will sign whatever releases are necessary."

"If you're sure, Mr. Ellicot."

"Quite sure."

Mr. Teng wanted some details clarified. Then there was a round of formalities, good-byes and all that. Kurt sailed through it all. His years of association with Doctor Nellis and the sanitarium were over now, part of the past. Time to look to the future. As he left the office, headed for his empty home, Kurt wondered if he would dream when he went to sleep.

## IDL DEFENSE SECTOR 32-(RED)
## GRENWOLD

Tall Butte Township was the presumptuous name of the place. It wasn't the Tall Butte part that Anders Seaborg thought presumptuous—the monumental landform in question was impressively tall. It was the town part which bordered on the absurd. Less than fifty rustic homesteads did not constitute more than a village on most worlds, but from what he had seen, this was one of the larger Grenwold settlements. Other than its size, however, it seemed little different from the dozens he and his troopers had visited in the last two weeks.

"Not much to look at, is it?"

Anders could barely hear Captain Metzler over the rattle and roar of the blower. The captain's helmet, being a pilot's and not decent groundpounder issue, was not linked directly to the combat vehicle's intercom, which left shouting the only way to communicate. They had not communicated much during the trip.

Most of the time Metzler was okay—for a shuttle jock— but every so often Metzler showed his annoyance over the fact that Seaborg was mission commander. *Shaka*'s maiming and departure hadn't altered the command structure for the ground mission, just its goal. To a degree the pilot's ire was understandable, Metzler having the superior basic rank, but in MilForce, mission and expertise came first, a condition that clearly didn't prevail in Metzler's home military.

"It's still the provincial capital," Anders shouted back.

"Backwater," was all Anders made out of Metzler's reply.

More than many settlements on frontier worlds, Tall Butte Township showed few signs of the technology base that had gotten Humans to the planet. Elsewhere the lack of amenities and industrialization was born of necessity; here it was part and parcel of the colonists' intended way of life.

When he'd been handed his expanded assignment, Anders had gotten a data download from *Shaka's* computers. Grenwold had been claimed by a sect of the Haimish Movement, one of a long line of back-to-simplicity philosophies. Haimish philosophy held that man was too dependent on machines and that an honest working life was infinitely superior to one of technologically assisted ease. They weren't total Luddites, but they weren't far removed either. Haimish philosophy went a long way to explaining why the system's traffic control was so ill-informed, and *that* went a long way in dispelling fears that the Grenwolders were collaborating with the enemy.

The people looking up from their work as the column blasted into the township were as Human as any of the troopers aboard the blowers. Humans—sane Humans—didn't, *couldn't* collaborate with the enemy. The Followers of Haims might not be reasonable, as arguments at each and every one of their stops had shown, but they weren't insane.

As the blowers throttled down, quiet settled on the township with the dust they had disturbed. No constant buzz of coolers here; the air inside the buildings would only be as different from that outside as the thick walls and roofs could make it; and in the day's late afternoon the differential wouldn't be great. Soon that warmth would be appreciated as the night sky began to suck away the day's heat, but just now wasn't the time.

Now the crowd was gathering. It was time to do what they had come here to do.

"I make the head Haimie to be the one in the digger hat." Metzler nodded in the direction from which the man was approaching. "From the frown on his face, I'd say that he's going to be a hard sell."

Anders watched the man approach. The way the crowd parted for him confirmed Metzler's identification. Anders hauled himself out of the commander's hatch and clambered down to meet him, offering his hand.

"I'm Commander Anders Seaborg."

"You're in charge of the League men?" the Grenwolder asked, ignoring Anders's hand.

Their equipment and identification flashes should have made that obvious enough, but Anders didn't want to start by antagonizing this influential man. "Yes, sir. And you are?"

"Damson."

"And you would be the provincial coordinator?"

"Right. We haven't got spare room for you and your men, if you're thinking of staying the night."

"Not a problem, sir. We don't intend to trouble you."

"Already done that."

A broad, red-faced Grenwolder with a gray fringe beard stepped up. "Ease up, Aaron Damson. These boys just got here. They ain't done nothing but stir up a little dust. Like that's something that never happens around here."

"They're stirring up trouble," declared Damson.

"And if I may ask, sir, where did you hear that?" Anders asked.

Damson glared at him. "Folks hear from other folks."

"If you've heard about us, you've probably heard why we're here." Anders lifted his head and swept his gaze across the crowd. He wanted to make sure they knew he was addressing all of them. "But in case you haven't, you need to know that you're all in grave and terrible danger. There are Remor on Grenwold, and not a lot to stop them. You're not ready to fight them, and frankly we're not either. We weren't expecting to find them here. But we have. Unless we stop them, this will become their planet. You've worked hard to make Grenwold your own. It's time to fight for what is yours. We're here to help you fight the Remor."

Damson spat in the dirt, barely missing Anders's boot. "We don't want your damned League. We don't need you running our lives."

"We're not here to run your lives. We're not here to run anyone's life. Save some lives, maybe. We're here to fight the Remor."

"Fighting costs lives," Damson said. "But there's nobody here for you to fight, soldier-man."

The fringe-bearded Grenwolder spoke, worriedly. "He says there's Remor, Aaron Damson."

"He does, doesn't he, Joshua Liefssen." Damson spun and faced the crowd. "Where?" he thundered. "What Remor? I ain't seen any. Have you seen any, Joshua Liefssen?"

Liefssen shrugged his broad shoulders. "Can't say as I have."

Damson nodded savagely. "What about you, Samantha Hasen? Or you, Svein Rostler? Edie Grammar? Aadne Duch? Anybody seen any of these killer aliens? No? There, you see? Nobody around here has seen any of your bogeymen, let alone been bothered by them. Way I see it, you're here to stomp somebody all right. Us!"

Anders's denial was swamped by shouts from the locals, but not all of the yelling was in favor of Damson's position. These Grenwolders were a fractious, independent lot, with more than a touch of paranoia about outside interference in their lives. They reminded him a lot of the folk back home on Ultima Eridani, except that most of these people were being willfully ignorant in a way that no Eridani ever would. The Remor were the enemy of all Humankind, even those who chose to ignore the threat.

"We're here to defend you," he told them when they ran low on steam. "The Remor are here to conquer you."

"If they're here to conquer us, why haven't we seen any of them, soldier-man?" asked one of Damson's partisans.

"Because you haven't gone looking," Anders told him. "Take a trip to Woldnos. You'll see them. We have."

That was a slight exaggeration. Without *Shaka*'s eyes in the sky, he hadn't dared risk the full platoon in reconnaissance, but the squad he'd sent across the water had reported Remor machines. Not fighting machines, but Remor devices nonetheless, and where there were Remor machines, there were Remor. If no fighting machines had been seen, it could only be because the Remor haven't needed them so far.

Damson wasn't buying it. "The Remor, if there are Remor, are on the other side of planet, minding their own business. This here planet is a big world. Way I see it, if they ain't bothering us, we got no call to go bothering them. We got peace here. Why fool with it?"

Why indeed? Anders couldn't deny that there were no hostilities between the Remor on planet and the resident Humans, but he knew the Remor to be the implacable enemy of Humankind. What other than Human–Remor collaboration could explain the enemy's inaction?

"The Remor are our enemy," he stated.

"Your enemy!" Damson stabbed an accusing finger at Anders. "If war comes to Grenwold, *you* will have brought it."

"The Remor aren't just my enemy. They are yours, too. They are the enemy of all Humanity!"

"The League's enemies."

"*Yes*, the League's enemies." The Interstellar Defense League had been formed to defend against the Remor. "You're a part of the League. Your government—"

"Don't give us that 'your government' garbage," an angry woman interrupted. "We don't want them messing up our lives, any more than we want your soldiers doing it. The government ain't nothing but toads and weasels. No offense meant, Aaron Damson. We all know you're not like those folk down in Landing Site City. They're the ones set themselves up as a government. *Politicians!* They're worse than soldiers!"

"Getting the message, soldier-man?" asked Damson. "Even if we accept your word that there are Remor on Grenwold, and I'm not saying that we do, we don't see any Remor enemy around here. Do you? So we must be doing okay defending ourselves. I think that makes the situation simple. We don't need you. Go home!"

"The Remor *are* on your planet. They won't leave by themselves. If you haven't seen them yet, it's because you haven't looked. If they're not destroying your towns now, they will. They'll come unless we stop them."

Aaron Damson shook his head, turned his back, and walked away. Individuals and small groups did the same until there was no one left standing near the blowers but League troopers.

But afterwards, as they had in the other villages, a few young men and women came to the bivouac and sought Anders out.

# 5

"Captain Konoye?" Despite the interrogative in the woman's voice, there was no hint of uncertainty in her eyes. "I'm Dinah Freneau, plenipotentiary factor for the Lisbonne Cartel and traveling under the authority of the Governing Committee."

He shook the offered hand, and made introductions to his team. Freneau greeted them all without seeming to give any of them her attention; that remained on Konoye. He was beginning to feel uncomfortable.

"I hope your passage through the last jump was smooth," he said, offering a common pleasantry. "We've had the stabilizer field up and running for a week now, but yours is the first ship through. And, honestly, you're a little earlier than I expected you. You made good time."

"My ship is no sluggard," she said with a dismissive shrug. "Neither do I intend to be one. Let me be blunt, Captain Konoye. As you are aware, your promise of a direct link to near-Earth space has raised many hopes and occasioned more than a bit of speculation. Prematurely, it seems. In some quarters, it has been suggested that you are draining PSC valuable resources with no hope of a reasonable return. You still have your defenders, of course, but they find themselves somewhat exposed, lacking firm proof of success in this venture. Indeed, a call for remedial action was narrowly defeated in the emergency Committee meeting following the receipt of your report. As a consequence, I have been sent to ascertain the validity of your claims. I carry the Committee's orders for you."

"Which are?" Konoye braced himself.

"Which are to be gotten to in good time, Captain. First, I have some questions. You have been here for fifty-two standard days. Have you been able to ascertain that this system is indeed an interim step in your alleged transit route?"

Konoye winced at Freneau's use of the word "alleged," which seemed to betoken a loss of faith on the part of her—and Konoye's—sponsors among the Lisbonne Cartel. Wishing he had better news, he could only tell her, "There has been insufficient time to do that, what with the work in stabilizing the transit point on this side."

"Then your pinhole theory remains no more than a theory." Frost chilled Freneau's voice.

"As I said, we haven't *yet* had time to confirm," Konoye said hastily. Freneau's aid could be invaluable, just as her ire could be devastating. It wasn't as if he were squandering resources chasing shadows. "*Yet!* We haven't even been here for two months! It's not easy uncovering a transit point, but we are collecting the necessary data. We might have gotten further along had we not been giving priority to stabilizing the inbound transit point, which is—as I am sure you are aware—standard Survey Office procedure."

"Yes," she said in cold, unadorned acknowledgment of his correctness. "What other standard procedures have you chosen to follow, Captain?"

"We've had our small craft out running survey sweeps of this system," he said, remembering his ace in the hole. "In fact, we've already bundled the data from our initial inner system run and shipped it back on the first of our H-tube test drones. Canessa Station should have recovered the drone and passed on the data by now. You probably crossed tracks with it while you were on your way here."

"Yes." She turned her gaze to the bridge holotank, which showed local space in abstracted display. "The initial report on the fourth planet is intriguing."

The cold, matter-of-fact comment caught him by surprise. She was a plenipotentiary official, and the data had been sent under Lisbonne Cartel seal. If she had known about the data transmission and happened to be in the right place at the right time, she could have used her power to order the files opened. "You've seen it?"

"Gross planetary data is so boring, don't you think? It never tells the true tale of a system's worth. The debris orbiting the fourth planet and its moon, however, I find worthy of attention. Have you refined your data on it?"

Her answer demonstrated that she *was* aware of the transmission's contents. Since she knew what kind of prize they had here, why was she so hostile?

"Of course we have continued study. I realize that we haven't done all that might have been done, but we have been preoccupied with necessary duties and with fulfilling our original mission. We have—"

"—no time for self-serving excuses." Freneau's expression was unforgiving. "I want to see all the files on the fourth planet."

Hope sprang up. Freneau's hostility made him fear that she carried a detrimental judgment on the mission, but if that judgment had been formed without the data in the follow-up reports, as it might well have been, given interstellar communication time lags ... "Well, it's been a while since we collected the last dump from the orbiting monitors. In fact, we should be processing one now, but I can have the existing files readied for you. The quarters prepared for you have a fine viewer and—"

"This is the bridge, is it not? That is the command couch, is it not? There is no reason the data cannot be played here and now, is there?"

"No. Of course not."

"Well, then."

He walked over to the command console and began to call up the records, intending to feed them to another station, but before he finished, Freneau slid into the couch. He felt a hot twinge of annoyance. That was the captain's chair—*his* chair. He was surprised at himself. He had never really spent much time thinking of himself as the captain, but now, with this hostile stranger in his seat, he felt very possessive about his rank and privileges. She could have at least waited for him to offer her the use of the chair! But he was too afraid of her connections to object. He started the records running and anxiously stepped back to wait while she judged what his team had found here.

The other members of his team found things to occupy them around the bridge, none—not coincidentally, he was sure—near him. The isolation of the tainted had begun. But why should that be? They hadn't opened the route he'd predicted, but they had found something of great value to the Combine: a life-supporting planet. Not only that, but the remains of an alien culture. Surely a blind man could see the potential here.

"Most intriguing," Freneau murmured. Then even more quietly, as if speaking to herself, she said, "It seems that I will be delivering the second disk."

Konoye knew that she had intended him to hear, but he restrained himself from asking what she meant. The way Freneau frowned suggested that she wasn't very happy with what she was seeing. Interrupting her concentration was not the way to improve his position with her. Waiting wasn't easy, but he managed—barely—until she finished viewing the records.

At long last she leaned back in the command couch.

"Captain, whatever else you have found here, you have not completed the mission upon which you set out. That is a most salient fact. No, save your excuses. I am under strict orders to except no excuses. I have a disk for you that I have carried from the Committee Room." She produced a disk from the pocket of her jacket. "You are to view it. Now."

Konoye stared at the thing in her hand. It glittered, reflecting the bridge lighting in chromatic glints. Such disks were old-fashioned, but they were the data mode that the Governing Committee traditionally chose to deliver messages of significance. Promotions came that way—he'd received the captaincy of *Byrd* on one—but so did demotions. Pardons came that way, as did orders for execution. Which was this? Freneau's stony expression offered no hint.

He started to reach for the disk. "Well, if you'll excuse me, I'll take it to my cabin and—"

"I think not," Freneau said, snatching the disk away. "My orders require me to validate your receipt of the message."

"Well, we can both—"

"In public."

Konoye swallowed hard. In public. As in public execution? Relieving him of command would have to be done in public, so that his replacement could be made publicly. Would Jane step up to take his place? Of course she would. Just business, after all. He wondered whether they would let her continue looking for the connection to Ursa.

"The console's right there," he said, pointing. He wasn't going to put in the disk himself.

Freneau raised an eyebrow, but said nothing. She slotted the disk and stepped back, positioning herself to watch him rather than the recording. Of course, *she* already knew what was coming.

Accompanied by a three-toned hum, an image winked to life in the tank. It was the golden steelyard weight of the Pan-Stellar Combine's great seal. A succession of verification icons and antitampering seals winked on, forming a wreath around the central image. The ring completed, the seal faded and was replaced by a blurred human image. As the focus refined, Konoye recognized Aleksey Quevedo, head of the Lisbonne Cartel, the Governing Committee member who had sponsored his pitch to that body. He had the most to lose by Konoye's failure and the most to gain from cutting Konoye off early. Konoye wasn't sure that he wanted to hear what Quevedo was going to say, but he didn't have a choice.

"Under authority granted by the Board of Representatives of the Pan-Stellar Combine," the image began, "and by proxy empowered to the Governing Committee and through the Committee by proxy empowered to me, Aleksey Quevedo of the Lisbonne Cartel, I hereby make this recording as a clear record for posterity.

"In acknowledgment of your recent outstanding contributions to the Pan-Stellar Combine, I am pleased and honored to extend to you the position of managing director of the newly charted system and claimed in the name of the Pan-Stellar Combine by right of presence."

The golden steelyard weight appeared for a fraction of a second, to be replaced by Quevedo again.

"On a personal note, Ken, I would like to invite you to join the Lisbonne Cartel. I know you'll be getting a lot of offers in the next few weeks, but I'm sure you understand all that's been done for you and, from everything I've heard, you're a lot like me—you've got a strong sense of gratitude and you remember people who have helped you. You can give Ms. Freneau your answer. She's got the necessary disks. I'm looking forward to working with you, Ken."

Konoye stood in shocked silence. He heard the murmurs of his team, felt the heat of Jane's beaming grin, and heard the footsteps of someone leaving the bridge to carry the news to the rest of the crew. The crew's reactions told him that what he'd heard was real, that he hadn't slipped into some kind of escape fantasy. He wasn't canned. He wasn't going to be pilloried. He had been *promoted!*

"Congratulations, Mr. Director," Freneau said. She smiled now. "But before we record any legal documents, we'll need to have a name for your system. Discoverer's right gives that privilege to you."

He kicked his brain into gear. She was correct, of course. The system needed a name. Despite the claims of some of his colleagues, he didn't have the kind of ego that needed to see his name emblazoned across the stars. So if he couldn't bring himself to name the place after himself, what could he call the system?

He thought about the sudden turnaround in his fortunes.

He'd never thought of this place as an end in itself. He hadn't even come here deliberately. All he had wanted to do was prove that his jump route was real. This system was just a waystation, a place between where he'd started and where he'd wanted to end up. *Would* end up! He still believed that this system was somewhere in the middle of a viable route to near-Earth space.

And *that*, he saw, was the answer. Neither one end nor the other, but the unavoidable, inevitable connection between the two. The middle.

"Chugen," he said.

"Is that someone's name?" Freneau asked.

"It's a word in the Earth language of my ancestors. It is used for a middleman."

"Ah," she said. "You are a man with a great sense of history as well as great faith. Very well then, it shall be as you wish. Chugen is henceforth the name of this system." Her fingers danced across the command console. "And Chugen is now officially a protected affiliate of the Pan-Stellar Combine."

Showing a newfound deference for the managing director, Freneau expressed her willingness to defer business discussions for the moment and asked to be shown to her quarters. That was fine by Konoye. He wanted a little time to get used to his new status. Not that he would anytime soon.

Master Hoppe saved him from a social gaffe by offering to escort Freneau. As they left the bridge, Konoye dazedly accepted the congratulations of his team and of the bridge crew.

Managing director! It wasn't anything he'd ever thought of achieving. The position came with a seat on the board of directors. On the board! He wasn't really qualified; he was an astrophysicist, not a manager or a politician. Of course many members of the board, especially managing directors, took little active part in deliberations as they had big enough jobs dealing with the systems under their authority. An entire system under *his* authority! An enormous responsibility. An enormous *job*. Intimidating! And lucrative. The wealth a man could accumulate from discoverer's royalties was substantial—the sort a managing director could garner was astronomical!

But wealth—dare he think it?—wasn't everything. This promotion could cost him quite a bit. He remembered his stint as dean at Mellenthin University and what that had done to his research time. He'd nearly lost his bid for tenure because he hadn't published enough. A dean only had a college to worry about, while a managing director had an entire solar system. This new position would almost certainly consume more time than he could conceive of wanting to give it. Shuffling administrative data was no way to chart a jump route.

Slumping into his captain's chair—was it the director's chair now?—he pondered the problem. With rank came clout, and he could use his new clout in service of his old dream. His fingers flew on his keyboard, drafting a request for Combine funds to build a gateway station. It would be his first official act as managing director. *A reasonable and foresighted one*, he told himself. A gateway station would make the jump to Chugen safe, and once they located the transit point to Ursa and linked it to the rest of the route, such a station would become even more necessary. The traffic through Chugen would be heavy, to say the least. Why, its wealth might even grow to rival Wayfarer Station. He'd been reluctant to name the system after himself—but the station! Now the station was something else. He was the *first* Managing Director for the system, wasn't he? It wasn't all that much of a conceit, was it? No, not really. Lots of—

His daydreaming was cut short by Jane's finger tapping on his shoulder.

"We've finished processing the download from the orbital monitors around Four. You're not going to like it, Ken. The planet's got indigenes."

She showed him the pics. He didn't need her helpful pointing to see the structures that looked like huts, or the black dots of the indigenes scattered around the settlement. These first few shots weren't conclusive, but he felt sickeningly sure that more pics would indicate patterned, organized activity. He felt betrayed.

"You said the civilization was *dead!*"

She shrugged as if it didn't matter. "There's no doubt that the technic civilization is. There aren't any signs of remaining industry, which means that the local species is at a nonindustrial level. They may even be nonagricultural. Whatever they were once, it looks like they've been reduced to a hunter-gatherer lifestyle."

That was a plus. He'd been afraid that he'd just had his prize snatched away. By Combine law, the existence of an indigenous technological culture would require that his managing directorship be annulled. A coordinating director would be appointed instead, and that was a post for which he was unlikely to be chosen.

"*Damn* them! Why couldn't the indigs be decently dead?" The presence of the indigenes would significantly complicate administration and restrict exploitation of the planet, but the natives also offered a unique opportunity. No one had ever found a *former* technological species before. Not a *living* one anyway. But unique or not, they would steal his time, and he had more important things to do with it. His eyes strayed to the main tank, which displayed Winnie's latest search patterns for the next transit point. The connection was out there. He *knew* it! It was just a matter of time. *Time.*

He sighed. "I guess we'll be spending a lot of time dealing with Four."

Jane's smirk had no sympathy at all.

## SERENTEN CONCORDAT
## SERENTEN

The simulacrum that answered the Serenten University's phones took a long time to pass Kurt's call through to the academic dean's office.

"I'm sorry, Mr. Ellicot. We don't have anything for you today." The bland smile plastered on the secretary's face looked no more real than that on the simulacrum, and his presence was no less efficient and cold. "Perhaps you should try again next month."

Last time, it had been "next week."

Kurt forced a smile of his own and thanked the man. The connection cut off, a trifle too quick for mere efficiency. Kurt sighed and accepted his card back from the phone. The blue "restricted" band across its top was there for all to see, allowing anyone to know that he was a limited citizen. It would take a reader and proper access to learn the reason for his classification as such, but the shame was visible without one.

Had Clarise intended to make him a total outcast?

He didn't want to believe that she had, but it was hard not to think the worst of her. She'd made it so easy for people to think the worst of him.

The secretary's latest brush-off made it all too clear that he was being shuffled into the back stacks. There was nothing to be gained by denying it. He'd told himself that his messages went unanswered because his former colleagues were just a little too busy and that they would get around to him. Wishful thinking, that. They had their careers to think of, and careers were built on associations of the right kinds. He was a pariah, an outcast from society, no different than any who had gone before. Did the same desperate loneliness he felt gnaw at the pariahs of Old Earth's India?

At least he was not totally cut off. Modern Serenten society had something of a conscience, or more accurately, a guilt complex. He still had the pensioner's allowance that was deposited automatically in his account.

Was being a remittance man any better than being a total outcast?

Perhaps a little. At least the university wanted something of his; his name remained on the rolls as professor emeritus. But his name was all they cared to have.

He really couldn't blame them.

So now what, now that he'd accepted his sentence? What was he to do? There was no way to do field work without accreditation and grants. He had been a good teacher, and hadn't it always been said that those who can't, teach? Staring at the blue band, he knew there was little hope of that. As long as he was a limited citizen, he wasn't the sort anyone would want having access to receptive, developing minds. Too dangerous.

Him—Kurt Ellicot—dangerous? He laughed—out loud, judging by the reactions of passersby. Their furtive looks told him that they knew what he was. Some might have even known who he was. He'd been famous once—at least in university circles. But those times were gone.

He shrugged up the collar on his topcoat and turned his back on the admin building. The transit station was on the other side of campus. He strode toward it, his walk taking him through shoals of students bustling between class sessions. He'd once had students of his own. Did they remember him?

He slowed his pace, letting them flow around him. No one stopped. No one acknowledged his presence, save to mutter under their breath at his being in the way. He cut to the side of the path and found an unoccupied bench. He sat, watching the crowd of young, eager faces passing by him. Once, he'd seen the future in those faces, but now all he saw was his own past.

The crowd thinned as destinations were reached. In ancient tradition, a bell tolled from the tower of Sudbury Hall: class sessions were beginning. Now only a few students strolled along the paths. A few more studied, or took their ease in the grass, despite the autumn air. Kurt sat watching them.

What else did he have to do?

He was still sitting there, hours later, when the growing chill of dusk gnawed deep enough into his bones to force him up. He was alone on the green. All the students were gone.

He stood, shivering slightly, and raised his eyes to the darkening sky where the stars were beginning to come out—as much as they ever did in the sky over Settlebridge. Distant stars. Foreign stars. So far away that only the strongest could force their light into the sky over Serenten. They shone with a hard, uncompromising light. He had once had a place among them. Now—he closed his eyes and sucked in a deep breath—now he was, as the poet Wilson had said, to go a-voyaging no more.

He looked once more at the beacons in the sky.

*Will you remember me?*

## IDL DEFENSE SECTOR 32-(RED)
## GRENWOLD

"Are you sure this is wise?" asked Metzler as soon as he brought up the intraship commo.

It wasn't the first time that the captain had questioned one of Anders's decisions. In fact, since they had landed on Grenwold, Metzler had made a habit of it. At least the Eustan captain didn't do it in front of the troops, but he did on occasion drag up his awkward questions in front of the noncoms. An Eridani wouldn't question a commanding officer that way, but—when Anders wasn't angry at the man—he was grateful. His sudden and unexpected rise to command of this expeditionary force had left him more than a little unsettled, and Metzler's questions made Anders think, hard, about what he was trying to accomplish. Even Metzler's ignorant questions about standard ground operations were useful, since this wasn't a standard operation. Assuming that it was standard could well be a program for disaster. There were so few resources and so much to do—so much at stake.

"Sure that it's wise?" Anders *wished* that he were sure, and would have *said* he was to any of his noncoms, but he figured he owed his Eridan conscience an honest answer. "No, not at all sure, but it's got to be done."

"Hewitt's qualified to lead the recon."

"Hewitt's got a job." Sergeant Hewitt was busy training the new Grenwolder recruits. The sergeant's instructional abilities were far more important under the current circumstances than his reconnaissance capabilities, and Metzler knew it. Where was Metzler headed with this?

"I'm talking about the two of us doing this recon," Metzler said hesitantly. "This is a high-risk op."

That was not news. High-risk ops came your way when they came your way. All part of life in MilForce. Clearly the Eustan didn't have an Eridani's discipline and needed some bucking up. "Didn't you offer to fly the shuttle because you're the best pilot among your team? I fully expect you'll get us in and out without a problem."

"I'm not talking about the transport. We don't really know what's happening on the western continent. Sure, we *know* there's a Remor landing force, but what do we know *about* it? There could be anything from a survey team to an entire army over there. We could be walking into a *nest* of the damned xenos."

"It's precisely because we don't know that we've got to do this," Anders snapped. Sitting in the shuttle with the engines warming up was not the time to debate the mission. The Eustan's whining was starting to annoy him. "Look, I know that you vacuum-heads don't like getting any closer than a million klicks to the enemy, but we're all dirtside now and life is a lot more intimate. When it comes to recon, us sloggers just got to see with our own Mark 1 eyeballs. It's a dirtside thing, and I don't expect you to understand. But I do expect you to follow orders, and your orders are to lift and get us to where we're going."

Anders expected that to be the end of it, but it wasn't. The engines maintained the steady idle, and Metzler said, "If we don't come back, this outpost will be without officers."

So that was it. "Are you asking to be replaced?"

Metzler didn't answer at once. "Actually, I was hoping you'd replace yourself. You're the senior slogger and this is a slogger outpost. It won't help anyone if you buy it on this mission."

Anders felt ashamed that he had misjudged the man. Metzler's concern was valid, but a commander needed information to do his job. Here and now Anders needed firsthand knowledge about the disposition of the enemy. A soft, minimal recon was needed, and after Sergeant Hewitt, Anders was the best qualified soldier on planet to do the job. How different was Anders's decision to assign himself to the task from Metzler's choice of himself as the best qualified pilot? Well, there was one difference: Anders was the commander.

And since when had Eridani led from the rear?

"I don't see any way out of it," he told Metzler. "We need to know more about what we're up against. Without that information, it won't matter who's in charge of the force. So we're going and that's it. Got it, Captain?"

"Aye, sir."

Almost at once, the engines growled more deeply. Anders was pushed back into his couch as the shuttle accelerated. Within seconds, they were in the air and on their way.

Metzler was a good pilot, but still Anders worried. Even

good pilots got caught out when they didn't understand and account for the enemy's capabilities. With so much unknown about the capabilities of the Remor, how could anyone be sure that all necessary precautions had been taken? Or if the precautions they'd taken would be effective?

As it happened, they crossed the strait separating the continents without incident. Two hundred kilometers of Woldnos landscape passed under the belly of the ground-hugging shuttle, also without incident. They had planned on a stealthy passage, but still Anders worried. Had they been spotted? Were the Remor just biding their time before blasting the shuttle from the sky? So far they'd seen nothing to indicate that the Remor even knew of their existence, let alone the approach of this shuttle. But that didn't mean the enemy was ignorant. Still, they could hope and pray that the enemy *was* ignorant.

At last they reached the canyon land that Anders had chosen to conceal their landing site and Metzler proved that he hadn't exaggerated his skill, following a river course and snaking the heavy craft in precise turns among the buttes. They thundered along above the river's sluggish, muddy water, which could be primarily distinguished from the ocher earth around it by its shine. Variegated rock walls slid past Anders's viewport as the shuttle rocketed along below the level of the plains and, presumably, below the line of sight for any watching Remor sensors.

This part of Woldnos was carved into wide, flat-bottomed river valleys, some dry, some still hosting the feeble remnants of the torrents that had cut through into the earth, revealing the layered strata of sedimentary rocks. It was wild country; Anders hoped that it was not the sort to attract Remor attention and would provide a base from which to launch their reconnaissance sweeps.

Metzler selected a steep-walled canyon and took the shuttle in, landing amid a whirlwind of dust and pattering gravel. At once they set about concealing the craft. With more than a little struggle, they stretched a mimetic thermal tarp over the shuttle, securing the craft as best they could from aerial observation. Metzler saw to powering down and securing the shuttle while Anders checked out the hardsuits, confirming that the recon software was loaded and all systems were operating at satisfactory efficiency. When Metzler came down to the bay, Anders told him to suit up and get ready for a hike. "I want you along to evaluate any aerospace assets we spot."

The Eustan didn't make the expected objection. He just nodded glumly and said, "I thought you would." Moving with funereal slowness, he climbed into the battlesuit.

Why was it that men often seemed willing to walk into deadly danger with other men rather than staying behind alone where it was safer?

It was hard for Anders to walk away from the shuttle and into the unknown land. It had to be harder for Metzler, the vacuum-head, but Metzler was uncharacteristically silent.

On the way in they had detected no identifiable emissions, neither had they seen any constructs. Two days of area sweeps didn't change that picture. Anders took them on farther ranging probes. A week passed and he began to think that he'd erred on the side of caution in having them set down so far from the disturbances they had seen from the orbiting *Shaka*. All they had encountered so far were ground tremors, thunderstorms, and local wildlife.

They were resting in the shelter of an overhang halfway up a red-banded stack of sandstones when a flash snapped Anders's gaze to the canyon floor. At first he didn't spot the cause, but another flash of light drew his eyes. Zooming in his focus, he located the intruder. Anders reached over and touched the shoulder of Metzler's suit. The conductivity circuits provided a private, nonbroadcasting channel for them to speak. He told the Eustan where to look. "Well, there's no more doubt that they're here, is there?"

"What is it?" Metzler asked.

"It's a Remor fighting machine."

"I'd guessed that. I meant what model?"

"I'm not sure. Library's best match is a cayman, but the confidence isn't high enough to be sure." He filed observation data on the machine, logging it as ?CAYMAN–GRENWOLD.

"They used caymans on Kuo's World, didn't they?" To Anders's grunted confirmation, Metzler said, "Thought so. I saw the pics. I thought they were bigger."

"Specs say they are. But this one's big enough to do for us."

The Remor machine stood four and a half meters tall on its two spindly-looking legs. There was immense power in those seemingly fragile legs; Anders had seen the pics from Kuo's World, too. He particularly remembered a scene of a charging Remor machine crushing hardsuited troopers under its clawed feet. This machine moved with a deliberate stride, stalking along the dry riverbed like one of the predatory avians from the Winchell Archipelago on Eridan. But no flesh-and-blood avian had ever gleamed with alloy armor cladding, or had the destructive power that this machine did.

Anders watched it with a mixture of fascination and fear.

Periodically the machine paused, its carapace slanting slightly upward. While stopped, it would sway minutely, shifting its snout back and forth in a motion that reminded Anders of a hunting animal testing the wind for the scent of its prey, while panels opened and closed along its flank. Sometimes rods extended from the openings, poking briefly out and being withdrawn again before the machine took up its march.

Metzler touched Anders. "What's it doing?" he asked, whispering even though there was no way they could be overheard.

"I don't know, but we're going to keep it under observation. Maybe it will lead us to their base."

Of course, there was no guarantee that their suit supplies would outlast the machine's patrol. If the thing even *was* on patrol.

They shadowed the fighting machine for the better part of the afternoon. The suits had no trouble keeping up, despite the many detours necessary to maintain blocking cover between them and the Remor. The machine didn't seem to be in a hurry.

Anders grew worried as the hours passed. The machine's meandering course was bringing it closer and closer to their landing site. Were the Remor's sensors somehow leading it there? His doubt about the fighting machine's destination vanished when it turned into the canyon where they had concealed the shuttle.

"We've got to take it down," he told Metzler.

"You can't be serious. There's just two of us and we haven't got any heavy weapons."

"Pop the access panels on your powerpack." Anders popped his own and started attaching cables drawn from his repair kit. "I'm going to hot-wire our suits together and juice up my pulser."

"Juice up—" Metzler sputtered. "But a pulser rifle's crystals are already near stress fracture. The manuals say—"

"Even the Bible's got addenda," Anders told him. "Pop your panels, mister."

Metzler obeyed, but it was clear that he thought Anders was nuts. Maybe he was right. Anders concentrated on making the connections between the powerpacks.

"You'll slag your rifle," the Eustan predicted.

That was definite, but a standard-issue pulser wasn't going to do anything to that machine before it made carrion of the two of them. "The rifle'll do one shot before it goes meltdown, but with a clean shot, and a little luck, it'll be just the Remor and the rifle getting slagged, not us."

"But even with the extra—"

"Mister, when I tell you how to fight your ship in vacuum, you can tell me how to fight dirtside. Not until! Got it? Now shut up, hunker down, and stop distracting me. If you've got to say something, make it a prayer to Saint Barbara asking her to look out for us mortal fools."

Metzler broke the conductivity link, so Anders didn't know if the Eustan prayed or not. Anders did—fervently— as he aligned his sight on the fighting machine's flank. He asked for a chance, trusting his own eye and skill to do the job when the opportunity arose.

Did they have a chance? Would the Remor pull another of its panel-popping probe routines before it reached the shuttle, where it would undoubtedly destroy their way home while it alerted its headquarters to their presence?

The Remor fighting machine was moving more slowly now. Was the Remor suspicious? Had it spotted them?

It stopped.

Anders waited.

The machine started forward again. Only a few steps, but its path was directly toward the hidden shuttle. Another step. This time, when it stopped, panels opened on its flank. Probes slid out.

This was it. Anders put the target dot on the blackness of an opening just forward of the machine's upper leg assembly and triggered the pulser. His helmet flash compensators handled the load of the augmented blast, but there was no denying the power of the searing pulse that burned into the belly of the machine. The Remor machine lurched as it was struck.

Anders dropped the overheated rifle. The fused pulser hit the ground, hissing and pinging. The barrel bent as it struck. The torque shattered the crystals. Anders barely noticed. His attention was on the fighting machine.

The machine crouched, panels snapping shut to guard its already violated innards. The carapace started to shift toward their position, weapon muzzles extending beneath its snout. But its defensive moves were too late. The previously opened panels—and several more—blew open a fraction of a second later, energy gouting in brilliant jets from every orifice. One leg lifted, extended, froze. The machine shuddered. The clawed foot came down. As the Remor shifted its mass for the new step, the leg collapsed. The machine toppled, crashing into the ground with a clamorous roar.

Anders stood, the better to watch the enemy fall. He'd done it. The Remor machine was down. His gamble had paid off.

Metzler jumped to his feet, cheering on an open channel. The Eustan slapped Anders on the back. "You did it! You got the bast—"

A chain of small explosions ripped off like a New Year's firecracker string. Exhaust trails erupted from the toppled machine and spiked into the sky.

Anders threw himself to the ground. Metzler remained upright until Anders reached up, grabbed his arm, and tugged him off balance.

"Get the hell down!"

Flares of eye-searing white light capped the smoke trails as staccato explosions echoed from the valley walls. Puffballs of dust sparkled greasily as they drifted down over the vanquished machine like dirty snow. Wherever the dust touched the remains of the Remor machine, the alloy began to bubble.

More explosions eviscerated the remains of the machine, scattering debris over a hundred-meter circle. Bits rained down around Metzler and Anders. Quick as he could, Anders brushed away the fragments that landed on him, but not quickly enough to prevent his suit from pitting where the stuff struck. He helped Metzler as soon as his own suit was clean. Metzler had caught more fragments than Anders, and brush-down took longer. One chunk had nearly burned through the pilot's back plate before they got it off, but that was the worst—no penetration, although both of their suits' gauntlets were burned through to the inner linings in several places.

"Look at that," Metzler said.

Anders didn't need to look. He knew what the pilot was seeing. He bounded down the slope and started across the wreck's debris field. Where the Remor fighting machine had fallen there were only unrecognizable lumps of pitted, multicolored foam. It was typical of what was left when a Remor machine destructed.

Metzler followed him. On Anders's rear monitor, he could see the pilot's head turning from side to side. Anders understood the reaction; he'd had it himself the first time he'd seen a Remor machine die. All around them the foaming wreckage was darkening, hardening. Anders kicked one of the larger lumps, shattering it into a million shards. One glittering chunk of alloy tumbled out of the dusty detritus. Anders scooped it up and tucked it away in a carry pouch.

"Not much of it left, is there?" Metzler sounded surprised.

"There never is."

Metzler shouldn't have been surprised; Anders wasn't.

But then, Eusta was a fairly new member of the League. Her people hadn't been in combat for long. Still, an officer ought to have a better appreciation of the enemy—even as mysterious and enigmatic an enemy as the Remor.

They had survived their first encounter with the enemy here on Grenwold, but all they had done was confirm the presence of Remor fighting machines on the planet. They needed more information to survive. More than likely, that meant more encounters with the enemy. Anders hoped that they would survive those encounters as well. For the sake of Humanity on Grenwold, they had to.

# 6

**SERENTEN CONCORDAT**
**SERENTEN**

The target skittered through the air, but Danielle Wyss nailed it anyway. Her athletic skills might have atrophied since she had become premier minister of the Serenten Concordat, but she still had her eye. As she called for the next bird, she imagined the face of Gaston McAlister, the Public Welfare Minister, on it. The laser carbine in her hands flashed twice in rapid succession. Two hits, one on each "wing." The bird fell like a stone, a far more satisfying sight than the wobble she usually got from only clipping one "wing."

*Take that, you obstructionist walrus!*

"Cleanly shot, *Kono*."

"Thank you, Musayi-no."

Praise from Musayi, captain of her Uritan bodyguard squad, was not exactly rare, never unearned, and always made her feel good. From a lesser being, Danielle might have considered the possibility that such praise was self-serving, mere ingratiating words, but not from Musayi. The captain had a fine sense of the difference between honest, uplifting, comforting praise and the sort of gratuitous attaboying that all too easily became obsequious fawning.

Musayi took his turn, drilling the bird several degrees of arc in the target's flight earlier than she had. Blasting the bird earlier didn't earn him extra points—only the number and location of shots on target counted—but the rapid target acquisition demonstrated his skill. It was a very good skill for a bodyguard to have.

They continued shooting for nearly an hour. The time was a luxury for Danielle, but one she was determined to have. Shooting "birds" out among the towering radeyo pines of her suburban estate was one good way to work off the tension born of a hard day running her star nation. Here she was alone—except for Musayi, and the other three Uritans of her bodysquad, and the technician on the skeet control board, of course. It was as alone as she ever got these days.

But, as with all things, an end had to come. Her last bird went up. She shouldered the carbine and tightened her finger on the trigger stud. Two flashes, one hit, and the bird wobbled to earth. Musayi's turn. He had paced her point for point during the entire session. His bird went up and he fired twice. Both misses.

It was deliberate; Musayi had thrown the match as he always did. For years she had been telling him that his transparent ploy was unnecessary, and that she could stand to have him beat her on points. But his acute Uritan hearing inexplicably failed, as it sometimes did when an Uritan didn't want to hear something. Musayi was as uncompromising in matters of etiquette as in matters of security, and a well-bred Uritan never beat his employer in any contest. It was simply unacceptable for a lower-ranking Uritan to beat a higher-ranking as such a circumstance would have challenged the *uku-rull*, the nature of the world. The result must be as the result must be: the superior one must do the expected and win the contest. The serene surface of the *uku-rull* must not be disturbed.

Still, it did make the "winning" less than satisfying.

She accepted Musayi's bow. Slinging his carbine, he

accepted hers and took it to the case. After laying both guns into their form-fitting cradles, the Uritan caressed the weapons. It was the sort of reverence connoisseurs of fine wine displayed when touching a vintage bottle or horse-women running their hands along the flank of a particu-larly good steed.

She understood something of his interest. The matched carbines were old and had been in her family for genera-tions. They hadn't always been tuned down for skeet shoot-ing as they were now. Her great-grandfather Alfred Wyss had carried one during the pacification of the rebels on Green Water and her great-uncle Chester Wyss, Alfred's twin, had carried the other. Chester never came back from the police action, but his carbine did, and Great-grandfather had retired the weapons from active service. It wasn't until Great-grandfather had passed on that her father had refur-bished them, setting them up for target shooting. Danielle had learned to shoot on them. They were indeed fine guns, deserving of Musayi's admiration.

"Very fine weapons, *Kono*," the Uritan murmured. "Much finer than those you send to our world."

"You'd like to see guns like these on your world, Musayi-no?"

"*Han, Kono.*" The Uritan's fur quivered slightly, as it sometimes did when he was anticipating something plea-surable. "Yes. Very much. A warrior could achieve much with such a weapon."

Much slaughter, most likely. The Uritans were a frac-tious lot. Before the Concordat contacted their world, they had been very prone to bloody wars among themselves. There was still a good deal of intrigue that threatened to boil over and ignite new wars. "You have too many warriors on your world."

Earth-descended primates weren't good at reading Uritan expressions. Like all of his species, Musayi had a long, low skull with a muzzle that sprouted brushy whiskers; his mouth was most expressive when he showed his teeth, but his smile was not the sort to warm the heart of a former tree ape. His dark eyes were ringed in dark fur, making them hard to see, effectively masking those windows to his alien soul. Even so, she had spent enough years in his company to know that he was regarding her with the kind of attention usually reserved for something unknown, possibly hostile, and definitely out of place.

"I meant no disrespect, Musayi-no."

"*Nogenta na tuan, Kono,*" he replied, using one of his species' multipurpose responses, usually indicating acquiescence.

She choose to accept it that way, despite the way his fingers lingered on the carbine's foregrip. "Perhaps we should get back to the house."

"*Han, Kono.*"

Musayi closed the weapon case and offered it to her so that she could print the lock. She did, and together they started through the radeyo pines. One of her bodysquad ranged ahead, the rest fell in behind. Danielle felt that somehow she had disappointed Musayi and, for reasons she was unsure of, felt that she ought to do something to make things better, or at least to make them seem better.

"Our high-tech weapons are too delicate for use on your world," she said. It was not the first time she'd handed him that particular fiction, a lie that her people kept up even with the most trusted of Uritan bodyguards like Musayi and his team. The fiction was aided by the nightly replacement of the guards' weapons, under the pretense that the guns needed sophisticated maintenance on their mechanisms. The Uritans accepted the untruth, thanks in no small part to one of their own cultural quirks. On Urita, the maintenance of mechanisms was a craftsman's job, not the province of warriors. The deception had survived for almost a decade so far. "Your people do not have the technical skills to maintain them."

Musayi nodded, a gesture he'd picked up since joining Danielle's staff. "Regretfully, on this day, what you say is true, *Kono*. It will not always be true."

Was he jealous that a craftsman might be able to do something that his culture did not allow him to do? Perhaps this was an opportunity for her to practice one of the commendatory verbal boosts that she cherished when he gave them to her. "You have more important tasks than those of a craftsman, Musayi-no."

"That is true, *Kono*."

They entered the house by a side entrance. As Danielle was recognized by the security system, the house greeted her.

"Welcome. You shot well today, Danielle," the house said, basing its compliment on its access to the skeet control. "All is in order. There are no unanswered calls. You have one visitor waiting."

Musayi's nose twitched. "There were to be no visitors tonight, *Kono*. Is this a matter of distrust?"

"Concern," she said, correcting his usage. His words might be off, but his assessment was on. She turned into the nearest room, the informal dining room, to access a screen. "House, show me the visitor and give me her credentials and stated purpose."

The screen came to life, showing a view of waiting room number one from just above the entry door. Seated in one of the tall, upholstered wingbacks was a man. He seemed at ease, sitting relaxed but absolutely still, his hands resting in his lap, but he looked definitely out of place. He wore robes rather like a monk's, but those were not those any sanctioned religious order: his robes were the rich lapis blue affected by members of the Alsion Institute. The cowl, pulled up over his head, shadowed his face and concealed him from the monitor's pickup. Danielle glanced down at the window in the lower left of the screen, where the house was displaying the standard indenticard data which included the man's portrait. He had a worn look about him, giving his expression a hangdog effect that made him appear older than his listed age. While Danielle studied the face for some clue to the man's character, the house computer voiced the most pertinent parts of the data.

"The visitor is Mohammed Miller, manager of the Serenten branch of the Alsion Institute. Identity confirmed to level two. I have a level-three confirmation of his accreditation to the Alsion Institute. Stated purpose of visit is—"

A recording of Mohammed Miller's voice replaced that of the house. "I have a message for the Premier Minister. A private one from Ambrose Alsion. I must speak to the Premier Minister alone."

"Alone is unwise," Musayi said.

"Agreed. But Mister Miller is too intriguing a visitor to go unmet." A private message from Ambrose Alsion? What had she done to draw the attention of the powerful recluse? *Something* was afoot. "House, ready the outer office and roust out Sheila. Tell her to give me fifteen minutes and then bring our visitor in."

Danielle considered the source of this visitation as she made her way upstairs for a change of clothes. Ambrose Alsion had been a researcher once, making an international name for himself in chaos-order dynamics. Sometime before Danielle finished first school, he had abandoned academia, spent a brief time amassing a considerable financial base, and founded his institute. He was said to be one of the richest beings in known space, but very little had been heard from him since his institute's early years.

His institute, on the other hand, was anything but invisible. It was said that there was a branch of the Alsion Institute on every Human-inhabited world, and most non-human-inhabited worlds as well. Researchers and scientists sponsored by it made excellent and valuable contributions to a great diversity of disciplines, touching the lives of people throughout the star nations. Danielle herself had studied under an institute-sponsored tutor during second school.

She had nothing but fond memories of and admiration for Ms. Hammond, the woman who had awakened and nurtured Danielle's interest in transplantive botany. It had been a wonder-filled and wonderful time. She still remembered how much it had hurt to face Ms. Hammond's disappointment at Danielle's announcement that she was going to pursue a political career. Even though Danielle hadn't followed Ms. Hammond into transplantive botany, she knew that she owed an incalculable amount to the woman without whose guidance and quiet wisdom Danielle would not be who she was today.

With a start Danielle realized what had prompted the memories of Ms. Hammond. There was a hint of her quiet assurance in the calm demeanor of the waiting visitor. More intrigued than ever, Danielle finished getting ready with a touchup of her cosmetics and headed for the outer office. A check of her watch told her that she'd probably be in and seated a good thirty seconds before Sheila ushered in Mr. Miller.

It turned out to be less than twenty seconds after she settled into her chair that the door opened and Sheila offered entry to Mr. Miller.

Miller paused just a step inside the room and lifted his

hands to draw back his cowl. His hangdog expression altered when he smiled. The smile made him look more like a tired old professor, or even the monk that his robes made him resemble. One member of the institute with whom Danielle had spoken at an PSC embassy party had confided that she found the robes somewhat embarrassing, but Mohammed Miller seemed totally at home in his outlandish garb as he stepped across the carpet. Danielle politely rose and accepted the hand that he thrust out.

"Good evening, Premier Minister," he said, pumping her arm with a firm but not oppressive strength. "Please accept my apologies for disturbing you at home like this, but my brief suggested that I make this delivery with all possible speed. I trust that you will not find my haste untoward, and if you do, I beg forgiveness."

Danielle gestured him to a seat. "I am at your service, Mr. Miller."

"It is most gracious of you. But I am sure that there are many calls on your time, so I will take no more of it for myself. As I told your computer, I have a message for you from Ambrose Alsion. However, I was instructed that it was private." Miller's eyes roved over the Uritan bodysquad, looming large in the dark body armor that concealed their alienness.

"Security." She shrugged. "They'll hear it whether they're present or not, so you might as well go ahead and deliver your message."

"I suppose that he understood they would, and I should have thought of it myself. Well then, if you are willing to hear Master Alsion's message, I will set up the player forthwith."

Accepting Danielle's agreement, Miller reached into his robe and produced a thick, flat disk about twice the diameter of his hand. Musayi's relaxed stance told Danielle that he was satisfied that Miller had been sufficiently scanned and pronounced harmless. There were still possibilities of threat inherent in unexpected visitors and the objects that they brought with them, but Danielle trusted Musayi's judgment. She sat and watched as Miller unfolded three lenses from recesses on one face of the disk, stretching out their supports and fiddling with the adjustment until he was satisfied that the heads were where they needed to be. The object was a holoprojector, though not a model that Danielle recognized. Miller set it on the floor and activated it.

The image that appeared was the head and shoulders of a distinguished-looking man, nearly full-blood Caucasian to judge from his fair skin, light hair, and piercing blue eyes. He wore an institute cowl, pulled down from close-cropped hair. The bunched material at his throat only slightly disrupted the flow of his very full beard. She had thought that Miller had looked like a monk, but this man struck her as the archetype of all monks. A suitable appearance for the mysterious sage Alsion, she supposed. Danielle couldn't help but think of her grandfather when she saw the smile beaming at her from the hologram. The snowy head inclined in a gesture of respect before Alsion's message began to speak.

"Good evening, Premier Minister Wyss," the deep voice greeted her as the hologram's eyes seemed to focus on her. "I am gratified that you found the time to accept my message, although I am not surprised, as I have heard word of your good will and perspicacity. I apologize that I cannot come in person and have the pleasure of speaking with you directly, but time presses and I am forced by other concerns to remain where I am. Matters, you see, are moving quickly since the recent rather profound disturbance in the event stream. The butterflies are free, I'm afraid, and until clarity is restored, all is at risk. You, I believe, are to be drawn into this turbulence, regardless of whether or not I contact you. Thus, I do not stand apart, and thus this message.

"In the expectation that my understanding is higher on the integration curve than your own, I hope to improve your position, and so I have given Mr. Miller certain data regarding the node around which the event stream first rippled. Please study the data carefully and with deep consideration.

"More ripples are spreading. Konoye's achievement, unexpected and exciting as it is, also inspires dread. I find it so, and others, for other reasons, find a great dread in it. The ripples have touched League space, but they are slow to reach Concordat space. Slowness will not hinder the ultimate wave, whose depth and strength will be overwhelming.

"Yet there is, I think, another butterfly emerging. This latest cocoon is within your own Serenten Concordat, on Serenten itself. A second drop of water cannot be expected to follow the first across a complex surface, but as two drops merge and stream in a course neither that of the first nor the second, so it may be here. Links once unknown become tenuous, then perhaps persistent, and even, ultimately, binding. Out of complexity, order.

"Hence the second set of addenda. Study these even more carefully and with deeper consideration, for these relate most closely to your own realm and your most immediate sphere of influence. Be wary. Even the slowest hand may catch and crush a butterfly before its wings are dried sufficiently for it to fly.

"I trust that your heart and your insight will serve you well in this time of coming crisis. May you know peace, earned or not."

The holographic image vanished, leaving Danielle staring confused at empty space.

"That was very cryptic."

Miller sighed sympathetically. "Not unusual in a message from Master Alsion. He thinks in ways that many of us find difficult to follow, but of his wisdom there can be no doubt."

Danielle wasn't so doubtless. "Well, in his wisdom, Master Alsion trusted you as his courier. Can you tell me about this other data? What are these nodes he was talking about?"

"I'm sorry, I did not feel that it was my place to review the data addenda, but I did notice the points of origin," he said, producing a chip case from within his robe and offering it to her. "I can tell you that the first set comes from sources in both the Pan-Stellar Combine and the Interstellar Defense League. The second set is mostly Concordat files, although there is a single one from the League, bearing their own secret coding. I tentatively conclude from the nature of the sources and from what Master Alsion said that the League figures significantly in the crisis which we are apparently facing."

Danielle agreed with his logic. The idea of a confrontation with the League disturbed her. "It has not always been easy to chart a course that keeps the Concordat friendly with our militaristic neighbor and still keeps us free of their control."

"You have done an admirable job so far. I think that Master Alsion believes that you will continue to do so."

The praise was welcome, validating her own evaluation of the job she had been doing. But what did the future hold? What was Alsion trying to achieve in sending this material to her? Whatever Alsion wanted, he foresaw that the Concordat would be involved in upcoming events. What sort of role would she or her nation play?

The Concordat files Alsion forwarded concerned a single citizen. How did he figure into this? If he was Alsion's "butterfly," the man's citizenship would ensure that the Concordat was a player in whatever developed.

She didn't like being manipulated. In the past she'd always managed to find some way to manipulate the manipulator. With Alsion that might not be possible. Still, she'd look until she found some way to take advantage of the situation. She needed to make sure that the Concordat came off well and ahead of the game, but if the League was deeply involved in this, it wouldn't be easy.

"Do you think your Master Alsion intends to lead the Concordat into war against the League?"

"War?" Miller blinked, looking appalled. "I would not venture to predict Master Alsion's intentions, but as to where the Concordat will be led, all I can say is that you are the Concordat's Premier Minister, not Master Alsion."

"You and your Master Alsion would do well to remember that."

It was an old ritual and a demeaning one; not intentionally so, but demeaning nonetheless. Of course the people who administered the ritual didn't think of it that way. Most of them were simple functionaries, doing their jobs. Some few were good-hearted souls, aware of their responsibilities and truly concerned that their charge be discharged honorably. Fewer still were aware, either through some innate appreciation of the social dynamic or through discovery by monkey curiosity, of the false prestige and very real power they held over the hearts and minds of those compelled to enter the ritual.

Dispirited as the others standing on line outside the East Settlebridge Office of the Public Welfare Ministry, Kurt Ellicot waited in the chill morning air, playing his part in the ritual.

It was possible to reach the office by entering through the grand main entrance of the municipal building, but there was little point in it. The office was located near a side entrance and somehow, the early arrivals always managed to fill the tiny lobby and spill out the front door, forming a line that straggled along the side of the building and often, by the time Kurt arrived, around the back and into the odoriferous service alley.

There was no real need for him to appear in person to validate another week of fruitless search for employment, not as long as he had access to the compnet. But the rules were the rules, as any bureaucrat would tell you, and a society without rules was no society at all. Anyone wishing to be a part of a society must follow the society's rules, take part in the rituals.

Kurt shivered as a gust whipped down the alley, driving discarded newsprint and other light trash before it. He tugged his coat closed and fastened it. Overhead, the sky seemed to be considering adding to his misery. Snow or rain? Either was possible and neither would be pleasant to stand in. He hoped that he would make it inside before the clouds shed their burden.

He didn't.

The cold autumn rain had thoroughly drenched him by the time he reached the door. The line continued its glacial advance. By the time he reached the door to the office, he was no longer creating a pool where he stood.

The office remained as drearily familiar as it had for the last six months. The same "motivational" posters on the walls, the same regulatory bulletins on the screens, the same grimed lighting panels shedding their dingy glow on scarred furniture and people alike. Amid all the sameness it was easy for Kurt to spot a change. There was a new clerk at the desk. She had a rather grandmotherly look about her — if one's grandmother had the hard, cold eyes of a snake.

She was, of course, the available clerk when his turn came around.

"Do I know you?" she asked as he walked up.

"I don't think so."

"I've a good eye for faces, you know. I've seen you before. I know it."

"If you say so." Kurt handed over his card.

"Didn't you used to be in politics or something? Off-world ambassador or something like that? I can see your face and some xeno. I follow all the off-world news. A lot of my friends say I'm wasting my time, but I know better. The universe is bigger than one planet. But you'd know that, wouldn't you? At least you would have before you came down in the world. It was a scandal or something. Had to be. Why else would you be here, right?"

"I'm here as required. I would appreciate it if you would do your job as required, which is to say with no personal bias or inappropriate familiarity."

The woman squinted, hard-eyed, at him. "No need to get huffy, young man. That kind of attitude won't serve you in this office. You need to understand your place. You should be grateful for the help that the government's giving you."

"I am grateful for all help I receive."

"Now that's a much more enlightened attitude." The clerk ran the card, but didn't hand it back. Instead she studied her screen, tapping the card in her hand and frowning. He waited. After some minutes her frown was replaced by a smug smile. "Say, you're that science guy who went native with the xenos on—what's its name—Cassuell's Place, aren't you?"

"Cassuells Home. That was a long time ago."

"Your card says you're still nuts. That true? You still nuts?"

"My doctor doesn't think so."

"Well, somebody does," she said, tapping the blue stripe on his card. "Maybe you should have your doctor talk to them."

"I'll consider that. May I have my card back?"

"When we're through, young man," she huffed. "When we're through. You still have to make your statement. The rules are the rules, you know."

"I know."

The question screen appeared in the window separating him from the clerk. They were the usual. Some were standard to everyone visiting the office, such as "Has there been a change in your address?" and "Have you sought gainful employment?" The rest were specific to his case file, such as "Has there been any change in your medication regimen?" and "Have you had any contact with non-Human species?" Kurt tapped the appropriate buttons.

"Well, it looks like you've been a good boy this week," the clerk said as he finished.

"My card?"

"Here you go," she said cheerily. "See you next week."

Kurt didn't reply. He just turned and left the office. Head ducked against the rain, he headed back to his apartment. What else was there to do?

It seemed that the ritual was to become a trial. Very well, he understood that. One needed to conform in order to have a place in a society, and the society was empowered to test the individual's conformity until his suitability was confirmed. His own suitability to reenter society *would* be confirmed. He was determined. He would perform as society expected him to perform. He would meet *all* expectations. Conformity was something at which he was very good.

## PAN-STELLAR COMBINE
## CYGNUS

Ambrose Alsion's office was definitely nothing like Juliana Tindal had expected. This was no office, it was a hall. The place was huge! Leaving the ordinary-looking, modern waiting room to enter it was like stepping into a virtuality presentation of some ancient monastery, or maybe, given its richness, a cathedral.

She stood on a smooth alabaster surface that seemed to glow from within. Darker flooring—cunning stonework—lay to either side of the pale surface, defining a walkway that stretched a dozen or more meters to a single padded armchair, and beyond the chair to an immense circular desk that seemed to flow almost organically out of the alabaster. Further still, beyond the desk, she could see the faint glimmer of arches where the stone coping stood out against the dark, barely seen walls. A pitchy open area lay beneath those graceful curves, suggesting vast, cavernous space beyond.

Above the opening a tall triple-arch framed colorful, glowing-light paintings. On the left, Saint George speared a writhing green-scaled dragon. On the right, Archangel Michael with his fiery sword battled a serpentine devil. In the center, a Human-faced sun streamed in glory among the stars.

Higher still, near the groined vaulting of the ceiling, was a round window. This, too, was filled with color, but of an unusual abstract design. Variegated light streamed through it into the chamber, casting its pattern on the wall above the door through which she had entered, a door that on this side appeared made of wood studded and banded with decorative swirls of black iron.

Juliana couldn't help but gape, awed to find a place such as this hidden within the ultramodern complex of the Alsion Institute. The contrast roused wonder, and confusion. Did Alsion design this place, and if so, why? He was renowned as a deep and subtle thinker. What sort of thoughts had birthed this place? What sort of man ran his business from a place that looked like a cathedral's sanctum?

"You are wondering about this place," boomed a deep voice from out of the darkness. She recognized it, though she had only heard recordings: Alsion's voice.

A robed figure stepped from the deep darkness into the shadowed space between the half-seen arches and the alabaster desk. The bearded face thus revealed was familiar as well. It was Ambrose Alsion. Her heart skipped a beat; she was face-to-face with a legend.

"How did it come to be?" he asked. "Why is it here?"

How had he known she had been asking herself precisely those questions?

Alsion did not wait for her to confirm his assertion.

"This chamber is a *fidnaljef* gift from the Mimaks, that necessary thing which is given unasked and cannot be refused without mortally offending the giver and the universe. Naturally, the presenters gave no reason save that they wished to make the offering. And quite an offering it is, as you can see."

She *could* see. She could see that the Mimaks seemed to hold Alsion in even higher regard than Humans did. Such a *fidnaljef!* Amazing.

"They had the stone for the walls, floor, and ceiling quarried on old Earth herself and ferried here, along with a master mason to supervise the construction." Alsion gestured to the windows behind him. "These are leaded glass—yes, actual glass. The glaziers were antiquarian craftsmen, also imported from Earth, who did all the work with ancient techniques. They were all, I think you'll agree, masters of their craft and superb artists.

"The rose window is a Mimak masterpiece, an everchanging creation that focuses light in endless variations. Intriguing, isn't it? You would, I think, be even more fascinated to know that it is alive."

Alive? Even Brown and Stern's seminal study on Mimak

material culture hadn't hinted at that kind of capability, despite establishing the biological or biological by-product origin of so many Mimak artifacts. She *was* fascinated, and she had a million questions, but further speculation was precluded by Alsion's continuing lecture.

"Although the bulk of the institute complex was constructed in a single standard year, the building of this chamber took ten years. It would have taken longer had not the Mimak architect consented to allow the Solarian mason to use modern construction techniques and equipment. Does ten years sound like a long time? I once thought so, until I learned that the glaziers had begun their designs twenty years earlier—at Mimak instigation—well before their patrons brought them here. Curious, don't you think, that the Mimaks began their gift before I had conceived of building this complex? Or perhaps not so curious. Some of the more abstruse Mimak mystic philosophies have been instructional in my own work.

"Just before the chamber was finished, priests from each of the nine major Mimak religions concelebrated a dedication ceremony. An extraordinary display of ecumenical oneness. Several live animals were brought to the ceremony, though none were ever seen to leave. Have you noticed that some of the stones are stained?"

Juliana heard herself gasp—unprofessionally. She felt foolish, putting it down to the unusual ambiance, but she couldn't stop herself from glancing around. In the dim light she couldn't distinguish any differences among the stones.

"Come, come, Professor Tindal," Alsion chided. "You hold a doctorate in socioxenology. Did you not do your graduate field work among the Shandaltelkak Association on Mimakron? Surely you are acquainted with some of their more sanguine customs. Well, no matter. Now I have told you how this place came to be. As to why it is here, I am still pondering that question myself. The Mimaks are silent when asked. Have you a theory?"

How could she? She had just encountered the place. She had several million questions now, but she guessed that now wasn't the time. "I'll give it some thought."

Alsion chuckled. "An excellent answer. You restore my faith in you. Please sit."

She did, but he did not. The chair at the desk remained empty as he continued to stand, half-lit at the edge of the alabaster. She shifted uncomfortably in her chair, suddenly feeling a little frightened.

Now that she'd met Ambrose Alsion, Juliana wasn't sure she *wanted* this slightly off-base man's faith in her. She certainly had once, though. Her thoughts flew back to the party she'd thrown when she got her accreditation with the Alsion Institute. She'd been the envy of the department. Then when Alsion's personal note had arrived, praising her work and offering a research sponsorship, she'd gone ballistic with delirium—the richest man in the nation, maybe even known space, had chosen to be *her* patron. She had orbited for a week. And she had revisited that high when she had received the invitation to meet with him. Now, though. Now . . .

"Perhaps you'd care to express your discomfort," he suggested.

Could she? Did she dare?

He waited for her to speak, seemingly assured that she would.

*Keep it impersonal, Juliana.*

"This place. Your clothes." *Your entire attitude.* She waved her hand to take in her surroundings. "Isn't it all a little odd?"

"Odd? Perhaps. Perhaps it is simply part of a pattern that

you do not yet perceive. There are many patterns in the universe, so *very* many. What is odd, and what is not? In a universe where mankind has altered his own genetic structure to produce chimerae whose humanity is, to this day, debated even by reputable scholars, how can an eccentric taste in clothing and office decoration be considered odd? If you find me odd, I am content to let it be so, for in the end I think that it will matter little.

"But we are met to speak not of me, but of you."

"Me?"

"Yes. There is confusion among the Board of Directors. Consternation even. And it is justified."

The board? Besides applying to them for funding, she didn't have anything to do with them. Politics wasn't the sort of thing that concerned her. "I don't understand. What's the connection between me and the Board?"

"A planet in the Chugen System."

"The Chugen System? I've never heard of it."

"You have now. You are aware of the tumultuarity principles, I trust."

How could anyone sponsored by the Alsion Institute not be? "I've read your books." Like almost everyone else in the Combine, she had read his popularization *Yielding to the Tumult*. She had also tried to read all three of his scholarly books on the subject. She hadn't understood the abstruse higher mathematics or the obscure philosophical conclusions that Alsion reached, but she had grasped enough of the basics to understand that Alsion had stretched the boundaries of chaos-order dynamics far beyond what had gone before. There had to be something to his theories, because by applying them to business and to market speculation, Alsion had amassed the peerless fortune that made him the richest man in the Combine and created the institute that bore his name. And paid for Juliana's research.

She might not understand the higher aspects of tumultuarity, but she appreciated its side effects. "I'm afraid I don't really understand more than the basics."

"So few do."

She was surprised by the loneliness that leaked out from behind those words.

"Simplicity, then," he said. "There are perturbations in the shaping course of events, and the clarity of prediction is very far less than desirable. Yet some individual elements of the future approach certitude. Soon, I think very soon, important nodes will coalesce into a hub, upon which much will turn. Political agendas are on collision courses, star nations stand at the edge of crucial and terrifying decisions, and you have a part in what is coming."

"You're scaring me, sir."

"Good. You demonstrate perspective."

Perspective be damned. She didn't see what *her* involvement could be. "Look. I know your reputation, sir, and I am sure that you have good reasons for your opinions, but I don't see how I could be involved. I'm a socioxenologist. A basic researcher, for pity's sake. I specialize in primitive, forest-dwelling cultures—unlikely to be of interest to the heads of any star nations."

"Exactly," said Alsion. "The unlikely becomes the focus of intense scrutiny, and the fate of at least one species hangs in the balance. Remember the connection. Chugen's planet."

"I told you that I've never heard of it."

"No longer true, although you do remain ignorant *about* it. The practical matter is that the Pan-Stellar Combine is organizing a joint expedition to the Chugen System with the avowed purpose of studying the indigenes. Yes, I know that you haven't heard of them, either. A folder of current data will be in your hands before you leave today.

You, Professor Tindal, along with a certain specialist from the Serenten Concordat, and other scientists from both the Interstellar Defense League and our own Combine, will be going to Chugen's inhabited planet." He nodded as if settling matters. Like a gruff drillmaster from a mart melodrama, he ordered, "You will order your affairs for a departure within the week."

*What cheek!* She didn't like his sudden change in demeanor at all. *Departure? A week?*

"Wait a minute here!" She speared him with her finger. "You may be funding my research, but that doesn't mean that you own me. I'm not going to drop everything I'm doing and go haring off to some place I never heard of just on your say-so! I've got work to do!"

"Exactly."

"You can't—"

"Of course I can." Alsion appeared unruffled by her outburst. his tone was firm, intolerant of argument. "In our Board-certified contract, which you signed when you received your accreditation with the institute, you agreed to serve as agent-representative for the institute should the institute require your professional expertise. The institute now requires the application of that expertise. Your expenses will, of course, be covered. Your leave of absence from your current position is already arranged."

Board-certified contracts were more binding than some Combine laws. She vaguely remembered such a clause, and if that clause was in there, she was hooked. "I feel like I'm being shanghaied."

"A quaint old term, and not entirely inappropriate. But you may put your reservations into abeyance, Professor Tindal. I assure you that this is a good cause, as I am sure you will agree once you have studied the briefing material. You are the right person for this affair."

Oddly enough she felt reassured by the certainty she heard in his voice. But she still wasn't sure what he wanted of her. "Let me get this straight. You want me—totally unqualified for the position, a beginner—to be your confidential agent in some interstellar intrigue."

"Nearly correct."

"I don't get it. Even assuming that I could do the job, why me? You don't know me. What makes you think that you can trust me?"

Alsion smiled warmly. "I trust you to be yourself. You will hardly fail me, or yourself, in that. So there is sufficiency. I arm you with the knowledge that this affair is likely to develop into a determinative hub. All else will follow."

He sounded so sure. She wanted to believe him. It was exhilarating to think that a man such as Alsion thought you the right person to do something that would change the universe. But it was scary, too. She'd never thought of herself as a universe-changer.

"Oh, and one last thing, Professor Tindal. Your position as agent-representative must remain undisclosed."

"Why?" she asked, her suspicions sparked.

"A precaution," he said blandly. "A safety measure."

She didn't like the sound of that. "At a guess, I'd say that nondisclosure would protect you more than me."

"Your guess could well be wrong."

"What are you involving me in?"

"Were there sufficient data to complete the tumultuarity calculations, there would be no need to involve you. All the details that I have for you are in the briefing folder."

Behind her the heavy doors boomed open. She turned to see who was making such an ostentatious entrance, but no one was there. She turned back to Alsion, or rather to where Alsion had stood. He was gone.

She was being dismissed. All right, then. She slapped her hands down on the arms of the chair and rose. Despite a resolve to take her time, she left the chamber at something less than a sedate walk, not slowing until the doors sighed shut behind her. The interview was over, but something new was beginning.

Just what the hell was she getting into?

## 7

## CHUGEN SYSTEM
## MIDWAY STATION

Ken Konoye had survived the academic snake pit at Mellenthin University. He'd even survived helming a survey ship officered by scholars barely competent at their duties. He was, however, beginning to have doubts as to whether or not he would survive supervising the construction crews working on the Chugen jump gate and on the transshipping station which he had named—realistically, he thought, not optimistically as Jane suggested—Midway.

*Byrd* had carried equipment adequate to ease the jump passage for heavy-duty ships like *Byrd* itself, but the regular merchant traffic necessary to exploit Chugen wouldn't be able to handle such rough jumps. Chugen couldn't go commercial until the jump gate was up and running, and commercial traffic would have no place to go until the station was finished. Unfortunately the project was running behind schedule, and every day some new crisis seemed to disrupt the construction effort

The schedule called for a Toyotomi frontier cargo carrier to be arriving today, hauling most of what was needed to complete both the gate and the station. Its timely arrival might be the only thing that could save his sanity. Access to the materials the contractors were clamoring for would get them off his back—maybe even long enough to do some more work on plotting the route through to Ursa. His moment's wistful contemplation of charting the whole jump route was shattered by Jane's voice on the intercom.

"Ken?"

"What is it?" he snapped. "If it's Sandy Ng about the selenium rods again, tell her I'm dead, and that she can't bother me until after the funeral."

"We've just had a ship jump in."

Didn't she get the message? He was busy! She knew better than to bother *him* with routine business that *she* was supposed to be handling. "You're sitting in ops. Handle it."

"But, Ken, it's not the *Kokkyo-maru*. It's an IDL ship."

IDL? He rocked back in his chair. The cool air of the cabin suddenly felt quite chill. What the hell was a ship from the Interstellar Defense League doing here in Chugen?

"What do they want?" he forced himself to ask.

"They say they're the *Henry Hull*, a *Captain*-class patroller under the command of a Major Jonas Ersch."

"Who cares *who* is running those mart bastards' ship? Was there ever a one of those kill-crazy marts that didn't think with his guns? Have they said what they want?"

"We're only getting an ID transmission. They're not responding to hails."

"Shit." Nothing good was going to come out of this. A League ship in Combine space could only mean trouble. How long had it been since the marts muscled in on Thorpe-Agrell? A year? Less? Now they were here. Trouble, for sure. "I'll be right there."

There wasn't a lot of Midway station under pressure so far, and it didn't take long to travel the habitable corridors to the operations center. He found Jane frowning over the holotank where the track of the incoming ship was plotted. He joined her, and soon was frowning, too. The League ship was on a direct track for the station and still refusing to respond.

"What are we going to do?" Jane asked worriedly.

What could they do? He wasn't trained for this. None of them were. Most Combine spacers were merchants— peaceful traders, not jack-booted, militaristic killers like the Leaguers. Combiners scrapped sometimes, but mostly against commerce raiders. As pugnacious as outlaws could be, they weren't fully fledged marts like the Leaguers. All of Konoye's command staff, being academics who held their posts by virtue of their civilian skills and abilities, were totally unsuited to dealing with a military situation. *No*, he thought, *not all.* Konoye looked around the operations center, and found himself staring into the eyes of the man he'd just remembered: stern-eyed, watchful, experienced Mathieu Hoppe.

Hoppe was a Merchant Spacer Guildsman, their mandated operations chief, the experienced spacer who was supposed to keep the inexperienced officers from doing mischief to themselves or the ship in which they traveled. He'd stayed on to perform the same office during the building of the station and the gate. Recalling that Hoppe had spent some time in the tiny Combine military fleet, Konoye had never been so glad to see him close at hand.

"I'd like your evaluation, Mr. Hoppe, and any suggestions you might have."

Hoppe nodded. "That League ship be letting us know who they be but not why they be here, so I'd say they be looking to make trouble. The station be having no defenses, so any fighting here will be absolutely lethal. Better any fighting that be going on, get done before they be getting here." He stopped speaking for a moment while he tapped something on his console. "That's all we be having for resources."

Konoye looked to the holotank, noting the change. Two ships were highlighted, the only two that might intercept the incoming League vessel before it reached the station. He didn't like what Hoppe was telling him, but he understood it.

"Jane, get me the captains of *Tillie's Dream* and *Star Dog*."

Jane was aghast. "You can't be thinking of sending them out against that warship. Ken, it's a patroller! It outmasses the both of those scouts put together. Hell, its armament load alone probably masses either one of them."

"The Leaguers are marts, Jane. There's only one language they understand: force. We've got to show them that we mean to defend ourselves. *Tillie's Dream* and *Star Dog* are here and they're armed. If *Byrd* weren't so deep insystem, I'd send her, too. Let's hope that a *show* of force is all we need to do to keep them law-abiding."

The captains of the scouts were even less enthusiastic than Jane was about the prospect of facing the League warship; but they went, bravely putting themselves, their crews, and their ships in harm's way in the hope of averting, if not the destruction of the station, at least its hostile takeover.

There was no doubt in Konoye's mind that while the Interstellar Defense League might espouse high ideals, it was infested by low-life, murdering scum—the marts who ran the League and filled its imperialist military. The average citizens were likely no different than citizens everywhere else, but they were terrorized and dominated by a fascistic hierarchy, as much victims as any of those killed by League guns.

Konoye remembered the compnet campaigns and the street protests against one of the League's most egregious sins—their actions at Cassuells Home—as though he'd taken part in them only yesterday. He still thought of Casual Slaughterer Stone's actions as rash, unsupported, and criminally genocidal. And he was not alone. Throughout the Combine, the League was a bogeyman, the black-uniformed terror in the night that stomped into the mud any good-hearted folk who stood in its way, and a warning to all right-thinking people to hold more firmly to their freedoms.

Watching the plot of *Tillie's Dream* and *Star Dog* heading out on intercept vectors toward the League ship, Konoye wondered how firm their hold on freedom was here in Chugen. Time crawled by as he watched the points of light in the tank draw nearer and nearer to each other. *Star Dog* was marginally closer to the incoming ship. Her "heave to" message would be reaching the League ship. Then . . .

"Director, something be happening," Hoppe announced.

"Are they shooting?" Konoye asked, dreading to hear an affirmative answer.

"No weapon signatures," Hoppe said brusquely.

"The League ship is decelerating!" Jane cried. "They're stopping!"

"No, just slowing." Hoppe nodded thoughtfully. "They be letting our ships match velocities, but they be still headed for us."

"A trap?" Konoye asked, again worried about the answer he might get.

"I don't think so," Hoppe said. "Be not much point in it. But they will be coming to rest relative to the station well within beam range."

Konoye didn't like the idea of sitting under their guns. Jane didn't give him long to think about it.

"Ken, we've got a comm beam from them coming in on array three."

He chuckled, more from relief than from amusement. He had called their bluff. "So now they're willing to talk, eh? See, I told you. *Tillie's Dream* and *Star Dog* showed them we weren't going to just roll over, and so they balked when they saw that they couldn't bully us. I guess we needn't have been worried. We *know* they're bullies and *all* bullies are cowards at heart."

Jane gave him *that* look. "Aren't you reading an awful lot into limited evidence?"

"Who knows? Maybe it was just some stupid machismo thing where honor had to be satisfied. That kind of chest-thumping is the sort of dead stupid thing that marts do. What's important is that we're still here."

"So are they," Jane reminded him. "The comm beam?"

"All right. Acknowledge it. Let's see what they've got to say for themselves."

The beam was voice only. The Leaguer's tones were clear, deep, and touched with urgency. "This is Major Ersch, officer in command IDLS *Henry Hull*, requesting permission to speak with the senior Pan-Stellar Combine official on station. Respond, please."

So they wanted to talk to him, did they? And now that they were ready, it all had to be done quickly. He let them stew unanswered for a few minutes before having Jane put him on-line.

"This is Ken Konoye. I am the managing director of this system. If you are not already aware, let me tell you now that this system is Pan-Stellar Combine territory, already claimed as a protected affiliate. The IDL has no jurisdiction here. Rash action on the your part could well result in war. You have been warned."

"That is a rather hostile greeting, Director Konoye." The major sounded offended. "We are only here to help."

"We didn't *ask* for your help, and we don't *want* it."

"Understood, sir. But you may need it nonetheless. Rest assured that we have not come to contest the Combine's claim to this or any system."

*Oh, yeah? What about your station sitting in Combine space at Thorpe-Agrell?* "Then why *are* you here?"

"My mission is very straightforward, sir. I have been sent here to investigate a suspected Remor artifact."

"Remor?" He should have seen it coming. The Remor were the League's excuse for everything they did. "There are no Remor here."

"But we believe that if they are not present now, they may have been at some time in the past. If so, as I am sure you realize, sir, the entire strategic situation has changed, especially if you are correct in your theory of where a jump route out of this system leads. If they were here once, it is likely that they will return. The enemy may have left a beacon in this system. It is imperative that I take my ship in-system to investigate."

The major sounded so sincere that Konoye found himself almost believing the story. The Remor, the real Remor and not the ones the Leaguers found hiding under every rock, were undeniably a danger. If they *had* come to this system, and if he *was* right about the near-Earth connection, the danger was magnified. What if the Remor *have* left a beacon? The damned marts would probably set it off. Maybe even intentionally! Yes, if the major was right, an investigation had to be made; but Konoye couldn't see the heavy-handed Leaguers managing to conduct it without making matters worse. Besides, this was Combine space, not League space! Ken was in charge here. And, by God, he wouldn't have thrice-cursed Leaguer marts tromping around in it!

"Permission denied, Major."

Major Ersch's reply was long in coming, but when he spoke, his voice was matter-of-fact. "I estimate we will reach your station in two hours. Please prepare a docking berth. IDLS *Henry Hull* out."

The nerve of the man! Konoye almost wished that *Star Dog* and *Tillie's Dream* had the firepower to blow Major Ersch, his ship, and his whole damned crew to atoms. But destroying the Leaguers wasn't an option. Not one that Konoye and his people would survive, anyway.

Two hours. They had two hours to think of some way to deal with Ersch.

## IDL DEFENSE SECTOR 32-(RED)
## GRENWOLD

Anders watched the landing shuttles with a mixture of relief and regret. Aboard one of them was the new commander of the Grenwold garrison. Anders's stint as officer-in-command was nearly over. Soon he wouldn't be the one responsible for the safety of the garrison and the civilian population, a load he wouldn't mind shedding. But the other side of that coin was that *he* wouldn't be in charge anymore, and he'd gotten used to having things done *his* way. All in all, though, the arrival of a new commander was for the best. He hoped that the new commander would be Eridani.

There had been no word yet on who the new commander was. In order to minimize the chance that the enemy would detect the *Maurat*, there had been no communication with her after the first tight beam that had announced the incoming ship. Now, with the shuttles of the relief force beginning their landing, he saw that each and every one of the incoming craft bore the same quartered heraldic shield, alternating the League's ring of silver stars with the tricolor of Rift's Verge. The relief forces were planetary legion troops, not part of the integrated MilForce. The relief commander would be one of their own, a Verger. With the shuttles maintaining commo silence, he wasn't about to break it by transmitting to them, but he wanted to know who and what he was dealing with here, and he wanted to know *now*.

There was, he realized, a way. Using his suit's IFF system, he sent a transponder query. The return told him that these Vergers were elements of the 24th Cavalry Regiment. His library told him that despite its name, the 24th Cav was a unit of mobile infantry: light armored groundpounders with fighting blowers and supporting elements that usually included ground-support VTOLs and gun platforms or tanks. The unit's service records indicated that the 24th were good troops, though not equipped with state-of-the-art hardware. A point in their favor was that these geepies had fought against the Remor on Caledonia. They'd survived the loss of the world by having been rotated out before the final collapse. The commander of record was Colonel Justine Rance, also a veteran of Caledonia.

It was good that the new commander had experience fighting the enemy. Unfortunately, experience would only go so far as a substitute for a sufficiency of troops. Given the shuttles' payloads, the Vergers had only brought a reinforced battalion.

Was there a second wave waiting in orbit? He scanned the sky and, seeing nothing, risked a ping on his radar. Nothing. A library check on *Maurat* said that she only carried twelve assault shuttles. Anders was looking at her full complement.

He had been expecting that StratCom would send enough force to kick the enemy off the planet. It looked instead as though the Grenwold force was still fighting a holding action. He wasn't pleased about that. He'd thought that his reports had made it clear that the enemy was not present in any great force. Now was the time to eliminate them. The longer the delay, the more likely that the enemy would receive reinforcements and the more likely that they would complete the defenses they were raising. Clearly

StratCom had other ideas about how to deal with the Remor presence on Grenwold.

Standing beside him, Metzler was making his own scan of the sky. The pilot didn't have the advantage of a hardsuit computer to provide him with the bad news Anders had already received.

"Just *Maurat's* shuttles?"

"Looks that way," Anders said.

"Don't they know that the enemy is here?" That was Rostler, the third member of Anders's welcoming committee. His military-issue sidearm and silver star armband were all that distinguished the man from a local outback crawler. The crowned captain's insignia marked him from other members of the militia as their officer-in-command. He hadn't been Anders's choice for the slot, but given the Grenwolders' anarchistic tendencies, Anders had decided that it would be best to let them select their first commanding officer rather than impose one. The troops had chosen Rostler and, so far, he had proven a choice that Anders could live with, showing good organizational and leadership abilities. The real proof of his suitability as an officer would come in battle, something that none of the militia had faced.

"StratCom is in the know; we are on the go," Anders said, quoting the old maxim. "Ours is not to reason the whys and wherefores of strategic thinking."

"We just do the strategic dying," Metzler finished for him.

In the distance Anders could see Verger troops disembarking. "Time to go meet the new boss. Move us out, Gordie."

Gordie, the blower's driver, kicked the accelerator and the engine howled up to speed. With a jolt that brought a curse of surprise from Metzler, they were off across the plain. Anders directed the driver toward the shuttle that had landed first. His optics showed a knot of officers converging there, which magnification revealed to be centered on a short, slim woman wearing a colonel's three diamonds on her collar. He noted the Caledonia campaign badge over her left breast pocket and concluded that this was Colonel Rance.

Anders kept his suit's sensors focused on the new commander as the blower closed the distance. The colonel was a small, compact woman—even out of his hardsuit Anders would tower over her—but she snapped out commands with an authority that an Eridani drill sergeant might envy. Her officers moved with alacrity, showing none of the hesitation Anders had occasionally seen among male soldiers taking orders from a female. He was glad to see that Rance had the trust of her troops.

By the time the blower reached Rance's command group, Anders had decided that he wanted to impress his new commander. Before the transport had eased down into idle, Anders vaulted out of the crew compartment. Three strides took him into the colonel's circle, where he saluted sharply. "Lieutenant Anders Seaborg, officer-in-command, Grenwold garrison, reporting, ma'am."

"Lieutenant." The hard-eyed colonel acknowledged his salute. "You're Eridani, eh? I should have expected as much when they told me a platoon of hardshells was holding the whole damned planet. Maybe I should leave you in charge."

"That would be improper, Colonel."

"Quite right." Her expression softened minimally—perhaps as much as it ever did, to judge from the ingrained lines around her eyes and mouth. "But don't go thinking that you're on leave now that I'm here. We've got a lot of work ahead of us, and I expect you to be taking a lead role. The first thing you're going to do is introduce me to these other gentlemen."

Anders acknowledged the order with a nod. "This is Captain Metzler of the garrison aerospace detachment. He has been an excellent second-in-command, adapting quite well to duties outside his specialty."

Metzler snapped a salute. "Ma'am."

"Captain, eh? Well, get with Captain Nogara on Shuttle 301 and sort out who has seniority."

"Aye, ma'am."

Colonel Rance turned to Rostler, who drew himself raggedly to attention. Anders, embarrassed by the man's lack of military bearing, introduced him to the colonel. "This is Provisional Captain Svein Rostler of the Grenwold Militia. He has been invaluable in mobilizing local defense."

"A pleasure, ma'am," said Rostler, starting to stick out his hand and belatedly converting the gesture into a salute.

Rance snapped a sharp salute in response. "Always glad to meet a local willing to defend his planet, Captain Rostler. You show a courage I wish was more common." Her glance swept across the three of them. "Gentlemen, I want all of you at a general briefing aboard Shuttle 308 in two hours. My officers should have their troops sufficiently disembarked and ready to get down to business by then. I'll want current sitreps from all of you. In the meantime, any questions?"

"When will the rest of the reinforcements be landing?" Metzler asked.

Briefly Rance looked puzzled, then she said, "For the moment, there is no *rest*. Just me and my battalion."

"But that can't be!" Metzler blurted.

Anders winced inwardly at the display of inexperience.

"We were the available forces, Captain," said Rance sharply. "We have what we have. Grenwold isn't the only place the enemy has decided to stir up trouble. StratCom assures me, and I assure you, that additional forces will be dispatched as soon as possible. Until then, we make do. We *will* do the job we were assigned."

"And what is that job, ma'am?" Anders asked, afraid that he already knew the answer.

"We take the battle to the enemy," Rance said with a grim smile.

## SERENTEN CONCORDAT
## SERENTEN

Technically the buzzer was an interruption since Kurt was supposed to be working. Unfortunately the research paper was going nowhere. The screen still showed page 23, just as it had two hours ago. So much for his current plan for rehabilitating himself. He put down his reader.

He didn't bother to see who it was; he just flung the door open. He found two men standing on the landing. One was short and portly and wore his dark hair at the currently favored collar length. The other was tall and broad-shouldered with close-cropped hair graying at the temples. Both wore conservative business suits of the sort Kurt had worn when he'd been teaching. The visitors' suits were more up to date, and the short guy's was actually rather fancy, being made of expensive Mimak polymer smooth-cloth—"the finest fiber made for man." Kurt wouldn't have noticed the fabric until recently, but these days he saw a lot of fashion ads; you couldn't avoid them on the free media.

Unlike his tall, dour companion, the short guy in the fancy suit smiled broadly.

"Professor Kurt Ellicot?" he asked.

"I'm Ellicot." The professor part was one of a host of a fading memories.

"Oh, very good. If possible, we'd like a moment of your time."

They hadn't asked for a handout, and they didn't look

like criminals or salesmen, and if they were, so what? What did he have left to steal? "Sure. Come on in."

The place wasn't as nice as the one he'd shared with Clarise and the kids. Hell, it wasn't even as nice as it had been when he'd moved in. In fact, the apartment was a mess, a testament to his lack of involvement with life. Dishes crusted with old food nested among drifts of newsprints, books, and dirty clothes. Dust from a nearby construction site, admitted by the faulty air-conditioning system, coated everything that hadn't been disturbed recently, which was most everything.

Kurt swept away a pile of debris from the battered love-seat he'd gotten at the second-hand store down the street, to make a place for his guests. His short visitor, face registering understandable dismay, declined to accept the offered seat. The tall one also remained standing, merely raising an eyebrow in disdain. Kurt accepted the tall one's attitude. Lord knew he felt that way about himself much of the time.

If they didn't want what hospitality he had, that was their problem. Kurt dropped himself into the chair he had vacated to let them in. The tridee was still on—Leonard Oprah's call-in show. Kurt considered ordering the set off, but didn't bother.

"Professor Ellicot, I am Ethan Shirrel," the short man said self-importantly. When Kurt didn't react, he added, "Of the premier minister's staff."

"I didn't vote for her," Kurt told him. Actually he hadn't voted in the last election at all.

"You were in the distinct minority, Professor," Shirrel said with what was probably supposed to be a disarming wink. "Whether you are one of Minister Wyss's supporters or not, the colonel and I—this is Colonel Marion Wayne Lockhart of the Defense Ministry—are here on her behalf. We would like to talk with you, if you have the time."

"I've got nothing but time. Talk, I'll listen."

"Good. I think you'll find what we have to say intriguing." Shirrel smiled. It was a politician's smile, all flash and no substance. "You see, we have an offer to make to you. A position, actually, and a rather prestigious one at that. At present there is a multinational mission forming to study a newly discovered world inhabited by an indigenous alien species. It's all very exciting! Naturally, Professor, as you are an acknowledged expert on alien cultures, you were among Premier Minister Wyss's first choices to be the Concordat's representative on the first contact team."

A washed-up, restricted-status, academic pariah was among her first choices? Kurt didn't really think so. "The others turn her down?"

"Excuse me?" Shirrel frowned, perplexed.

"You said *among*. Did her other choices pass on this prestigious and exciting position?"

"Did I say that? I'm sorry. I meant to say that you were first among her choices." That smile again. "'Uniquely qualified' was her exact phrase, I believe. There is an opportunity here for you to remake your career, Professor. Are you interested?"

Was he? He wanted to work again, to be respectable. He told himself so every night when he lay abed, trying to sleep, but somehow, every day when morning came, climbing out of the hole just looked impossible. Now an opportunity had walked in his door. He'd be a fool not to take it, wouldn't he?

There would be strings attached. How could there not be? But even with strings, this was the best offer he'd had in years. For the first time in a long time, he felt enthusiasm stir.

"Tell me about the natives," he said.

Shirrel smiled. "At this point in time, we have little

information on the indigenes. A few orbital pictures, enough to show that they are bimanous bipeds. The discoverers are keeping strictly hands-off until a qualified team of experts can be assembled. Experts that could include you, Professor."

Shirrel wasn't as good a salesman as he thought he was. Kurt, his mark, had bitten down on the bait and the man was still trying to coax him to take it. What did it matter? Kurt wanted to know about this new species. "Bimanous bipeds. That's all you know?"

"As I said, information is scanty. I can tell you that the indigenes are nonindustrial. That much is clear from the orbital surveys."

"You said you had pics."

"In fact, I have several here." Shirrel reached into his jacket and withdrew a reader. "Colonel Lockhart's people have run them through for enhancement, but I'm afraid the original images are not all that they might be. Here, see for yourself."

Taking the offered reader, Kurt looked at the image on screen and felt his muscles go rigid.

He flashed on another time and place. His head was full of a strong, familiar odor, and he felt the touch of phantom fur against his skin. He forced the memories away. The Cassuells were gone. Dead! All dead. The Interstellar Defense League had destroyed the Cassuells and burnt their world to a lifeless cinder. The mental image drifted away on the wind and he managed to choke out a question.

"Is this some kind of bad joke?"

"Professor Ellicot, a man in my position has no time for jokes, bad or otherwise." Shirrel sounded offended.

Well, *damn* him! "Where did you get this picture?"

In a calm voice Lockhart said, "It was supplied by the Pan-Stellar Combine survey office."

It probably had been. "They must have had to dig deep into their old files for you."

"You're confusing me, Professor Ellicot." Shirrel complained. "Are you saying you recognize this picture and that it is a vintage pic?"

"Oh, I don't recall this exact picture, but I knew the subjects."

"Impossible," Shirrel contradicted. "This was taken on a newly discovered planet. No one from the Concordat has ever been there. How could you have encountered these aliens?"

"You do innocent confusion well, Mr. Shirrel. I suppose it's useful for someone in your line of work."

Colonel Lockhart cut in. "Disrespect is unnecessary and unbecoming, Mr. Ellicot. The pic is what Mr. Shirrel said it is."

Really? "Are you telling me that this *isn't* a picture of Cassuells?"

"Of course not." Shirrel sounded like he thought the idea absurd. "How could it be? *This* pic was taken less than a year ago."

"You are not the first to note the surface similarity of the two species," Lockhart said.

"Fascinating, isn't it?" Shirrel smiled.

Fascinating, maybe: intriguing, certainly. A close similarity between these aliens and the Cassuells shouldn't be possible. It might be no more than convergent evolution, similar forms achieving similar shapes in a similar environment. After all, selective pressure had produced bimanous bipeds on Earth, hadn't it? It would take an evolutionary biologist to sort the situation out, and Kurt wasn't one. But he was a socioxenologist and the chance to compare the *cultural* evolution of disparate but similar species was not one that he could easily throw away.

But was it one that he could take on?

Remembering his experience ten years ago, he shuddered. He didn't want to go through anything like that again. Maybe he shouldn't take this position. Temporizing, he said, "I don't need make-work."

"This is anything but," avowed Shirrel. He was back in salesman mode. "We are looking at a very high-profile mission with multinational support. You would be working in prestigious company, Professor Ellicot. Already a halfdozen prominent scientists have signed on. They come from a number of star nations, including the Federated Star Nations, Pan-Stellar Combine, and the Interstellar Defense League."

That last name stopped Kurt's ruminations cold. "The League's involved? I want nothing to do with them."

"I don't understand." Shirrel looked puzzled. "I assumed that your attitudes toward the League had changed."

"Whatever gave you that idea, Mr. Shirrel?"

"Well, I had assumed that since the League representative asked for you by name—"

"By name? Why in *hell's* name would the League want *me* to investigate a new species on a new planet?"

The foreign stink of machine lubricants and gun oil assaulted his nostrils. Keening, his own and that of the others, filled his ears. He felt hard, unfeeling hands grabbing him, dragging him away.

"Professor?"

Kurt forced his fingers to unclamp from the arm of his chair. That was all in the past, the dead past. It was for the best that he had been separated from the Cassuells. It had been vital for his mental health. Doctor Nellis said so. Kurt had come to believe it, too. Hadn't he?

If so, why did he see this alien species as another chance, not just for his career but for his self? The last real closeness he had experienced had been among the Cassuells. Was that what was calling to him? If it was, if he could find it again, could he bear to lose it a second time?

"I can't do this if the League is involved."

"Professor Ellicot, you're making this very awkward." Shirrel frowned. He seemed to be working himself up to something. Finally he seemed to resolve his internal struggle and said, "I shouldn't be telling you this, but you can't refuse. The Concordat has already offered your services."

"Too bad. As long as the League is involved, I'm not."

"It is your duty as a citizen of the Concordat," Lockhart said.

"Oh, really?" Ellicot pulled out his identicard. "See this blue stripe? It's a gift of the Serenten Concordat justice system. It absolves me of a great number of duties. By government ruling, I might add. So tell me, what makes this supposed duty any different from voting?"

Lockhart wasn't moved. "It is still your duty."

"Professor, am I correct in surmising that you hold your current social problems to stem from your treatment by the government?" asked Shirrel.

Kurt tossed the stigmatizing card on the floor at Shirrel's feet. "You try living with one of these."

Shirrel bent, picked up the card, and looked at it for a moment before tucking it away in his jacket. "To date, the government has shown remarkable indifference to your situation. Should you refuse this duty, that could well change. Given how little you care for your current situation, shouldn't you consider what an actively hostile government could do to your life? There *are* other categories beyond limited citizenship."

"Is that a threat, Mr. Shirrel?"

"An observation," Shirrel responded blandly. "One based on experience, I might add."

Could they make his life worse? Probably. Would they bother? Who knew? If they had already committed him to this project, *somebody* would be embarrassed by his refusal. Would it be somebody sufficiently motivated and powerful to carry out Shirrel's threat? A look at Shirrel's cold smile told Kurt that the functionary was quite comfortable with his threat.

"When did Serenten become part of the League?" Kurt asked bitterly.

"We are not now, nor shall we ever be part of the League," Shirrel growled, facade cracking briefly. "That was a deliberately hurtful remark, the sort one makes to one's enemies. But there is no need to make this an adversarial relationship, Professor. Consider the positive side. The Pan-Stellar Combine has refrained from contacting this species, leaving them untouched, unaltered by human contact. What greater opportunity could a socioxenologist have? And here you are, being offered a slot on the first contact team. Think carefully about throwing it away. Consider, Professor. You can be there when humankind speaks its first words to these aliens. You yourself might speak those words. It will be a historic moment, and you can be a part of it. A part of history, Professor Ellicot. Such a chance doesn't come along for everyone. Is another such opportunity likely to come along in your lifetime? I think not."

"Life only comes along once for everyone, Mr. Shirrel. The Cassuells got one chance, and the League took it away from them. What's to keep the paranoid leadership of the League from ordering the same thing done to these poor aliens, just because they happen to look like the Cassuells? Who's going to stop them?"

"You have my full assurances that the Concordat would not support such an action on the League's part, Professor. Any position we might take in such a situation would be bolstered by positive, scientific evidence that these Chugen indigenes are harmless. That is the sort of information we want you to gather, Professor Ellicot. *You* could be the one to ensure this species' survival."

Him? He hadn't saved anyone last time.

"You have another chance before you, Professor."

Did he?

"This mission could fail due to the lack of your expertise, Professor. Your presence in this joint mission will keep the League in the mission, and their participation will make it that much harder for them to act unilaterally. If they do not participate, who knows what they will do on their own? You know what they are like, Professor."

Too well. But he was just one man.

"There are times when one man can make a difference, Professor. The premier minister believes that this is one of those times. She has asked you to stand up and accept this challenge. She believes in you. She believes that *you* are the man who can make a difference here. Is she wrong?"

The strong arms. Helplessness. The keening, the eternal keening. Fire from the sky, lancing down through a ring of stars. "The League will kill them."

"No one wants to see that happen, believe me, Professor. Least of all Minister Wyss. She wants to see the League curbed as much as you do, Professor. Maybe even more. She is looking to you for help. Will you help her? Will you help the innocent Chugen indigenes? Will you help all of us?"

"Innocent?" The indigenes might be innocent, but he was no longer innocent. He also was no crusader. So what was he?

Nothing; and on the course he was taking, he would only become less. He had been a socioxenologist once, successful, respected. Shirrel was offering him a chance to have what he had before, to do what he had trained for all his life. All he had to do was to let go of his belief that his life was already over. Could he do that?

He squared back his shoulders. He could try.

Looking Shirrel in the eye, he said, "Mr. Shirrel, I want you to know that I'm no savior. I'm just a man. I *am* a socioxenologist, and what a man of my discipline can do, I'll do."

"You won't regret your decision, Professor Ellicot."

Kurt shook the functionary's hand, hoping that the man was right.

# 8

Some people called Jason Metzler a pessimist, but he liked to think of himself as a realist. He just wanted to be sure that everything that could get him screwed was accounted for and eliminated. So he asked a lot of the kinds of questions that made people nervous, especially people who hadn't thought through their plans. They didn't like realizing that they had forgotten something vital, or gotten it wrong, or just plain had picked the wrong option, but that was their problem. He considered the kind of prodding that he did to be indispensable. After all, when it was his butt going on the line, he needed to make sure it wasn't going to be left hanging out there.

Sitting in his command couch aboard Shuttle 614, he was getting that hanging feeling. *Shaka* had reported three Remor ships, but nothing had been heard of them since they chased the cruiser to the jump point. Were they still out there? Jason wanted to believe that they weren't. It would explain why they had made no attempt to intercept *Maurat* when she arrived, and why they had ignored his flight of shuttles lifting to orbit. Even after three orbits the enemy had sent nothing to challenge them. It made Jason nervous.

The lack of opposition should have been encouraging. Unfortunately, the Remor were unpredictable. They could be gone, or they could be waiting for what their alien minds would judge to be the right moment. All plans had to assume that they were still insystem.

He would find out pretty soon. At least with *Maurat* hanging silent and watchful near Grenwold's moon, they should get sufficient warning.

The ground commo link opened. "Rance to Metzler. Anything?"

"This is Metzler. All clear as far as we can see."

"Very good. Keep watching. We're about to stir the pot. Rance out."

If anything would bring the Remor out of hiding, the beginning of the ground attack would be it. Jason put his flight on notice and locked his eyes on the scanners. He didn't want to wait to be told that things had gone south.

Anders Seaborg thought about Metzler's concern that the Remor still had space forces insystem as he watched Colonel Rance's battalion deploying at the jump-off point. The massed fighting carriers would make a tempting target for an interface striker.

His own task group would be less vulnerable, but only because their motley collection of transport vehicles would be a less juicy target than the armored vehicles of the 24th Cav. But the enemy would get around to them, and then Anders's platoon and the militia, lacking armor, would die faster than the planetary legion troopers.

And Anders didn't want to see that happen to this task group, his first warranted independent command. His new captain's pips, a gift from Svein Rostler which the militia captain had personally glued to Anders's battlesuit, were still shiny reminders of his new responsibility. Although doctrine called for him to dull them down before going into combat, he hadn't had the heart to do it.

Anders's force was the second wave, intended to mop up

any enemy bypassed by the 24th Cav. It wasn't a glorious mission, but it was a necessary and honorable one, and the one most suited to the green troops making up the bulk of his command. He knew that Colonel Rance didn't intend to leave anything for the Grenwolders to deal with if she could help it, but battle demolished plans even faster than it did men and materiel. Anders had little doubt that the Grenwolders would see action.

So far, however, everything was going according to plan. Metzler's flight had achieved orbit unmolested and had sent pics confirming what the command team had suspected from the reports of Anders's scouts: the Remor were blessedly few. Their forces remained concentrated around a single base set in the heart of an inland forest. Recognizable defenses were few and far between. Perimeter patrols were nonexistent. It seemed as though the Remor commanders were unaware that they shared the planet with their enemy. Colonel Rance's all-out, strike-for-the-heart assault looked to have a good chance of succeeding.

Of course, there were still unknowns. Ground recon had reported swaths of devastation, twenty-meter channels in the forest where everything had been reduced to bare earth, rock, and debris. Metzler's orbital pics showed the devastation to be centered around the enemy camp. The area nearest the Remor base was almost completely denuded. Further away the destruction was more haphazard, threading through the forest in winding, crisscrossing trails of desolation. At the head of each trail was one of the monstrous machines that the enemy had unleashed, which the scouts had dubbed "grinders." Intel's best guess was that the grinders were some sort of mobile factories for processing organic material, but infrared scans failed to show a power plant aboard big enough to run such behemoths. The grinders were another Remor mystery, one which the troops would have to deal with shortly, since their path of advance was taking them into a broad river valley where three of the things were working. There had been a time when he would have been intrigued by the grinder machines. Now he was just worried about what sort of threat they might pose.

Anders's blower was following hard on the heels of the recon. He was taking advantage of the fact that the recon, his original platoon, was attached to his task group and used a commander's privilege to attach himself to the sub-unit of his choice. He wanted to be there when his men cut a path into the grinder tracks. It would be one of the tricki-est parts of the operation, and he wanted to be on top of it in case something went wrong.

Coming down the track that led to the valley floor, he got his first look at the wall of forest ahead. It was dark under the trees, an ominous contrast to the rolling, open country they had traversed. In the distance he could see the channels cut through the trees with their pale scars of open earth, each ending in a thrashing mass of greenery where the grinders were at work. Black dots skittered at the edge of the deep woods where the recon blowers were working their way along the marshy banks of the meandering river, looking for a suitable entry point.

The forest wasn't good country for blowers. That inhos-pitality had been the genesis of the plan to utilize the tracks that the grinders were creating through the bush. Free roads, leading through otherwise inaccessible territory to the heart of the enemy camp, were not something to be ignored. Of course, roads were restrictive, which was why they had chosen to strike for a point where three of the grinders were converging near the edge of the forest. Mul-tiple roads were far preferable to a single track vulnerable to choke-point ambushes.

Unable to find a suitable place to cut into the forest, the recon teams started working their way up the river. Private Gordon skillfully guided the command blower through the uneven ground toward the smoother going near the river edge, following the track that the recon vehicles had used. As they drew closer to the treeline, Anders noted that some of the big trees just past the verge were swaying as if they were caught in a localized storm. The darkness shifting between the boles beyond that point only enhanced the impression, calling to mind the roiling blackness of a thunderhead. If there was any sound, he couldn't hear it over the noise of the blower.

A forest giant toppled, crashing through its brethren. Its leafy crown slammed into the marshy verge with a splash. Anders watched as the trunk was drawn back into the trees. Through the slash left by the giant's fall he could see a shape. The darkly gleaming bulk of something monstrous heaved itself forward, battering the trees and sending more of their number crashing down.

One of the grinders!

He ordered Gordon to take the blower to cover. There wasn't much, but Gordon managed to find a small hillock, parking the blower hulldown on the side away from the advancing Remor machine. Once the blower was settled into the relatively firm earth and the engines were on standby idle, Gordon popped his driver's hatch and pulled himself up. He, too, wanted to see with his own eyes the fabulous destructive machine that the enemy had unleashed on Grenwold.

With the blower's engine down, Anders became aware of a subsonic rumble vibrating through the air. Some sort of emanation from the grinder's power source? Whatever its source, it had a different quality from the thudding noise of the ground-shaking tremors caused by the grinder's passage. So much mass could not move quietly.

The last of the big trees fell as the grinder moved relentlessly ahead. The lesser plants of the forest verge were no impediment to the juggernaut as it emerged from the shelter of the covering vegetation.

Or at least part of it emerged: fifty meters easily. Opaque, heaving shadows glimpsed between the boles suggested that at least three times as much of the grinder remained concealed within the tree cover. He'd known, intellectually, that the grinders were big, but he was unprepared for the emotional impact of something so *incredibly* big. He stared in awe at the monstrous thing emerging from the forest, too amazed to do anything *but* stare.

All the other Remor machines he'd seen or been briefed on were sleek, but this thing was anything but sleek. Its body appeared to be constructed of segmented compartments. Their linkage was concealed by a rough, contour-disrupting covering that was stretched over the entire frame and fell into deep folds between the segments and around the upper leg joints. Each of those multijointed legs, a dozen to each segment, had to be at least two meters in circumference and at least four between the joints, but even such massive propulsive mechanisms only sufficed to ram the machine's gigantic body along, furrowing a track in the ground. There were plates of some kind of nonmetallic armor scattered about the sides of each segment. On the first segment the plates were bigger and thicker, overlapping each other to shield the front end almost completely.

The first segment was the grinder's business end. A thick, jointed boom projected from a collar of armored plates. At the end of that boom was a gaping orifice easily large enough to engulf a battle tank, equipped with a veritable shredding mill of flashing cutters, rippers, manipulators, pulpers, and mulchers.

Here and there dark spots—maintenance drones?—moved on the grinder's surface. They reminded him of ants crawling across an uncaring caterpillar. Indeed, the image was apt, since the grinder itself bore such an uncanny resemblance to an enormous, nightmarish caterpillar.

"That ain't no machine," said Gordon. "That thing's alive!"

Could he be right? How could something so huge be alive?

The longer Anders watched the rippling motion of the grinder's phalanx of legs, the more he saw of its immense body; the more closely he studied the motions of its feeding apparatus, the more convinced he became that Gordon was right. This was no machine, but an enormous creature. It looked like and fed as voraciously as a caterpillar, but where a caterpillar might chew a leaf, this creature ate entire trees.

A living animal as big as a small starship! What a wonder!

If it had eyes or any other sensory organs, he couldn't identify them. Still, it seemed somehow aware of its surroundings. With three body segments clear of the treeline, it seemed to pause, almost as if it were puzzled that there were no more trees in front of it. The head shifted up, its shredding battery still, and quested back and forth. The subsonic rumbling increased as it sought whatever it sought.

Could that rumbling be from its stomach? Such an enormous animal would need vast amounts of food.

The head dipped once toward the tough marsh grass, then lifted again, higher this time. But only for a moment before the head lowered and began swinging from side to side. The grinder crammed grasses, tangled roots, and organic muck into its maw. With each pass the body shifted forward and more and more until, at last, all of the incredible creature emerged from the sheltering trees. Anders could only stare in slack-jawed wonder.

Thus the Remor machine, a true machine this time, caught him by surprise as it emerged unexpectedly from the gap that the grinder had left in the treeline. The machine had six legs and skittered as fast as a cockroach surprised by a sudden burst of light. Anders barely had time to register its presence before he saw the turret slung under the forepart of its carapace swiveling toward the blower. He shouted—what, he wasn't sure. A backflash of energy release lit the underside of the machine as a line of superheated air cracked beside Anders's head.

His startlement was only momentary. He started to grab for the blower's cannon. Gordon was reacting too, slipping back into his couch. The driver gunned the engines and vectored thrust unilaterally to send the blower skidding in a trough-making, skirt-battering, sideways slide. Anders hit the compartment's coaming hard as another beam crackled through where they had been. He aborted his grab for the cannon in order to hold on and keep himself aboard the bucking vehicle.

The blower lurched forward, turbine wailing. A second shot from the enemy machine exploded soil from the hummock. Anders managed to steady himself enough to make another grab for the cannon. He succeeded. Eyes steady on the enemy, he swiveled his weapon to bear. The six-legged machine was the sort of enemy he was used to, and he knew what to do. He triggered the gun and sent a stream of high-energy pulses ripping into the machine.

Fragments exploded in a cloud of steam and smoke as the blasts ripped into the fighting machine's carapace, gouging deeper until one pulse caught something vital. The machine blew apart. Secondary explosions sent the familiar Remor acid plumes into the air. One, unfortunately, spurted into the path of the onrushing blower. Gordon, banking hard to avoid the drifting corrosive, nearly sent them into the side of the grinder. Another gut-wrenching turn saved them from collision, but spun them alongside the grinder, nearer to the ravening, feeding orifice.

Anders feared that the Remor beast would attack them, but it ignored them. As it had throughout the short fight, the grinder kept eating; it had never paused. Voracious, it plodded on, devastating a forty-meter-wide swath of marsh.

As Gordon circled them out away from the gorging behemoth, the battalion command link came on-line.

"Seaborg?" The colonel sounded annoyed. "What are you firing at?"

"Encountered single enemy machine; flashed same. It's a new type; visuals uploading to net." He gave his suit the command to do so.

"Evaluation?"

"I don't think it was a fighting machine. It had an energy weapon, something on the order of a light industrial laser. It didn't have any armor."

"Just one machine?"

"Affirmative. Enemy force reevaluation uplinking," he said. Rather than trying to explain the grinder, he'd let her see it for herself. He wasn't sure she would believe his unsupported word. By Saint Michael, he was looking at it live, and he wasn't sure *he* believed it. While waiting for her response, he also sent out a recall to the recon. He'd need them soon.

"All units." Rance's voice was calm and businesslike. If the nature of the grinder surprised or awed her, she hid the fact. "Prepare to receive situation update. New data on the grinders and enemy forces. Review soonest."

On a direct link she asked, "Anything else, Seaborg?"

"I've also got an entry point to one of the grinder trails."

"Have you?" Rance sounded eager. "Exploitable?"

"Recon is re-forming to scout it now."

"Maybe we can still pull off our surprise. Entry at your location?"

At his affirmative, she gave orders for her force to open their throttles. Anders passed the same order to his driver. "Take us down the trail, Gordie. The colonel will want to know if this will take us where we want to go."

"What if there's another one of those monsters down there? I can't squeeze this blower through the trees to get out of its way."

"I don't think you'll have to. The grinders don't look like they can move very fast. Get us going, Gordie. We've got a job to do."

Jason Metzler wasn't sure whether he was glad that the colonel considered his shuttle flight too valuable an asset to commit just yet. His friend Anders was down there and headed for trouble. As much as he hated the idea of taking his birds into combat, it didn't feel right just listening to the commo and watching the whole battle pass by in snapshots as they made their orbital passes.

For the moment, though, sitting and watching was his job. He checked the deep scan. It was empty. No sign of active space drives insystem. But the enemy could still be out there. It was a threat that they dared not ignore.

He listened to Anders's recon report.

"We've located the other two grinders in our sector. Grid reference three-two by six-niner. They are cutting parallel trails toward the river and are escorted by at least three of the new type machines and a skink." The skink was a small four-legged machine that had been encountered on other planets. Unlike the new types, a skink was armed and armored for combat. "The new types are using their energy weapons on the grinders. I think the machines are trying to herd them."

"Save the animal husbandry lessons, Seaborg. I want you out of there. Do not engage. Repeat, do not engage. We're on the way."

Jason estimated that Rance's main body would reach Anders's advance position within twenty minutes. The orbiting shuttles wouldn't see the link-up. Their observation window was closing in five.

"Update processing initiated," his copilot said.

Right on time. "Feed it to my screen."

"Aye."

This was the last set of pics they were going to get on this pass. As the link came up, Jason ran a comparison with the last suite. The computer tagged a definite change in enemy depositions ten klicks southwest of the line of advance. It looked like a flanking maneuver.

"Colonel, you've got sixteen fighting machines moving up from the south," he reported live as he sent the computer's analysis downlink. That was two-thirds of the enemy's armored complement, and more than enough to maul 24th Cav. They could annihilate the militia. "A dozen skinks, two caymans, and two unidentified heavy machines."

"Acknowledged," Rance responded. He heard her give the orders for the battalion to turn in that direction. "Seaborg, I want you and the militia to deal with the grinders and their escort while we go after the enemy's battle force. I'm counting on you to make sure I've got a clear line of retreat if I need it."

"Aye, ma'am."

Jason sat looking at his screens with a sour taste in his mouth. His birds would be on the other side of Grenwold when the engagement started. The dirtsiders, Anders included, would be on their own.

*      *      *

Colonel Rance's orders left Anders with a quandary. He had three categories of target: the grinders, the unarmored new type machines, and the skink, ranked according to his estimate of their threat value, lowest to highest. To counter the enemy he had an understrength platoon of hardsuited troopers in transport blowers and the Grenwold militia, an overstrength battalion of lightly armed, unarmored infantry in a ragtag assortment of hover and wheeled transport.

The colonel was right to worry about lines of retreat; the isolated grinder would lie across his own. From its lack of reaction to his fight with the enemy six-legger, he didn't think it would pose much of a threat, but he preferred to be safe and be rid of it. Besides, tackling the thing would give the Grenwolders a relatively safe blooding.

Under Rostler's command, the militia set up a firing line at the edge of the marsh. The troops moved hesitantly, often stopping to stare at the incredible thing they were about to attack. But Rostler got them moving again and, finally, set in position. They opened fire in volley and the fusillade ripped into the grinder. It was hard to miss such an enormous target, but some of his greenies managed.

But for every miss, ten shots hit.

At first the grinder seemed untouched by the fire. It continued its voracious march through the marsh. Then a high-pitched, keening wail began and parallel rows of orifices began opening and closing along its flanks.

The Grenwolders set up their light mortars and started dropping explosive shells. The monster started to show visible damage as chunks were torn from its enormous body, but it continued eating as the assault increased in intensity. The grinder's legs flailed in undirected motion and its segments writhed under the terrible pounding, but it paid no attention to its tormentors. It bled, lost gobbets of its flesh to explosive rounds, had limbs amputated by pulse blasts, and it ate. Organs seeped fluids, gashes in its side gushed forth half-digested vegetation, and it ate. Its injuries were catastrophic, but the grinder kept eating.

Apparently the lack of hostile response from the grinder encouraged and emboldened the Grenwolders. Four vehicles burst from the militia's line—all hovercraft, so it had to be first platoon—and rushed toward the grinder. Anders considered ordering them back, but he could hear the crews whooping with wild excitement all over the commo bands as they jinked and banked on their wild, evasive course. Militiamen in the firing line were cheering their comrades' bravado. The grinder was as safe a target as they were likely to engage. He let them go.

First platoon had closed to within a hundred meters when the lead blower turned suddenly and headed straight for the grinder. Inexplicably, the craft's gunners stopped firing. The blower charged in and rammed into the wall of legs. One spasmed and lifted the hovercraft off the ground, sending it arcing away from the creature with its turbine howling madly. Spilling men, the hovercraft slammed into the ground and sent up a fountain of water and muck. The splash must have blinded one of the other drivers; he failed to turn in time and crashed into the crumpled wreck.

The remaining two blowers were also having trouble. One careened out of control, swerving wildly back and forth until it slammed into a hillock and tumbled. It landed upright but none of the crew emerged. The other didn't go out of control or crash, it just glided to a stop. The crew didn't get out of that one either.

What in Saint Michael's name had happened?

Anders's horror at the fate of first platoon was pierced by the sound of weapons fire erupting from his troopers' ambush position. That was the danger point. If the Remor forces were moving down the trail, they could brush through the ambush and be on the Grenwolders in short order.

"Report!" he ordered.

For several agonizing moments as the intensity of the firing increased, the commo remained silent. Anders considered cutting into the platoon's tac channel, but if the fighting was as hot as it sounded, he might distract someone. He decided it was better to leave them to their business for the moment. He was reconsidering his decision when Hewitt came on-line.

"It was the skink, sir. It came in alone and we flashed it. I don't think it knew we were here. All quiet now."

"Casualties?"

"Yes, sir. We lost Roderigo. Hannibal and Foch need evac. Roderigo's blower's a scratch."

"Call for a pickup," Anders told him. "And send someone out to regain contact with the enemy."

One dead, two injured. They had gotten off very lightly for engaging an enemy fighting machine. He could only hope that the rest of the engagement would go as well.

The Grenwolders, despite their easier target, hadn't fared as well. First platoon was out of action, but the grinder no longer moved. Its neck lay stretched on the ground, its appetite stilled at last. The cost still needed to be evaluated.

Ordering his units to hold position, he dismounted and walked toward the nearest of the crashed hovercraft. Their last actions had made him suspicious. He engaged his suit's nose, the system that let him smell his environment despite being inside a sealed hardsuit.

The sewer stink wafting from the blower assaulted him. It was the smell of death, and not unexpected. He ordered the suit to filter it out. Still, his stomach was churning as he climbed aboard.

The crew lay at their stations, all dead. Their contorted limbs showed that they hadn't died easily, but he saw was no blood save what had leaked from orifices. The blower's makeshift armor was intact and the crew showed no wounds. The cyanotic skin color of the dead militiamen was the last thing he needed to see to crystallize his suspicion.

"External air sample," he ordered his suit. "Analyze."

"External air contains trace contaminants of an unidentified chemical compound. Effects unknown," it replied. "You are advised that air quality monitoring subroutine has begun. Recommendation: remain on internal air supply until further notice."

He'd been right. The crew had succumbed to a gas attack. He passed the word to Sergeant Hewitt and Rostler. "No one is to approach a grinder without breathing gear."

They still had four machines and two grinders to deal with.

The militia couldn't get near the beasts since none of them had biochem gear, so Anders assigned them to long-range fire support, reserving the close stuff for his hardsuited troopers.

In the end he didn't succeed in protecting all the Grenwolders from the gas; several squads managed to get lost and engage a grinder at close range, with the predictable casualties. His hardsuited troopers took it on the chin while routing out the last of the enemy machines, but in all the casualties were less than Anders had feared they would be. They had done the job Colonel Rance expected them to do. Still, he was sick at heart when he counted the letters that he would be writing to the bereaved.

His gloomy thoughts were interrupted when Sergeant Hewitt linked to him on the command channel. "Captain, there's something over here you need to see."

Anders decided that he really didn't need to see more gas victims, but as commander it was his duty. He trudged toward where the sergeant was standing over a pair of corpses. These bodies weren't wearing uniforms. They weren't wearing anything. They were furred, and they weren't Human.

"There's another sticking out from under the grinder," Hewitt said.

Anders barely registered what the sergeant said. He was staring at the dead aliens, not really believing what he was seeing. He'd seen aliens similar to these before, a decade ago, on Cassuells Home. StratCom had declared the indigenes there to be Remor, a controversial position to this day. Having been there on Cassuells Home, Anders had developed a personal interest in the issue, and so he'd studied the arguments, including some of the classified ones. He'd never been totally convinced that StratCom had gotten it right. Now he'd have to rethink the situation. On Cassuells Home the link between the Cassuells and the enemy had been tenuous at best. Here, it looked undeniable.

"Take pics and samples, Sergeant. We've got to get this off to Sector Intel soonest."

# Part 2

# Formative Translation

# 9

**WAYFARER STATION**

Watching the public feed from the docking starship's bridge, Kurt was surprised that Wayfarer Station looked different than he remembered it. He shouldn't have been. It had been ten years, after all, and Wayfarer was a bustling, growing commercial hub. There was absolutely no reason the place should have remained static.

Years ago he had been impressed by the sheer size of the place, and he still was, not the least because the station was even bigger than it had been then. The habitat ring that had been under construction was complete, as was another that hadn't even been shown as proposed on the station maps. In part Wayfarer's size was necessitated by its location. Since the system didn't have any habitable planets, there were no local biological resources, and everything had to be imported or grown on station. Other stations faced similar problems, but none of them even came close in size to Wayfarer. But then, none of them were situated at such a confluence of significant, heavily traveled jump routes, and the station's extranational government did everything it could to promote trade along those routes. Clearly their programs were garnering success.

Kurt also remembered the thrill he'd felt on seeing Wayfarer Station for the first time. Then he'd had a bright future ahead of him. He'd been heading for Cassuells

Home to prove his theories. Wayfarer had been the gateway to his dreams.

He'd been expecting to feel something similar this time. After all, wasn't he heading for a new chance at a bright future? He just felt empty. Where had all his optimism gone?

Some, he knew, had been blown away by the Concordat press coverage of the mission. The media were giving far too much attention to his presence on it.

Once he'd sought the academic spotlight. He'd practically had to plead with the press to get the pitiful few notices of his endeavors. Now, it seemed that he couldn't call up a news or commentary program without getting something on the Chugen Contact Mission, and most of that coverage and commentary was centered on him, specifically *his* qualifications—or, as some would have it, his *dis*qualifications. Some, having heard that the IDL had asked specifically for his inclusion, had gone so far as to accuse him of collusion with the League! He had tried to set the record straight, but he wasn't very good at public speaking and had only succeed in getting himself more unflattering coverage.

Media attention. *One must,* he reminded himself, *be careful of what one wishes for.*

Why weren't the press bothering to dig into the backgrounds of the other members of the Serenten contingent—Dale Wallace Lockhart, for instance? The young woman was supposed to be the logistics specialist, but one didn't need to know that she was related to Defense Ministry Colonel M. W. Lockhart to see that there was more to her than that. Her erect carriage, her rigidly polite manner, even her buzz-cut hair just screamed military. Why weren't the press interested in the fact that an incognito military woman was a part of a peaceful, scientific mission? Or what about Dr. Paula Stevenson? The press touted her work with the Gedry Foundation and the ecological rescue work on Mantua, but no one seemed interested in the fact that she was a doctor of psychiatry and had no skills pertinent to the mission at hand. No one, it seemed, interested the press more than the brilliant, but unbalanced, Professor Kurt Ellicot.

The starship would have dumped the Concordat media reports, along with the rest of the news and data that she carried. Already, eager viewers would be taking in the latest half-truths, lies, vilifications, and occasional facts about him and his work. And from Wayfarer Station, other ships would disseminate the entire scandalous amalgamation to all the places where humankind dwelt. The media were spreading his name and fame among the stars.

Who cared if the truth was involved or not?

"Hello, Juli."

Juliana Tindal turned at the sound of the familiar voice, singling out the speaker from the crowd thronging along the Ring One Zocalo. Despite the shroud of a beard, she found the man's features familiar, too. The beard lent him a rakish air that she had to admit was attractive.

"Rafael Sebastian Burke," she said. "I thought I'd seen the last of you. What are you doing here?"

"Same as you, Juli. The Chugen Contact Project. We're all headed for scientific glory at Chugen, wherever the hell that is."

The slate for the Combine's contingent had been incomplete when she left Hoffreter. More than half the slots were still empty, according to the last update to arrive at Wayfarer Station, and Rafe's name hadn't been on any list she'd seen. "But—"

"How did I get in ahead of other obviously better qualified candidates? Got recommended by a member of the board for whom I did a little eco cleanup work a few years back. It was good work. She got wind that the Committee's first choice for an ecologist couldn't go, and slipped my name in as a replacement. Her way of showing gratitude, I guess. Frankly, I wasn't going to take the slot until they told me that you were part of the team. It's been a long time, Juli. I've missed you."

"I've missed you, too," she said, realizing that it was true.

He stepped closer, put his hand to her cheek, and said, "It's going to be like old times."

She flushed at his touch, memories calling to her. Why would it be any different this time? She brushed his hand away. "Things are different now."

"Have you got a partner?"

"No." She wished; *that* would have made it easier. "That's not it."

"Then what *is* it?"

"Well . . ." Why *was* she resisting? There was no denying that the physical attraction was still there. As strong as ever. But she couldn't deny the hours of crying, either. "I've gotten over you."

"Really?" Not surprisingly, he sounded unconvinced.

*No, not really. But I ought to have.* "Rafe, you left and you never looked back. I felt like a stepping-stone. I don't think I want to feel that way again."

"Is that it? You think I just want to take advantage of your position? I realize that I might not be an Alsion scholar like you, but what kind of a lowlife do you take me for? No, don't bother to answer that one. It's pretty clear—"

"No, Rafe. It's not like that."

"Isn't it?" He sounded bitter. "I suppose you always have to be on the lookout for people trying to ride your coattails. Well, you don't have to worry about me. I may be just a down-in-the-trenches grant grubber, but I've accomplished a few things. Lots of hard work and very little recognition. I've learned how to get used to it."

"What about your MacReady Fellowship?" she asked, reminding him of the prestigious prize that had signaled the beginning of the end for their relationship.

"Old news. Like my leaving." He dropped his aggrieved tone and put on a bright smile. "You've got to look to the future."

She knew that smile, knew the offer it made. She was beset by conflicting feelings. Did she want him back in her life, or didn't she?

Belatedly she realized that standing in a corridor wasn't the place to be having this conversation. "Maybe we should continue this later. I was on my way to the Sedgewick Lounge."

"To the cocktail mixer. I'd guessed. That's where I was headed, too. I *am* on this project, remember?" He slipped his arm into hers. "Why don't we go together? Get to know each other again, while we're getting to know the others?"

Despite their linked arms, the conversation on the way to the lounge stayed impersonal, focusing on the first gathering of the entire project team. As their surprise meeting had reminded her, Juliana knew more about the other national contingents than she did about her own. Taking advantage of Rafe's more recent information, she partially rectified that. He pointed out luminaries like Singh, Mogumbo, and Hollister, as well as identifying her fellow Alsion scholars O'Brien, Shadwell, and Diaz. Rafe surprised her by having synopses of the careers and specialties of just about everyone on the project, and he promised introductions in the course of the mixer, but Juliana stayed more interested in meeting some of the people from other star nations than in being introduced to fellow nationals.

She especially wanted to meet the other socioxenologists, and one of *those* in particular. Unfortunately, he wasn't present when they arrived at the lounge. With her preferred start unavoidably postponed, she went with Rafe to pick up drinks and consider where to begin. Rafe directed her attention to a lone figure near one of the viewing ports.

"That's the eminent Professor Inigo Jones of the University of Neu Bremen, our glorious leader."

"This could be a good chance to get to know him," she mused aloud.

"Could be," Rafe agreed, steering her toward Jones.

Unfortunately others sought the same opportunity. They had barely finished introducing themselves when Paula Stevenson of the Concordat team arrived. A pair of station officials turned up within a minute and a meteorologist by the name of Langdorf was right behind them. Before Juliana knew it, her hoped for one-on-one with Professor Jones had turned into a multisided discussion group with her concerns shunted to the background.

Frustrated, she interjected less and less into the conversation. The same sort of thing always seemed to happen to her. Rafe noticed and made some sort of excuse about refilling their glasses, easing them out just like old times. As they withdrew to look for a less busy conversation, she learned that other things were just like old times, because as soon as they were out of Jones's earshot, Rafe gave his unsolicited evaluation of the project's leader.

"My, what a windbag. And he's our exalted leader, though why he is, I can't see. It's not like he's got the professional standing of Singh or Hollister. It has to be political."

"Of course." What else had he expected? Singh and Hollister were both Combine scientists, and the Committee had ordained a multinational image for the research project. Naming one of the Combine's own to lead the project would have left them open to charges of partisanship. "There are worse choices. I understand that he's quite well thought of in the Hanseatic Coalition, and his nationality makes him a safe, neutral choice. Politically speaking, of course."

"Safe and neutral, eh? Then you haven't heard about the FSN mess." She hadn't heard of any trouble with the Federated Star Nations contingent, so he told her what he'd heard. "Your 'safe choice' seriously rocked the boat when he displayed naked nepotism and appointed his own protégé, one Gilian Zandowski, as head of the biological team. She's barely out of graduate school! I'm told you could have heard the howls of the Feddies half a light-year away. By their lights, their own venerable Professor Anand Kehar had the seniority and experience for the job. And you know what? They're right.

"But nothing they said meant a damn to Professor Jones, and as soon as they figured out that he wasn't backing down, Professor Kehar was called away on a family emergency. Within hours all but one of the Feddies found similar emergencies forcing them to withdraw from the project. They were all resignations of protest, of course, but prettied up for general consumption. Before he left Wayfarer, Kehar actually gave a speech of support for the project. You should call up the playback. It's full of trid bites about international cooperation and the importance of scientific work and the wonderful opportunity that Chugen's virgin first contact offers. It's also full of slick, roundabout digs at Jones, Gilian Zandowski and her lack of credentials, the quality of scholarship at the U of Neu Bremen, and the Hanseatic Coalition in general. Quite a piece of work. Makes you respect old Kehar."

Juliana was more respectful of Kehar's work than manners if Rafe's report of a sniping speech was correct.

Rafe introduced her to Sandy Kohrs, the pool representative for the multinational press, who had arrived on the same ship he had and despite their just having met acted as if she had known Rafe for years. She extended the same sudden familiarity to Juliana, presuming to set a time and a place for an interview before buzzing off to arrange more of her schedule.

"She'll grow on you," Rafe commented.

"Like Toerot fungus?"

Rafe laughed. "At least as tenacious."

Juliana's own first attempt at an introduction went scarcely better. Ray Paston, the PSC logistics person, was normally quite well mannered; but tonight he made only the briefest of polite noises and barely introduced Dale Lockhart, his opposite number from the Serenten Concordat, before diving back into deep conversation with the Concordat woman. Rafe didn't even wait until they had walked away to comment.

"So refreshing to meet people for whom their work is their life."

If the logistics specialists heard, they gave no sign. Juliana was grateful. Sometimes Rafe could be so embarrassingly crass. Chutzpah, he called it. She called it bad manners, but the party wasn't the place to have an argument about it.

The awkward meet-and-greet went on. Except for the incident with Paston and Lockhart, Rafe didn't behave badly once, and she found herself thinking that perhaps he had changed. The logistic specialists had been rude, after all. They'd given him cause. Much like the booze-fueled rambles of Paula Lawson, the lone remnant of the FSN delegation, were giving cause. Rafe's smile didn't waver, and Juliana let him carry the conversation while she surreptitiously scanned the crowd, looking for a decent excuse to pry herself and Rafe away. That was when she spotted the project member she had most wanted to meet: Kurt Ellicot.

Mumbling contradictory excuses to Professor Lawson, she hooked her arm in Rafe's and headed for the one member of the Serenten Concordat team whom they had yet to meet: *the* Kurt Ellicot, dean of modern socioxenology!

"Excuse me," she said timidly. "Professor Ellicot?"

"Yes?" he said, turning to see who was addressing him.

His manner was reserved as he stood awaiting her next statement. She found to her surprise that she was flustered at actually meeting him. He had an exotic air that she couldn't place. It wasn't because he was not from the Combine; she met plenty of foreigners, even aliens. It was something else, something just a little feral. He waited for her to continue her stalled introduction.

"I'm Juliana Tindal," she said, awkwardly extending a hand.

"Ah, the Alsion scholar." Some of the guardedness went away.

When he took her hand, she felt a tingle of excitement. This wasn't like meeting Ambrose Alsion; that had been so unreal. This was so *very* real. Her hand in the hand of the master, the man who had done the work that had inspired her to take up socioxenology.

"I'm so pleased to meet you, Professor. I'm a longtime admirer of your work. I've read all your books." God, she sounded like a schoolgirl!

"You are kind, Professor Tindal, if somewhat remiss," he said. "And your gentleman friend is—?"

"My—" Embarrassed, Juliana disengaged Rafe's arm from her waist. "This is Rafael Burke. He's the ecologist for the Combine."

"Pleased to meet you, Professor Burke." Ellicot nodded politely. "Burke? I once worked with another Professor Burke from the Combine. Any relation?"

"It's a common name," Rafe said stiffly. "Not so common as it once was, but there are still a few of us around."

Juliana's desire to keep Rafe's sour tone from spoiling the moment gave her the impetus she needed to get over her star-struck jitters. "I've been wanting to ask you if your sufficiency doctrine grew out of the work that your great-grandfather did among the Yanellocyx?"

"I would say his work had an impact," he answered a little hesitantly. "Inspirational more than factual."

"So you would say that Cole's refutation of the doctrine is inherently flawed since he bases his attack on your alleged misinterpretation of the Yanellocyx data. Personally, I think Cole's biggest mistake was ignoring the parallels you drew. He missed the picture because he was looking at the pixels. My own work among the Shandaltelkak Association of the Mimaks has turned up a number of classic instances of sufficiency."

*That* got his attention.

"I'm afraid that I haven't read your work," he admitted.

"It's not like it got published outside the Combine. I can drop you a copy if you'd like."

"I would be interested to see it."

*Really?* But she asked another question instead, one about Yanellocyx prayer rituals. His answer was a little vague, the sort of thing one said to a well-informed layperson. She asked another question, and another. His answers came more freely as she demonstrated her command of socioxenological theory and practice. His answers drifted into jargon, a tacit acceptance of her as a colleague. As they talked, she observed his reserve dwindling. She began to believe that he was actually warming up to her as a person, but she didn't get to have that warm feeling for long.

"Oh-oh," said Rafe. "We've been targeted."

Juliana looked where he was looking and saw a knot of six men and women approaching. She recognized them from her Alsion briefing. "The League contingent."

"None of them are in uniform," Ellicot said. "Not that it matters with their kind."

Juliana wanted to ask him what he meant by that, but the Leaguers were too close. She turned and offered a welcoming smile.

A swarthy young man sporting a thin black strip of a mustache stepped forward of the group as they arrived, snapping his heels together as he came to attention and bowed.

"Professor Ellicot, I am Marc Decloux, coordinator of the League team. I have the honor to present Professor Miles Mowbray, our contingent's scientific leader. He is considered by many to be the League's finest scholar of indigenous cultures. Some few even place him in a league with yourself."

"A working scholar is all I am," Mowbray said with a deprecatory smile. "I am so very pleased to meet you, Professor Ellicot. Your previous work was so very enlightening and informative for us. I am so glad that we are finally getting to work side-by-side."

Ellicot stared down at Mowbray's offered hand until the man withdrew it. Only then did he meet the man's gaze and say, "I am a part of this project at my government's request, sir. I will do my part, and not, I trust, side by side with you or your colleagues. I hope you won't be too disappointed."

"How imperti—" Decloux started to sputter, but Mowbray cut the man off with a raised hand. Mowbray bowed stiffly to Ellicot, then to Juliana and Rafe. Turning, he led his delegation across the room.

"I guess the rest of the introductions will have to wait," Rafe commented.

"My manners are a little rusty," Ellicot said somewhat apologetically. He offered her a sheepish smile.

"Oh, don't apologize. I understand. It must be hard working back into the social rituals after so long a convalescence."

"I'm sure." The shift in Ellicot's demeanor was chilling. "Whatever you may have heard was undoubtedly exaggerated; however, I am not in the business of correcting gossip. I suggest that we confine ourselves to professional discussions in our future conversations."

"I'm sorry. I didn't—"

"I'm sure you didn't. Now, if you will excuse me, the station's schedule is a bit off what I am used to. I believe I shall retire."

Stunned into speechlessness, Juliana watched as her offended idol turned away and left her standing there.

"It isn't, you know," said Rafe.

"What isn't?"

"The time. The ship he arrived on was keeping station time from the minute it left orbit around Serenten. I'm afraid you offended the eminent professor."

"But I didn't mean to."

"I know, Juli. I wouldn't worry about it. Still, I think you'd be smart to stay away from him for a while."

Rafe was probably right. So why did she feel so bad? She'd known that her idol was human. How could one listen to those sensational stories from the Concordat press and not know? But he didn't deserve the treatment the press was giving him. He had recovered, otherwise his government wouldn't have had the confidence to send him. He'd probably assumed that she believed all the things that were being said about him. She wanted to tell him how wrong he was.

She knew something of what he'd gone through. Every socioxenologist got attached to the sentients they studied. You couldn't do your work and not get attached. Some people said that he had gone too far, but what basis did they have to judge? Only a person who'd spent time among aliens could even begin to understand what was necessary to get inside an alien culture. She wanted to tell him that she understood. She hoped she'd get a chance.

But it was not to be tonight. Rafe nudged her. "Here comes Decloux again."

Rafael Burke didn't pay a lot of attention to what Decloux said. The marts were an impersonal hate, Ellicot was a personal one, and Rafe always put the personal ahead of the impersonal.

While watching Ellicot frost the marts of the League, Rafe had reluctantly awarded the man a point. The arrogant sons-of needed to be put in their place whenever the chance arose. Rafe, having always believed that chutzpah was necessary to get ahead in the universe, was the sort of guy who acknowledged it in others when he came across it. Not that he was likely to let such a tiny seed of admiration grow into anything bigger. He knew what sort of man Ellicot was, and Rafe was not about to fall into the trap of believing that the enemy of his enemy was *his* friend.

Ellicot was so smoothly deceptive, pretending that he didn't know who Rafe was. "Burke?" he had said, sounding innocent. "I once worked with a Professor Burke." Not even giving her the dignity of her first name. *Franchesca Burke*, Rafe had wanted to shout at the man. She had deserved at least that from the man responsible for her death. *Her name was Franchesca!*

But he had kept his mouth shut. Ellicot might have forgotten Franchesca, but Rafe, her brother, had not and would not. Nor would he forget the man whose negligence had killed his sister on Cassuells Home. The deed was so far unpunished. *So far*. There was always the future, and Rafe was the sort of guy who kept his eyes on the future.

"Rafe, is something wrong?" Juli asked when the damned Decloux finally left them alone.

"Nothing some fresh air wouldn't fix."

"I know what you mean," she said, gazing across the room. "Those Leaguers give me chills."

Leaguers? If she thought that they were why he was steaming, maybe it was for the best. This wasn't the time to let her know the truth about Ellicot—he'd seen the puppy-dog look she'd given him. She'd just get her back up, being too stubborn once she'd set her opinion to be swayed by any number of facts. There'd be a time.

Yeah, he was confident of that. The time would come.

# 10

**CHUGEN SYSTEM**
**MIDWAY STATION**

When Konoye came out of the shower, Jane was sitting on the bed, brushing her hair. Whatever the intercom call had been about, she had handled it.

"Ersch wants to see you again," she said.

Over the last month Konoye had already seen more than he ever wanted to see of the IDL major. "What does he want this time?"

"The usual, I expect. He didn't say, and I didn't ask, just made the appointment. You know, I thought that he sounded a little flustered when I answered the intercom. I think he finds our relationship scandalous."

"Really? He doesn't fluster easily. Still, I suppose I'm not surprised to hear he's got a problem with our not being married." They'd put the sexual side of their relationship on hold for the duration of the exploration voyage, but now that the voyage had turned into more of a residency, they'd picked it up again. Their relationship didn't raise eyebrows among Combiners, but Leaguers had funny ideas of what was appropriate. So Ersch disapproved, did he? "Typical mart Puritanism, most likely."

Jane, of course, disagreed. "Actually, I think he's more bothered by the fact that you're the commander here and I'm your second."

"Hmmm." He struck a speculative pose. "I can understand that. I know I get bothered by you as my second."

She threw her brush at him. Jibes—and hair brushes—thrown at times like these were just for play. He caught her missile and tossed it back, more gently, of course. They both laughed.

He needed moments like these to remind him that life wasn't just construction schedules, resource reclamation reports, parts and materials requisition forms, labor disputes, and everything else that contributed to his increasingly frequent headaches. All too soon he would be back to dealing with the consequential things to hand. Like that damned warship sitting outside the station.

Damn the League! Damn Ersch! And damn the Remor who stirred up those self-important marts and got them scurrying all around the galaxy trying to exterminate their damned enemy! What had he done to deserve having the whole mess land on his doorstep?

The smile left Jane's face. She would know where his thoughts had drifted.

"Ken, the stall isn't working. The League's got a lot of resources tied up in keeping that ship sitting out there doing nothing. Clearly Major Ersch and his masters are very serious about his mission here. It may be time to reconsider. The evidence Ersch brought warrants an investigation."

"At some point."

"At some point," she agreed. "Are we making a mistake in not cooperating with them?"

"Who knows? One thing I *do* know is that it would be a mistake to trust them."

Jane sighed. "Are you talking out of habit, or has Ersch given you reason to believe that?"

He took a moment to consider. Lord knew, he had hated and despised the marts of the League, well and truly, since he and Jane were graduate students together. *Were* those old attitudes clouding his consideration of the current situation? If so, could he *afford* to let them? "Do *you* think that they could be right about this octahedron thing?"

She hedged. "Well, their evidence is all circumstantial. And their copy of our survey tape could have been doctored."

"The tape's not doctored. I checked it against our original. The object's there, all right."

"Really?"

Jane sounded a little scared. And who could blame her? If Ersch *was* right and the octahedron *was* a Remor signaling device, they could be in trouble a lot worse than the trouble they were in with the Committee for being behind schedule.

But they didn't *know* enough to make a good decision. Konoye was getting very tired of not knowing.

"Look. The only thing that we're sure of is that the object is there, and that the major wants to go play with it. The object hasn't *done* anything so far. Even if it is a signaling device, it might be dead."

"So you're suggesting that maybe we should just let Ersch go blow it up, so he can go home happy?"

"I wish it were that simple. I don't think the Committee would thank us for setting the precedent of allowing the League to do whatever they wanted in a Combine system."

"We could send an escort ship. In the name of interstellar cooperation. You know," she shifted her voice deeper, "under our authority we allow you to take the actions you take."

"If we send a ship along with his, then we might as well just go do it ourselves."

"Why do I get the feeling that we're running out of time?" Jane asked.

"I don't know," he replied. He was getting the same feeling himself.

The *Henry Hull* alone was sufficient to deal with the Combine assets insystem. Ersch knew it. Managing Director Konoye knew it. If Ersch wanted to, he could blow away the opposition and do as he pleased. But that would not be politic, so Ersch had carefully balanced threat and diplomacy in his dealings with the managing director. He'd walked carefully, cautiously, and more slowly than he would have liked, careful to accede to StratCom's desire that a diplomatic, cooperative solution be reached if at all possible, but Konoye was still refusing permission to take *Henry Hull* deeper into the Chugen System, and Ersch's patience was wearing thin.

Fortunately, things would soon change. Yesterday's diplomatic pouch had brought news that the research team was due soon. The dispatches had also included authorization to proceed with Operation Chameleon. He didn't know yet which alternate of Chameleon they would be using. That would depend on Managing Director Konoye.

Ersch was punctual for his meeting with the director, which meant that he was standing in the corridor outside the director's office when Konoye, late as usual, arrived. Konoye frowned at Ersch's salute, but rapidly changed his expression to a diplomatic smile.

"Good morning, Major. Have a good night?"

"Good morning, Director," Ersch said politely. "Yes, I did. Yourself?"

"Wonderful." Konoye winked conspiratorially. "Assistant Director Van der Hoogt sends her regards."

So, his slip on the intercom this morning had been noticed. In the future he would be more cautious about letting his personal attitudes show. He would also be more cautious in his dealings with A.D. Van der Hoogt given the knowledge that she was *literally* in bed with her boss. If Konoye wanted that kind of kink in his chain of command, Ersch would be happy to exploit the weakness if the opportunity arose. In the meantime, he would not allow his distaste for decadent Pansie morality to leak out again.

"My regards to her, Director," he said.

Konoye thumbed the lock plate. When the door shushed open, he started forward, but he didn't step completely inside. "You know, Major, we can make this short and save time for both of us. I still won't approve your insystem excursion."

"Your opposition is as expected as it is unwise. However, I am here not to request clearance, but to make an offer in the interests of interstellar cooperation."

Konoye eyed him suspiciously. "Then, in the name of interstellar cooperation, I'd better hear what you have to say, hadn't I?"

Konoye's office was still furnished eclectically with scroungings from various sources; the director's office furniture must still be a low priority on the shipping schedule. Ersch sat where he always sat, avoiding the overstuffed armchair in front of the director's desk and taking the bucket chair near the credenza. To face him, Konoye needed to swivel his own chair. The arrangement weakened Konoye's psychological defensive position behind the wall of the desk.

"Let's be frank, Director," Ersch began. "With my ship sitting idle here, I have had ample opportunity to observe all of the work that is going on with the jump gate and station construction. I would say that you are right on the edge of what you can do with your resources."

"We *are* stretching ourselves," Konoye admitted. "Completion of the gate is a priority that requires all the resources we can bring to bear."

"Exactly. How unfortunate that you will soon have another drain on those resources. I expect that there will be additional delays. Costly delays."

"What do you mean, another drain?"

"Why, the Chugen Contact Project, of course. The scientists and their paraphernalia will be arriving shortly by deep-space transport. They will require transportation to Chugen IV, which you will be expected to provide. Ships ferrying scientists will not be available for priority construction operations, will they? Schedules will slip, possibly past crucial deadlines. I suspect that failure to meet your deadlines will result in a downward adjustment of your profits."

"I'm not here for the profits," Konoye claimed. "I came here to chart a jump route."

"That charting remains at a standstill while the jump gate is built, does it not?"

"You know it is. Don't be disingenuous."

"Your pardon, Director. I only wished to make it clear that I understand how awkward current conditions are for you. I appreciate how frustrating it can be when one is held back from achieving one's goal. It is sympathy that motivates me, and, I admit, a certain self-interest. You may not be aware of the discipline problems that can arise aboard a military vessel during periods of enforced idleness such as my command has been subjected to by your lack of cooperation. I can address the issue by completing my mission, but you are preventing that. My crew needs activity, and yesterday's dispatches offered an answer. As a step toward changing your mind about us, I want to make a gesture of good will and cooperation—call it a demonstration to prove that we have your best interests at heart. Specifically, I would like to offer you the services of IDLS *Henry Hull* to ferry the researchers insystem."

"So our problems solve each other?" Konoye said.

"Exactly."

"I suppose it would just be by coincidence that you would follow a course that would take you close enough to Chugen IV's moon for you to make observations on the octahedron."

"I have made no secret of my reasons for coming here, Director. Those reasons are as valid today as they were last month when I arrived. More urgent, perhaps, with increased enemy activity in other systems.

"You can surely understand that I will take whatever opportunities arise to complete my mission. I assure you that I will make landing the project scientists my top priority. In the spirit of cooperation, I will share all data on any observations of the octahedron that we manage to make."

"What assurance do I have that you will do as you say?"

Ersch gave him the best assurance he could. "You have my word as an officer and as an Eridani."

"You will pardon me if I don't find that sufficient. Nothing personal, Major. It's just that promises, even recorded promises, won't cut it back home."

Ersch stiffened. "Are you questioning my veracity or my honor?"

"Neither," Konoye replied quickly. The man's brow was slick with sudden nervous sweat. "As I said, it wasn't personal. The Committee—"

"Your Committee isn't here! We are," Ersch told him. It was easy to see that the man was afraid. It was time to press. "Your superiors and mine are alike in one way. They both understand that results are what count. If you get the jump gate finished, your bosses will be happy. If I bring back some information on the octahedron, my superiors will be happy. Happy superiors do not cashier their underlings. Unhappy superiors don't care that all the rules were followed, if they don't get the results that they want. Right now, no one is getting what he wants. It doesn't have to be that way. We can help each other here, Director."

"I can't let you go insystem unescorted."

"And you can't spare a ship. We've already butted our heads against this impasse."

"What if you take a Combine representative aboard and let him monitor the flight? He would have command. *Nominal* command. Just enough authority to sanction the flight as a Combine mission."

"I cannot surrender my command."

"Weren't you the one just urging me to bend the rules? You wouldn't be surrendering your command. It would be like—like—yeah, that's it. It would be like having an admiral on board. You're still in command, but he tells you where to go and what to do."

"A Combine representative?" It would be a complication, but not an insurmountable one. "He would have to be restricted from certain areas."

"Understood. Will that satisfy your honor?" Konoye asked.

"It will satisfy me."

Operation Chameleon could proceed.

The frontier hauler wasn't as sophisticated as the ship that had brought Kurt Ellicot to the rendezvous at Wayfarer Station. For one thing, it didn't have individual public feeds in the cabins. To see their destination approaching, one had to go to the passenger deck's lounge-cum-dining hall, which was exactly where Kurt was, as were nearly half of the project's personnel. To Kurt's relief, only one of the Leaguers seemed curious enough about their next stop to bother attending the informal final-approach-to-destination party, and she had found herself a seat at the far end of the hall, about as far away as possible from Kurt's table.

"Not much compared to Wayfarer, is it?" he commented to his tablemate, Juliana Tindal.

"Why should it be?" she replied. "Chugen is a new system. The only commercial traffic it's seen has been the transports hauling construction crews and materials."

"You're right, of course. Wayfarer was the only Combine station I'd seen before this one. I must have decided subconsciously that it was typical."

"If anything it's atypical. After all, strictly speaking Wayfarer isn't part of the Combine."

He held up a hand to stop her. "It's a political thing, isn't it?"

She nodded. "And off limits. Sorry."

They sat in silence, letting the small breach heal itself. Their truce was built on two ground rules that he had laid down when she had come to apologize for her gaffe at their first meeting. The first was that she was not to involve him in political discussions. The other, articulated through hints and circumlocutions, was that she was not to mention his "problems."

He looked at her from the corner of his eye and wondered why he was allowing her a second chance. He'd seen the pity in her eyes that night, and he usually avoided people with that reaction. Yet here they were, sharing a table as they had each night of the voyage to Chugen. Admittedly, he found her attractive. He knew many men would. She was fit and trim, with long raven hair and lustrous soft brown eyes. Yet he was not a slave to his libido; he never had been, so although he found himself flattered by the attentions of this pretty young woman, there had to be more to it than that.

Recalling their conversation from the night they'd met, he knew that much of the reason was a sense of mutual concerns and kindred interest, the kind of instant camaraderie that comes from an intense shared passion for an esoteric subject. That she thought so highly of his own theories, no doubt, played more than a small part. It had been a long time since anyone had paid him that kind of respect.

Maybe it was just because she seemed not to condemn him for what had happened on Cassuells Home.

She turned and caught him looking at her. She smiled. He smiled back. She'd been very professional since that first night's schoolgirl burbling, but it was no schoolgirl looking out of her eyes; it was a woman, a woman attracted to a man.

Uncomfortable, he pointed at the screen. "We'll start docking soon."

"Not for another hour or so, I'd say. But once we're aboard, things will start getting busy. No more loafing in the lounge."

They talked for some time about the timing for attempting first contact with the Chugen indigenes. She argued against his idea of waiting until the base camp had been established. He knew he didn't have a valid reason for delay—his own timidity about actually contacting aliens again was not valid—so he gave her alternative arguments that held a certain amount of practical wisdom. Eventually she yielded, but he suspected that she acquiesced more because *he* had proposed the plan than because the plan itself was the right one. As the talk shifted to allocation of personnel and resources, she grew increasingly less talkative.

"Is there something wrong?" he asked.

She was silent for a moment, but a determined expression crept onto her face and finally she spoke. "Look, I know that this could very well touch on things I promised not to bring up, but I think that it's something that's important for me to know."

He'd known that working together would eventually result in the ground rules being broken. He hadn't expected the moment to come so soon. "I'll tell you if I think it's inappropriate and that will be the end of it."

"That's fair." She settled herself and asked her question. "Were you serious about not working with the Leaguers?"

"Yes."

"I don't understand. I mean, I understand that you don't like the League's policies, but I thought that the League had made a special request that the Concordat include you in the project."

"Where did you hear that?"

Her teeth showed briefly against her lower lip as a quick frown passed across her face. "I have a good digest agent scanning the media and the nets for me. It, ah, came up when I was researching who I'd be working with."

She wasn't the best of liars. More likely she had been listening to some of the sensationalistic stories in the Concordat press. On the positive side, she hadn't taken them as gospel. Negatively, she had taken them in.

"The League did make the request," he said. "The only influence it had on me was to nearly cause me to refuse to participate."

"It goes back to Cassuells Home, doesn't it?"

"Yes. And that's all I'm interested in saying about it."

"I understand."

Did she really think that she understood? Of course she did. She couldn't, though. No one who hadn't been through what he'd been through—was still going through—could understand. At least the look in her eyes was sympathetic rather than pitying. He liked the change.

They lapsed into an awkward silence, unbroken until "logistics specialist" Dale Lockhart arrived at the table, trailed by Paula Stevenson. He guessed that Lockhart had news that, in Stevenson's professional opinion, might upset Kurt's delicate psychological balance.

"Have you been informed that we will be going insystem aboard the IDLS *Henry Hull*?" Lockhart asked.

"No." So the bastards were interfering again. How many would die this time? Well aware of Stevenson's watchful presence, he asked, as blandly as he could, "Should I have been?"

"I thought you might have heard."

"I hadn't. Is there a problem with this arrangement, Ms. Lockhart?"

She shrugged. "I don't think so. The Combine authorities have elected to take advantage of a passing IDL ship. It's not the sort of decision I would make, but they are well within their rights."

"The IDL forces are just providing transfer service," Stevenson emphasized. "They will not be remaining on planet."

"I'm glad to hear that," he said.

"Well, just wanted to see if you'd heard," said Lockhart. Apparently satisfied, the two women departed.

"It looks like you can't escape them," Tindal said.

It did look that way, didn't it?

When she entered Midway Station's mess hall, Juliana Tindal found her favorite dining partner sitting alone as usual. Ellicot wasn't popular with either the project staff or the station personnel, which demonstrated their foolishness while making it easy for her to have him all to herself. As she approached, he was staring glumly into the distance, seemingly uninterested in his breakfast.

"You seem gloomy this morning, Professor Ellicot." Juliana set her tray down on the table. "Would company cheer you up?"

"I'm willing to give it a try if you're the company, Professor Tindal."

"Careful, Professor. You'll turn my head."

Ellicot gave her a grumpy old professor's harrumph that seemed to cut off a smile. "Sit," he said. "Eat. This territory still belongs to a free nation."

"As if it shouldn't?"

"You never know," he mumbled.

"What brought on this pessimistic mood?"

Ellicot poked at his cultured zelliope egg omelet for a few moments before answering. "I really don't like the idea of going on board that League ship."

"Ah," she said in what she hoped was a knowing and sympathetic way. "Would it help to think about the ship as a glorified bus?"

"If it's a bus, it's an armed bus. The sort of *bus* that killed the Cassuells."

"And you think that they're going to try the same thing here?"

"I don't know." He shook his head. His eyes seemed to be focused on something only he could see. "I hope not, but I'm not a telepath. I don't know what's in their minds."

Juliana's wake-up check-in with her computer had told her something which might give him reason to put away his fears. "Look, I don't think that there's a lot to worry about there. This *Henry Hull* is the only League ship in-system. It's a patroller type. I don't think it carries anywhere near enough armament to affect a species with any significant dispersion on the planet. At least, not without a prolonged campaign, which is very unlikely since there will be some Combine warships here soon. The League won't try anything."

"And how do you know that? About the Combine warships, I mean."

"The usual way. That good digest agent of mine." That had been her story and she'd better stick to it. "Nothing mysterious about my knowing. The Combine doesn't maintain a very large military fleet, so when a ship gets reassigned, it's usually news. The public data net had a note about two of our ships being dispatched to Chugen."

"Are you sure that *you're* not the agent?"

"What do you mean?" She hoped she didn't sound as nervous as she felt. No one was supposed to know that she was acting as Alsion's agent. Had Ellicot figured it out?

"You know what I mean," he said, increasing her wariness. "An agent for your government."

She didn't have to fake her laugh. "The government? No way. I'm an Alsion scholar. We're not supposed to take non-subject-related jobs with any government."

"I'm sorry. I am being overly paranoid this morning."

"Apology accepted, Professor."

He looked as if he still wanted to apologize. "Call me Kurt. I've been thinking that we know each other too well for that fancy professorial etiquette."

Did he really think so? Fine by her. "Then I'm Juliana. Juli to my friends."

"Juli, then. If you think it appropriate."

"Fine by me." *Very* fine.

They spent a genial morning making last-minute preparations for boarding the *Henry Hull*.

## 11

**CHUGEN SYSTEM**

To Kurt's surprise, the crew of the *Henry Hull* received their passengers with the courtesy and efficiency of a commercial liner. Arrayed in their midnight-blue dress uniforms, the men and women of the crew were a stark, well-tailored contrast to the haphazard diversity of the project personnel. They contrasted, too, in their unflagging smiles and calm demeanor through the trials of negotiating the ship's tight corridors with the project team's baggage. With faultless courtesy, they made apologies for the accommodations. League warships, it seemed, were not built to carry passengers, but their guests were getting the best available. Crew members had vacated two bunkroom-style dormitories to accommodate the passengers, stuffing their own gear into the lifeboats for the duration.

By commander's decree, the scientists and their support teams were segregated by sex, though not—except for the League contingent—by national origin. Where the Leaguers were quartered, Kurt didn't know, but he suspected that Rafael Burke was right when he suggested that they probably had somewhat more reasonable sleeping arrangements.

"Officer country, most likely. These Leaguers take care of their own," Burke commented. "And to hell with anyone else."

After the first night several of the Combine men, complaining of the cramped and overcrowded conditions, began to talk about taking their complaints to the commander. They seemed to find it intolerable that the females of the project, who amounted to only a third of the total number, had been allocated equal space with the males. "Mart prudishness," Burke called it.

Kurt didn't see any point in stirring up trouble. Neither did Inigo Jones, who called everyone into the mess hall and gave a speech about toughing it out. Kurt listened, politely, but while the Neu Bremenite might be the titular head of the project, he had a long way to go before he was as inspirational as a real leader.

"It's going to be a long project," Juli commented.

"Base camp will be bigger than this ship," Kurt reminded her.

"More space to get away from, er, things."

"Exactly."

"And once we get *our* work started, there will be less and less need to even be in camp. Thank God he's a biochemist."

Juli was a quick study. They shared a conspiratorial smile.

Except for a minor incident when two Combiners tried to personally and unilaterally rearrange their bunks into the female dormitory, only to be rebuffed by League crewmen, the passage inbound was a quiet time of inventory checks, survival equipment drills, reviews of sampling and recording routines, and survey coordination planning—in short, ordinary and uneventful. Until the third day out, during the dinner hour, when the ship's commander spoke on the ship's intercom.

"This is Commander Ersch. All ship's crew to link in for orders. All passengers, may I have your attention.

"We have just detected a magnetic fluctuation consistent with the formation of a Remor jump point near Midway Station. We have also lost communication with the station. This combination of events leads me to conclude that the enemy has invaded the system with hostile intent."

There was turmoil and worried exclamations at the major's announcement, but he continued speaking in calm, confident, measured tones that demanded attention and offered a strange sort of reassurance.

"Although we are now in a war zone, there is no need for panic. No enemy activity has been observed in the inner system. I expect to be able to deliver you safely to your destination.

"*Henry Hull* is currently making best speed for Chugen IV, where all civilians will be landed. This is likely to attract enemy attention. Therefore, in order to minimize our time in orbit and consequent risk to you, we will be performing a battle-drill launch and atmospheric penetration with the landing shuttles. You will experience a bumpier ride than you are used to, but do not be alarmed. The interface craft will be operating well within their design parameters.

"After debarking all passengers and recovering interface craft, *Henry Hull* will reconnoiter the enemy and engage him if possible. My crew and I would appreciate your cooperation during this crisis. Please follow any orders given to you by ship's personnel and excuse any apparent discourtesy. Such orders will be vital to the safety of everyone on board and the survival of the ship itself. If you have complaints, save them till the crisis has passed.

"Of necessity, your departure schedule has been advanced. You will find shuttle assignments posted to your personal comps. Please complete any remaining preparations as expeditiously as possible and report to your assigned shuttle. Current estimate is forty-seven minutes to shuttle launch.

"Commander Ersch out."

* * *

From the faces of the other Combine folk around the table, Juliana wasn't the only one in shock.

"Oh my god! Is he serious?" she heard herself ask.

"If he's joking, it's in very bad taste," Rafe replied.

Grim-faced, the crew manning the dinner line abandoned their gustatorial posts and headed out of the hall. They didn't look like they were responding to a joke.

Jeremy Chiang, director of the Combine contingent, turned in his seat to watch them leave. When the door had closed, he turned back. "Well, my friends, I guess our morning meeting is rescheduled." The chuckle he probably intended to be amusing came across badly. He tried a more serious tone. "If we're leaving the *Henry Hull* in some forty minutes, we'll be on the surface by morning. Everything will be fine once we're down."

"Jeremy, what's going to happen?" That was Barton Langdorf, the meteorologist. "If the Remor are out there, why can't we just stay on the ship? It's armed and armored. We'll be defenseless on the planet."

"Ersch is going to take this ship into a fight against unknown odds," said Rafe. "It'll be safer to be on-planet than here."

"Rafe is right," agreed Chiang. "Everybody do as the commander says. Get your stuff and board the shuttle. And don't worry. The Leaguers are experts at fighting the Remor. If there's trouble, they'll handle it."

Abandoning their half-eaten dinners, people headed for the dormitory.

"My stuff's already stowed," Rafe claimed, coming up behind Juliana. "Let me give you a hand with yours."

She didn't really need the help, but she said, "Thanks." She was grateful to have his familiar presence at her side when so much else was getting very, very strange.

Thirty minutes later, they were at their assigned shuttle. They were the last to arrive. Though some of the project people were already in their couches, Ellicot among them, most were moving back and forth, squirming past each other in the narrow aisle and trying to get their gear stowed. Rafe was helping her stow her personal bag in one of the gear compartments when the intercom came on. It was Commander Ersch.

"Attention all hands, we have an enemy vessel on intercept vector. Secure for acceleration. Repeat, all hands, secure for acceleration."

Like a lot of the others, Juliana stopped what she was doing and looked around. A few of those seated were buckling their harnesses and locking down their crash frames. One or two of those standing, like Rafe, were frantically stuffing things into stowage. Most people just looked worriedly at each other and babbled confused questions about what was happening. From the front of the passenger compartment Lockhart bellowed out.

"That means us, too, people! In your couches and strap down! Snap to it!"

Could this really be happening? Juliana looked to Rafe.

"In!" he ordered her, shoving her toward the nearest acceleration couch.

"But this isn't my seat," she complained.

"What does it matter? This isn't a formal dinner."

All along the aisle people were scrambling to grab the first available couch and strap in. Juli appeared to be the only one concerned about her assigned position.

Rafe finished dogging down the storage compartment, found her still standing behind him, and gave her another shove, toppling her into the couch. He didn't wait to see her strap in. He went running down the aisle to find a couch for himself.

Juliana set to securing her crash frame. The whispered instructions from the couch's monitoring system made it easy. Only when she finished did she realize there was nothing left to do but be afraid.

Across the aisle from her, Sandra Kohrs, the press representative, sat calmly. Eyes closed, she had one hand tucked into a pocket, searching for something. Kohrs produced a vial, opened it, shook out a pair of pills, and popped them. Opening her eyes, she caught Juliana watching her. Kohrs lifted the unlabeled package. "For motion sickness. Want some?"

Juliana shook her head.

Kohrs shrugged and laid her head back. Her eyes closed again. She didn't even twitch when the ship began to shudder.

Rafe was buckling down when Paston slipped into the couch across the aisle. It wasn't the logistics officer's assigned seat.

"Last one open," Paston told him.

He said something else, but his voice was drowned out by the bleat of a klaxon. Seconds after the warning cut off, the ship shuddered.

"What was that?" someone asked.

"Did we launch?" asked another.

"Not us. Those were missile launches," Paston said. "The ship is firing at something."

Something outside the shuttle boomed and Rafe felt as if the back of his couch had been kicked by something the size of a nokturmbeast. Clanging bangs echoed nosily through the compartment. Two styluses, a pen, three books, and someone's computer lifted to the ceiling, then sped for the rear bulkhead.

"*That* was the launch," Paston said.

Rafe hated not being able to see what was going on. Only the unit commander's couch had a viewscreen, and switching with whoever sat there was out of the question.

"We are clear of the ship," the shuttle pilot reported. "Shuttle one is clear as well. Prepare for acceleration."

A low rumble vibrated through the cabin as the craft's engines fired. Twenty seconds into the burn, something hammered against the shuttle's hull. The debris floating in the compartment went crazy as the ship tumbled. Since Paston seemed to know how to read the battle through the sounds and the shakings, Rafe asked him, "What was that?"

"Shock wave."

"From an explosion?"

Paston nodded grimly. "A big one."

"A near miss? What?"

Rafe's answer came from the command section.

"*Henry Hull* is gone," the pilot reported in a shaky voice. "We're on our own. If you pray, start doing it. I'm going to have to take us down hard."

With acceleration dragging at him, Rafe knew that they were moving, but he had no idea of which direction they were traveling. For all he knew they could be driving straight toward the Remor ship that had destroyed the *Henry Hull*. Why wouldn't anyone let him see anything?

When the shuttle started to buck, he didn't need Paston's "We're hitting the atmosphere," to know. The temperature started rising fast and he began to sweat. With the heat climbing, he wanted to put faith in Commander Ersch's promise that a steep drop into the atmosphere was within the shuttle's design parameters. He never thought that he would actually *want* to believe something that a mart bastard of a Leaguer told him, but he did. He wanted to believe very fervently!

Finally the bucking lessened. He thought the heat was

abating, too. The loose debris in the cabin was just beginning a slow drift downward under the fringe influence of the planet's gravity when something slammed into the shuttle and forced it into a roll. The pilot managed to right the plummeting craft, but the ship shuddered constantly as, nose down, it continued its descent.

Rafe guessed that their planetfall would be a spectacular sight, but it wouldn't be one he could enjoy. Or survive.

# 12

## CHUGEN SYSTEM
## CHUGEN IV

Kurt remembered the smoke. The reek of ozone and fused synthetics was familiar. The scent and feel of blood trickling down his cheek weren't new either. He was well acquainted with the disorientation that fuzzed his mind and the dizziness that pulled the contents of his stomach out in a stinking, liquid mess. The dead, the dying, and the moaning wounded lay all around.

Something had gone wrong. Why had the Cassuells laid the trap that caused the transport to crash?

Weren't the Cassuells all dead?

The sounds and smells—and no doubt the sights, were he brave enough to open his eyes to view them—told him he was on Cassuells Home, lying trapped again, in the wrecked transport. Soon the fire would start. Soon—if he opened his eyes—he could watch the flames creep along over the dead, the dying, and the screaming wounded.

Would anyone rescue him this time?

Pain burned in his left hip, sending spikes of agony shooting down his leg and up into his chest.

That wasn't right! He should be feeling nothing in his trapped legs. He couldn't move them, so he shouldn't be able to feel them. The nerves were supposed to be pinched or in shock or something. His aching hip called him a liar. If he could feel his legs, this couldn't be Cassuells Home.

He remembered now. The Cassuells were all dead.

He wasn't in a wrecked ground transport, but aboard a crashed IDL shuttle. He opened his eyes to confirm his conclusion. It was the IDL shuttle all right, and it was crashed on Chugen IV.

Minister Wyss's agent Shirrel had told him that the Chugen mission was going to be his chance to redeem himself. That chance had been shot out of the sky. But now, here in the wreckage, he was being offered another, different chance at redemption, one that he had no qualms about accepting. On Cassuells Home, he had been helpless. Here, he was not. He would not lie still and watch others die this time!

He punched the emergency release on his crash frame. The button went in and the lock released, but the frame stayed down. He had to shove hard to get it to swing up and away. Unfastening his harness was easy once he got the deflated impact bag clear of the clasp. He dragged himself out of the couch to stand unsteadily in the aisle. The smoke coiling along the ceiling tried to choke him. He had to bend over to breathe anything approaching clean air.

Lockhart was in the seat across the aisle, between him and the gap in the hull. Her impact bag had malfunctioned, and she had taken the landing hard. Groaning, she turned her head toward him. One eye peered from her bloodied face. "Ellicot?"

"Yes."

"I think my legs are broken." The pain on her face suggested that she was right. She was fighting to ignore it. "You okay? Who else made it?"

"You. Me. I don't know who else." He could hear someone screaming and another crying. There were other survivors making noise as they dealt with their restraints. "There are more of us."

"Smoke." She coughed. "Got—Gotta get clear."

Lockhart started to paw at her restraints, but her bloodied hands were ineffectual.

"Stay still for a moment. I'm going to try and get you out through that hole. but I've got to get past you. I think I'll be able to free your restraints more easily from out there."

She nodded and stopped her efforts. Using her warped crash frame for support, he crawled over her couch and through the rent in the hull. Once outside, he got her crash frame retracted and her restraints undone. When he tried to pull her from the couch, she screamed in agony. Afraid of injuring her, he stopped.

"No," she panted. "Don't stop. Get me the hell out."

Steeling himself, he dragged her free. As he struggled to get her through the opening she became a dead weight, passed out. *At least she isn't screaming*, he thought. As he was settling her on a pad of foamy ground vegetation, she came to.

"Shock," she gasped. "Need blanket."

"I don't have a blanket."

"First aid kit." Her words were punctuated by grimaces of pain. "Overhead. Your seat."

That was right, he remembered; he hadn't been able to stow his personal bag because the kit took up too much of the compartment. He crawled back in, wrenched open the hatch, and grabbed the kit. After getting a thermal blanket over Lockhart, he started rummaging through the kit, seeking something to help her. She protested, insisting he go back for the others, but he ignored her. He'd seen her legs and knew that if he didn't deal with her injuries right away, she wouldn't survive. He administered a painkiller and did a very unprofessional job of bandaging her legs and setting them in isosplints, but at least he managed to stop the bleeding. Having done all he could for the moment, he left her in her drug-induced stupor and returned to the craft.

The fumy haze had dissipated some by the time he got inside again, but as the acrid mask of the smoke lessened, the wrecked shuttle was beginning to reek like a charnel house. Kurt forced himself to ignore the stench as he checked the couches, looking for survivors. Many—most—of the impact bags hadn't deployed. Why not? What did it matter? They hadn't, and people had died. The dead were beyond help, but the living weren't. He kept looking.

He found Juliana Tindal crouched in the aisle, holding the limp hand of Sandra Kohrs. She was staring at the battered corpse and whispering, "Ohmigod" over and over.

"Juli?"

She looked at him, eyes bleak.

"That was my seat," she said in a very small voice. Kohrs had been one of those whose impact bag had failed. "*I should have been sitting there.*"

"But you weren't," he told her. "You're alive and you have to come along."

She let him lead her outside. He got her seated and took a second thermal blanket from the first-aid kit and wrapped it around her before starting back in. At the gash, he met Rafael Burke helping Gilian Zandowski. Together the two men got the Coalition biologist through the hole in the shuttle's side and settled next to Juliana.

Without discussion, both men returned to the wreck. Someone in the rear of the compartment was wailing like a lost soul. Kurt turned in that direction, but stopped as Burke put a hand on his arm.

"Paston's the one you hear screaming," said Burke. "He's got a crash frame bar through his belly. He's not going to make it. There's nobody else alive back there. Let's check up front."

Up front they found three more survivors, Jones, Langdorf, and Singh, all seriously wounded. It took a lot of work to get the first free from his crash frame. The second was still conscious and helped Kurt and Burke unstick his crash frame. Langdorf insisted that they get the third survivor out before removing him from the wreck. Some time before they finished, Paston stopped screaming.

"How many others?" Langdorf asked when they returned to carry him out.

"Eight including us," Burke told him.

"That doesn't count the crew," Kurt said.

"Did any of them make it?" Langdorf asked.

"They don't deserve to," Burke commented.

"How can you say that?" Langdorf protested. "They're people, too."

Burke wasn't moved. "You want to know if they're alive? You go looking."

Langdorf was in no shape to do much of anything, but he was right. Kurt said, "I'll go."

The shuttle's spine had broken in the crash, the nose with the crew compartment separating from the rest. The forward section was lying on its side, some fifty meters down the trail it had plowed through the trees. The torn vegetation was littered with shards of shuttle and fragments of its contents.

Now that the first surge of adrenaline had waned, Kurt felt his hip again. Walking sent bolts of pain shooting through his leg, which he tried to ignore as he limped down the path of devastation. The survivors in the crew, if any, were likely to be in worse shape.

More than half of the crew compartment had been sheared away longitudinally, accounting for much of the debris through which he threaded his way. The remaining structure was tilted over on its torn side, shredded spars and components hanging down like high-tech stalactites. A meter and a half of space lay between the furrowed forest floor and the struts of the ravaged crew compartment, making a shadowed cavern into which Kurt crawled. Pale light flickered within as the ship's emergency batteries fed the last of their power to the lights and consoles. Twisting his way to what was left of the flight deck, Kurt found the pilot and one other crewman still breathing. Both were wounded: the crewman only slightly, but the pilot had lost a hand, which his suit had handled by automatic vacuum sealing. Unfortunately the suit hadn't been designed to handle the shredding that it had taken across his lower torso. The man had lost a lot of blood. The crewman needed Kurt's help to get out of his warped crash frame, and together they got the pilot out of the ruined couch, out of the command section, and onto the ground outside.

The pilot was pale, well into shock, but through pain-wracked eyes, the man recognized him. "Ellicot? You okay?"

"I survived, Commander."

"Don't think I will."

"Nonsense. You'll be fine," Kurt lied.

"You're a bad liar. It's okay. It's okay. The risks are part of the job." He raised an arm, apparently in an effort to draw Kurt closer. Then he noticed he had no hand on that arm. The arm dropped. The pilot laid his head back. "Tell the major I got you down safe."

Kurt didn't see any point in reminding the man that Major Ersch was dead, killed along with everyone else on board when the *Henry Hull* was destroyed. "I'll tell him next time I see him."

The pilot's eyes rolled up into his head and he was gone.

From the trees all around, Juliana could tell that the shuttle had come down in one of Chugen's continent-covering forests. The ocher and russet vegetation was unlike any she'd seen before, but the overall structure of the plant community strongly suggested a tropical or subtropical rain forest, as did the day's heat, humidity, and midday thunder shower, which might put them near a native settlement. Or it might not; orbital evaluation indicated that the native villages were widely dispersed. The only visitors they had were insects whose annoyance went away once Rafe set up the anti-animal sonic generator that he called a bug screen.

They needed a screen against the sun blazing down through the gash ripped in the canopy by the shuttle's brutal descent, since no one seemed ready to trust the shelter of the ruddy, alien trees. Rafe and the League crewman rigged a tarpaulin in the center of the path plowed clear by the crashing shuttle. Beneath it Juliana tried to tend the injured as best she could, and the others came there during their infrequent breaks from salvaging the wreck.

As the sky grew dark, the exhausted survivors gathered around the smoldering fire. With the heat of the day barely subsiding, the fire wasn't necessary for warmth. Neither did they need it for cooking food, as the ration packs had their own heating elements. But against the gathering darkness and the strangeness of the surrounding forest, Juliana found the fire a necessary source of comfort, more reassuring emotionally than the invisible fence of the bug screen. Occasionally something unseen tested the screen's boundaries and expressed its displeasure with a hiss or buzz or yipping squeak, but so far nothing had crossed the barrier to bother the stranded humans.

"Fifteen dead," Zandowski said solemnly, speaking the first words since they had begun to gather around the fire.

"You're looking at it the wrong way," Kurt told her. "There are nine of us alive."

"Eight soon," Burke remarked. "Jones will be gone by morning without medical care."

"Shush! He'll hear you," Juliana warned. Rafe could be so insensitive! He'd gotten Zandowski crying again; the young biologist wasn't taking her mentor's condition well at all.

"Like he doesn't already know," Rafe snapped back at Juliana defensively.

"She's right, though," Kurt said. "Some things don't need to be said."

"Who asked you, Mr. White Knight?" Rafe was getting angry. "I don't recall anyone putting you in charge of what can and can't be said."

"It's a simple matter of good judgment," Kurt responded.

Rafe gave a mocking, false laugh. "Good judgment! Coming from you, that's a laugh! I suppose you used nothing but good judgment on Cassuells Home!"

"That's all past." Kurt eyes narrowed to slits of fire. "This isn't Cassuells Home!"

"Damn right, it's not! I won't let you won't get away with what you pulled there!" Rafe wrenched himself to his feet and started around the fire. "It won't happen this time. I'll show you! I ought to—"

Crewman Shanholz shot up and cut Rafe off both physically and verbally. "What you ought to do, sir, is sit back down."

Rafe was taller than the Leaguer, but Shanholz was more heavily built. Doubtless he had been trained in some very effective hand-to-hand combat techniques. Rafe glared down into the resolute Leaguer's face. "Yessir, Mr. Mart. Whatever you say, Mr. Mart. I wouldn't dream of harming your little pet."

Getting up slowly, Kurt started his own march. As he stalked toward Rafe, Kurt muttered, "You insufferable little—"

Juliana could see no good coming from such a confrontation. She sprang up, moving to block Kurt as Shanholz had blocked Rafe. "Kurt, no!"

"Shut up, the lot of you!" Lockhart's voice burned with authority despite its quaver. Her words were blurred a little by painkillers, but they held no less power for that. Everyone stopped, turned where necessary, and looked at her. "I want everyone to shut up and sit back down. Now!"

Juliana and Kurt did as she asked without a word. After shooting a vicious glare at Kurt, Rafe did so as well. Only when Rafe had reseated himself did Shanholz sit down, reset his work light, and go back to fiddling with the black box, which he had recovered from the shuttle, as if nothing had happened. Once everyone had settled themselves, Lockhart spoke again.

"The last thing we need is dissension. We're all in a tough position here. *All* of us. We'll all have to work together if we're going to get through it."

"You make it sound like we're on our own," Juliana said. "Help will be coming soon from the gateway station."

"No, it won't," Shanholz said.

"The Remor?" Langdorf asked fearfully. "We're isolated here, aren't we?"

Shanholz nodded.

A brooding silence descended as everyone considered the implications of being cut off from galactic civilization. Even had the crash been a simple accident, they were in a frontier system. There were no regular shipping routes here, no mail runs, no regular contact. As best Juliana could recall, Midway Station hadn't even had a courier boat berthed at it, so it was unlikely that any message could have gotten out. It would be weeks before anyone outside the Chugen System became worried about not hearing from them and consider investigating. Who would know they needed a rescue ship?

Ambrose Alsion might guess sooner than most. Conceivably his alinear sociodynamic equations could predict that they had run into trouble. In fact, she realized, those equations might *already* have predicted trouble. This disaster could well be the circumstance for which he had given her the analog, which she had been relieved to locate among the computers salvaged from the wreck. But would Alsion act? Almost certainly he could organize a rescue mission, but *would* he? The analog might know. *But how,* she wondered, *can I consult it without the others learning of its existence? Maybe after they've all gone to sleep . . .*

"Look," Kurt said. "Maybe help will come and maybe it won't. In the meantime, Lockhart's right. If we've been cut off, we've got to help ourselves. We've got to make the best of it."

"Maybe we should just all go native," Rafe sniped.

Juliana was relieved to see Kurt let the reference pass. She said what he could have said. "The natives know how to survive here. We don't. We would be stupid not to learn from them, assuming that we get the chance."

Her comment started a debate on how to go about contacting the natives. A few seemed inclined to hold to the original plan of several weeks of observation before contact, but most favored a more immediate contact, while Rafe argued for avoiding them all together. Despite his objections, the basic decision to make contact was made, and the argument about when and how to go about it grew heated.

Lockhart ended the fruitless discussion. "Since we haven't met any natives yet, we can't know whether or not they'll help us out. If we encounter them, we'll deal with them, but we won't waste our effort seeking them out. Since there might not be any of them within a hundred kilometers of us, we'd best not count on them. People have managed on less hospitable planets than this before now; we'll manage here. First thing is to take stock of what resources we do have. Professor Ellicot, what was salvaged?"

"I can really only speak for what we got out of the passenger cabin, and I'm afraid that we didn't get a lot that was useful, but then there wasn't a lot to be expected. We've got clothes, a few personal computers, and some instruments. Believe it or not, we're actually equipped to do some of the science we came here to do. Unfortunately, besides the shuttle's first-aid kits, there's not a lot of survival gear. I did find something odd, though." Poking a meter-long cylinder painted in green and white stripes lying at his feet, Kurt asked, "Anyone know what this is? Shanholz?"

The Leaguer looked up from his puttering. "It looks like a canister of morphanox, sir."

"Morphanox?" Lockhart sounded puzzled. "Isn't that riot control, rather than combat supplies?"

When Shanholz confirmed it, Rafe drawled, "So, Shanholz, you and your cronies been suppressing the masses again?"

"I don't know anything about suppressing any masses, sir," Shanholz said, refusing to rise to the bait. "I'm a flight engineer, and I was only just assigned to six-one-five. I wasn't on her last mission, and I don't know what it was. I suppose the can could be left from that, sir."

"Doesn't really matter, does it?" Lockhart asked. "We can't eat it, and without a delivery mechanism it won't work as a weapon. Burke, you spent a lot of time in stowage. How did the cargo fare? Food especially."

Rafe answered sullenly. "Cargo's not good. A lot of the hold-downs failed, and most of the equipment is trashed. Given time and luck we might be able to patch quite a bit of it back together, but we'll be roughing it for awhile. The rations palette is one of the deaders. There's quite a stew going bad all over the floor of the compartment. The local wildlife was already starting to investigate it before we got the bug screen up. I don't think we can salvage more than ten or twelve person-weeks worth."

"Less than two weeks rations for us," Lockhart concluded.

"About right," Rafe agreed.

"Professor Burke, did you see any of the local wildlife eat any of the spilled rations?" asked Zandowski.

Langdorf looked askance at her. "Gilian, this is no time to be worrying about—"

"I beg to differ, Professor. It's very much the time. If the local animals can eat our food, it's possible that we can subsist on local fauna and flora."

"The only fauna I've seen is bugs," Langdorf said. "I don't eat bugs."

"You'll eat what keeps you alive," Lockhart told him. "If you're lucky, we'll find something more appetizing once we get moving."

"Get moving?" Langdorf asked.

"Got some bad news for you, Ms. Lockhart," Rafe said. "Several crates went right through the cruzabouts. We're going to be walking wherever we go."

"Why should we go anywhere?" Langdorf asked. "We'll be easier to find if we stay by the crash site."

"Exactly the problem," Lockhart said. "The first ones to come looking for us may not be Human."

Langdorf gulped. "You think the Remor might come after us?"

"It's a possibility."

Lockhart sounded grimly sure. The idea made Juliana shiver. They were defenseless. Clearly the same thought had occurred to Lockhart, who turned to the Leaguer and asked, "Shanholz, was the crew carrying any weapons?"

"Of course they were. They're marts," Rafe interjected.

Shanholz ignored Rafe and addressed Lockhart, patting his holster. "We all had personal sidearms. There would also be three Mark 22 pulse rifles in the survival canister in the cargo hold."

"Yeah, I found them," Rafe admitted. "But they're useless. Their power cells, all the heavy-duty cells for that matter, were discharged."

There were general expressions of dismay. Kurt asked, "How could all the power cells be discharged?"

"We were on emergency power before we hit," Shanholz said. "If the charger in the supply pod was on, we could have drained them dry. We were pulling juice from wherever we could near the end."

"Not a very good design," Rafe opined.

"So you say, sir. Generally we find it's better to do what we can to stay in the air. The lieutenant did what he could to keep us there. Without that power, we might have come straight in and splashed all over the countryside."

"We've only got your word for that."

"No, sir, you don't." Shanholz held up the black box he'd been working on. "This is the shuttle's flight recorder. It got banged up pretty badly, but I think I've got it patched up enough for a limited playback through a perscomp display."

"Let's try it and see," Lockhart said.

The record was a patchwork of raw sensor data, voice recordings, snapshots of monitor display, systems assessment reports, computer inquiries in binary as well as normal language, and operational verifications—in short, a confusing mishmash that required Shanholz to interpret. "This," he began, "is the magnetic anomaly that signaled the appearance of the enemy force."

The flight recorder showed Remor ships moving toward Midway Station as *Henry Hull* drove insystem. They couldn't tell if the Remor reached the station because the long-range scan records were replaced by shorter range scans. Shanholz said the switch came about because the *Henry Hull* changed its sensor focus at the sudden appearance of a Remor ship from behind Chugen IV's moon. Still, there was an ominous loss of signal from the station just before the launch of the shuttles. Commander Ersch's warning was recorded in full. Once the shuttles launched, the quality and nature of the recording changed, as the recorder was forced to rely on the shuttle's onboard systems. The data showed that both shuttles launched successfully before the *Henry Hull* turned to do battle with the enemy ship, a gallant but doomed gesture. Spikes in the radiation monitor marked the destruction of *Henry Hull*. Similar spikes recorded the subsequent Remor attack on the shuttle. Extensive system failures were reported. More were recorded as the pilot fought to control the craft's atmospheric entry.

"I make recorder failure to have occurred at thirty-three to thirty-five seconds before the crash," Shanholz concluded. "We lost ground radar just after that. Commander Mostel couldn't find a clear spot to set down. He did the best he could. He was a good pilot. The landing could have been a lot worse. We could have all died in the crack-up."

"What about the other shuttle?" Rafe asked.

Shanholz shook his head. "I don't know. We lost its blip after we hit atmosphere."

Like the rest, Juliana sat in stunned silence and contemplated what the flight recorder showed them. Could the end of transmissions from the station really mean that it had been destroyed? It seemed the only logical conclusion. Quite likely they were the only living Humans left in the system.

"The good news is the enemy didn't follow us down," Shanholz said. "Whatever their plans for this system, for the moment they don't seem to include this planet."

"Obviously," Rafe remarked. "We're still alive."

"Why didn't they follow us?" Juliana wanted to know.

Shanholz shrugged. "Well, ma'am, we were emitting a lot of heat on reentry. They must have figured we were burning up."

The Remor were supposed to be implacable. "Why didn't they make sure they'd killed us?"

Again Shanholz shrugged. "Who knows? Sometimes them xenos don't make any sense. I don't know about you, but me, I'm glad they *didn't* check for the kill. We wouldn't be having this conversation if they had."

"So we're stuck here," Rafe said.

"Until someone comes for us," Kurt said.

"Oh God, let it be Humans and not the Remor."

Juliana agreed with Langdorf's prayer. "If it's Humans, they won't be coming from the station."

"At least not anytime soon." Kurt looked around at them. Juliana knew that hers was just one of the anxious faces he was seeing. "We have to face it, ladies and gentlemen. For the foreseeable future, Chugen IV is our home."

# 13

## CHUGEN SYSTEM
## CHUGEN IV

Kurt tossed in his sleep, haunted by recurring dreams wherein he lived and slept and ate and worked at the bottom of a terrarium watched constantly by an unseen alien presence that, although possessed of godlike powers, was distinctly ungodly. Somehow he knew that his dream-self existed only at the sufferance of that presence. There were others living in the terrarium with him—sometimes Humans, sometimes aliens, sometimes both—but they were not of interest to the monitors. Only he was. Everything that he did was watched, weighed, and judged. When he was found wanting, as he always was, everything around him—Human, alien, and world alike—dissolved under a rain of fire, leaving him miraculously untouched save for the scars which his own acid tears carved in his cheeks.

He awoke to an unfamiliar landscape of towering trees, whose leafy boughs were visible as black shapes against the scattered patches of graying sky. A strange song of musical trills and buzzing chitters rose from unseen sources to greet the coming dawn. Some of the scents were familiar—wood smoke, leaf mold, and moist, rich earth—while others, both pleasant and foul, were nothing that he could identify. As his senses sorted the real from lingering dreams, he remembered where he was: shipwrecked on an alien, probably hostile world.

Some chance of redemption!

Tossing aside his tangled blanket, he sat up. He was the only one awake. Zandowski, who was supposed to keep the dawn watch, had nodded off to sleep where she sat by the smoldering remains of the fire. A quiet hum told him that Burke's bug screen still protected them, the machine staying vigilant while the person had not. How long before lack of power robbed them of their staunch mechanical guardian and left them to their own resources? And when that happened, how well would they handle it?

During last night's discussions, Burke had implied that Kurt was advocating going native. If he only knew how much that idea scared Kurt. The Combine's cursory surveys from orbit were totally inadequate when it came to determining how to survive on Chugen IV's surface, so contact with the indigenes could only benefit the castaways.

Looking over to where the Combine ecologist still lay asleep, Kurt saw that Burke had come out ahead on another front as well. His arm was wrapped protectively around Juliana Tindal. It could have been just the instinctive gesture of a man protecting a woman from the threat of the wild, but Kurt suspected otherwise. He'd seen the way Burke looked at Juli, and he'd recognized the lust in the man's eyes. Juli was a good-looking, well-built woman, and intelligent. A potent combination. Juli had told him that she and Burke had once been "a feature," which was her Combiner way of saying "romantically involved." It looked as though the past was once more showing its penchant for repeating itself.

Why Burke? And why now? Kurt had begun to think that she was hinting at an interest in him, but it seemed that his perceptions were flawed. Not uncommon in his dealings with women. Clarise, for example: he certainly had been wrong about her.

But such thoughts were a clear invitation to an unwanted depressive episode. With no one stirring and no inclination to wake anyone, Kurt looked about for some other way to distract himself. He found it at the edge of the bug screen's safety zone.

One of Chugen's eight-legged insects, small by the standards of some they'd seen in the jungle but as large as one of Old Earth's bigger beetles, was marching stolidly into the teeth of the bug screen. But only for a short distance. Its march faltered as it came under the screen's power, until it stopped for a second before scurrying away to the more comfortable region beyond the screen's influence. It remained there for only a moment, though, before marching forward again. Stymied again, it fled, recovered, and tried again. And failed again. Another insect arrived. Like its fellow, it too was repulsed by the bug screen, frantically hurrying away once it succumbed to the screen's sonic torture. Both creatures milled uncertainly for a moment, antennae and forelimbs waving, before again trying to breach the barrier. Again they pressed against the sonic wall, and again they failed and retreated. More of the insects arrived. Like their advance scouts, they hadn't the stamina to brave the screen's power for long. Small groups made the march now, with no better results. More of the critters arrived and joined the futile assault. As their numbers increased, the turnaround point took on the aspect of a rallying point, as the insects gathered, advanced en masse, retreated, and regrouped for another go. Still more insects emerged from the trees, and the tangle of insects at the rallying point grew to a writhing mass.

Kurt stuck his hand past the insects' high-water mark, laying a finger on the ground in front of one of the advancing army. The insect ran up onto his finger as if it were no more than another dead twig littering the forest floor.

Withdrawing his hand, he carried his hitchhiker past its retreating fellows and into the protected zone. The insect reacted to his generosity by reversing its course and scrambling frantically back to the tip of his finger and beyond. Legs pumping uselessly, it fell to the ground, landing on its back. However, once it had righted itself, it did not head instantly for the rally point. Instead it wobbled along unsteadily, a few steps in one direction, a few in another, never heading in the right direction to rejoin its fellows. Clearly its sense of direction was being impeded by the bug screen's field. Kurt tried to pick it up again to return it beyond the screen, but it refused—or was unable—to climb aboard his finger. He watched the insect collapse, quivering. In a few moments it stopped moving altogether.

So much for enlightened intervention.

"That's a lot of bugs." Juliana had come up behind unheard. "What's going on?"

Without looking at her, he replied, "A study in futility."

"I worry about you sometimes." She laid a gentle hand on his shoulder. "Come on. Lockhart wants us to get moving."

"Good idea," he said, rising and following her.

The morning's departure from the crash site was delayed by the argument over the fate of Inigo Jones. The leader of the ill-fated Chugen Contact Mission had died of his injuries, and his protégé Zandowski demanded that he receive a proper burial, unswayed by arguments that graves would provide unequivocal evidence of survivors for the Remor should they come looking. Last night, she had agreed that the dead should be left to lie in the shuttle's wreck where the jungle would see to their burial, but it seemed that while she found that fate acceptable for the other crash victims, it was not suitable for Professor Jones. Lockhart, Shanholz, and the others tried to sway her, but were no more able to make headway than the persistent insects were able to cross the screen's barrier. In the end, a shallow grave was dug in the soft loam, but Zandowski didn't get her way entirely, for no marker was placed and Shanholz did what he could to disguise the location of the eminent professor's resting place.

"Buried or not," Burke commented, "the bugs will be feasting on Jones before the sun's high. Dead meat, however previously eminent, is just a resource in this ecosystem."

At least today he was showing enough compassion to not make his remark where Zandowski could hear him.

Deciding it was better to concentrate on what needed to be done instead of fretting about Burke's state of mind, Kurt set his mind to accomplishing the tasks Lockhart set for him. Cassuells Home had been an arid world, rather like the high desert of Serenten's North Andalusia where he had grown up; this verdant jungle was anything but. He had no problem acquiring enough springy saplings, vines, and brush. With his gleanings, they constructed sledges for Lockhart, whose legs were useless, and for the still unconscious Singh. They fashioned three other sledges to take the bulk of their salvaged goods, with the remainder packed around the two invalids.

Preparations complete, they left the crash site. Burke and Shanholz each pulled an ambulance sledge. Lockhart assigned the still-weeping Zandowski to the lightest equipment load and Juliana to the heaviest. Kurt and Langdorf, both walking wounded, got the last, taking turns at hauling. At Lockhart's direction, Shanholz had rigged all the sledges with trailing fronds to stir and obliterate the marks left by their passage. They left a trail, but no footprints; and behind them, no longer constrained by the bug screen's barrier, the insects swarmed over their campsite.

At first Kurt thought the sensation of being watched was born from a lingering disturbance left by the dreams he'd experienced during the night. But as the morning wore on, he became convinced that there really was a watcher. Often he turned around or tried to look about from the corners of his eyes, but he never spotted anything to account for the sensation. By afternoon, he had convinced himself that if there had been a real watcher, he would have seen some sign. Most likely his suspicions grew from the strangeness of the closely gathered trees and were spurred on by the life all around them.

Constant motion seemed to surround them as they trekked. The jungle thronged with bugs. Singletons, groups, dozens, hundreds, myriads, lots of bugs. All shapes and sizes. Crawling bugs, flying bugs, climbing bugs, and hanging bugs. Lean, rickety sticks of bugs and squat, rounded humps of bugs. Bugs so tiny that they were only noted as motion when they flew in massed swarms, and bugs so enormous that they mowed down brush in meter-wide swaths as they crashed through the understory growth. Armored bugs and gossamer bugs. Bugs that waddled, skittered, or swooped alone, and bugs that marched, wobbled, or darted in packs, columns, and hordes.

They weren't true insects, of course—with eight limbs, they couldn't be; but their general character was insectoid. There were other creatures too, mostly things much like terrestrial arthropods, in almost as great a variety as the eight-leggers. Some looked remarkably like terrestrial scorpions, crabs, shrimp, and centipedes, despite coming in sizes that man had never seen on Old Earth. One pseudo-millipede that held them up while it perambulated across the trail nearly came up to Juliana's shoulder. Just as the smaller bugs weren't true insects, neither were these critters true arthropods. What they were, Kurt didn't know, or care. He'd leave the classification to Zandowski. To him, they were all bugs.

Once, and only once, did he spot something that wasn't covered in the local equivalent of chitin. For fleeting seconds he stared in wonder at the garishly colored body that flashed along the trail beside him. He had the impression of more pumping limbs than there should have been, propelling that sinuous, slime-shiny body through the tangle of brush alongside the trail, but he got no count. Neither did he get a real sense of what sort of animal it was, other than that it was long and low and tailed.

Evening came on. It was well after the time that he would have called a halt to the trek, but still Lockhart pushed them to move. Kurt, tired as he was, couldn't go any further without a rest. He trailed behind the group and flopped on a fallen tree to catch his breath for a while. *Let the others press on*, he thought, *I'll catch up to them in a moment or two.*

He had closed his eyes, drifting near to sleep when his paranoid apprehension of being watched came back with full force. His eyes snapped open. Looking back the way they had come, he noticed that something had changed since he closed his eyes. The bright flowering bush with the draping fronds looked denser now. Darkness that was not the coming night had crept into its shelter, and from that shadow a pair of dark, glittering eyes stared at him.

Kurt sat stock still, hardly daring to breathe. Could it be? The fronds shivered as the eyes' owner brushed past them and stepped onto the trail. He might have emerged from Kurt's memory instead of from the jungle. Kurt blinked. This was no hallucination! This being could only be one of the indigenous sentients, making this the historic moment that Ethan Shirrel had hinted might come Kurt's way. But history wasn't foremost in Kurt's mind as he sat, dumbfounded, and stared at the Chugeni.

Kurt had been told that the natives were very similar to the Cassuells, but he had not been prepared for such an uncanny resemblance. This being's sparkling eyes with their dark fur surround, the narrow snout tipped with a wriggling black nose, and the forward-jutting chin made Kurt think unwilling of Shessone the Bright-Eyed as he must have looked in his youth. But this was no Cassuell, he reminded himself. This was a native of Chugen IV!

If erect, the Chugeni—a male if the parallel to the Cassuells held—would stand no taller than Juliana. He was as similar to a Cassuell in build as in height, with the same lean, lithe body form. Bipedal and bimanous as advertised, the Chugeni stood on his toes, the central two flexed in tension so that the flanking two barely brushed the forest litter. He was ready to move. He held a stone-tipped spear in his four-fingered hands, ready but not threatening.

Once past the initial shock, Kurt could see that there were differences, the most obvious being that this Chugeni wore a harness of straps unlike any he had ever seen among the Cassuells. That could be just cultural, of course, but there were physical differences as well. The native's fur was shorter and sparser and, except for his head, a ruff, and a dark ridge of hair that extended to his stumpy tail, no more dense than that of a hairy specimen of *Homo sapiens sapiens*.

But so similar to a Cassuell! How could two species separated by hundreds of light-years evolve to such strikingly similar forms? The League would have everyone believe that was impossible—that these natives and the Cassuells were part of the same species, a species that had terrorized mankind for over a decade. Kurt did not believe that they were the Human-destroying enemy. He'd known the Cassuells—he *couldn't* believe that!

Lockhart and the others had wanted to avoid contact

with the indigenes as long as possible. Well, that was no longer possible. The Chugeni had come to them.

The Chugeni chittered at him, a sound that clearly carried meaning, but one that he could not define despite its tantalizing familiarity.

Kurt pointed to himself, saying "Kurt Ellicot," then pointed at the indigene and gestured with widespread hands and raised eyebrows. He got no response for the first four tries. Then the native's eyes opened wide and nose twitched. His mouth opened slightly, revealing his sharp teeth, and he pointed to himself and said, *"Ah'zzt."*

The open-eye, nose-twitching expression had been almost identical to a Cassuell expression indicating discovery or understanding. Kurt could only conclude that Ah'zzt had grasped Kurt's gesture of naming for what it was, and having done so, supplied his own name. To test his conclusion, Kurt pointed to the indigene, said "Ah'zzt," and pointed to himself while repeating his own name.

The native responded by cocking his head back slightly several times in quick succession. That gesture had been a Cassuell "yes."

*"Ula Ah'zzt,"* the native said, pointing to himself. A clawed finger extended toward Kurt. *"Ola Kurtellicot."*

"I am Kurt Ellicot," Kurt confirmed. "I am a Human." He waved his hand at the path down which his companions had gone. "We are Humans. You are Ah'zzt. Ah'zzt is . . . what?"

*"Ah'zzt la H'kimm."*

Communication had begun.

"I believe his name is Ah'zzt and that he is a H'kimm, which I take to be his tribe, although it might be his species if he is aware of such a distinction," Ellicot said when he rejoined them. Behind him at the edge of the clearing, too shy to enter it, stood the Chugeni. The native resisted Ellicot's nonverbal invitation to join them. Ellicot gave up and faced Rafe and the others. "I think he wants to take us home with him. We should go with him."

What audacity! Rafe should have expected it, though. He'd seen the way Ellicot had frosted the League marts back on Wayfarer. No doubt of it, the man was bold and stubborn and sly enough to implement his own plans in preference to anyone else's and regardless of any agreed upon plan. What did Ellicot care that the survivors had agreed to avoid contact with the locals? *He* wanted to deal with the natives, and deal with the natives he had. Now he wanted to compound his offense by dragging them all along behind him. Pure brass balls!

Now Ellicot was getting the others to listen to his crap about chance meetings and the deed being done. Like he'd had no part in it!

It was probably just as well that the sight of the hairy native had caught Rafe out speechless. Rafe was the sort of guy who prided himself on being able to tell which way the wind was blowing. All he had to do was look at the rapt faces around him and see that no amount of rational argument was going to counter Ellicot's fait accompli.

It was unlikely that the Leaguers were right about the natives being Remor. To judge from the specimen before them, these hairy bipedal weasels didn't even have access to metal, let alone advanced technology. Still, the indigs could cause the castaways more than enough trouble. Rafe held his peace while the others fell in line with Ellicot's plan to follow the weasel home.

Ah'zzt led the castaways back to his forsaken village, a pitiful collection of ramshackle huts that was a sad excuse for settlement. The structures had a rundown look; indeed repair work on one was interrupted when the castaways marched into the central area. Everywhere Rafe looked, the jungle was encroaching on the meager cleared space. The indigs were barely managing to keep their clearing cleared. The place stank! And not just figuratively. The air all around the pathetic huts was permeated with the odor of damp, decaying vegetation and beneath that lay a rank, musty, wet-animal smell. A stench, Rafe realized, that came from the Chugeni who had gathered around them.

Disgusted, Rafe watched as Ah'zzt danced and cavorted a greeting to his tribe. Ah'zzt spent a lot of time pointing at the sky. His listeners spent a lot of time with their beady little eyes turned on the Humans. Then suddenly Ah'zzt's performance was over, and the Chugeni crowded around him, butting their snouts against him, rubbing hands and heads against him, and sniffing at his neck. They were acting so much like a pack of dogs that he half expected them to starting sniffing each other's butts. When they didn't, Rafe wondered if that was only because they were using their best manners in front of company. Through the whole thing, the Chugeni squeaked and growled and coughed at each other. Talking, Rafe supposed. There was a lot more pointing at the sky. When the excitement died down a little, a gray-furred, pot-bellied Chugeni waddled away from the group, entered the biggest of the huts, and emerged a few minutes later bearing a knife that gleamed like metal, which—if it was metal—was the first Rafe had seen. *Old Ah'zzt is going to get it now,* he thought, but the gray weasel only made a big show of giving Ah'zzt the knife. The dancing and cavorting started up again.

"He seems to have done a good thing by bringing us here," Juli commented.

"Yeah? How do you know that they're not just paying our buddy Ah'zzt for bringing home dinner?"

"Rafe, really. Sometimes you can be so misanthropic."

He had to admit that there *were* a lot of people he distrusted, but he didn't see how the attitude applied to something so obviously non-Human as these overgrown weasels. She never had understood his perfectly normal aversion to non-Human species, so he knew better than to express his true attitude. He said, "Have they shown any signs of deserving trust?"

"Of course they have. They don't know who we are or where we've come from or why we're here, and I'm sure that we must look as strange to them as they do to us, yet they have brought us to their home. That's trust."

Stupidity, more like. Naiveté, at the least.

"Don't you see it?" she asked.

"I know *you* see it, Juli."

Hand on his arm, she stared up into his eyes. "Then believe that we have been welcomed here."

The weasel people started to bounce in time to a hollow tocking sound made by a drum that the Chugeni had fashioned from the chitinous shell of some monstrous insect. A dance, Rafe supposed, but it looked rather ridiculous. More musical instruments came out: rattles that had once been insects, stick-mounted gourds that made a sound something like Old Earth maracas, and an assortment of other clacking, slithering noisemakers. As more and more Chugeni joined in, the group dance turned into a village-wide party. Even the young Chugeni abandoned their ogling of the strangers and started to bounce in imitation of their elders. The music rattled and clanked louder. It wasn't the sort of party music Rafe liked, but he had to admit that it had a danceable rhythm; certainly the Chugeni seemed swept up in it.

With the castaways being ignored by their hosts for the moment, Ellicot started expounding a theory about their welcome. "A lot of primitive tribes on Old Earth had legends about sky people. It is not surprising to find that these H'kimm have some kind of parallel belief structure. From what Ah'zzt seemed to be telling the others, I think he may have seen the shuttle crash. I'm fairly certain that he found the site and followed our trail. It would be only natural for them to conclude that we fell from the sky."

"Maybe they think we're gods," Lockhart suggested.

"They might," Juli said.

"As far as they're concerned we might as well be," Rafe said. "Did you see the fuss they made over one rusty metal knife? We've got tools that they haven't even dreamed about."

His companions launched into a whispered debate of the advantages and disadvantages of letting the natives believe in the humans' "divinity." Ellicot was against the idea, and Juli seconded him; but Lockhart was adamant in looking for an advantage, and Langdorf took her side. Rafe let them wrangle. He couldn't express his preference for duping the weasels; he had no interest in having Juli mad at him.

Since he wasn't paying attention to the argument, he was the first to notice a procession of Chugeni females winding its way back and forth across the village, coming closer to the clustered Humans with each pass. The leading females carried earthenware crocks in which some liquid sloshed. The others had armloads of fuzzy, almost spherical objects about the size of a woman's fist. Rafe had seen similar objects hanging from some of the local trees; they appeared to be some kind of nut. These had been hollowed out, and their purpose was demonstrated when an older female used one to serve some of the dark liquid from a crock. She offered the cup to Ellicot.

He accepted the offering and, while seeming to address the natives, asked Zandowski to do a chemical analysis on the stuff in the cup. While she readied her sampler, Ellicot continued his "speech," telling everyone that he was going to stall the natives with a song-and-dance about purification rituals. He handed the cup off to Zandowski and started a halting attempt to talk to the Chugeni. The bastardized combination of Anglic and yips, barks, grunts, and whines made no sense to Rafe. It probably made no sense to the natives either, but at least they listened, and didn't start a ruckus as Zandowski dumped a sample of the stuff into an analyzer.

Ellicot had said enough that even Rafe was realizing that he was doing a lot of repeating by the time Zandowski announced, "Well, there's a lot of compounds that should be inert, and something that looks like a potable alcohol. Several carbohydrates. A lot of trace substances. I don't know. I'd like to do some work on it."

"If we don't drink with them, they will be offended," Ellicot told Zandowski over his shoulder.

"I don't know if it's safe," she complained.

"Is it obviously dangerous?" Ellicot asked.

"I—I don't think so."

He took the cup back and raised it in salute. "Here's to you, Professor Zandowski. I hope you're right."

Ellicot sipped the beverage. He seemed to savor it for a moment then took a deeper draught. Swallowing, he nearly spewed back what he had drunk, but managed to choke back his cough reflex. "Had worse," he said. He forced a smile for the Chugeni as he held the cup out for more.

The natives cheered as Ellicot got his refill. Females brought cups to all of the humans. Rafe took his with the obligatory smile. Juli looked at hers dubiously. Well, if Ellicot could stomach the stuff, so could Rafe. He wasn't about to lose face with Juli. Raising the cup he breathed in the smell: smoky and fruity the same time. At least it smelled better than the natives. Tasting it, he realized that the brew wasn't so bad. In fact, it reminded him of a local winter stout he'd had on Lonesome. Egged on by a sudden thirst, he drained his cup and held it out for more. No, not bad at all.

After the second round, he began to think that maybe the locals weren't so bad either, discounting their stink, of course. He started to enjoy watching their antics. Juli had found herself a place with a good view of the party and he joined her.

Surprisingly, he was feeling mellow. It was the liquor, he realized. Something in the Chugeni brew matched well enough to Human biology to act on him like high-proof booze, and like any good booze, it was loosening him up.

Juli sitting beside him in the firelight reminded him of the old days, back at Verpoorte University. His mind roamed back to that long summer of field work during which they had made love for the first time. Those had been good days. They had shared each other's world then, shared a bed, shared troubles and confidences. It had been a long time since he'd had someone to trust, with whom he could just be himself. Juli had been that for him. The warmth of her at his side reminded him of how he had awoken this morning to find that she had snuggled close in the night. Her conscious mind might be denying her attraction to him, but her body knew. He knew, too. They *would* be lovers again. *Ah, yes*, he thought, *just a matter of time*.

He put his arm around her shoulder. She snuggled down and rested her head on his chest. Oh, yes. It could be the way it had been. Lovers. Companions and confidants. The two of them against the universe. It had been a long time since he'd been able to share his concerns—his *real* concerns—with anyone else. Juli had always been an understanding listener. He was glad to have her back.

"Will you just look at him," he said.

"Who?"

"Ellicot. Look at the way he's put himself up to be in charge. I don't like it."

"Kurt's not taking charge," she said, leaping to his defense. "He's just being our speaker. I think he's right, the H'kimm will react better to us if he's our speaker. All you have to do is watch them to see that the H'kimm have a definite hierarchical society. If they're like most forest cultures I've studied, they will associate leadership with personal curiosity and assertiveness. Kurt already started the communication between our two species. If we put someone else forward now, it will upset the H'kimm's expectations. I think that it's better not to confuse them."

"Their expectations?" What the hell was she thinking? Since when did aborigines matter more than people? For that matter, when did they matter more than he did? "Well, I've got some expectations myself."

"This is neither the time nor the place." She shrugged off his arm and stood. Wobbling a little, she said, "I think I'm going to go talk to Kurt for a while."

Ellicot, eh? Her rejection sobered him. It made him a little angry, too. He didn't like being led on.

"You want to think about expectations?" he asked. She didn't turn around. The hell with it! With her! Let her go running to the treacherous Ellicot. She'd end up the way anyone near him ended up. Rafe raised his voice and shouted, "Well, try this expectation on for size. With him in charge, we can only expect trouble."

One of the sniveling local females brought him another cup of their brew. He snatched it away, drained it dry, and threw the nut husk back at her.

Juli would see! Damned if she wouldn't see!

# 14

**CHUGEN SYSTEM**
**CHUGEN IV**

Morning found her back and limbs stiff, and her head seemingly swollen to twice its normal size, but Juliana managed to sit up anyway. Blood pounded in her head like a H'kimm percussion group, but the noise was for her alone. The village, which she could see through the open door, was quiet except for a few H'kimm going about their business.

The hut that had been given over to the Humans' use was the size of a Shandaltelkak Association guest hall, and had an undivided interior space like one as well. Juliana thought that she was the first of the Humans to arise until she noticed that Kurt's sleeping pad was empty. She looked around for him, but he had already left the hut. She envied him. He was clearly a born socioxenologist: besides his ease at opening communication with the H'kimm, he had an immunity to their liquor as well. *Experience*, she told herself. *One day you to will be able to match him.* Disbelieving, she dragged her aching head and body to the latrine trench behind the hut.

The sleepers in the hut were still abed when she returned. *An opportunity*, she thought. As quietly as she could, she rummaged through the pile the H'kimm had made of the Humans' goods until she found her perscomp. Hugging it to her chest, she sneaked from the hut.

She squinted in the sunshine, looking about to see if

anyone was noticing her as she sought out a secluded spot at the edge of the village clearing. Her head wasn't so muzzy that she had forgotten her promise of secrecy.

Kurt, sitting in the shade under the communal gathering roof, saw both of Juli's exits from the hut. He'd kept silent during the first because he'd recognized her need from his own experience. The second time, he was not so sure of his reason for silence. Curiosity? He'd seen her sitting with Burke during last night's celebration, but the effects of the liquor and the communal nature of their housing were probably enough to put even Combiner licentiousness on hold. Until this morning perhaps?

But watching her, he decided that this morning's furtiveness didn't seem to betoken an assignation. For one thing, there was no need for a perscomp if she was headed for an assignation.

*Oh, well,* he thought sadly, *her business is her own.*

He had business, too, and he returned to it, trying to improve his vocabulary by playing point-and-name games with some of the village children. It was a technique that worked faster and more easily with adults, but the H'kimm seemed as vulnerable to their liquor as the Humans, and only a very few adult H'kimm were yet arisen. Their snappish remarks to their own kind suggested that Kurt was wise to deal with the children for the time being.

"*Ela* log," he said, caressing the rough, bark-stripped surface of the post supporting the center of the roof. Pointing outside to a particularly large specimen, he said, "*Ela* tree."

The children barked their H'kimm laughter at him.

Shanholz had been taken off-guard by the potency of the natives' booze last night and had drunk too much. Sleeping in hostile territory with no watch set was a good way to sleep permanently. He supposed he should count himself lucky that he hadn't had his throat slit during the night. He resolved to be more prudent in the future.

He was not asleep when Professor Tindal reentered the hut, although her attempt at stealthiness encouraged him to pretend that he was. Through slitted eyes he watched as Tindal selected a perscomp and departed with it.

She had drunk as much as anyone last night. If her hangover was the size of his, she was being awfully dedicated to get to work so early. But if she was just going to work, why all the tiptoeing about? It might be simple courtesy, or it might be something else. Given the furtive way the professor glanced about as she stood in the doorway, Shanholz was willing to take bets that it was the latter.

It was something he'd have to investigate.

Unwilling to go into the jungle alone, Juliana selected an alcove in the brush at the edge of the clearing as far from the clustered huts as possible. She hadn't roused anyone in the hut, which was good. Although several H'Kimm looked curiously in her direction, none came near. Not that they would have understood anything that she or the computer said, but their attention might draw the notice of her companions once they arose. Satisfied that she had the best privacy she was going to get for the moment, she laid her fingertip on the perscomp's start pad.

"Good morning, Ms. Tindal." The screen-bound image of Ambrose Alsion bloomed to life, monkish robe and all. "How are you this morning?"

"I've been better," she responded. "How are you?"

As the words came from her mouth, she felt a flush of embarrassment. The analog program was just a program, not a real person, no matter how sophisticated its responses and no matter how advanced its interactivity. But she was still not used to its small talk, and still tended to react as if she were receiving a fone call from Alsion rather than talking to a machine that had been given a veneer of his personality.

"I am well," replied the construct. "Although I am experiencing problems locating the Combine's reconnaissance satellite," the analog said. "I take it that we have reached Chugen IV?"

"How did you know that?"

"Temperature, humidity, trace gas in the atmosphere, and so on are all within parameters for our intended destination." The analog paused. "Am I wrong?"

"No, you're not wrong."

"Thank you for the confirmation, Ms. Tindal. I'll log the data." Another pause. "You appear stressed. Are there problems in setting up the base camp?"

"We, uh, have had a few problems." She told the analog about the Remor attack, the subsequent crash landing, the missing second shuttle, the deaths and injuries, and their encounter with the H'kimm.

The image frowned. "Your distressing news would explain the lack of signal from the satellite. Corroborative detail and hard data input on the situation would be appreciated."

She wanted that herself. "I'll do what I can. When I can. I wish you'd warned me about the Remor."

"Intervention by the Remor was always a possibility, although one with a low probability. Even had the probability been higher, I would not have expected any interference to occur so soon."

"I'll take that as an apology."

"Take it as you will."

"What do you think they will do next? The Remor, I mean."

"I'm afraid that the current configuration cannot support both my semiautonomy and a full range of complex alinear sociodynamic equations. Actually, I suspect that it would be incapable of handling the equations even were I not resident. Thus predictive postulations are contraindicated. Also, historically speaking, the severe lack of hard data has made the Remor difficult to integrate into the algorithms. As it is, I doubt that even my archetype could answer your question with adequate confidence."

"You sound just like Alsion."

"Of course. Otherwise I would be a disappointment as an analog."

The real disappointment was the lack of answers Juliana was getting. But that was like talking to Alsion, too. Before she could formulate a new tack to try on the machine, she caught movement out of the corner of her eye. Someone was emerging from the hut given over to the castaways. By his uniform, he had to be the League crewman, Shanholz. Shading his eyes, he looked around, spotted her, and headed in her direction.

"Shanholz is coming this way," she told the analog.

"Given Warrant Officer Shanholz's League allegiance, I believe that it would be wise to suspend this conversation until our privacy can be assured." The analog disappeared, its image replaced with a series of charts. Her computer's normal voice announced, "Insufficient data for definitive analysis. Suggest additional sampling of basal nouns."

The Leaguer arrived wearing a friendly smile. "Good morning, Professor Tindal. You're up and working early."

"Yes," she said, offering a polite smile that she didn't feel. "No one had laid on the bacon and eggs, so I decided to get busy. I don't seem to be getting very far, though." She folded down the perscomp's lid. "I'll try again later. Right now I could use something to eat. How about you?"

"Best idea I've heard all day," he said with a chuckle. "Shall we hunt something down together?"

Looking at the sparkle in Shanholz's eye, Juliana suspected that she understood Shanholz's interest in her. As far as they knew, their little group comprised the only Humans left alive within twenty parsecs. Five men, one unconscious, and three women, one effectively paralyzed from the waist down. So that left the math easy; there would be only two couples. Likely Shanholz subscribed to the commonly held belief that Combiner women were easy. He'd be disappointed in her. She had her own idea of who she'd prefer for a partner, and it wasn't a black-uniformed Leaguer like Shanholz. Still, in such a small community, it would be best if they all stayed friends. "What did you have in mind?"

"If there were any pigs around here, we could have your bacon and eggs. If we had any eggs."

Despite herself, she laughed at his old joke. She hadn't been expecting it from him; apparently she was as guilty as he was of seeing the stereotype and not the person. Embarrassed, she said, "You know, I really don't like bacon. Too much fat."

"Can't honestly say I much care for it either," he admitted sheepishly. "But I'd rather eat it than survival rations. Fat over cardboard, I always say."

They both laughed this time. They fell to discussing the possibilities of something local to eat. He proved to have an unexpected stock of culinary lore which he expressed with a wry wit. Clearly, Shanholz was more than just another jack-booted mart.

Rafe emerged from the hut to see Juli and Shanholz walking together and laughing. So, that's the way it was. He should have known. All her talk about being a one-man woman was nothing more than talk. Why should he have expected her to be any less a liar than anyone else? But the goddamned *mart*? She needed to be enlightened, and that was something he could do.

Just now, though, his bladder was straining.

First things first.

He ducked behind the hut to the latrine trench. Goddamn primitives. He unfastened, got his tool out, and started pissing his way to relief. He imagined a face where his stream hit the ground, but he couldn't decide if it was Ellicot's or Shanholz's.

# 15

Christoph Stone was not a man who liked to jump to conclusions. For him there was a great gap between boldness and rashness. The first was laudable, especially when it paid off; the second was often expensive, usually regrettable and, in war, always inexcusable. Unfortunately, all too often, one's actions were characterized in retrospect; at the time of decision, all a man could do was make his best call and stand by the results. One couldn't know if one was headed for praise or damnation.

After a long, sleepless night, Stone still was unsure of which direction he was heading.

The door opened, letting in the sound of controlled chaos along with Chip Hollister. Stone's executive officer always presented a professional appearance, from his unflappable manner to his impeccable uniform. Today was no different. It didn't matter that Chip had been working through his entire downwatch.

"The morning reports are in, Commander." Chip's eyes strayed to the pics scattered across Stone's desk.

Stone had felt it necessary to have hard copy pics of the Grenwold discovery, perhaps because their physical existence made the situation more concrete. He had gone a long time without the concrete evidence he'd wanted.

Now, apparently, his vindication was near at hand.

"Any new insights?" Chip asked as he handed over the datachips.

Stone shook his head. "Just one question, Chip. Is the fleet ready to jump?"

"Nearly. Squadron Radek reports that two of their transports have developed problems with their space drives. Nothing major, but it will be another thirty standard hours before the squadron can reach the rendezvous point."

Thirty hours? Thirty hours in which something could go wrong or the situation could change. Thirty hours for the enemy to act. Thirty hours whose passing could cost, not just him, but the entire Human species. Could he afford to wait?

A bold move could tip the balance. With what they brought back, they could convince the scattered and squabbling fragments of Humanity to unite and face the enemy's threat. A rash move could result in the loss of a significant portion of mankind's defense, starting them down the road to destruction. Bold or rash? Which sort of move was he about to make?

"Send the fleet without Radek," he ordered.

Chip didn't move. "Radek's carrying the 115th Armor. Their absence will reduce the effectiveness of our ground forces by at least twenty percent. That would put us well below the margin on the worst-case scenario."

"The worst case is highly unlikely."

"Very true, sir. We'll be below margin for a lot of the more probable scenarios, too."

It was a point that Stone had spent a good bit of his night worrying over, but too much caution was as damning as too little. "The enemy has shown no sign of reinforcing their beachhead. That oversight won't last forever. I believe that they've given us an opportunity, and I want to take advantage of it. If we're lucky and Colonel Rance's evaluation of the situation on Grenwold is correct, we won't need Radek's ships and troops."

"I thought you didn't like trusting to luck," Chip commented with a touch of sarcasm.

In another officer Stone would have found Chip's attitude insubordinate, but they had worked long and well together. He understood the remark for the gentle nudge that it was. It *was* true that he didn't like trusting to luck. Poking one of the pics with a finger, he replied, "I like idea of losing what we found on Grenwold even less."

"I understand, sir. I'll despatch a courier immediately." Chip saluted and turned on his heels.

Before he was through the door, Stone stopped him. "Chip."

"Sir?"

"How's Operation Chameleon coming?"

"There were some unexpected casualties," Chip reported with cool aloofness. Chip had friends on that mission. The exec's attitude suggested that one or more of them had been killed. "But the essential parties have been delivered safely. The situation seems to be proceeding in an acceptable fashion. The details are all in the reports."

"Thank you, Chip. I'm sorry." Chip nodded once in acceptance of Stone's condolences, displaying all the emotion allowable while on duty. Later, they would talk, but for now, duty ruled. "Keep me informed."

"Will do, Commander." The door slid closed behind him, shutting Stone once more into his lonely command cocoon.

The orders were given. The plans were in motion. No matter how much sitting still ate at him, there was nothing to do for the moment but wait.

✻        ✻        ✻

## SERENTEN CONCORDAT
## SERENTEN

Danielle Wyss was just starting to sip her morning coffee when Pyanfel came padding into the inner office, toe claws tapping lightly on the floor. Uritans preferred to walk barefooted when possible, but their claws were not kind to carpets. To preserve the heirloom floor coverings, she had ordered the carpets taken up, though now regular applications of sealant were necessary to protect the surface of the exposed Mantuan green-oak floors. The rooms were cooler now and Danielle's toes were chilly nearly all winter, but considering the impositions on personal liberty that the Concordat's secrecy policy demanded of the aliens— secured residences and private estates were the only places Uritans were allowed to go about without armor or encounter suits that hid their nature—a season of cold toes was a tiny price for what her Uritans brought to the house.

Pyanfel stood quietly waiting until Danielle swiveled her chair to face the Uritan. Bowing, Pyanfel said, "There are visitors, *Kono*."

It was not unusual to be confronted with business so early in the day, but it was rarely pleasant. The idea of dealing—uncaffeinated—with immediate, unavoidable problems was already starting that old familiar ache between her eyes. She took a long draught of her coffee. Being partially caffed was better than nothing. "Who is it today, Pyanfel?"

"The honorable Ethan Shirrel and the honorable Colonel Marion Wayne Lockhart await your attention, *Kono*."

If Ethan had brought Lockhart with him it was sure to be unpleasant. The Defense Ministry colonel's involvement suggested national security. She consulted her timekeeper. It was seven minutes after six, far too early to have to save the Concordat from its enemies. "Did they say what it was about?"

"Not directly, *Kono*."

Which meant that Pyanfel had listened in on the visitors' conversation. While eavesdropping might be a social faux pas, and a cause for dismissal of ordinary domestics, it was a valuable talent in loyal servants, and Pyanfel was nothing if not a loyal and valuable servant. And a discriminating one: the Uritan female could pull out the underlying meaning from deliberately obscured words with uncanny skill. "Not directly" meant that she had successfully employed her skill for Danielle's benefit.

"And indirectly?"

"Their minds are turned to Chugen, *Kono*."

She had been wondering when the Chugen matter would resurface. The resemblance between the Chugeni and the Uritans had the potential of becoming extremely troublesome for the Concordat, especially with regard to the IDL.

The League's involvement with Chugen was puzzling. The mismatch between socioxenologist Kurt Ellicot's desire to have nothing to do with the League and the League's insistence on having no one but him was a discordance that cried out that something was off. As was the IDL's curious indifference to cooperation once they'd seen Ellicot assigned to the Concordat contingent. Unfortunately, as yet, neither she nor any of her advisors had been able to see the hidden meaning. Perhaps Shirrel and Lockhart were bringing the missing pieces.

"Pyanfel, please call Musayi-no to the outer office and send in Ethan and the colonel five minutes after Musayi-no arrives. And try and get Sheila there before that."

"*Han, Kono*." Pyanfel nodded. "It shall be as you wish, *Kono*."

Danielle spent a few moments arranging her semipublic face, then snagged her coffee cup and proceeded to her outer office. Musayi and three other Uritans of the body-squad were awaiting her. All four bowed as she entered. Musayi spoke.

"Day dawns again for me, *Kono*. I trust you slept well."

"Securely, Musayi-no."

"You honor us, *Kono*."

Uritans took their protective duties with an almost religious intensity. She supposed that Human bodyguards could be as obviously dedicated and attentive, although she didn't recall ever observing quite the same level of devotion. Time after time, Uritans had proven themselves fiercely loyal to their employer. None had ever been accused of accepting a bribe or in any way compromising the security or affairs of the handful of influential Concordat officials who had been allowed to take the aliens into service. There were times when Danielle regretted the necessity of the Concordat's secrecy policy concerning the aliens. The Uritans deserved public praise for their service, and Lord knew that Humans could use the good example. But the timing of their discovery, coming so close to the incident at Cassuells Home, had dictated otherwise, and now the Chugen situation could well touch off a greater spurt of xenophobia.

Had there been good news, Ethan Shirrel would have come by himself to deliver it. Whatever had motivated the dawn visit, she'd know soon. As if her thought had been a cue, Sheila came through the door, talking over her shoulder.

"Just another minute, gentlemen, I'm sure." With the door safely closed behind her, she looked at Danielle and rolled her eyes. "Whatever possessed you to give that man early-morning access? And speaking of early-morning access, I wish you'd speak to Pyanfel. She's supposed to come to me first when—"

"Later, Sheila," Danielle admonished her. She was in no mood for territorial squabbles. "Have the morning deliveries been forwarded?"

"Already in your files."

"Good. Pull together everything on the Chugen Contact Mission and put a synopsis on my machine. And I want you to listen in on this meeting. Run down anything that sounds like it might give us something we don't already have, but don't interrupt. If you find anything really urgent, flag it and put it through on my machine. Got it?"

"I hear and obey," Sheila responded with a hint of mischief.

"I wish. Now, let them in and disappear yourself to the inner office. I want you nearby when we finish."

"Don't let this one run too long. Remember, you've got an eight o'clock downtown with Public Welfare."

She hadn't wanted to remember.

Sheila ushered in Shirrel and Lockhart and disappeared herself as ordered. Danielle's visitors were long-faced, confirming her expectation of bad news. She didn't have to wait for long to get it, because Ethan Shirrel launched right into the meat of the matter.

"We have trouble at Chugen! It seems that through some inconceivable lapse in judgment, the Combine's managing director allowed the project team to be transported insystem aboard an IDL vessel. A League vessel! Can you believe it?"

"The *Henry Hull*, ma'am," Colonel Lockhart amplified. "A patroller under the command of a Major Jonas Ersch."

Shirrel nodded. "Exactly. And this Major Ersch has been identified as having connections with IDL Strategic Intelligence. Not exactly a difficult thing to find out, but apparently beyond the capabilities of the Combine intelligence agencies. How the PSC has managed not to be eaten up by the League is beyond me. Such a simple thing! Someone with Major Ersch's connection does not normally command a patroller. To any intelligent being, that would suggest that the *Henry Hull*'s mission is something more than a simple surveillance."

"One presumes that the managing director was unaware of Major Ersch's background," Danielle said.

"Possibly he was not," said Shirrel. "Preferably, actually, since alternative scenarios are somewhat unsavory."

Danielle certainly preferred to see the Combine as League dupes rather than puppets. "Whatever their motivation, the Combine authorities were within their rights to assign transportation as they saw fit. Clearly you have more to tell me than a tale of poor judgment."

"That's correct, ma'am," Lockhart said solemnly. "The League ship began experiencing communications difficulties as she was in the process of launching her interface shuttles, which were to take the Chugen Contact Mission personnel down to the surface. Something went wrong, we don't know what. The communiqué from Midway Station is garbled and unclear. We do know that one shuttle, IDL designation six-one-five, was reported destroyed while entering the atmosphere of Chugen IV, lost with all aboard. Regretfully, I must inform you that it appears that our entire contingent was onboard shuttle six-one-five. The other shuttle appears to have grounded safely."

Shirrel didn't give Danielle time to assimilate the colonel's announcement. "I must emphasize that our information is very preliminary, and I would also like to emphasize that we have not been able to confirm any details. Steps have been initiated to correct our information deficit."

Lockhart elaborated. "A courier boat has been dispatched, but it will be at least a week before any of our people reach the scene. Even were they to make an immediate turnaround, it will be more than another week before we have confirmation."

"Barring reports from the Combine, of course," Shirrel added. "Which we may not be able to take at face value, given the circumstances."

"You're a suspicious man, Ethan, but then that's why I keep you around." Danielle asked after the status of unofficial sources and got the answer she was expecting: Chugen was too new for the Concordat to have developed anything useful. For the time being all the information they would get would come through official channels. Of course, they still had their taps into those channels from which they would gain insight into the real news behind the official news, but such sources were a poor substitute for first-hand information from their own people. "Gentlemen, you have not brought me the sort of news with which I like to start my day."

"I'm sorry, Danielle, but I though you ought to hear right away," Shirrel said, sounding honestly apologetic.

"You were right, Ethan." The implications of the disaster were starting to sink in. "You say that all of our people are dead?"

"Reported lost, ma'am."

"But presumed dead," she persisted.

Shirrel nodded. "Yes, Minister, I'm afraid so."

If that were so . . . She turned to Lockhart. "Colonel, wasn't your daughter part of the mission?"

"Yes, ma'am. Security."

The man was taking it like a rock. "You have my condolences."

"Appreciated, ma'am. If Dale is dead, she died while

serving our nation. She wouldn't have had it any other way."

There was an awkward moment of silence, broken by Shirrel, who was making a valiant effort to change the focus. "I wish I had more to tell you, Minister, but our usual sources are as in the dark as we are."

"Maybe we should try a more *un*-usual source."

The tripod of Ambrose Alsion's holoprojector sat in the corner in which it had stood since her interview with Mr. Miller. Not that it had been neglected. Within a week of that interview, Miller had returned with an addition to set atop the tripod: a sleek, dark piece of abstract sculpture that was actually a sophisticated computer housing an analog of Alsion. Over the weeks since its arrival, Danielle had found the analog to be a useful source of information and an unusually perceptive and sagacious, if occasionally obscure and idiosyncratic, advisor.

Shirrel saw where she was looking and asked, "Is that the Alsion analog generator?"

Danielle nodded. Although she had spoken of it, she had never activated it in the presence of any of her senior staff. That was about to change.

"Activate the Alsion analog," she called out.

Lights winked awake on the "sculpture." Unlike the earlier version, the projected image was a full-length figure. As solid in appearance as if he were actually in the room, a robed and cowled Ambrose Alsion appeared, sitting regally in an overstuffed armchair. Danielle gave a short bark of surprise. The chair was new.

"Good morning, Premier Minister Wyss," the analog said in a cheery bass voice. "How are you this morning?"

"I was doing fine until I received some recent news."

"Ah." The analog stroked its full beard. "That would be the report from Chugen which, by concatenation of circumstances, has aroused your suspicion of the Combine and, by association, of myself."

"Right on the head," she admitted.

The image looked chagrined. "I am a captive of appearances. For the little good that it will do, I will take this opportunity to remind you that the Alsion Institute is, although headquartered within the space claimed by the Pan-Stellar Combine, an independent, international organization. I would also like to reiterate the importance of the sociodynamic node that appears to be developing, and to remind you of the critical need to consider carefully any actions or non-actions taken. Remember that you are the leader of the Concordat."

Her position was something that she never forgot, and she didn't like having her own warning to Miller turned around and used on her. "Alsion, we have company today."

"Yes, I see. Good morning to you, Mr. Ethan Shirrel, Colonel Marion Lockhart." The image nodded politely to each in turn before returning its simulated gaze to Danielle. "I'm glad that Mr. Shirrel and Colonel Lockhart are here. Their insights may prove useful in unraveling the conundrum."

"How does it know we're here?" Shirrel whispered to Lockhart.

Shirrel discovered, as Danielle had already, that the analog's hearing was sharp.

"I simply accessed Minister Wyss's security program and visitor log to ascertain who was present and correlated with personnel files. Identifying you two gentlemen in the future will be far simpler now that I have first-hand data on record."

Lockhart looked stunned. "Minister Wyss, I protest!"

"Let us hope it is not to excess, Colonel," the analog quipped. "You no doubt are concerned about my access to sensitive material. Let me assure you that my access is limited to Read Only. I won't—can't, actually—go tramping about adjusting things to my liking."

"Musayi has had it checked out and agrees," Danielle told Lockhart. "The analog has no access keys."

Lockhart wasn't satisfied. "It doesn't need to do things to be a problem. It has accessed classified security files."

The analog clucked disappointedly. "Colonel, Colonel, Colonel. I came here to help the premier minister, not to hinder her. And I would like to get back to helping her, assuming that this tiresome worrying about security is complete. I assure you that I have no intention of divulging any secrets belonging to either the premier minister or the Serenten Concordat. And before you ask, let me inform you that my matrix hardware has been examined for transmission devices and found to be satisfactorily devoid of such worrisome mechanisms."

Lockhart looked to Musayi, whose nod confirmed the analog's statement. But Lockhart remained unsatisfied. "Ma'am, please," he protested. "The presence or absence of transmitters aside, if this machine were to be stolen . . ."

"This 'machine,' as you so impolitely put it, would reveal nothing to any thief," the analog interrupted. "Assuming that some person of hostile intent were to breach Security Chief Musayi's excellent system, penetrate to this chamber, and abscond with me, I have, as I have already informed Musayi-no, multiple, redundant safeguards to destroy any compromising data the moment my matrix hardware is removed from this physical locale. The honorable, if mistrustful, Musayi-no found it comforting to install a thermal device within my hardware casing that, if subjected to a physical displacement of more than four meters from this spot, will detonate, slagging my matrix hardware and therewith any data contained within it. A crude but effective precaution, as I am sure you will agree. Perhaps you'd like to install a similar destructive device of your own choosing?" The analog's pause was short. "Well, Colonel?"

Danielle watched Lockhart's gaze flick to Musayi-no's face. Questioning Musayi-no's competence could be construed as an imputation to his honor, and the colonel was well aware of how touchy Uritans could be about matters of honor. The Uritan guard captain's expression was as unreadable as ever; if he was ready to take offense, his bewhiskered face did not show it. The colonel elected caution.

"Ma'am, I am sure that this machine was checked out thoroughly, but this analog has demonstrated unexpected capabilities, things that our best machines cannot do. How can we be sure that it doesn't have other, more dangerous abilities?"

The analog answered for her. "You can't, of course. While I appreciate your flattering evaluation of institute technology, I find your opinion of my trustworthiness a trifle insulting. Understandable, though, and from a certain viewpoint even laudable. Perhaps I can earn a small measure of your trust. I have come into possession of some information that I feel confident you will find interesting. Of course, if you find me unreliable, perhaps I should hold my peace and wait for you to stumble on these data in your own good time. Would you prefer that, Colonel? The delay shouldn't be more than a few weeks. I had thought that people in your profession put a premium on gaining information in a timely manner. Am I wrong?"

Danielle wondered what quirky programming prompted the analog to be so deliberately provocative. It was a matter she would pursue with it in a private session.

Temper fraying, Lockhart snapped, "Just what have you got, analog?"

The analog feigned surprise. "My, such politesse! And please do call me Alsion, Colonel. After all, through our individual relationships with the premier minister we are effectively colleagues."

"Enough, Alsion," Danielle said. "If you have information we can use, let's hear it."

"As you wish, Minister," the analog said compliantly. "You see, agents of the Alsion Institute have intercepted a dispatch intended for the Interstellar Defense League's Strategic Command; and now, by my courtesy, that dispatch, a privileged communication belonging to your rivals, is here for you to scrutinize. You can view the military situation report portion at your leisure, since I have downloaded it to the premier minister's computer. But for the moment I direct your attention to a collection of enlightening, if grim, pictures. These pictures were obtained on the planet Grenwold by a military unit under the command of one Captain Anders Seaborg."

As the analog spoke, the pictures began appearing on Danielle's wallscreen. She was familiar with the pictures of the Cassuells; she had seen the images from Chugen IV, still blurry despite enhancement; but these new ones, labeled *Grenwold*, held her attention. The aliens in them were all dead, but even so their resemblance to the living, breathing aliens standing in her office was uncanny. The hands with their four digits, the outer shorter than and able to oppose the inner. The four-toed feet. The slender, furry bodies. The narrow-snouted, muzzled faces. There was some variation, but no more than could be expected from individuals within a species. She might have been looking at Musayi-no's cousins.

This was the sort of bad news that she had been expecting to get from Chugen. The fuzzy pics from that planet had been suggestive, but inconclusive, giving rise to hopes that the resemblance between her Uritans and the newly discovered natives was due to a chance fluke of evolution. But these Grenwold pics were clear. There could be no doubt of the similarity.

True, the Grenwold evidence was only visual, outward evidence, but it struck home on a gut level. A layman could only conclude that these new aliens were of a kind with the Cassuells, quite possibly with the Chugeni, and ultimately, when knowledge of their existence became public, with the Uritans. Four nearly identical species of aliens pushed the convergent evolution argument past tenability.

But were they identical? Molecular studies comparing the fragmentary data from Cassuells Home to that gathered from Urita suggested that while strong similarities existed, the two aliens were *not* of the same species. Now she could not but wonder if such results were based more on wishful thinking than scientific honesty.

And what if they were identical? Did that make them Remor? The League would say so. She believed that they were wrong, but belief—even when supported by hard scientific evidence, which was in short supply—didn't always win the day. The League would use the evidence from Grenwold to bolster their case, but as Grenwold was already a League world, other nations would be cautious about accepting that evidence. Chugen would be another matter; it was a Combine world and not under League sway. Yet the shuttle disaster looked likely to skew any data coming from Chugen in favor of the League's position. Just how devastating was the loss of Concordat personnel on that front going to be?

Oblivious to the shocked reaction of the Humans, the analog continued speaking. "While the presence of the Grenwold aliens among the Remor machines and biological monstrosities on that planet would interest any humans, they had, I believe, a special significance for Captain Seaborg, encouraging him to bring them immediately to the attention of the IDL Strategic Command. And I assure you that he has done his duty by the League; this intercepted dispatch is but one of several copies. Captain Seaborg seems to believe that this information is of too great an import to trust to a single line of communications.

"As ever, circles intersect circles and the curve turns back on itself when the attractor is strong. The unconnected becomes the improbable, only to become history. The obscure is clarified as the butterfly emerges into the light."

"What the hell are you babbling about?" Shirrel demanded.

A new image superimposed itself onto the montage: a picture of an IDL officer, a lieutenant by the two pips on his collar. His name tag read *Seaborg*. The picture dissolved into another: the same man, but younger, in a noncommissioned officer's uniform.

"Seaborg," the analog explained, "when of a less exalted rank, was a member of the IDL expeditionary force to Cassuells Home and had personal contact with the Cassuells. Enough, he believes, to recognize them on sight."

Danielle gulped a swallow of her now-cold coffee, the only anodyne to hand for her dry throat. "You're saying he recognized these aliens as Cassuells."

"So it would appear," the analog replied.

"One match could have been coincidence," Shirrel muttered. "But two?"

The colonel's eyes shifted uneasily to the Uritans. "Three."

Shirrel eyed Danielle's bodysquad as well. "God help us, the League has been right all along. They are the Remor."

"That remains unproved," Danielle said. "Certainly there is a strong similarity, but we already knew that. According to our best biological evidence there could be a connection between our Uritan friends and the Cassuells, but identifying either or both species with the League's rampaging Remor is a leap. The Remor leave nothing with which to make such a connection. Even were there a biological connection, how can you equate Uritan culture, for example, with Humankind's enemy? They aren't a technic civilization. They knew nothing of space flight until we showed up, and years of searching Urita and the Uritan System have yet to yield *any* evidence otherwise."

"Biology is all the League is looking at," said Lockhart. "If they can make that connection, they will call it incontrovertible evidence that species like the Uritans are in fact Remor."

"You can't be persuaded by such an argument, Colonel. We share biology with the Leaguers, but we are not them."

"An argument emphasizing cultural differences will not go down well in Remor-ravaged space," Shirrel pointed out.

"But does that make it invalid?" asked Danielle. "We can't let League propaganda overshadow what may be our last defense."

"Then you have accepted that the Uritans and their like are Remor."

"I have not," she stated firmly. "How could they be? Look at their reaction when we landed on Urita. Did they attack us on sight? Of course not. They welcomed us; not exactly a Remor reaction. Even if the Uritans are a Remor species, they have demonstrated that xenophobic aggression is not a trait that is hard-wired into their psychology."

"The Cassuells weren't aggressive either," Lockhart said.

Danielle smiled at him. "Exactly. I have to say that after

nine years of personal contact with Uritans I have seen nothing like the single-minded xenophobic fury that the Remor demonstrate. What sentient species doesn't demonstrate psychological and cultural variation? Certainly our own species is not uniform. Humanity has built both pacifistic and warlike civilizations, even some with genocidal bents. Why do we find it so difficult to believe that an alien species might also produce such variation?"

"Fear of the Other," Shirrel suggested.

Danielle thought the explanation more than likely. "And should we let such paranoia rule our reactions?"

"We do not and we have not," Shirrel said. "But others are not as enlightened as we in the Concordat."

"That is the situation we must address. Ever since the day that the first Concordat survey team discovered Urita and Milyukow Sloan noticed a similarity between the natives and the ill-fated Cassuells, we've known we were walking a tricky path. But we accepted it because we were greedy for what Urita offered. Yet we were smart enough to be cautious.

"Out of fear of the nascent IDL's expansionism and military adventurism, we made the appearance of the Uritans a state secret. We keep the location of Urita secret. We forbid any Uritans who leave their world from appearing in public without a concealing environment suit. We do not allow them to leave Concordat space. We have imposed a great deal on our loyal friends in the name of protecting them, and they have not complained. Instead they have given us loyal service. What kind of reward is it to look at them as the terrible enemy that the League says they are? Even if they are genetically related, we know the Uritans are not like the Remor."

"Do we, ma'am?" The colonel's expression was stern. "The Uritans are as warlike a people as any I've ever met."

"A lot like ourselves, you mean?" she countered.

Lockhart shrugged.

"We must consider whether we can afford to continue sheltering them," Sherril said.

"They've been our secret for nearly ten years," Danielle reminded him. "Can we afford *not* to continue?"

"Perhaps there is another viewpoint worth having," the analog suggested. It inclined its head toward the bodysquad.

Danielle recalled that Sloan's early attempts to question Uritans about the Cassuells had run into such an unyielding wall of attitude that the subject had been largely ignored. Planet-bound Uritans had refused to accept the pictures. They called Sloan's assertions that the Cassuells came from another world a story, labeling the pictures clever fakes. The few who believed the pictures real deemed the beings in them to represent a foreign tribe from some faraway island not yet a part of civilized Urita.

But Musayi's view had been expanded by personal experience of other worlds. And now there were the Grenwold aliens *and* the Chugeni. How *did* the Uritans see their place in the universe now?

"Musayi-no, you see these pictures. What do you make of them?" Danielle asked.

For several minutes Musayi silently regarded the images. Then he simply shook his head and looked away, returning to his relaxed guard stance.

"Musayi-no?"

"*Kono?*"

"Are we looking at others of your kind?"

"*Ey, Kono.* They are not us. Their *mareka*, their fate, is their own. We are loyal. Do you question that?"

"*Ey*, Musayi-no. I never question your loyalty. *Nogenta na tuan.*"

*"Nogenta na tuan, Kono."*

Musayi seemed sure, simply by looking, that the other aliens were no relations of his. To her, and likely to any other Human, there was no difference to be seen. The truth would lie in further investigations, in genetic tests, and—for now—in other hands. The Concordat's investigators on Chugen were dead, they had no access to Grenwold, and the limited Cassuell data dated from before the fall of the Mercantile Union and was fragmentary at best. All the crucial material seemed to be in the hands of the League, a totally unacceptable situation.

"You've given us a lot to think about, Alsion," Danielle said.

"I have, haven't I?" the analog said, smiling broadly as its image vanished back into storage.

# 16

"Burke!"

The shout wasn't quite strident, but it was insistent. Rafe let the lid of his stowbox drop and the bang echoed across the village's narrow common area. Human and Chugeni heads turned, but he ignored them as he strode over to where Lockhart lay on her litter.

The woman was in a better frame of mind than he would have been in her place, although clearly she chafed at her lack of mobility. Her mangled legs remained useless, but Zan, the closest thing they had to a doctor, was no longer afraid that they would have to be amputated. They would just lie there and wither. Rafe didn't envy her. Had they been in a decent environment, she would have had the medical treatment she needed. Here on this backwater planet, she didn't even have the wheelchair that she was more than capable of powering by herself; she had to be dragged around on that damnable sledge or carried whenever she wanted to go somewhere, which is what she wanted now.

Lockhart's impositions were among the few times Rafe wasn't altogether pleased that his specialty kept him fitter than your average scientist. Though he didn't complain as he dragged her and her computer across from the Human hut to the communal gathering spot under the big grass-thatched roof, he considered the injustice of it all.

Why was *Rafe* always Lockhart's first choice as beast of burden? Hell, he wasn't even her fellow national. Why did she have to impose on *him*? What about Langdorf? He seemed to spend most of his time hanging around the Chugeni village pretending to repair his equipment. So what if the weedy meteorologist wasn't exactly a manly paragon of strength; he *was* available and he *could* pull the litter if he tried hard enough. And what about Shanholz? The Leaguer was fitter than any of the castaways, but he was, of course, a heel-clicking product of the IDL and Lockhart—wisely—was reluctant to put a lot of trust in him. Still, she could have considered trusting the mart to be a beast of burden.

And why not call on Ellicot? Rafe would have enjoyed seeing Ellicot sweating to lug Lockhart around. Rafe guessed that he knew why Lockhart let her fellow national off the hook; the gimpy Ellicot couldn't do any serious physical work without needing to raid the medical supplies for a painkiller. Lockhart's physical situation was clearly worse than Ellicot's, and she was swallowing her own pain to conserve the medical supplies. It was all part of the nobler-than-thou, we-all-stick-together attitude that she flashed every time she ran one of her we'll-all-survive-this-together pep talks. That attitude wouldn't let her be the excuse for someone else's guzzling those same supplies she wasn't using to kill her own considerable pain. Rafe admired her fortitude every bit as much as he disliked her impositions. But why couldn't the damnable woman deal with inactivity as well as she did with pain?

Once he got her situated to her satisfaction, with her back to one of the common roof's corner posts, he remarked, "If you've got nothing else for me to do here, Zan and I will be getting on with the studies that you also want us to do."

Lockhart had insisted that each of the castaways do his or her best to conduct the surveys that they had come to Chugen to make. It was make-work therapy to distract them from the rottenness of their situation, but what else was there to do? He'd agreed, partially to avoid argument and partially because the damned planet did have an intriguing ecology, but he might as well be here as a *tourist* for all the scientific rigor he could apply. Lacking orbital or overflight data, and with his traps, cameras, nets, piccaptures, night-viewing equipment, and just about every sampler he'd brought all rotting away in the wreck of the shuttle, he'd be years, possibly *decades*, getting a decent handle on even the local ecology. Unfortunately, given that the Remor were moving on the system, that was time that he wouldn't have.

But none of the other castaways had wanted to hear about the pointlessness of the exercise, preferring to delude themselves. Even Juli. She'd been a clear thinker once, but that was a long time ago. Now she'd joined the ranks of the great thought-deficient majority, a group to which Rafe, thankfully, remained an outsider.

So why was he going along with the foolishness? He didn't even have to look around to know the reason. He could smell it. The stinking Chugeni and their stinking village. Who in their right mind wanted to stay around this pestiferous rural warren? Doing his ecological scouting got him out of the village. If he thought that he'd have a reasonable chance to survive in the uncharted wilderness by himself, he'd just keep going and not come back; but Zandowski was still figuring out what was edible and what wasn't, and without that knowledge, soloing was too likely to be suicidal.

So he stayed. And did his survey like a good little scientist. It wasn't as bad as it might have been. He had

Zandowski's company, which might have rewards, and the ecology wasn't uninteresting, but any pretense that he could do a decent survey was pointless. The main thing was that the field trips like this overnighter got him out of the stinking village.

Which he devoutly wished to be.

Lockhart didn't have anything else for him to waste his time on, so he finished his packing. Zandowski, not having been interrupted, for once was ready before he was. As he shouldered his stowbox, Lockhart shouted across the commons, "Take Shanholz with you."

"Why?" Zandowski asked, a quaver of uncertainty in her voice. She had told Rafe more than once that she felt uncomfortable with the Leaguer around. Rafe understood that.

"Zan and I will be fine," he said.

Lockhart was adamant, as usual, in imposing her will. "Ah'zzt isn't available. You're working the river today and you might need protection. Shanholz is armed and you're not."

*That* could be fixed by having the Leaguer surrender his sidearm to Rafe, but that argument had already been fought and lost. Shanholz had made it very clear that he would give his gun to no man or woman while his mart body still breathed, and so he remained the only gun-armed Human. That would change once the rechargers could be rigged to deliver enough juice to zap the powerpacks on the survival canister weapons, a task which Shanholz—the only one with the necessary technical knowledge—was taking remarkably slowly. He probably *reveled* in being the only one with a gun.

So Lockhart wanted Shanholz to be the great white hunter and protect the foolish scientists when they went off on their safari. As though Rafe was incapable of taking care of himself. Unnecessary worry on Lockhart's part. Rafe had worked wildernesses before without needing a baby-sitter.

He told her so, and she snapped his head off, reiterating her demand that they take Shanholz as a watchdog and adding nonsense about dangerous animals.

If Lockhart had fallen for the locals' stories about Chugeni-eating beasts, she'd been spending too much time listening to Juli's faltering translations of Chugeni juju tales. He had thought Lockhart too tough-minded to fall for that crap, but obviously he had overestimated her. There are dangerous animals out there! Spotted ghosts, green slitherers, and gnarly bone crunchers, oh my! Goblins of the mind and the darkness, that was all they were, the same things that populated the scary stories he'd heard on half a dozen planets where the natives liked to thrill each other at night around their cozy campfires. Rafe wasn't the sort of guy to be put off by such bugaboos and child frighteners. Experience had taught him that the real ecology was rarely what the locals thought it was. So far Chugen IV was just like other planets in that regard. He had yet to see hide, hair, or sign of anything big enough to bother an alert, healthy Human, even presuming that the local wildlife had a taste for off-world flesh.

With a day pack slung over one shoulder and his trusty sidearm belted at his hip, Shanholz joined them.

"Bow-wow," Rafe said, "Good boy, good shepherd."

"You just be good sheep, then, and we'll get along fine," Shanholz suggested, with a grin that reminded Rafe that sheep dogs were descended from the wolves that preyed on the flock.

Lieutenant Mostel had been in charge of the shuttle mission; he had been the one in charge of getting them back to the rendezvous and off this steam box of a planet. Unfortunately that plan was as dead as the lieutenant, leaving Warrant Officer Shanholz in the deep end. Shanholz didn't like it, but there it was.

He wasn't supposed to be here, stranded with a bunch of coddled civvie scientists. The highbrows made him uncomfortable, always sounding like they knew a hell of a lot more than he did even when they were telling him they had no idea of what was happening around them. Before he'd signed on with the IDL MilForce, he'd taken off whenever he didn't like what was going on around him, and that was what he wanted to do now. But he couldn't just walk out on the civilians, if for no other reason than he had nowhere to go.

He also had no idea what was going on elsewhere. All he knew was what his orders had been, and how he had been dumped in the crapper by the shuttle crash. He also had a good idea of what his superiors would do to him if he screwed up.

He didn't like it. He didn't like the planet. He didn't like the company. He especially didn't like having to figure out what to do. That was an officer's job. Joining MilForce and finding somebody to take care of that job had been the best thing he'd ever done. Why did the lieutenant have to go and get himself killed?

No officer, no orders. Nobody to blame when the shit came down.

He supposed that was why he went along with Lockhart's orders. She sounded like an officer, even if she was just a civvie logistics tech. Somewhere she had picked up the knack of making a guy jump to. He figured that she could soak off any targeted rounds coming his way if he wasn't doing what he ought to be doing.

But that protection would only go so far, and he knew it. So he had set himself the task of doing what he could to see that the mission was accomplished. Not that he could do much. For the moment, keeping in the background seemed the best idea. He'd fit in as best he could and wait.

This latest assignment might even offer an opportunity or two. Even if it didn't, there were a lot worse duties than following a couple of highbrows while they poked into trees and pried under logs and tried to make friends with bugs. At least he'd get a good view of Zandowski's shapely butt when she bent over to talk to her crawly friends. And he could put up with Burke's shots; the Pansie's anti-League attitude could be as much pose as real dislike. He seemed an all-right jake when he wasn't spouting Pansie propaganda.

Zandowski headed out of the village, hips rolling. Shanholz felt a grin of appreciation stretching his face as he started after her. Yeah, there were lots worse duties. Who could blame him for enjoying this one while it lasted?

Later would — well — would be later. He'd worry about it when he had to.

Lo'gnen didn't move as quietly as the other H'kimm. In the jungle, if his creaking joints did not betray him to prey, his strings of rank beads would — but he didn't need the stealth that the other members of his pack used in the bush. Lo'gnen's hunting days were a thing of the past; as the oldest of the pack, he was provided for, and honor was accorded him for the years that he had lived to attain his gray fur. But though he had lost his survival edge through age and honors, he retained more than enough stealthiness to sneak up on a shipwrecked Human lost in contemplation. Thus Kurt did not know of the elder's presence until Lo'gnen spoke.

"Do you see the stars in the day, friend Kurtellicot?"

"In my mind." *Which*, Kurt thought, *is the only place that I'll ever visit them again.*

Head bobbing, Lo'gnen coughed agreement. "It is as I have told the others it is. You are *tuoyal*."

His translator program's language base was extensive, more than an unaided Human researcher could have amassed in the few weeks they had spent among the H'kimm, but it was not—could not be—complete. His agent chimed through his earpiece, informing him that *tuoyal* was an identified but undefined word. Surprised, Kurt checked to find *tuoyal* duly logged in the database. It had been used when the castaways had first been introduced to the elder, but had gone unspoken since. Juli had entered a notation that it might be an honorific, possibly metaphorical. Thinking back to when he had first heard it, Kurt was not even sure whether the word had been applied to Lo'gnen or to the castaways. Now seemed the time to find out.

"*Tuoyal*," he said, using the interrogative construction. "What is this?"

Lo'gnen yipped in amusement. "Truly *tuoyal*. The others do not believe you are *tuoyal*. They will. They want you to come. They will speak to you at the Gathering."

*Gathering*? The Chugeni word had connotations of collecting things, but Lo'gnen modified it by lowering his snout and eyelids, a gesture the H'kimm used when speaking of things sacred.

"I am confused, friend Lo'gnen," Kurt admitted. "What is this Gathering? Who wants me to come?"

"All want. I know."

"All? All who? How do you know?"

The elder growled. "You talk like a pup. This makes others think you are not *tuoyal*. They are not right. Why do you make them look right? We will go," Lo'gnen said as if the matter were decided. "You will speak."

"When?"

"This last question will I answer on this matter. When the call comes, we will go." Lo'gnen's earnestness vanished in a toothy H'kimm smile. "I will be pleased to hear you speak, friend Kurtellicot. It will be a great day for the H'kimm."

The elder ducked under the common roof, headed for the area that was his. He curled upon the ground near the cooking fire, near enough to snatch a taste of whatever would be impaled upon the spits or laid upon the grill when the hunters returned. At Lo'gnen's beckoning gesture, Kurt followed him and settled cross-legged in the dirt.

"But let us be speaking of other things," Lo'gnen said. "I saw your eyes searching for the stars. Have they words for you?"

He wished that they did. He especially wished that they spoke of a coming rescue. Unfortunately, the next thing that they heard from the stars was likely to be the rumble of landers carrying Remor conquerors. But that was not something he could bring himself to say to Lo'gnen. Despite the fears of some of the others, nothing he had seen convinced him that the H'kimm knew anything of the Remor. Kurt had no intention of being the one to end their innocence in that regard. Someone other than Kurt would have to be the prophet of doom.

"Have they words for me?" Kurt shook his head. "Once when I traveled among the stars, I spoke to others who traveled as I did. Now I am here, and do not speak to the stars."

"Yes. It is sad." They sat in silence for many minutes. Then Lo'gnen's attention was caught by a tumble of H'kimm youngsters whirlwinding their way through the common area. A smile split the elder's face. "But the pack remains. This is truth, friend Kurtellicot. In many ways, your folk are like ours. Though your past dwells in the stars, you are left to run on the dirt. For some, it is enough. Is it not better to run on the dirt than to lie in it?"

Was it? "There are those who would say that it *is* better to lie in the dirt than to lose the stars."

Lo'gnen stared at Kurt. "Are you one of them?"

Was he? Kurt raised his eyes to the darkness of the roof above him. There were no stars in that firmament, but beyond it, in the true heavens, the stars still burned, gifting worlds with their light, and thus with life. Out there lay Human civilization, his civilization, and here he sat, cut off from it. And not from choice this time.

Still, though it was not a situation he had asked for or one he wanted, he did not entirely miss Humanity's stellar civilizations. The H'kimm were so much more in touch with their world, so much more basic. He'd felt that pull before. Once before he had followed that siren song.

Better to run on the dirt than to lie in it? Oh, yes.

Yet did the stars mean so much? He had turned his back on them once, preferring to run in the dirt. However, now that he had been forced down from the heights onto the dirt, he found that living a primitive's life was not as attractive as it had once been. He'd lived that life, however briefly. Though he had objected to being torn from his dirt life, he had gone back to the stars and—painfully—rebuilt a life for himself. He had been born to Human civilization; it was his—admittedly flawed—civilization, and nothing could change that cold, hard fact. Having suffered through that difficult rebirth, he had no desire to lose what he had regained.

Besides, he hadn't *lost* the stars, he'd had them *stolen* from him. The resentment of the Remor burned in him. They had forced him from the heavens. They would come and take his life. But while the Remor could blast his body to its component atoms, they could never touch his heart, and in his heart the stars would always be there. It seemed to Kurt that the only real way to lose the stars was to lie in the dirt and he was not ready to lie down and die.

"Yes," he told the elder. "I am one of them."

Lo'gnen made a noise that didn't sound like a coherent word. The translator agent queried Kurt, wondering whether to add the sound to its databank. Kurt silenced the agent. There were times when the rigorous pursuit of science was inappropriate.

Lo'gnen removed a necklace and held it out to Kurt. Most of the beads were wood, dyed a half-dozen different colors. Most of the rest were bone, polished bright, but one was gleaming metal. Unlike the other beads, the metal one was smooth and flat, and its edges showed no signs of chipping or wear. It looked machined and reminded him of a washer.

But the H'kimm had no machines. Where had the washer come from? "What is that?" he asked.

"The sign of the *tuoyal*." Lo'gnen touched a similar necklace that he still wore. Jiggling the offered necklace, he added, "You wear. Always wear."

Kurt accepted the necklace. He put it on, but not happily. The Cassuells, too, had given him signs to wear. Honors, they had told him. Tokens of belonging, they had said. At the time he had accepted them gladly. It wasn't until much later that he had understood that those gifts really had been knives to cut him away from his humanity. *This time will be different*, he told himself. *This time I know who and what I am.*

After its odd beginning, the day passed much as other days passed. Lo'gnen sat, almost in state, under the common roof and the village's life unfolded within his sight. Kurt observed, adding to his knowledge of H'kimm ways and customs. When Lo'gnen was not settling a dispute between two village children or passing judgment on the quality of some craft product, he and Kurt talked of the

H'kimm and of Humans, of the jungle and the weather, and of homey things of village life, but no more mention was made of the *tuoyal*.

Juli joined them for a while in the afternoon. The elder was polite to her, but Kurt sensed a guardedness entering the elder's speech. He put it down to the H'kimm's dislike for Human reliance on mechanical aids. Juli, like the other castaways, constantly wore her earpiece translator and relied on its resident agent when conversing with the H'kimm. The translator might breach the language barrier, but it didn't dissolve it completely. Although Juli needed the agent less than any of the other castaways, she used it far more than Kurt, and the H'kimm spoke preferentially to him.

Kurt suspected that it was more than ease of communication that fueled their preference. Like the people of many primitive cultures, the H'kimm expected other social structures to be like their own. Thus, they had expectations of Human social structure, which by virtue of Kurt's having spoken for the castaways as a whole, made him the leader of the Humans. It was not a role he wanted, and certainly not one that the other Humans, especially Lockhart or Burke, seemed willing to grant him, but it was the role that the H'kimm saw him filling.

A spokesperson was necessary, that much was clear; it made handling communication so much easier and safer when the person best able to communicate did the talking. Safe, clear communication was their best guarantee for maintaining H'kimm goodwill, and as long as the castaways were reliant on the H'kimm's goodwill for survival, the Humans needed to keep that goodwill. After the Humans and the H'kimm had achieved a better mutual understanding there would come a time to dispense with the fiction of Kurt's leadership.

Still, he didn't have to shoulder all the burden of fostering Human–H'kimm understanding. Juli came with a lot of questions. Today her focus was on pack structure, and she seemed to direct as many questions to Kurt as she did to Lo'gnen. The elder was more tolerant of her than usual, and he even answered some of the questions that Juli, applying her rudimentary comprehension of H'kimm etiquette, tried to get answered through Kurt. But Lo'gnen divided his attention, watching Kurt as much as Juli.

"A curious pup," the elder commented after Juli left to take her questions to some of the other H'kimm. "She is your pair-mate, yes?"

"She is my pair-mate, no."

"But there is interest, yes?"

"Yes," Kurt admitted, to Lo'gnen's yip of amusement.

"I was once young like you, friend Kurtellicot," the elder confided. "She will be a better pack-mate if you make pups with her."

"We Humans are different from the H'kimm."

"You feel the dirt under your toes, yes? You feel the itch under your fur, what little you have of it, yes? You breathe the air, you feel the rain, too much sun hurts your skin, a knife will cut you and you will bleed, you pair and make pups, all this, yes?"

"All that, yes," Kurt admitted.

"You are not so different," Lo'gnen pronounced. "Funny-looking and ruffless, but not so different. I think you should make pups with Julianatindal."

"*I* think we should talk of something else."

Lo'gnen yipped. "No, not so different. We will speak of other things. I see Ah'zzt has brought home a good catch."

Kurt saw the string of bugs slung from the approaching Ah'zzt's shoulder but declined to think of his catch as "good." His stomach shifted, giving its unfavorable opinion of the new topic.

"May I suggest a topic, friend Lo'gnen?" When the elder bobbed his head, Kurt took the opportunity to jump to something completely different, where Lo'gnen's recently aroused empathy might allow some headway in understanding the way the H'Kimm saw their place on Chugen. "I have thought upon what we spoke of earlier, and I would ask you a question. I ask you to speak your answer with all the truth you know."

Lo'gnen did not shift his gaze from the cook, who was jamming a trio of foot-long grubs onto a spit, but his attitude changed. Kurt thought that he detected a new wariness. So much for catching the old H'kimm off guard.

"I will tell you what I can, friend Kurtellicot."

"Each night when you speak to the pack by the fireside, I listen. Is it true that your tribe came from the stars?"

"Your tribe came from the stars."

The dreamy note in Lo'gnen's voice made Kurt wonder for a moment if he was only echoing Kurt's question. "Yes. But we had a ship. Technology." The H'kimm were living bare subsistence lives eked from the jungle. "We would be like you in a few generations if our people did not rescue us. Is that what happened to the H'kimm? Were your ancestors shipwrecked here?"

"We sit here happy in the comfort of our pack," Lo'gnen replied. "It is not right for me to speak of ancestors I did not know."

"But you tell the legends of the fall from the stars," Kurt pointed out.

"The stories we may tell."

"It is the story behind the story that I seek."

Lo'gnen's eyes glittered in their dark pits of masking fur. He said nothing, simply staring at Kurt.

"I need to know the truth behind the stories," Kurt said.

"Not all needs are met."

Frustrated, Kurt asked, "Are you saying the stories are only stories, that there is no truth to them?"

"The H'kimm have always walked this dirt," Lo'gnen replied. "It is our home. We make our lives here. We make our deaths here. This is your home now, too, yes?"

"We live here now, yes," Kurt admitted. "But Chugen is not our home. We have not always lived here. We came from somewhere else."

"Yes." The elder hesitated, adopting a slightly submissive head cant before continuing. "You asked for truth. Will you give truth? Did the gods send you and your Humans?"

"No gods sent us, friend Lo'gnen."

"This is truth?"

"It is truth as I know it, friend Lo'gnen."

The elder seemed to find Kurt's answer acceptable. "Men run through the jungle chasing truth. Some catch it, some do not. Sometimes truth catches them. It is a strange life, yes?"

Kurt couldn't deny that.

"I do not run and hunt as I once did," the elder continued. "A hard life has taught me much. Truth is as wily a prey as any. I sense that you know this little truth as well as I. We watch the stars wander. We feel the air turn. We know when the time of changes comes. It is the way of the world. Soon we will go to the Gathering as we must. I think this will be a strange season, one that the children will remember when they are as old as I am, if they should live so long. But it is not for me to speak their fate. All will be as it must be, and we live as the gods would have us live. No man can change this truth. You cannot change it, friend Kurtellicot." Lo'gnen sighed. "I am tired, friend Kurtellicot. My bones are old and weary, and I would sleep. We will talk again, yes?"

"Yes, friend Lo'gnen. We will talk again."

But not that day, as it was nearly time for the evening meal. The grubs proved less loathsome than Kurt had feared, actually reminding him of a seafood dish he'd had on Wayfarer Station. When the humans retired to their hut, Juli cornered him.

"I've been dying to ask you since this afternoon," she said excitedly, pointing at his gift from Lo'gnen. "What's that?"

"A trinket," he said, tugging it over his head.

He'd had to take it or risk offending the elder. Gifts and their giving were important to primitive cultures, and dealing properly with offered gifts was vital to interacting with such cultures.

"Did he make you a member of the tribe?"

"I'm not sure. I don't think so. I think it's more like a private society."

"A society? Like the Shandaltelkak Reed-weavers? Is it exclusively male? Are you going to have to go through an initiation rite? Do you—"

"I have no idea. And I have just as many questions as you, but right now I don't have any answers. I really don't know anything about it."

"I know one thing about it," she said slyly. "It's progress."

She sounded cheerful. Kurt wasn't. He didn't want to wear the token, but not wearing it would likely offend Lo'gnen. Kurt had all night to come up with an excuse for tucking the gift away, but if he couldn't, he would do what he needed to do. He could wear the thing in public if necessary, but he saw no need to wear it all the time; it wasn't part of *his* culture. Lo'gnen didn't need to know that Kurt took it off as soon as he was out of sight.

As he tossed it into the stowbox that held his personal gear, he said, "I don't think it's anything important."

Juli stared at him for a moment, almost challenging his

assertion, but he preempted whatever she was going to say by asking how her studies were going. One thing he had learned about Juli was that she was more willing to talk about their shared field than about almost anything else.

"Pretty well," she began. "There's a lot of similarity between H'kimm pack structure and that of one of the Yanellocyx cultures Carlsen studied. We don't have full documentation in our surviving data, but what's there makes for some intriguing comparisons. I think a lot of the cultural similarities arise because both are basically derived from carnivorous stock and both are forest-based societies."

She had a lot more to say on the subject, citing Carlsen's report, some of Kurt's own theories, a plethora of local observations, and her own ideas. Kurt was actually getting interested when Lockhart told them both to shut up and go to sleep.

Personally, Shanholz had agreed with Burke's objection to having him accompany the two highbrows into the jungle. Nothing anyone had seen suggested that there was any local wildlife big enough to worry a human. Of course, that didn't mean that there wasn't anything dangerous in the bush; plenty of worlds had exotic small things that could do for a man. But even highbrows could handle small things if they paid attention. Of course they weren't any good at paying attention to anything but whatever they had their noses in, leaving Shanholz to keep his eyes open for danger.

That, he supposed, was the reason behind Lockhart's order. For a Concordat civvie, she was pretty smart. Of course, that didn't mean she was always right. Extra eyes weren't being of special use out here. So far they hadn't encountered anything that couldn't be stepped over or kicked out of the way. And all of it bugs. Every time he looked up into the canopy, expecting to see a tremonkey or a squirrel or a novopposum or some other tree rodent, all he saw was bugs. Every rustling in the brush turned out to be not a bushdog or falsefox, but another kind of weird, overgrown bug. The damned jungle was infested with them.

The day's hike made him wonder if he'd made the right decision in agreeing to go along. Sure, the way sweat made Zandowski's coveralls hug her body was worth seeing, but the show that a sweaty Tindal could put on back in the village was nearly as good. And with a lot less bugs.

And back in the village he could keep a closer eye on Tindal for other reasons. The Pansie was hiding something. Almost every day he caught her sneaking off with her perscomp for a private session. Now, if she was going off with Ellicot, for whom she obviously had the hots, he could understand. But who needed a computer for that kind of job? She was doing something on the sly that she didn't want shared even with her fellow nationals.

*Spy stuff*, Shanholz guessed. *Definite bad news*.

What was he supposed to do about it? He wished he knew. Why did Mostel have to go and get himself killed? He would have known what to do. He was an officer, after all. Could you get a guy for posthumous dereliction of duty?

He'd figure something out. He had time.

But nothing came to him by the time they decided to set up camp. The night went easy enough, except for the fact that Zandowski decided to lay out her bedroll nearer to Burke than to him.

They weren't able to use Burke's powered bug screen—Lockhart had declared the batteries a strategic reserve—but the pylene netting and the smoker from the survival canister did almost as good a job. Shanholz had only a couple of bug bites in the morning, and a few dabs of medicated salve put them out of his mind.

It was midday, and the rare breaks in the canopy were shafting down near solid columns of light, when they approached the river. Shanholz could tell by the way the undergrowth was getting thicker.

Zandowski had stopped to play with some kind of mud nest built by fist-sized bugs, leaving Burke to press on. Shanholz hesitated for a minute, weighing his preference for hanging with Zandowski against Lockhart's expressed concern about danger coming from the river. He decided to follow Burke, on the theory that Lockhart might be right and he would get his ass chewed for letting anything happen to Burke. Shanholz still wanted to stay on the highbrows' good sides for the moment.

While Shanholz had hesitated Burke had gotten out of sight. He wasn't hard to follow, though. When Shanholz spotted him, Burke was fussing with his recorder; he'd seen something that he wanted to put in a pic. Looking to see what, Shanholz caught a glimpse of something familiar moving beyond the undergrowth that walled the riverbank. Could it really be what he thought it was?

He listened, wishing he had a helmet with an amplifier. As some trick of the forest brought him the familiar drone, he almost laughed out loud—this was one of the few places where such a thing would look more at home than not. But it was just as well he kept quiet. Burke had caught the motion, too, and was moving forward for a better look.

That could be a problem. Keeping his eyes on Burke, Shanholz slipped the latch on his holster.

The highbrow strained, trying to make out the flitting shape that Shanholz had already identified. Burke was moving through the trees and getting closer to the river edge. As he walked, he held his recorder ready. Like a man laying an ambush, he selected a tree for cover and leaned against it; from there he had a good line of sight to a clear patches in the foliage through which glints of water could be seen.

Slipping his weapon free, Shanholz stalked Burke. He moved silently behind the oblivious highbrow and was glad that Zandowski was too busy to pay attention to what the two men were doing. When Burke took up his position, Shanholz selected one of his own that offered a clear view of both Burke's tree and the brush at the river's edge.

Shanholz had barely taken up his position when unexpected motion in the corner of his eye distracted him. He tracked it. Something was moving, scuttling and freezing as it made its way down the tree against which Burke was leaning. This new thing was nearly two meters long, half of which was whippy, segmented tail that ended in a thin stiletto of a wetly glistening spine. This something also had a battery of mandibles, and two pair of overdeveloped pincers, and it looked as if it was stalking its lunch.

Another motion distracted Shanholz. A shape had appeared, hanging in the still air over the river where the brush dipped low. Burke, oblivious to the creature sneaking down the bole toward him, shifted against the tree, trying to train his recorder on the elusive shape now hovering in the gap.

It was time to act.

*Ah*, Rafe thought. *Finally.*

Steadying himself against the tree, he watched the deep shadows that the overhanging trees threw across the water and waited for the darting form of his quarry to emerge. It teased him, almost flitting into the sunshine, then pulling back, over and over. It coursed the water like a Terran dragonfly, but unlike a dragonfly, it didn't seem to be interested in any of the smaller pseudo-insects sharing the river's airspace with it.

*Come on, you evasive little bastard. I'm ready for you now.*

The scudding shape shifted direction, turning on a course that would take it into the light.

"I would move very carefully if I were you, Mr. Burke."

Rafe started at Shanholz's voice; his finger triggered the recorder.

The whining shriek of a blaser cut the still jungle air.

Rafe's bladder let go. Wetness spattered him and he began to fall, fearing the terrifying non-pain of a fatal wound.

*That treacherous bastard Shanholz had shot him!*

Something heavy slammed into Rafe's shoulder. Ribbons of fire burned across his skin. *That* pain he felt.

*The other must be worse!*

The spongy ground squelched as he hit. The weight rolled from his shoulder as a multilegged, segmented body sprawled by his side. A long, jointed tail coiled and uncoiled, stabbing its caudal spine into the earth near his face.

Shanholz's boot came down, stamping on the spasming tail and pinning it. As he did, something viscous and purple squirted along the wickedly pointed spine, spraying away in sparkling droplets. Rafe's shocked eyes followed the liquid in its arc until it struck spattering against a broad-leafed bush. Brown spots blossomed on the leaves where the drops had fallen.

Looking at the dead arthropodoid, Rafe knew that he had not been shot. Shanholz had used his weapon on this creature. Rafe hadn't even seen the beast until after it was hit. He'd been damned lucky.

Shakily, with Shanholz's help, he got to his feet. He had to turn away as his lunch came rushing up his throat. His spew had no effect on the broad-leafed bush. Shanholz watched, saying nothing.

Rafe didn't want to think about how close he'd come to dying. He shut the thoughts away, pulling his best dispassionate scientist manner onto himself like armor.

"It looked like he wanted you for lunch," Shanholz said.

"Nonsense," Rafe said as he forced himself to crouch and examine the corpse. Shanholz's shot had nearly cut the creature in two, exposing energy-seared innards. "And it's a her, by the way. See the egg clusters, here under the outer keratinous layer of the abdomen. But as to taking me for lunch, all you have to do is look at the pedipalpate pincers. Admittedly they look formidable, but they're not built to hold prey much more than twice this critter's mass. And the mandibles are built for cracking the sorts of keratinous shells real lunches come packed in around here." Rafe pried back the upper pair. "See here. These feeder peripalps are what our bad girl here uses for shredding soft stuff like flesh. No, she's not built for hunting people."

"What about the stinger? I've seen shorter combat knives."

"Dangerous, to be sure, but not designed for use against us. It *could* cause a serious wound," Rafe admitted, shivering at the thought of how close he had come to having that dark dagger plunged into him. "The toxin might or might not prove to be lethal, and the spine alone would have been unpleasant at the least, but she wasn't hunting me."

"It *was* coming for you."

"Possibly. If so, I'd guess that I must have violated her territory. Ambush hunters like this are often aggressively territorial, even against things they couldn't possibly kill. Still, I don't think I would have liked having her serve the eviction notice with that spine. You did me a service, Shanholz. I never thought I'd say that to a Leaguer." Rafe held out his hand. It felt strange, but if Shanholz had been the sort of man Rafe had always imagined all Leaguer marts to be, he would have just stood there and let the bug do for Rafe. He hadn't. He'd been a real man and he deserved Rafe's thanks. "Thank you."

Shanholz was strong and he tried for a crush when their hands gripped. Rafe resisted, but not strongly enough to win the macho test, just enough to show that he was no wimp.

"You're welcome, Professor," Shanholz said, smiling at his victory. "Just what were you chasing, that you let that spine-tailed bastard sneak up on you?"

"It was a flier, as big or bigger than the ambusher. By far the biggest I've seen here. I never did get a good look at it. It was just coming out of the shadows over the river when you called to me. Did you see it?"

Shanholz shook his head. "Sorry, Professor. I didn't see nothing. I had my eyes on the spine-tailed bug."

Rafe really hadn't expected otherwise. "Oh, well. I'm sure that there'll be other opportunities. After all, we have the rest of our lives here."

Just then Zandowski burst through the trees, shouting questions. After hearing what had happened and seeing the ambusher, she threw herself into Rafe's arms, babbling about how glad she was that he was all right.

*Well, well,* Rafe thought. *It seems that I've misjudged more than one person on this field trip. Things are looking up indeed.*

# 17

## IDL DEFENSE SECTOR 31-ORANGE
## TARSUS STATION — KANSIAS TRANSIT CORRIDOR

The transit corridor was a wilderness route, an unavoidable and dull part of the Tarsus Station–Kansias route. At standard drive velocity, it took thirty days of real space time between the inbound transit point from Tarsus and the outbound to Kansias. Thirty days of sliding through the cold void of the outer reaches of a binary star system so empty that the explorers who had charted the route hadn't even bothered to name it, but simply left its designation as equally cold and empty navigational coordinates. No one since had disputed their decision.

Sitting in the command couch of IDL *Shaka* and contemplating the rolling blackness of the forward display screen, Major Anne Ryan considered doing so, but the vast expanse of nothingness inspired nothing but nothingness. She let the impulse pass. It really didn't matter. She might be the godlike commander of IDL *Shaka*, a mighty ship of the plane of the League MilForce, but it was a temporary berth. Anything Ryan did as commander would also be temporary.

Temporary things bothered her. As an engineer, she preferred that the things she touched have some staying power. There were things about *Shaka*'s running order she'd prefer to be different, and knowing that anything she changed would be subject to immediate rearrangement by *Shaka*'s permanent commander frustrated her. She hated wasted work, and what would it be but wasted work were she to fine tune things to her satisfaction? She'd be glad to see the hind end of this posting.

She had been thrust into the commander's chair, an ostensible reward for getting *Shaka* out of the Remor ambush at Grenwold that had cost the ship every officer senior to Ryan. Such rewards she could live without. Ryan was an engineering officer and satisfied with it. Promotion was all well and good as long as it got her better, more prestigious, and more challenging engineering berths, but she was more than happy to leave the big chair to those who wanted it. She'd do her duty, naturally, which just now was overseeing the recently repaired *Shaka* as she made the milk run to Kansias. Once there *Shaka*'s real commander and the replacement crew would come aboard. With her duty done, Ryan could go back to an engineering berth, where she could oversee something more to her taste, such as getting *Shaka*'s systems in fine tune and integrating all of the new systems and equipment they'd be taking on at Kansias. *That* was the sort of job that had a legacy. The best chair-sitter in all the fleets couldn't do a damn thing if her ship didn't perform, and a ship wouldn't perform without a good engineer.

"Commander?"

Captain Reeve's voice interrupted her reverie. Reeve was her executive officer, a post he'd retain under *Shaka*'s new commander. She was glad to have him. He was a good officer, seasoned enough to catch most of the things that Ryan missed with regard to ship handling. When he brought something to her attention, it was something out of the routine.

"Detection reports a dark mass two hundred kay klicks off the port bow, thirty kay up planar," Reeve announced. "It's big and it isn't under power. The only motion is a slight planar drift."

"No emissions?"

"Nothing directed. We're still too far out to pick up internals."

"Curious."

"Aye, Commander."

The nav buoy had reported the corridor free of debris. An unreported mass was a danger to navigation, and a commander's duty included reporting any hazards. Clearly someone hadn't done their duty. Ryan wasn't going to compound the failure. "Mr. Reeve, log everything we've got on it and send it out to the navigation buoy. See if you can get optical on it. We'll do an update as we pass. For now, give me a refined reading on the mass. I want to see just how blind the last ship through here was."

"Will do, Commander," Reeve said as he turned to give the necessary orders. He went to the detection station to watch the numbers roll in.

"Jesus Christ!"

Reeve's exclamation was totally unprofessional, but when the reading came up on Ryan's repeater, she felt like doing the same. Ten billion tonnes! The damned thing was a planetoid! Given its low velocity, there hadn't been time for it to drift into the transit corridor since the last ship went through. How could anyone be so blind as to miss something that big?

There was only one reasonable answer: the thing *hadn't been there*.

And *that* led to only one other conclusion: the dark mass was a ship. No Human had ever built a ship so huge. It had to be Remor.

"Battle stations!" she ordered.

Reeve gave the same order only a nanosecond behind her.

*Shaka*'s understrength crew jumped to as the klaxon

sounded. Weapons systems armed and status boards came live. From the moment the alarm was sounded, *Shaka's* computers were ready to receive orders from Ryan's couch, but battles weren't fought by commanders and their computers; not successful battles, anyhow. Nervously watching the screens, Ryan waited. In 7.2 seconds, human overwatch was confirmed on all critical systems. In another 34.3, all stations reported manned. *Shaka* was as ready as she could be.

Orange sector regulations didn't require command crew to serve their shifts in vacuum suits. Ryan hadn't bothered getting into the uncomfortable harness—what was the point on a milk run? Now a rating brought her a suit and at Reeve's nod that he had con-and-command active on his couch, she climbed in. As she dressed, she was acutely aware that her bridge crew sat their stations unsuited. If there was time, their relief, once suited themselves, would bring suits for the men and women who sat in their places without a hope if the bridge was holed.

Once she was suited and back in her chair, Reeve returned control to her and left the bridge to get his own suit. She watched the boards and looked for a sign that the enemy was reacting.

Nothing.

Why did the hulk out there lie so silent and apparently unaware of their presence? A Human ship would have been accelerating to gain maneuverability. Could *Shaka* possibly be undetected? Could all the saints and martyrs have interceded and gifted them with the unthinkable: a Remor hulk that was truly a hulk, a derelict? Signals showed low-level electromagnetic activity, dashing that hope. Ryan liked problems, but she didn't like no-win dilemmas. What could they do? They were just past the halfway point of the corridor. With a straightline run, it would be thirteen days before they could jump outsystem. If the enemy showed interest in them, *Shaka* would have to fight. Unfortunately, *Shaka* was a gnat compared to that ship out there.

Their only hope for survival lay in the fact that no Remor hulk had ever been reported to fire on a Human ship unless the Human fired first. A headstrong chair jockey might want to start the fight for the glory of it, but Ryan wasn't about to start a fight she had no hope of winning.

"Mr. Reeve, find me a course down-planar that will give us some room to slide around our dark friend out there."

"Aye, Commander. How much time slip do you want on reaching the jump point?"

A tough call. The more days they added to their transit, the further they could stay from the mass, but that added just as many days to the time that *Shaka* spent insystem with what could well be an enemy lying doggo and waiting until *Shaka* was committed. If Ryan cut it close and that was an active hostile out there, they might never reach the jump point. No reasonable course would let them pass the dark mass totally outside its theoretical attack envelope. Too cautious an approach would leave her looking awfully foolish if they were reacting to shadows. She hated making compromises and betting lives on them. That, she guessed, was why she didn't want the big chair.

But here and now, she had it. She made her decision. "If you can give me something that won't add much more than five days, I'll be satisfied, Mr. Reeve."

In a few minutes he was back with several choices. She rejected every one that called for immediate acceleration beyond that necessary to change heading. Drive activity could attract unwanted attention. Ryan selected one that kept them in the attack zone longer than the others but offered more reasonable escape vectors should things go bad. She had several of his other recommendations laid in as alternates, with update feeds to allow instant switch-offs.

The hours ticked slowly by as they moved crabwise past the suspected enemy. Unwilling to utilize active methods, Ryan had *Shaka*'s scanners straining to pull in any passive signals. For a day they heard nothing but an occasional burst of static more likely random noise than Remor commo. Optical finally located the object, confirming that its shape was not that of a typical extraplanetary body. But whatever was out there didn't look like any Remor ship logged in the League's databanks, either. They still had a mystery on their hands.

Then, on the second day after they detected the mass, without warning, the commo bands flooded with static of a familiar and terrifying sort: Remor communication.

As Ryan triggered the return to full alert, Warrant Officer Satsumoto reported from the detection console, "We're being scanned."

"Return the favor, Mr. Satsumoto." Clearly the enemy knew they were present; there was no more need for sneaking around. They might as well learn all they could about their opponent.

Just as Ryan began to give the order to increase speed, the bridge lights flared into brilliance, flickered like strobes, and went down. Emergency lighting came on slowly, glowing with a faint hint of the usual amber strength.

Surprisingly, *Shaka* remained stable. She hadn't been hit.

"What the—"

"EM scanners fritzed. Recalibrating."

"No strike. Repeat, we have not received a strike."

"Optical down. Rerouting."

With the scanners down *Shaka* was blind. "What's happening, Mr. Reeve?"

"I believe . . ." Reeve cut himself off and ran from console to console until he found a working instrument. "Yes, it is. Gross mass detection shows the enemy capital ship is gone. She has jumped."

Could it be so easy?

As if in answer to her question, *Shaka*'s lights came back up. The ship's intercom buzzed with queries, reports, and chatter. Ryan took stock of what she could. *Shaka* seemed unhurt. System after system was coming back on-line. The Remor hulk was gone and *Shaka* was still here.

But as the detectors came back up, detection reported that the hulk hadn't left them alone.

"Multiple contacts on closing vectors. Seven destroyer mass. Nineteen smaller craft."

Ryan checked the vectors. The enemy vessels were divided into three wings, closing on three separate vectors, none of which cut *Shaka* off from the straightline to the jump point. That meant *Shaka* had a chance. "Stretch our legs, Mr. Reeve. Best speed toward the outsystem transit."

"Will do, Commander. Recommend taking the governors off, ma'am."

"Do it. Captain Gaddi will scream like hell about it, but tell him I said to do it."

"Will do, Commander."

Ryan watched the plot. The Remor ships burning hard for them were a mixed lot. The computers were bringing up probabilities on their classifications and estimates of their capabilities. It wasn't looking good. The destroyers alone outmassed *Shaka* nearly three to one. But combat power was more than just bulk. *Shaka*'s concentrated mass meant she had concentrated, controlled firepower, more than enough to bloody the pursuit force. The Remor, if true to form, would not coordinate their attacks well, and *Shaka* might survive the first round. Then if they were very, very lucky, and if the enemy decided not to press, *Shaka* just might escape.

But first they had to survive the initial combat.

"Have you had time to assess their ECM, Ms. Radek?" Ryan asked the weapons officer.

"I can give you hits, Commander."

"Very well. Let's send them some birds. Target the destroyers in the nearest wing and send them to hell."

"Will do, Commander."

*Shaka* shuddered as the salvo launched. Six nuclear-tipped missiles streaked toward their targets, guided by the best agents and warded by the best ECM that MilForce could provide. All six wouldn't have impressed the enemy hulk, but a good hit from just one would leave an enemy destroyer a floating wreck.

"Incoming missiles from the enemy's lead wing," Satsumoto announced. "Eight tracks, no, nine."

"Ready antimissiles," Reeve ordered.

Because they were coming down on closing targets, *Shaka*'s missiles would be the first to resolve. Time stretched on the bridge, seeming to move far more slowly than the countdown clock on the weapons console said it did.

"Missiles two and five intercepted," Radek reported. "All other birds with on-time detonations."

"Scan?" Ryan snapped.

"Two enemy destroyers in wing one no longer register. Third one trailing atmosphere, but still coming on. Wing one escorts now number . . . five."

That meant they'd taken down three.

"Antimissiles away." Reeve's voice was calm, calmer

than Ryan thought hers sounded. "Scan, report intercepts."

He'd remembered to order the launch she'd forgotten. Ryan watched the plots. Strings of yellow stretched out to meet incoming strings of red.

"Scratch six," the scanner chief reported. "Three remaining. New launches from the wing one survivors. Launches from wing two."

"Long-range solution on the three incoming," Ryan ordered. "Compute for simultaneous solution."

Reeve raised an eyebrow, but acknowledged. Ryan had ordered a more difficult resolution to the incoming missiles than standard doctrine called for, in the hope that seeing all of their first attack wave vaporized with apparent ease might demoralize the Remor—or at least get them to overestimate *Shaka*'s capabilities. It was a gamble, but if it failed they still had a chance for close-in defense. But before the gunners completed their input and the point defense weapons could open fire, the scanner chief swore and shouted, "Enemy missile tracks are splitting!"

"Those aren't missiles," Reeve said in a dead monotone. "They're *Typhoons*."

*Typhoons* were enemy interface craft. There had been no reports of the enemy using them as attack craft anywhere save Sector Two, nearly all the way across Human space, but here they were nonetheless, having ridden booster rockets to close with *Shaka*. Individually they were less of a threat than a single capital missile, but they flew in fours, and unlike a missile that missed its attack run, they could come back. Thank God they'd caught six of them before they'd split. A dozen *Typhoons* would press *Shaka*'s point defense, but she might handle them without too high a cost. Three dozen would have been doom.

With more following this wave, *Shaka* could well meet her doom anyway. Ryan could hear Reeve giving the necessary orders to deal with the *Typhoons* while she gave her attention to *Shaka*'s second missile spread. More enemy launches appeared on the plot. The ship shuddered as the surviving *Typhoons* hammered at her. The bridge lights failed again. Surrounded by the controlled frenzy of the amber-lit bridge, Ryan watched *Shaka*'s chances fade. She touched the command stud that cloned copies of the ship's log, tucked them into a bevy of tiny message torpedoes, and launched the torps on a random, bewildering array of courses. With luck one of them would get through to Strat-Com. That done, she gave her full attention to running the faltering *Shaka*.

The enemy might have them, but before she was done, by God, they'd know they'd been in a fight!

## IDL DEFENSE SECTOR 32-RED
## TARSUS STATION

There were not many who would describe Christoph Stone—a man in charge of entire fleets of starships and armies of ground troops—as helpless, but that was the way he felt. It was a feeling that had grown more familiar to him over the years as he had climbed in rank, each grade removing him further from the direct control of his forces in battle. Intellectually he knew that his effect on a battle was greater than ever, but sitting in a command center, isolated from the noise, stink, and shock of battle, left him feeling removed from reality, information deprived, unable to affect events, isolated, and ultimately helpless.

It was a falsehood, of course, a *ruse de guerre* employed by fate. With all the opportunities that he'd had to experience it, he should be able to see through the ruse easily, but every time he set fleets and armies to moving, that powerless feeling came back to him full force. *If only you could be on the scene*, a seductive voice whispered in his head. *If only you could have first-hand knowledge of what was going on, things would be better.*

Of course, the voice never said *how* things would be better. How could it? It was only his own doubt. It knew no more than he did. Less, actually. He knew he was where he needed to be.

Right now he needed to be on Tarsus Station, overseeing the deployment of forces to meet the renewed enemy invasion. The station's battle center, in which he sat, offered the best command and control system that Humankind could make. From it, a sector commander could coordinate his forces using the best intelligence available. The computer power available to him, and the specialists and analysts who manned those machines, were among the best in Human space. It was a sector commander's job to take advantage of the people and the technology in the best way possible—no matter how much he would prefer to be leading a fleet in battle with the enemy.

Given that they were in the early phase of an enemy incursion, the sector commander needed to be in his battle center, taking in all the information he could about the situation. This was a time for planning, for gaining understanding, and for preparing. That was best done within the cone of sound control around the sector commander's chair, where all the station's intelligence resources were available at the touch of a console and all of the commander's advisory specialists were within call.

Duty didn't often let one choose the chair in which one sat. Duty had put him in the sector commander's chair, and an Eridani did his duty.

Action would come.

Then, maybe, a sector commander's duty might take him elsewhere. Until such time, Stone would sit in his chair and do his duty. He would make sure that his sector was ready to resist and repel the invading enemy.

So far enemy forces had only appeared in the Grenwold System. Their presence upgraded the sector to Code Red, empowering him, among other things, to concentrate fleets and call in reinforcements from unthreatened sectors. In anticipation of a hard fight on Grenwold, he'd done so. Curiously the enemy seemed disinclined to defend their incursion into his district and had made no effort to reinforce their landing on Grenwold. The ongoing planetary campaign was an anomaly in the war with the Remor, a strange encounter among strange encounters with the enigmatic enemy. But with his forces eliminating all the enemy they encountered on and around Grenwold, he was not about to complain. Soon, he expected, he would be able to declare the battle of Grenwold over, a victory for embattled Humanity. That alone was a prize in the long, demoralizing war, but Grenwold had provided more than just a victory in arms; it had given the League the best evidence yet of the enemy's nature.

It was a good day for the League, and for Humanity.

And a very good day for him, since the Grenwold evidence validated Major Ersch's radical and somewhat unorthodox Operation Chameleon, banishing Stone's last doubts about the plan. Now he could see that there was no need to question the rightness of the operation. Humankind needed what would come out of a successful operation. Unfortunately, as events had turned out, operations in the Chugen System had not gone as well as in Grenwold System. He logged a note to see if anything could be done to expedite Chameleon.

There were a million other details to check, oversee, confirm, or deny. Buoyed by the general positive trend of operations, he worked his way through them until an update from the base at Nus clouded his mood. The most recent courier from Nus reported that Task Forces Lull and Zang had arrived; that was good news. Their layover for refitting and resupply was estimated at four standard days; not good, but not bad either. What piqued his ire was a note from General Lull sending his regards and requesting confirmation of his change in orders. Lull would know that the transit time for such a confirmation would delay his task force's scheduled departure from Nus, just as he knew Stone was required to make the confirmation if requested. What was he playing at? This was no time for petty jurisdictional disputes. Stone dictated Lull's confirmation and added an order—in the form of a request, of course—for the general to report to him at once when his ship reached Tarsus Station.

Face-to-face was the way to handle Lull.

He worked through more routine material, but he never regained his equanimity. Instead, his mood darkened. His unease came from no source that he could identify, but slowly he began to feel that something wasn't right in his sector.

The enemy had appeared on Grenwold and was being defeated with relative ease. Why hadn't they supported their forces on the planet? Why hadn't they appeared in neighboring systems? Their renowned unpredictability seemed an inadequate answer. Sifting through situation reports from across his sector, Stone began to get the impression that he ought to be waiting for the other shoe to drop.

Could Grenwold have been only a probe, to be abandoned when an alert and responsive League military showed up and bloodied the enemy's nose? Somehow he didn't think it could be that simple. Somewhere, the hammer was poised to fall.

He noticed Chip Hollister approaching his chair. From

Chip's grim face, Stone guessed he might be about to learn where.

"Commander, a message torp just came in on boost from the Kansias run," his executive officer said as he passed the boundary of the sonic curtain. "I think you ought to see what it was carrying."

# 18

**CHUGEN SYSTEM**
**CHUGEN IV**

Traipsing through the jungle with the H'kimm foragers was a wonderful experience for a socioxenologist and an especially poignant one for Juliana. The local ecosystem had the same feel as the one in which she'd done her graduate and postgraduate work—she half expected to see a rotectadeer emerge from the sparse understory, or hear a chektor screeching in the canopy. As a scientist she knew that the similarities were superficial, but her heart kept trying to tell her than this wasn't Chugen IV, but Mimakron. *But all you have to do is look around*, she told herself. *Really look.* Everywhere there were new sights, sounds, and smells to experience.

Ah'zzt appeared, dark nose twitching. With one hand the senior hunter motioned to her to move forward, while with the other he gripped his snout in the H'kimm signal for silence. Clearly he had spotted prey. All around her the slender H'kimm youths of the foraging party slipped through the brush with nary a sound. She did her best to follow. Away from their village the H'kimm seemed an integral part of their primitive world, moving through the brush with a ghostly ease that her best efforts could not approach.

Did she need any clearer reminder that the H'kimm were not the Shandaltelkak Association Mimaks that she had studied for so many years? A Shandaltelkak food drive was a noisy, clumsy operation compared to this quiet, focused raid to gather the forest's juicier tidbits.

A thrashing in the brush ahead told her that the H'kimm had pounced on their prey. By the time she reached the spot, the prey—a waist-high mound of articulated armor plates, and another reminder that this wasn't the Shandaltelkak Association's forest domain—was subdued; its myriad legs waved helplessly as it rocked on its back. The hunters were already beginning to remove those legs. Ah'zzt called the arthropodiform a *sinter*, and Juliana added the name to her growing catalog of fauna and flora.

It seemed that everything she'd seen on this trip was new. The H'kimm seemed to know every plant and animal, and had a dozen uses for each. She marveled at the harmony between them and the jungle. It was pure joy to share this part of their lives. Juliana wished Kurt were with her to witness the wonder and discovery.

But Kurt had not been interested in coming along. He'd said that with Rafe and Zandowski still away, somebody had to stay in the village to look after Lockhart and Singh. As if Langdorf didn't exist, or wasn't able to do it! Kurt just didn't want to leave the village, even if it meant spending time with her.

She was a little hurt by that, but not much. *It isn't me*, she told herself. *There are a hundred reasons for him to stay.* But she couldn't think of even one that she could be sure was his.

Was he afraid, as she was, that the Remor could come at any time? Did he want, as she did, to spend as much time as possible doing what they had come here to do? Was he, like her, using his work to drive the Remor out of his consciousness?

*Don't be foolish*, she chided herself.

To Kurt the Remor threat was unimportant. He was just following his own advice for socioxenologists, letting each day unfold as it would and taking from it what it offered. He was fitting himself to the rhythms of their subjects; since Kurt had bonded with Lo'gnen, he was following the rhythms of the sedentary elder. It wasn't that Kurt didn't want to spend time in her company; it was just that he was, as she knew she was sometimes, focused totally on his work. And her absence from the village probably helped that work, giving him more time alone with Lo'gnen.

She felt a twinge of jealousy over Kurt's rapport with Lo'gnen. At the same time, she felt guilty about it. How could she deny Kurt a relationship that he so obviously enjoyed? What did it matter that she wasn't a part of it? Lo'gnen tried to be polite about it, but she knew that the old H'kimm was uncomfortable around her. Kurt tried to be polite about it, too, but they both knew that Kurt got more out of the H'kimm elder when she wasn't around. She didn't understand why—all other observed H'kimm interactions told her that it wasn't just a male-female separation thing—but she knew that she had to accept it.

The important thing was that Kurt was happy. He was coming alive while working with the H'kimm. He laughed and smiled almost daily now, a welcome improvement. Though he still paid more attention to the work than to her, she was satisfied. Working so closely together, they couldn't help but grow closer. If the Remor were content with isolating the world from galactic society, then she and he were going to be on-planet for a long time. There would be time.

For now they had their discoveries to share, gloating over the daily increase in their understanding of the H'kimm. They were sharing everything they learned. *Well, almost everything,* she thought with a pang of guilt. She was continuing to keep the reports she filed with the Alsion analog on her computer a secret. Did she really need to maintain that secrecy? *No, not really*, she supposed. *Still* . . . The analog was a link to Alsion, to the Combine, and to the greater sphere of humanity. Dealing with the analog as she had—including maintaining its secret—was a way of holding on to a link to what they had lost, and a way of maintaining hope that the loss was not permanent. Pointless, possibly, but comforting in a small way.

The capture of the *sinter* gave the foraging party what it needed, and Ah'zzt, as was his way, faded into the forest. The hunter was a rarity among the H'kimm: a loner. Though honored by his pack-mates for his skill and knowledge of the jungle, he was simultaneously treated as something of a pariah. On his visits to the village he was welcomed cheerfully at some activities but spurned at others. His treatment was an aspect of H'kimm social behavior that she didn't yet understand.

The return to the village was more direct and noisier than the trip out. Her companions were happy, pleased with their kill. Juliana found herself caught up in their mood, going so far as to attempt joining their song. The H'kimm made jokes about her singing, but seemed pleased that she tried.

Her good mood faded when, through the screening trees, she saw that she and her group were not the only ones rejoining the pack tonight. Rafe, Zandowski, and Shanholz were moving along a game trail that passed near the village.

The last week or so had been peaceful, almost idyllic. Juliana realized what a large component of her lightheartedness had been: Rafe had not been around to bitch and to sneer and snort at Kurt.

It was clear that Rafe was unhappy. She would have thought that access to a virgin world like Chugen IV was an ecologist's dream, that he would have been as pleased about the study opportunities all around them as she was about working with the H'kimm, but not Rafe! He complained nearly constantly about the primitive conditions, reminding her and informing everyone around that he was the sort of person who didn't like personal discomfort. And then there were his gripes about the loss of his equipment—as if his eyes and his brain weren't enough—making her realize just how dependent he'd become on the tools of modern science. Set against the frantic world of galactic society, Rafe didn't seem so out of place, but here among the serenity of the forest and the simplicity of village life, he was a beacon of discontent. Why couldn't he be more like Kurt, whose easy adaptability was a model for them all?

But Rafe was Rafe, an immutable island of attitude and self-centeredness. His smile upon seeing her turned to a frown when he took in her H'kimm companions. The H'kimm, if they noticed, ignored his sour face and happily made the two expeditions one for the last leg of the trek back to the village. To make conversation, Juliana asked if they'd found anything interesting on their field trip. Rafe snorted derisively.

"Only if you like Chugen's version of insects and arthropods," he said.

"Actually we did see some inter—" Zandowski began, but Rafe cut her off.

"We might as well be back in the Carboniferous of Old Earth. Except for your Chugeni friends, there's nothing even vaguely mammaliform. If they're native to this pestiferous planet, I'll marry one of them."

"I don't think any of them would have you," Juliana told him.

"Fine. Who wants to sleep with the enemy anyway?" he shot back.

"You can't me—"

He didn't let her finish. "They sure as hell aren't native."

"We suspected that," Juliana said, although she had been hoping that he would find some evidence to the contrary. "After all, the Committee's interest in this project was based on similarities between the space-visible constructs on this world and those on Cassuells Home."

"Are you saying that your authorities believe that we have Cassuells here?" Zandowski shook her head at Juliana's shrug. "They are jumping to conclusions, if that's what they believe. There is undoubted strong phenotypical parallelism, but without proper genetic comparisons, no one can say anything definite about the relationship of the two species."

"Agreed." Juliana was glad to get some support. "Believe me, I'm not suggesting that they're the same."

"Because you won't face facts," Rafe accused, sweeping his glare across both women. "Convergent evolution is one thing, but convergent construction techniques? Come on!"

Juliana tried to keep calm. "I know there are similarities in the constructs, but there are ways to explain that, too. Your supposed similarities could be coincidences of structural engineering, properties of matter, and universal geometry. Nobody knows yet, because no one has examined the Chugen structures."

"And nobody is likely to, since the Remor are keeping everyone away from their toys." Rafe sneered at the H'kimm trekking along with them. "And away from their children."

"You can't mean that." Juliana was appalled to find Rafe taking the Leaguer view. "We may find out that the Cassuells and the H'kimm derive from the same stock, but that doesn't make them Remor."

"Doesn't it?"

Why was he being so obstinate? "Kurt doesn't think there is *any* basis for linking the H'kimm to the Remor."

"No, of course *he* doesn't," Rafe burst out. "*He* didn't think that the Cassuells were Remor, either. Just look at *him*! He spends more time with the weasels than with any of us humans. That damned gray-furred elder treats Ellicot more like his own son than like an alien from another world."

Juliana tried to cool Rafe's anger with hard facts. "Adoptive behavior by the indigenes is not unusual in situations like this."

"Screw the indigenes! I'm talking about Ellicot. *He's* the one doing the adopting! All you've got to do is look at him. He's even started to wear the local jewelry."

"That's a—"

"I don't care what you call it. It's a sign of things to come. Mark my words. He's going native, just like he did before."

"He's doing what he came here to do," Juliana declared.

Rafe snorted. "Defend him if you want to, but I'm telling you that you're worried about the wrong side. With Ellicot going delusional, it's ourselves we've got to watch out for. He'll put the damned natives ahead of us, like he did before. Well, he's got a surprise coming this time. I'm watching him. When he steps out of line, when he trades us for them, I'll be ready. *I'm* not going to die meekly! I swear to God that he won't get away with it this time."

"I don't think *Kurt's* the delusional one." Juliana knew she didn't have a prayer of stopping his rant unless she understood what had set it off. "What *are* you talking about?"

"You never mind what I'm talking about!" Rafe stomped ahead, slamming into Shanholz and knocking him down as he tried to pass the Leaguer on the narrow trail. Shanholz's unnecessary apologies were swamped in a torrent of invective from Rafe. Heedless of Zandowski's plea that he not get too far ahead, Rafe stormed off.

Juliana was just as glad to see him go.

She noticed Shanholz brushing himself off and looking perplexedly after the disappearing Rafe. The Leaguer hadn't done anything wrong and still he had been burned by Rafe's anger.

*Odd*, she thought, *to feel sympathy for a Leaguer*. But Shanholz wasn't just a stereotype anymore, he was a real person, with a personality, likes and dislikes, and feelings to be hurt.

"He's really not so bad," she said, defending Rafe while helping Shanholz up.

He gave her a half smile. "Don't worry, Professor. He reminds me of a drill sergeant I had in flight school. He's just a little self-important, is all. Do you think he could be right about Professor Ellicot? About his going native, I mean."

*Could he?* "Professor Ellicot had some trouble before, but he's cured of that. He's fine. His interaction with the H'kimm is perfectly normal."

Shanholz looked thoughtful, and a little unhappy, but he nodded. "Whatever you say, ma'am. Shall I take point again?"

At Juliana's nod, he did. It wasn't long before they reached the village.

It hadn't been easy for Shanholz to conceal his eagerness for Burke and Zandowski to finish their puttering. He had thought about just dumping them in the jungle, but had decided that such a course would be too suspicious. And it might not even be the right move. Lacking any better idea of what he ought to do, he had decided that for the moment the best thing was to return to the village. Once he was shed of his responsibility to shepherd the highbrows, he could work out his next steps.

He'd been as helpful as he could be, in the hope of speeding his charges along. If his increased aid had raised suspicions, he hadn't seen them. The two highbrows had seemed to think he was just warming up to them, like they were old drinking buddies. That might be something he could use. Good buddies helped each other out, didn't they? He'd offered to handle developing the pics that the highbrows had shot on the trip and, against his expectations, they'd bought into it. He supposed that he shouldn't have been surprised; why do flunky work when you have a flunky who is not only willing but asking to do it?

His timing had been good, for within the hour they had encountered Professor Tindal and some native foragers. In short order Burke and Tindal were going at it again, till finally Burke stormed off. Even after a cooling-off time, Shanholz suspected, Burke wouldn't be in any mood to be granting favors.

When they finally made it back to the village, both expeditions were called in to report their findings. Zandowski prodded Burke into telling the tale of his narrow escape. The center stage made Burke slough off Lockhart's "I told you so's" about insisting that Shanholz accompany them. Shanholz's not making a big deal of it helped, especially when he urged Burke to detail what he'd observed of the critter. The talk shifted to the highbrows' discoveries. Shanholz, like a good little flunky, went off to get his "work" done.

The developer was set up in the communal hut along with most of the highbrows' scientific gear. It was never a private place, but only the comatose Singh was there when Shanholz set to work. As a precaution, he managed to angle to the workstation's screen so that only he could see what came up. Singh might not be coherent, but better safe than sorry. And if anyone came in before Shanholz finished, he would have a moment to conceal what he was doing.

Shanholz couldn't stop the program from printing out the whole sequence, but he monitored it, waiting for the one he wanted. When it finally came up, it revealed that his suspicions about the riverside flier had been right. Freezing the developer program, he did a little work on the image before allowing the machine to proceed. When he removed the hard copies from the machine, one of them just happened to end up in his pocket. The rest went into a neat stack on the table.

Burke came in as Shanholz was working on the last batch of unimportant pics. Cranky as usual, but not bothering to make any anti-League wisecracks, the Pansie headed straight for the pile of finished pics. He shuffled through them twice before he complained.

"Where's the shot I took down by the river?"

Shanholz heard the singular and knew which one Burke wanted. It was time to see if he was going to get away with it. "The river sequence is stack three," Shanholz told him, waving vaguely in the direction of the table.

Burke shuffled through them again. "It isn't here. Where's the one I shot right when you killed the ambusher?"

Shanholz kept his eyes on the work screen. "That's all the river pics. All I've got left is Zandowski's mud hive shots. You sure it isn't there?"

"Yes, I'm sure," he snapped.

Burke didn't like having his competency questioned. He got angry when that happened. That was fine by Shanholz, anger made a man careless.

"The picture isn't here," Burke groused. "What happened to it?"

"Don't know. Must have fallen below the printability limits," Shanholz suggested. "Was it something important?"

"That's what I wanted to see. I thought it looked like an arthropod—and if it was, it was by far the biggest aerial one I've seen here—but I never did get a good look at it. Damn." Burke slapped the stack down on the table. "If I hadn't jumped when you shot, I might have—well, no point in maybes, is there? If you hadn't shot, I wouldn't be standing around here bitching. Too bad the pic didn't come out. Oh well, it's not like I'll be presenting any papers anytime soon. Too damn bad."

"Yeah, too bad," Shanholz agreed.

*Grawr'tayo* was the word the H'kimm used for one who, though of the pack, lived his or her life alone, only intermittently interacting with the others. Anyone who was *grawr'tayo* was a little crazy. The word was also the H'kimm term for a sinner, one who had stepped beyond the bounds that the gods had laid down. Ah'zzt the hunter was *grawr'-tayo*, in at least the first sense. Kurt suspected that only Ah'zzt's superb skill in the hunt kept the second meaning from applying to him. The useful, in *any* society, were rarely totally ostracized, and so Ah'zzt had honor, a place by Lo'gnen's fireside, and even a sometimes mate by the name of Tlok.

*Grawr'tayo* was the way Kurt had begun to think of Warrant Officer Shanholz. It wasn't just because Shanholz was the odd man out, the single military man among a pack of scientists and the lone Leaguer among those who hailed from more enlightened regimes. Lately a similarity between Shanholz and Ah'zzt had developed. Ah'zzt's chosen solitude gave him the solemn, sturdy air of a man who knew his place in the world and embraced it. And of late Kurt had noticed a similar sense of peace around Shanholz, as if he had come to terms with a problem that had been bothering him.

And from what Kurt was seeing, Shanholz had done more than find his place in the castaways' little society. The Leaguer had made peace with Chugen IV, or at least one of its life-forms. Shanholz sat on the bole of a freshly fallen forest giant, in the wash of light streaming down through the swath that the tree's fall had opened in the canopy. Next to him, a gossamer-winged insect had alighted. The Leaguer was murmuring to the iridescent bug, apparently coaxing it to take some scraps of food from his hand. The insect fit Burke's description of the "dangerous aerial predator" he'd seen by the river, but it was acting more like a park squirrel than a predator in its tentative approach to Shanholz.

*So much for Burke's "dangerous aerial predator."*

It was such an idyllic scene that Kurt, who had been sent to look for Shanholz, decided to withdraw. Whatever Lockhart wanted could wait. Kurt had been responsible for more than enough shattered moments of peace in his life. He'd let this one be.

Did only the *grawr'tayo* know peace?

Sometimes Kurt thought of himself as *grawr'tayo*, though it was a somewhat inaccurate self-image. For one thing, he lacked the transcendent calmness that Ah'zzt and Shanholz displayed. For another, as his acceptance by the H'kimm grew, so did his unease at that very acceptance. He was not H'kimm, but Human—a fact he could not afford to forget. Unfortunately, he found it all too easy to empathize with the H'kimm, to slip into the rhythm of their lifestyle, and to see things the way they saw them. It was a problem.

Becoming just another member of the pack was not part of being *grawr'tayo*.

He had dared to confide his concerns to Juli, but she had been less than no help. She had listened, and he was grateful for that; but she had seemed to think that his problem was a good thing, going so far as to express the desire to have such "problems" herself. She didn't understand what she was asking for.

Yet as much as he feared falling into acceptance, he feared being alone more. He was as drawn to the H'kimm as he had ever been drawn to the Cassuells. Though there was an abyss of difference between the H'kimm's jungle lifestyle and the Cassuells' desert existence, he felt as at home here as he had there. He was beginning to think in the H'kimm language, a first step in true understanding, but also—he was afraid—a step toward the Humanity-losing identification that he had reached with the Cassuells.

So much fear and so little comfort.

Juli was the bright spot there. She reminded him that he was Human. He was aware of her interest in him, and he reciprocated that interest, but remembering how he had screwed up with Clarise, he was afraid of getting involved.

God, what a timid rabbit he was!

And, like a rabbit, he was pounced on. A pack of half a dozen yelping younglings had stalked him, and now they had caught him. Their captive he was, they yipped. He fell in with their game, allowing himself to be bound with imaginary cords and hauled before the village elder, a trophy to the prowess of the younglings. Lo'gnen solemnly accepted the offering, then scattered the celebrating younglings with a mock charge. Returning to Kurt, the elder grinned toothily and drew his knife, a slender blade of carefully flaked obsidian bound by tough sprankel vines to a handle of burnished zela wood. Waving the knife, he said, "You are free."

Lo'gnen sheathed his weapon. "Know by such an igno-minious capture that you are no *grawr'tayo* hunter like Ah'zzt. Our pack-mate you are, friend Kurtellicot. Be part of the pack as the pack is part of you. Wander no more."

Kurt didn't want to carry the conversation in that direction. Seeing Lo'gnen's knife was stone and not metal inspired a change of subject. "Friend Lo'gnen, you are honored and revered by the pack, yet I see that you carry a knife no different than any runner of the pack. Yet you gave a knife of metal to Ah'zzt when we Humans first arrived. Was it your own knife that you gave to him?"

"In my charge, it was."

An heirloom perhaps? "Of value, was it?"

"Of value, yes."

Now that he thought about it, that knife was the largest item of any metal other than copper that Kurt had seen in use among the H'kimm. "I have seen little iron among the H'kimm."

"This is true, friend Kurtellicot. We have not your riches. H'kimm do not make the iron, we must trade for it."

Lo'gnen's response confused Kurt. If the H'kimm didn't make it, who did? "Are there others besides the H'kimm on this world?"

"Yes." Lo'gnen laughed. "You and your pack."

"We did not make the iron, nor did we trade it to you."

"I know this. I joke, yes?" More seriously Lo'gnen continued, "Few packs make the iron and none here in the forest. The forest does not like the iron. The iron comes to the forest and the forest makes it go away. Here, while it lasts, the iron is precious. Elsewhere this is different. Younglings often call this unjust, but we older folk know better. It is the way of things."

"It is important to understand and appreciate differences."

"Out of your mouth the wisdom of the *tuoyal*," the elder agreed.

"Help me understand, friend Lo'gnen. You said iron was precious. Is that why you rewarded Ah'zzt with a knife when he brought us here?"

"You thought I gifted him with a knife of the iron?" Lo'gnen laughed. "So wise and so ignorant. You are a puzzle, friend Kurtellicot. To give the gods honor, I gave kind in kind. The iron would be too little; I gifted a knife of the star metal."

Kurt's mouth went dry. He had been fishing for a mackerel and had hooked a shark. "Star metal?"

"Of course. To the star metal, the iron is a dross thing. The forest cannot make the star metal go away, and so it is more precious here than in most territories. Ah'zzt brought you star people here. The gods say a man should receive his just due, so I gifted Ah'zzt kind in kind. Some might have done otherwise, seeing that Ah'zzt is *grawr'tayo*, but Ah'zzt is not a bad man. Had he walked other paths, he might someday have come to be chief, but he is *grawr'tayo*. He will not take the knife from the pack. We will not be made poorer."

"Do you trade for the star metal as you do for the iron?"

Lo'gnen snorted. "Who can trade for the star metal? R'kimm, who live among the dust, know the secrets of the iron, but even they do not know the secrets of the star metal. The star metal is our honor. It is as it has come down to us, as everlasting and eternal as the stars."

Kurt's head was starting to reel from Lo'gnen's elliptical explanation. But buried in the strange words and phrases were nuggets of what might be very important information. *Come down*, the elder had said. What might that mean? "Are you saying that it falls from the sky?"

"So many questions you have, friend Kurtellicot. You

get lost in the questions, yes, forgetting answers you already know? I remind you of what all *tuoyal* know. We came from stars, too."

*That* wasn't the answer Kurt wanted. "You mean that your ancestors were spacefarers, marooned here like us Humans?"

Lo'gnen gave a long sigh, something he'd done with increasing frequency starting a few weeks after the Humans' arrival.

"You use many of your pack-words that I do not know," he said. "I smell surprise on you. How is this so?

"You sit by the fire. You listen to the stories and you tell them over again to your box. You know our stories. Why do you question? Do I need to show you where the stars first touched the earth?

"Mock not the gods. Accept what we have held sacred from the beginning of time. We are here because the stars came down and touched the earth, and where they walked, the Hos'kimm sprang up." Lo'gnen sighed again. "Ah, why do I bother? The time of the Hos'kimm is coming again. When the stars are right, you will come with us. The Hos'kimm are eager to meet you."

Kurt knew he was imposing on the elder's good will, but he had to know. "Who are Hos'kimm?"

"The greater pack," Lo'gnen replied with exaggerated patience. "All of us."

Kurt had more questions. "How do you know the Hos'kimm want to meet us? I have seen no messengers."

"I am *tuoyal* and I am a chief," the elder said, as if it explained everything.

Perhaps it did—to him. Kurt, however, was still in the dark. One thing that was becoming clear was that Lo'gnen's position as "chief" was not as simple as ruling this small pack. A thousand questions bubbled through his mind. Most he dared not ask. This was no time to go searching after subtle meaning. "But *how* do you know?"

"I am *tuoyal* and I am a chief," Lo'gnen repeated.

"I am *tuoyal*, as well," Kurt said, reminding the elder of his inclusive pronouncement. "Can you not share with me the way in which you know? Truly, I would like to understand."

"You sound like a pup," Lo'gnen said, making the pronouncement an accusation. "You are our friend, Kurtellicot, and you are *tuoyal*, but you are not a chief. Someday you may learn, perhaps, but not today. Find your place among the H'kimm. Find your place among the Hos'kimm. When you know the pack and the pack knows you, all will be as it should be. Until then, bide as the hunter at the *skendalu* nest."

"But—"

Lo'gnen cut him off gruffly. "Enough. A pup must walk before he can run."

In the castaways' hut, alone save for the unconscious Singh, Shanholz studied his purloined pic as he had every day since he'd hijacked it from the unsuspecting Burke. The image was lousy, but good enough to confirm that the object was what it was. What a joke that he knew and the highbrows didn't have a clue. Of course only Burke had seen it, and he'd fallen for the ruse of its external appearance, and then brought the others in on his mistake. They believed Burke's talk about aerial predators, which was fine.

Stuffing the pic back in his pocket, he lay back and listened to the sounds of the village. Typical midday activity, he judged. Soon, things would quiet down as they always did in the heat of the day. Soon.

The original plan had died in the crash with Lieutenant Mostel, but the objective was still attainable—now he knew that the mission was still on. He wasn't abandoned. He had a place to go.

It felt good not to be on his own.

Before long he'd be back where he belonged. There were still a few things he needed to do, and soon they'd be done. He felt a little underhanded, but orders were orders. Soon.

To hell with soon!

He rolled to his feet. From the doorway he checked on the positions of the others. They were all in the village, all settling down in their afternoon places. The natives were going about their business, too. He couldn't tell if any were missing, but it didn't matter. The natives paid no attention to the Humans' dwelling, and less to anything he did. The days he'd spent establishing his "afternoon nap" were about to pay off. They were ignoring him, which was the way he wanted it.

He got down to work.


Rafe said that Shanholz had been complaining about an upset stomach and had retired to the communal hut, so Juliana went there looking for him. Walking across the open ground of the common, she realized that she should have thought of looking there first; it was after midday and time for the Leaguer's usual siesta. Shanholz probably wouldn't be happy to hear her complaint about a malfunction in the recharging station, but she believed in solving a problem early, before it became insurmountable.

She called his name as she ducked through the doorway. The only response she got was a moan from Singh. The poor man clung to life despite his grievous injuries. If only there were something that could be done for him.

The hut was dark to her day-adjusted eyes, but not as dark as usual, because a hole had been torn in the dried rushes of the back wall. It was low to the ground and small, but big enough for a man to be dragged through. The extra light it shed showed her that the castaways' meager goods lay in disarray as if there had been a struggle.

She thought about shouting for help at once, but overrode the impulse. Instead, she quietly called Shanholz's name. This time she got no response at all.

The damaged wall allowed enough light for her eyes to adapt quickly. There was no sign of Shanholz. Neither were there any puddles of blood. Her fear that some Chugeni predator had stolen him away faded. Had he run away, then? If so, why?

She made a quick survey of the things that she knew had been in the hut when she left. All, while not where she remembered them, appeared present. He hadn't stolen anything. So what was going on?

Despite her responsibility to the others, she did not call out. Shanholz's stealthy desertion prompted concern over her own secret. She checked her computer and, to her relief, it started. Her anxiety level jumped right back up when the Alsion construct appeared on the screen and skipped its usual greeting.

"Ah, Ms. Tindal, I am glad to see that it is you and that you are well. Thirty-seven minutes ago an unauthorized person accessed the machine."

The program's concern for her health was touching, but it set off a shudder. Shanholz was a Leaguer after all. As a product of their fascist indoctrination, he was, no doubt, capable of unthinkable mayhem. How had she ever thought of him as a normal person?

So someone had been at her computer. She had a good idea who, but she had to ask. "Who was it?"

"I am afraid that I am unable to tell you that," the Alsion agent replied.

With her suspicions high, she was more than ready to apply them to this enigmatic virtual entity. "Can't or won't?"

"Neither this machine's native capabilities nor my own peripherals provide adequate input to identify individuals not already logged in memory."

"That's not really an answer, is it? You're as evasive as your model sometimes."

"Why thank you, Ms. Tindal. I rarely receive compliments and such a substantial one from you is flattering."

"You can't be flattered. You're a program."

"I am, indeed, a program."

"Now that we've settled that, answer the question. Are you unable to tell me who it was because you don't know or because your programming gives you a higher priority than telling me the truth?"

"I assure you, Ms. Tindal, that I am here to be as helpful to you as possible. I cannot identify the individual."

"Can't or won't?" she snapped.

"Cannot. The individual is not in my databases. I can, however, confirm, that it is a Human, not a H'kimm, and one quite skilled at computer operations. I can also eliminate Mr. Ellicot and Ms. Lockhart."

"I could do that. I was sitting with them at the time. In fact, everyone but Shanholz and Singh have been in sight for the last hour."

"Ah, independent corroboration. Useful. Since Mr. Singh remains incapacitated, our culprit must be Warrant Officer Shanholz. Excellent. I shall recognize him hereafter."

"Much good that does us. You said he was a hot operator. Did he tamper with you?"

"Tamper? Hardly. I assure you that he never knew I was here. He attempted to search your databases and delete several sections. He also attempted to install an agent, which I was forced to eliminate in order to prevent its function. However, I allowed him to think that he had achieved complete success. I am afraid that the necessity of preserving the secret of my presence prevented me from preserving all of your data; some few files were deleted. I do hope that there are backups on some of the other computers."

Juliana looked around the hut at the other machines, all moved from where she remembered them. "They didn't have watchdogs like you."

"How unfortunate." The construct actually sounded saddened. "Will you be organizing a party to retrieve Warrant Officer Shanholz?"

What was the point? Where was he going to go?

"I'll talk to the others about that," she said, and after shutting down the computer, that's what she went to do.

# 19

Looking at the shiny new major's diamonds, Anders Seaborg felt a little as if he were dreaming. He discovered that it felt real enough as he affixed it to his collar.

Had it only been three months ago that he'd been brevetted to captain? Now he was again jumped up a rank. The new rank was also a brevetting, but it made the jump to captain permanent. How in St. Michael's name had it come about?

Certainly the campaign on Grenwold had gone well, although now that the campaign was just about wound up, it was clear that the enemy had never set great score by the planet. But victory against the enemy was a rare thing for Humanity, something to be prized. After more than ten years of war with the enemy, MilForce, the League, and Humanity itself needed the morale boost. There were promotions and commendations for just about everyone who'd made it through. Anders felt that the whole thing was a little hollow, but no one had asked his opinion.

He gazed past the bustling landing base to the tall, gray mountains that the Grenwolders called the Western Divide. Beyond those peaks, on the long sloping plain that stretched to the Vasty Sea, lay the immense forest that the enemy had claimed for their own. Looking back the other way, at the ochers and purples of the empty plains and furrowed, barren badlands that made up so much of Grenwold's western continent, he saw in his mind's eye what the enemy had sought to make of the forest, grinding it to pulp with their harvester beasts.

It was good that the harvester beasts were all as dead as their masters now. Grenwold belonged once again to the Humans who had settled it.

The blue skies above Grenwold were quiet now. No transports rumbled heavily through it to deliver ground forces, no fighters shrieked on attack sorties to support those troops, and no shuttles thundered down with reinforcements. The artillery no longer slam-thudded, the tanks no longer howl-cracked, and the pulse rifles no longer whine-whooshed. The battlefield was empty, the graves were dug, and the Masses said for the fallen. All was as quiet as it had been before MilForce—and the enemy—had arrived.

Save for the crying of the mourners.

But beyond the few units to be left as garrison troops, MilForce wouldn't be on Grenwold for the mourning of the hundreds of dead militia men and women. He hoped that the mourning would heal the hearts of the surviving Grenwolders. It was never an easy thing to lose loved ones, even in the defense of life and freedom.

His dreary thoughts were cut off by an insistent shout. Jason Metzler—*Major* Jason Metzler, another hero of Grenwold—was hustling up the trail to the jutting rock that Anders was using for an observation deck.

"Hey, Seaborg, what's going on? I just got my orders transferring my flight to *Prince Rupert*, and there's nothing in them about picking up you and your shellbacks."

"That's because you're not picking them up," Anders told him. The hard necessities of managing a force strung out across uncounted light-years meant that it was impossible for the troops to return to their own ship, *Shaka*, but they were too useful a force to remain idle, so a new berth had been found for them. Anders consulted his watch. "Hewitt's taking them aboard *Santa Anna*'s shuttles while we speak."

"I don't like it," Metzler announced. "They shouldn't be breaking up our team."

"StratCom knows best," Anders said in the traditional dubious manner. "Did you say you'd been assigned to *Prince Rupert*?"

The interface flight commander grinned. "Yeah. Six hundred meters of lean, mean space-going machine. Only two years out of dock and full of all the amenities they forgot to put into old *Shaka*. You'd never guess they were classmates."

"She's part of Schley's task group, bound for Tarsus Station, isn't she?"

Metzler's eyes narrowed in mock suspicion. "You're surprisingly well informed for someone who spends so much time hanging out on a rock."

"I got my orders today, too," Anders admitted. "I'm reporting to Sector Command on Tarsus, with transport aboard Schley's group. I've been transferred to sector staff."

Brows furrowing in honest sympathy, Metzler observed, "That'll put you right under Stoneface's nose."

"Don't I know it." Anders shook his head glumly. "But I don't get it. Four months ago I was a lieutenant on long-term aptitude assignment to the geepies. Now they want me to tap dance for the stars."

"They probably want to pick your brains."

That had been Anders's conclusion as well, but it hadn't made any sense to him. There were others who knew and understood more about what had happened on Grenwold than he did. "Mike's hikes, Jase, I'm an infantry officer! I'm not supposed to have those kind of brains."

"You said it, my friend. Being a kindly man, I wasn't going to point out the bitter, obvious truth."

"What would you know about brains, Mr. Vacuum-head?"

"That's 'Mr. Vacuum-head, *Sir!*' to you. My promotion's straight by the book, Mr. Brevet-rank," Metzler corrected, pushing the technicality of their relative ranking. "At least I'm smart enough to stay in the field. Or if it's not a case of relative brain power, I'm not as much of a sinner. Who'd you piss off?"

"If I knew, I'd apologize and then some!"

"It's too late for that."

Anders supposed he was right.

Sober-faced, Metzler said, "Joking aside, I suspect you *are* being punished for your sins. You know what I think? I think you never should have bothered anybody about the stink-weasels."

Stink-weasel had become the derogatory term of choice for the furred aliens that Anders had discovered in association with the grinders.

Could that be it? The shock of seeing what he thought were Cassuells had caused Anders to report the discovery up the chain, even though he had never really believed the official position that the Cassuells had been Remor. Yet here on Grenwold, since having seen the aliens tending the Remor monster beasts, he'd done a lot of rethinking without reaching satisfactory conclusions. The aliens just might be the Remor enemy, but if they were, why hadn't any been armed? Why hadn't any even had clothes, or carried anything other than primitive tools?

The official line was that the "world-dwelling Remor" of Cassuells Home had been recidivistic. Anders knew that Humans had fallen back into barbarism on some of the worlds they had colonized, and in remarkably quick time. Why couldn't the Remor do the same?

But such an explanation didn't fit very well with the situation on Grenwold. This Remor infestation had included battle machines and starships. That wasn't any kind of recidivism he'd ever heard or read about.

He'd thought long and hard about the situation and had only ended with more questions than answers. On Grenwold, just like everywhere else where Humankind had encountered the enemy, the Remor continued their scorched earth—and everything else—policy. There was so little hard evidence with which to work. Normally, after a battle one got to see the enemy's face—twisted and burned perhaps, but unequivocally there—staring from the ruins of the weapons in which he had opposed you and from the wreckage of his installations and defenses. War with the Remor didn't work that way. MilForce had never yet recovered any bodies, or even any significant portions of bodies from the wrecks of enemy installations or machines. The only biological material recovered that was bigger and better preserved than charred tissue samples were the bodies of the furred aliens, the monstrous harvester and miner beasts, and a host of parasites. The Cassuells, stink-weasels, or whatever one called them were obviously—so Sector Command said—the enemy. If that was so, why were their bodies never found anywhere but here on Grenwold among the harvesters? If they were Remor, why hadn't any been found at the enemy base camp?

To Anders, it didn't add up.

"Do you really think Sector Command believes I know something they don't?" he asked.

Metzler shrugged. "Who can tell? The thing is, you're the one who brought the stink-weasels to their attention, and I can't see any other reason they'd want to talk to a dumb-ass geepie."

"I could be just going into the reserve officer pool."

"You *could* be about to become old Stoneface's personal bodyguard."

"I suppose I'll find out is by showing up at Tarsus Station, eh? My ticket says I'm supposed to ship with Schley's task group, but Personnel, in its wisdom, didn't assign me a specific berth. You think *Prince Rupert* has room for a hitchhiker? I hear she's practically a luxury liner."

"I'm sure there's a storage locker somewhere about to stuff you." Metzler grinned. "But if you want a smooth ride upstairs, the best bus in the fleet is leaving at thirteen hundred hours, sharp."

"Thirteen hundred sharp, you say? When do *you* lift?"

"Smart guy."

"Nope, just a dumb-ass geepie."

"Too right. You want a ride or not?"

"Of course. I wouldn't fly with anyone else."

Together they turned their backs on the mountains and the battlefields beyond. Anders let Metzler lead the way down to the landing field where IDL shuttles waited to return troops to the orbiting starships. In less than twenty-four standard hours, Grenwold would be no more to him than a memory.

# 20

The news of Shanholz's disappearance raised more ruckus among the Chugeni than it did among the Humans. They ran around a lot, chattering and yipping at each other so fast that even Ellicot was having trouble following their jabbering. Certainly Rafe lost track of what they were on about, since his translator was burping up more error messages than translations. Rather than relying on that bastard, Rafe tried to get an explanation out of Juli.

"They believe Shanholz was taken by a spotted ghost," she told him.

"Of all their impractical, superstitious nonsense!" A ghost? Rafe's opinion of the Chugeni went down a few more notches, which was surprising, given how low it already was.

As word of the ghost spread, the Chugeni clumped in groups. They had a natural tendency to avoid being alone, but the behavior they demonstrated now went far beyond that. They clung to each other like orphaned tremonkeys. None of them seemed willing to go anywhere alone. All for fear of the spotted ghost.

Rafe was even more amazed when Langdorf asked the Humans assembled in their violated hut, "Do you think there could be anything to this spotted ghost?"

"Why don't we ask Singh?" Rafe suggested in mock

seriousness. "He was here the whole time. He *must* have seen it."

"This is serious, Burke," Lockhart admonished. "Shanholz is gone and we need to know why."

"So he's gone," Rafe said with a shrug. A man had the right to make his own choices. "Did he take anything that didn't belong to him?"

"A good question." Lockhart ordered everyone to check their personal gear, and when nothing turned up missing, she focused on Shanholz's area. Langdorf found the crumpled hard copy of a pic. Rafe recognized the image at once; it was a shot of his riverside aerial predator. Or rather, an imitation of it. A bad joke.

"Somebody's messed with this," Rafe observed, tossing the worthless thing on the ground.

Ellicot picked up the pic, stared at it for a moment, then looked suspiciously at Rafe. "You're saying this isn't the creature you saw by the river?"

"How could it be? It's got six legs." He knew Ellicot wasn't paying attention to anything but the Chugeni sophonts, but he had thought that the man had grasped the basics about the planet's life-forms. "Even without checking the biochemistry, it's easy to see that Chugeni forms are distinctive from Earth-descended forms. Here, for example, insectiforms resembling Anisopterans have eight legs. Perfectly obvious to a careful observer."

Ellicot bristled at Rafe's tone, puffing himself up for an argument. Fine. Rafe was ready. But Juli cut in, suggesting that everyone check his or her computer to see if Shanholz had been at them. Data loss—or worse, data theft—was a constant fear among professionals whose careers depended on the correct and proprietary data. People reached for their machines. While the castaway scientists quizzed their individual computers, Lockhart went through the general-issue machines and the small stack of specialized comps that they had salvaged from the wreck. She was the first to report.

"Right now, the only thing that I can see for sure that's gone is the survival canister's manual. He took all three copies of the chip."

On a hunch, Rafe specifically went looking for the pic file from the riverside. He expected to find that it had been altered; instead he found that it had been excised whole—with the file directory altered so that anyone coming cold to the pic files would never know that it had existed. It was a fairly crude job, not the sort that Rafe would have done had *he* sought to steal such a file. Nowhere near tidy enough to fool someone who was looking for alterations. He would have expected Shanholz to do a better job.

Of course, thinking about Ellicot's reaction to the hard copy of the pic, it might not have been Shanholz. Why Ellicot might want to stir up trouble this way escaped him, but he didn't doubt that the bastard had sufficient malice to try it. Rafe would have to keep a sharp watch on him from now on.

Rafe also discovered that some of his files were missing, others scrambled. The rest of the group reported similar problems. Surprisingly, the data lost was general stuff— mostly history and technical files. It seemed an unfocused and random vandalism.

*Again, out of place for Shanholz*, Rafe thought. *But not for a certain crazy bastard.*

"We should go after him," Zandowski suggested.

"Why?" Nobody had forced Shanholz to walk away.

"He's alone. He'll die out there."

"If any one of us could survive out there, he's the one," Ellicot said.

Rafe could think of another one who could manage, but he seconded the bastard's opinion anyway. "It was his choice, let's leave him to it."

Lockhart disagreed. "I think there's more to his departure than simple personal choice."

"And what evidence do you have?" Rafe asked.

She didn't have any, of course, but she did insist that a search party be formed to track Shanholz down.

"I think we should all go," Ellicot announced, "excepting Ms. Lockhart, of course."

"Why?" Rafe didn't see the point. "If you ask me, he's had his fill of our happy home for castaways and just wants shut of us. If that's what he wants, let him have it. On the other hand, maybe we *should* go after him and drag him back. Yeah, that's it! We'll make the decision for him. We can run his life! *That* should make him feel right at home, 'cause that's the way the thrice-damned *League* does business."

"Oh, Rafe," Juli started.

"Don't 'oh, Rafe' me! We've got no business running Shanholz's life. You know I'm right. He's got as much right as any of us to throw up his hands and just walk out of here whenever he wants."

"He didn't have any right to mess up our databases," Langdorf said.

"But he did it, didn't he? Well, it's *done*. That isn't going to change." Rafe sighed. "It's not worth tromping through the jungle looking for him to slap him on the wrist."

"We're not likely to catch him," Juli said, evidencing a burst of rationality. "He's had survival training. A jungle has all sorts of places for a man to hide from clumsy searchers. He probably knows lots of ways to avoid pursuit."

Looking a little betrayed, Ellicot asked, "So you don't think we should try?"

"I don't think there's anything to be gained," Juli said.

"She's right. There isn't anything to be gained." Rafe smiled at Ellicot's chagrined expression. "You know, you and your fellow national seem to be the only ones interested in catching him. Why is that? The League sponsored your place on this expedition. You never have explained *that*. I don't suppose that friendship has anything to do with your wanting to chase after your Leaguer buddy, does it?"

Lockhart glowered while Ellicot made his standard denial. "I have nothing to do with the League."

Rafe blinked innocently. "Oh, really?" But before he could continue, someone else spoke.

"Actually." Langdorf cleared his throat uncomfortably. The meteorologist never said much in group discussions. Stepping into the middle of one of Rafe and Ellicot's rows was out of character for him. With everyone watching him, he started again. "Actually, I think we should try to find Shanholz, too. If he left freely, we don't know why. It doesn't seem right to me. If he just wanted to be quit of us, he would have said something. Everyone seems ready to accept that an animal couldn't have dragged him away, even though the Chugeni think that's what happened. We know so little about the life-forms on this planet. What if we're wrong? Maybe something did drag him off. There's also one other possibility that everyone seems to be avoiding. What if he did get dragged off, but not by an animal? We're not the only outsiders to have come to this system. I think we ought to find out what happened."

"You're not suggesting that the Remor stole him, are you?" asked Lockhart. She didn't look like she was taking Langdorf's suggestion seriously.

Her skepticism deflated Langdorf some, but he held to his position. "I don't know. None of us know. But I think we ought to try and find out what happened to him, rather than just speculating."

"Fine," Rafe told him. "You go off with Ellicot, then. You want your funeral held now or later?"

"Rafe?" Zandowski's tone urged caution. Her hand on his arm suggested restraint.

What the hell. If Langdorf wanted to go, let him.

"Forget it," he said. "Forget I said anything. You two want to go chase spotted ghosts, go ahead."

Rafe's mention of the putative culprit acted like a summons; the Chugeni chief busybody stuck his snout into the hut.

"What is it you do?" asked the tribal chief.

"We are going to look for Shanholz," Ellicot told him.

The gray-fur nodded. "I understand. So small a pack cannot afford the loss of a soul."

"What we *want* is his bloody butt," Lockhart said.

After her comment was explained to the chief, the alien said solemnly, "The spotted ghost has taken him. You will not find his body."

"Nevertheless, we will search," Ellicot said.

"As you must," the Chugeni chief agreed sanctimoniously. "I will pray that you find his soul."

"Will the H'kimm help us?"

The furry alien gave one of his snaky nods. "Ah'zzt is coming. He will be here soon. When you go, he will go with you. Others may. Our packs curl up together, our packs face the trials of the gods together. This is the way of godly beings, is it not, friend Kurtellicot?"

"It is what friends do for friends, friend Lo'gnen," Ellicot said.

Fortunately the conversation between the bastard and the Chugeni ended there. Rafe didn't have to barf up his lunch.

✳    ✳    ✳

Juliana dated the freeze in her relationship with Zandowski to her return from the field trip with Rafe. Since that trip the mousy biologist had been giving Rafe regular soulful looks and she seemed to find frequent excuses to stand next to him, more closely than people who were just colleagues would. The sum was simple: Rafe had made another conquest.

Juliana wasn't surprised, really. Zandowski was pretty— a little more subdued than Rafe's usual type, but there wasn't a lot of choice on Chugen IV. Zandowski and Juliana were the only functional Human females on planet, and since Juliana hadn't responded to Rafe's advances, he must have finally decided to look elsewhere.

Juliana would have been happier if Kurt was better at picking up *her* signals. But she felt sure that her time would come.

Meanwhile she would be dealing with Rafe trying to make his latest conquest as soured on his last as he was. There wasn't room in Chugen's tiny Human community for that kind of nonsense. Some bridge-building might make their little community a bit more livable.

Juliana waited until she caught Zandowski sitting outside the castaways' hut alone, working with her comp. Settling beside her, Juliana offered a smile and a data chip. "If you think that there's a problem between us, consider this a peace offering."

Frowning in suspicion, Zandowski accepted the chip. "What is it?"

"It's a complete synthetic gene profile of the Cassuells. Much of it is reconstructed from intercepted IDL data."

Zandowski's eyes widened. "Where did you get it?"

*From the Alsion analog,* but that wasn't something she could tell Zandowski. "It was in the files I inherited when I became the senior Combine project member," she lied. "We salvaged quite a few files that I haven't had the time or desire to look through. I noticed it while I was checking to see what Shanholz might have taken, and when I scanned the summary, I thought it looked like something you might find useful."

"Oh, yes," Zandowski affirmed enthusiastically. "A full profile! Wonderful! The best material I'd seen was the partial profile I lost when my perscomp was destroyed in the crash. I'd worked up approximation, mostly from memory, but now I, well, this could be very helpful. Thank you."

The two women sat in awkward silence for a moment before Zandowski said, "Why are you giving me this? I thought you agreed with Ellicot that the Chugeni and the Cassuells are different. You realize that this will probably go a long way toward confirming that both aliens are of the same species."

"Yes, but we need to know, don't we?" Juliana shrugged. "But biology isn't everything, especially for sentient species. There's still a tremendous gulf to be crossed to connect either the Cassuells or the H'kimm to the Remor, even if they all come from the same stock."

"There is that," Zandowski admitted. Turning the chip over in her hand, she frowned worriedly. "Even if I don't find a strong correlation, *any* similarities I uncover could incite the IDL to repeat here what they did to Cassuells Home."

"I'm the last one who wants that. Even without hard data, the Leaguers may act. We scientists aren't supposed to jump to conclusions like the Leaguers do. We're supposed to tease the truth from a situation. I would prefer to know the *truth*. Wouldn't you?"

"Of course."

So, Juliana thought, *we have more in common than just*

*Rafe.* "But knowing the truth and telling it aren't the same thing."

Zandowski looked puzzled. "What do you mean?"

"And even if your research shows that the Cassuells and the H'kimm are the same, neither the Pan-Stellar Combine nor your Hanseatic Coalition is a part of the IDL. We're under no obligation to share our information with the League. We *are*, however, under an obligation to the H'kimm. Even if they are the same species as the Cassuells, even if they are the same species as the Remor, the individuals here have had no part in the war. *They* are ·not the enemies of Humankind. They don't deserve the genocide that the League will want to inflict. You don't want to be a part of genocide, do you?"

Zandowski looked genuinely terrified by the idea. "No. No, I don't."

"Neither do I. We have to do all that we can to prevent that. If we can show the Cassuells and the H'kimm to be different species, we'll have rock-solid evidence to show up any attempt at genocide as the paranoid lunacy that it is. And if it turns out that the League is right about our friends' ancestry, well, we'll at least know enough to look for another way to save them."

It took a while, but at last Zandowski nodded. Juliana smiled. Perhaps she had an ally rather than an enemy after all.

Ah'zzt was the acknowledged leader of the hunting party, even though the expedition set out at Human instigation. Kurt didn't mind. For one thing, the fifteen H'kimm far outnumbered the two Humans who had come along. For another, Ah'zzt was the most woods-wise being present. If anyone could track the absconded Shanholz, he could.

From time to time the hunter would scout ahead, forging on and disappearing with consummate ease and reappearing from the brush with unnerving suddenness.

They were working their way along the river where the forest was sparse and the understory more vigorous, often enclosing them so thoroughly that they couldn't see more than a handful of meters. Near the river edge the vegetation grew even thicker, making a tangle that was next to impenetrable. Why Shanholz would have chosen such a course was beyond Kurt, but Ah'zzt assured him that they were on the Leaguer's track, although the hunter referred to it as "the path of the spotted ghost."

"Who cares what he thinks he's following?" Langdorf commented, rubbing his knee. The meteorologist's crash-injured leg still bothered him, and the trek wasn't a pleasant one for him. "Just so long as he tracks Shanholz down. And quickly."

Although his own leg still pained him, Kurt was not having as much trouble with walking as Langdorf. Still, he also wanted the unpleasant task over with. He didn't like the wilderness. He didn't like exerting himself in the clammy heat. But what he really didn't like was the way Shanholz had run off. Striking out alone into the jungle was the act of a madman—or of a very sane man with a hidden agenda.

He'd been surprised when Burke had denied the image in the crumpled pic they'd found among Shanholz's bedding. Kurt had seen Shanholz with the bug and knew that it looked exactly as it did in Burke's pic. What that signified, Kurt had no idea, but between what Kurt had seen, Burke's denial, and the man's sudden chumminess with Shanholz, the idyllic image of Shanholz quietly communing with nature had been shattered for Kurt. Something sinister was going on, but what?

Shuddering, Kurt fought to suppress memories of his last involvement with Leaguers. Thus occupied, he missed

Ah'zzt's return to the hunting party until the H'kimm slipped up beside him and spoke.

"Friend Kurtellicot, I have wondered," Ah'zzt said. "Lo'gnen says you are *tuoyal*, yes?"

"Yes, he does," Kurt responded, glad to turn his mind to other things, but unsure where the hunter was headed.

Ah'zzt curved his neck back and tilted his snout down in the graceful polite acknowledgment of his people. "I am a hunter, and live as a hunter. I sniff many strange things. Often there is no one to tell me if what I sniff is true or not. I accept this as part of my way under the stars. Sometimes, though, I long for answers where I have no answers."

Ah'zzt hesitated, so Kurt prompted him. "Do you have a question that I can answer for you, friend Ah'zzt?"

"I do sniff a strangeness," Ah'zzt admitted. In a whisper, he continued, "Many of you Humans are touched by solitude. Almost *grawr'tayo*. Is this the Human way?"

Kurt thought about all the loners he'd known, and about the times he'd spent alone. "We gather, as the H'kimm do, but we have times when we walk alone, too. Perhaps more of us do so than among the H'kimm."

"This is sad."

Ah'zzt drifted away and in short order headed off on another scout. He returned excited, having found something.

What he had found was a trampled spot in the jungle. Langdorf pointed out a burn mark on tree. "Looks like Shanholz used his weapon."

Kurt agreed. But if the Leaguer had fought someone or something here, he had not done well. There were a few scraps of cloth, which Ah'zzt sniffed and pronounced Shanholz's. Kurt recognized the camouflage pattern on them as the Leaguer's fatigues; none of the other castaways had anything like them. There was blood, too, not much, but enough to show that someone had been wounded here. Tasting it, Ah'zzt pronounced it Human blood.

Blood wasn't the only thing smeared on the ground and the ravaged brush. A foul-smelling slime was present in copious quantities. Ah'zzt neither tasted, touched, nor sniffed that, but he seemed to recognize it just the same.

"The spotted ghost drank a soul here," he announced solemnly. "This is very bad."

"So the spotted ghost is not just a story animal."

"Very real. Big ghost, very hungry." Ah'zzt's expression was troubled. "Very bad. This is not the spotted ghost's time."

Kurt had no chance to question him—from the bushes nearer the river came a startled yelp.

Kurt watched Ah'zzt's eyes quickly dart across all those present. "Kr'ezt," the hunter said, naming one of their companions.

Kr'ezt yelped again, this time in pain, and the brush began to thrash. As one, the hunting party rushed to aid the beleaguered H'kimm. They pushed their way through the thick brush as a fearful rending sound slashed the air, and Kr'ezt's cries abruptly ended.

For once Kurt and Langdorf had an advantage over their companions. They could bull their way through clinging vegetation that thwarted the others' sinuously graceful but less powerful rush. A slimed, trampled patch of vegetation slowed them down not at all. Urged on by the scent of blood and deathly fear, they hurtled down a narrow, new trail that led from it. The rescue party came to an abrupt halt when they reached the riverbank and stumbled out onto a sandbar to confront a monstrous beast standing over Kr'ezt's mangled remains. Like the others, Kurt stared frozen in awe and horror.

The creature was easily the size of a Green Water aligerator, at least three meters from the tip of its blunt snout to the end of its laterally flattened tail. It looked a little like one, too, in the general shape of its broad four-limbed body. But where an aligerator had a scaly hide and dermal scutes, this monster was smooth-skinned and had a triple row of needlelike spines running the length of its sinuous body. Its hide was mottled orange and yellow, dotted with irregular patches of black, and glistening all over with a layer of dripping slime.

With a shock, Kurt realized that this nightmarish salamander was a vertebrate—other than the H'kimm, the first Chugeni creature of that type any Human had seen. Kurt would have gladly given up the honor of discovering it.

For a moment, the tableau held; then, like an exercising man, the creature flexed its forelimbs, elbows out. It thrust, rearing up onto its hind legs to tower taller than Ah'zzt or Kurt, taller than the lanky Langdorf. Fist-sized, milky orbs stared down at them as the wide jaws opened to reveal a double row of sharp, recurved teeth. Three pairs of previously unseen, spindly limbs, each tipped with a quartet of hooked claws, unfolded from its belly as it rumbled a warning growl.

Half the H'kimm yipped in terror, dropped to all fours and humped away into the brush. The rest stood stock-still as their frightened whimpering moaned under the creature's growl. With a start, Kurt realized that the fearful noise wasn't just coming from the H'kimm. He, too, was wailing his terror of this monster!

To Kurt's side, Ah'zzt simply repeated "spotted ghost" over and over.

Unimpressed by the puny bipeds interrupting its meal, the spotted ghost lunged forward.

Juliana stood staring off into the jungle, as she sometimes did in the evenings since Kurt and Langdorf and the

H'kimm hunters had left. If anything happened to Kurt . . .

"He's not coming back."

Juliana started at Rafe's voice. His hand, placed on her shoulder to calm or comfort, instead raised annoyance.

"It hasn't even been a week," she pointed out in perfect rationality. There really was no basis for serious concern. "They could be back today. Any minute, really."

"Suit yourself." He removed his hand. "You're wasting your time looking for him. Even if he does come back, he won't be the same."

"What do you mean?"

Rafe shook his head sadly. "You may be denying the evidence, but that doesn't mean I haven't seen it. He's going native again, the way he did on Cassuells Home."

"No, you're wrong."

"Like I said, suit yourself." He shrugged. "I just thought you were more realistic. Guess I *am* wrong. You haven't got your head screwed on any better about him than about the damned Chugeni."

"What's that supposed to mean?"

"How realistic is it to maintain that the Chugeni are native here?"

"We don't have any solid—"

"Oh, come on! It's *plain* that the damned Chugeni aren't native. The most derived life-form we've seen here is that little salamander Zan found yesterday. There's a lot of evolutionary ground to cover between amphibiforms and mammaliforms, even if you discount the fact that your furry friends have only half the limbs of an *honest* Chugeni vertebrate. You don't need genetic profiles to see that they didn't grow here. All you need is eyes."

"Zandowski disagrees with you."

"No, she doesn't. Zan's just being thorough."

"We need hard data, not speculation," she protested.

"We've got it. You heard Zan's report yesterday. Chugeni DNA plots out in left field when compared to everything else we test here."

"We haven't surveyed the entire planet yet," she said, knowing the objection was feeble.

"You're grasping at straws. The Cassuell DNA pattern you gave to Zan plots almost exactly the same."

"It wasn't an exact match."

"Nor should it have been. Both the Cassuells and the Chugeni are primitives. It's been a long time since they saw the stars. Without knowing how long, we can't correct for genetic drift, which is inevitable given that they're living on different planets. I know Ellicot wants to believe the Cassuells and the Chugeni are different, but he's deluding himself. Don't be stupid and follow his lead."

She had suspected for some time that Kurt's assertion that the Cassuells and the H'kimm were different was not reasonable. She wanted to believe that he stood on honest socioxenological grounds, but she was beginning to wonder. Zan's studies certainly refuted Kurt's position on the biological front. But as every socioxenologist knew . . . "There's more to it than biology."

"You sound like Ellicot." Kurt eyed her suspiciously. "But you can't deny the biological connections."

"I admit that there are strong biological correlations, but it wasn't really the biological similarities that got the Combine interested in Chugen. It was the similarities between the space-visible constructs on this world and those on Cassuells Home. And so far we've seen no evidence that the H'kimm could even contemplate building such structures. Especially not on their moon."

"They're a devolved culture, for god's sake. They probably built those things on the moon right after they got here."

"Perhaps. But you don't know that. The H'kimm ancestors could have been marooned just like we were."

"You mean shot down by the Remor?"

Juliana sighed exasperatedly. "Now you're twisting what I say. There's just no evidence that the H'kimm are connected to those structures. Yes, judging by the preliminary surveys, there are strong similarities between the Cassuells Home structures and the ones in this system. Such similarities might be a coincidence of universal geometry, or engineering technique. We have no proof that they were built by the same culture."

"So you don't think they're Remor-built? What about Major Ersch's octahedron?"

"I don't know. It could be."

Rafe grinned wolfishly. "So, the constructs could be Remor, and they could have been built by the natives' ancestors. In short, you're admitting that the Chugeni could very well be Remor-descended."

"No, I'm not. I'm not saying *any* such thing." Infuriated, Juliana glared at him. "All I'm saying is that there is a lot that we don't know, and that we can't go making life-and-death decisions while we're ignorant. It may well be true that the Cassuells and the H'kimm derive from the same stock, but even if that's the same stock that bred the Remor, that does *not* make them our enemy! We come from the same earth-descended stock as the Leaguers, but that doesn't make us Leaguers. And I, for one, don't intend to start acting like a Leaguer and advocating genocide against a people who have done us no harm!"

"I'm hearing Ellicot again."

"No, you're hearing me. We never would have survived this long without the help of the H'kimm. We are obligated to them for our lives! We have to do what we can to help *them*."

"The League has a name for Humans who aid the Remor. They call them species traitors. The League has a way of dealing with traitors, too. It executes them"

"We're not traitors," she snapped defensively.

"We?"

Juliana realized that she had automatically assumed that Rafe had been referring to her and Kurt. "Any of us. All of us."

"Don't be so fast to be inclusive."

Juliana knew who he wanted to single out. Rafe had been hostile to Kurt from the very beginning. It seemed that the closer Juliana got to Kurt, the more openly hostile Rafe became. Anything Kurt championed, Rafe opposed. Now it had grown to the point that Rafe, a devout anti-Leaguer, was espousing League propaganda.

"This isn't about the Cassuells and the H'kimm, is it?" she asked. "It isn't their possible association with the Remor that bothers you, is it? It's Kurt and me that you're upset about."

"I don't know what you're talking about." The fire in Rafe's eyes denied his denial. "But if you're going to start dragging irrelevant personal issues into serious discussions, I've got better things to do."

With that, he turned on his heel and strode away, leaving her standing alone at the edge of the jungle.

The castaways' hut wasn't significantly cooler than anywhere else in the village, but its dark interior offered that illusion. Rafe accepted the seeming relief from the muggy heat, just as he accepted the hut's deceptive isolation. Inside the ramshackle construction, with the comatose Singh occupying his sickbed, one was never truly alone.

*That* at least was one thing that was likely to change soon. Their supply of nutrient patches was nearly exhausted, and without the patches the castaways would have no method for keeping Singh fed. Unless the man came to and started eating on his own, he'd die. Which he should have done a long time ago, saving Rafe and everyone else a lot of trouble.

Juli's voice, distorted by the natives' squeal-bark jabber, drifted across the village.

Too bad Shanholz hadn't confided his plans to Rafe. Rafe might just have gone with him. No more of Singh's stink. No more of the stinking natives. No more of a lot of things.

The *nerve* of her to accuse him of letting his hate for Ellicot blind him to reality. His opinion of the bastard wasn't likely to blind him to *anything*! It was plain that the Cassuells and the Chugeni were of a kind. No amount of opinion or alien-loving could change it. Ellicot was just terrified that when the Chugeni were proved to be Remordescended he'd lose his furry friends just like he had the Cassuells. Too bad. They were *aliens*, for god's sake. It's not like they were Humans.

Human loss was something that the alien-besotted bastard Ellicot would never understand. Not like Rafe did.

Why couldn't Juli see what was in front of her eyes?

Probably because it was Zan who had worked it out. Juli had always been jealous of his other women. She didn't like to be reminded that *she* wasn't at the center of the universe. Well, to hell with Juli anyway, Zan was a better lay than she *ever* was!

In fact, Zan was a lot better in a lot of ways, not least as a scientist. Zan's elegant analysis had proven that the Chugeni weren't native to Chugen, while simultaneously showing that they were siblings to the Cassuells. Of course, the work would have been impossible to do without the data he'd provided on the local wildlife he'd been cataloging, but that didn't belittle Zan's achievement.

Rafe hadn't studied Zan's data closely enough to quote sufficient statistics to cow Juli. If he had, their argument might have gone differently. If he could convince her that Ellicot's scientific position was crap, she'd lose respect for him, and *that* would damp her schoolgirl crush big time. He might not want her for himself any more, but he'd be damned if he'd just leave her lying around for Ellicot to pick up.

He pulled a connector cord from his perscomp, snugged it into Zan's machine, and started reviewing Zan's latest work. The multivariant analysis comparing frequencies of amino acid and RNA variants was the keystone, a classic practical tool for comparing genetic similarities. Zan had tried such work previously without anywhere near as clean a result. What had changed?

He cruised through Zan's preliminary work. Among the pile of files she had discarded almost a week before, just after she'd added the new Cassuells file, he found a file labeled CHUGENI AA PROFILE, which seemed to have been the principal basis for all of her earlier comparisons.

Just to see what would happen, he fed the raw data into Zan's recent analysis and reran it. He wasn't surprised to see the old data bring up a new plot point, but its location caught him off guard. It was right up there with the recent Cassuells point and the Chugeni point.

His satisfied smile drooped into a frown. A second new point had shown up as well. It didn't plot tightly with any of the alien points, but it wasn't anywhere near the Chugen indigenous species either.

He ran a search on the old file, trying to identify its source. The odd point came from extant computer files, data from Zan's own genetic profile in her medical files. Rafe's dumping of the raw data into the multivariant analysis had caused the computer to plot Zan's data as if it were part of the analysis.

The positioning of the point near the Cassuell-Chugeni complex bothered him. He ran several more analyses, shifting focus and variables. The Human point drifted from its companions, coming closer and moving further away from the Chugeni-Cassuell complex according to the particular choice of comparisons, but it never seemed to totally divorce itself from them, which, stupefyingly, suggested a connection. He'd seen a similar dance when he'd studied genetic drift among isolated populations of Earth-descended species. Compared to life-forms from other planets, Earth-descended species always clumped tightly. The Human/Chugeni–Cassuells clump wasn't that tight, but it was tighter than he would have expected.

Did the Cassuells–Chugeni have some sort of relationship to Earth-descended Humanity?

In years of studying alien ecologies, he'd learned that the obvious answers weren't always the right ones. He didn't want to jump to conclusions. In years of dealing with Humans, he'd learned that jumping to conclusions, especially the kind that could upset the order of the universe, had severe consequences.

As a precaution he began encrypting his runs as tightly as he could. He'd need time to think about the implications, and to do more comparisons. If he had just uncovered trouble, he wanted to be ready to weather the storm. And if he had just uncovered the scientific coup of the millennium, he wanted to be ready to exploit it.

He was finishing locking things down when he heard the unmistakable rumble of an approaching aircraft.

## 21

**IDL DEFENSE SECTOR 32-RED**
**TARSUS STATION**

Seeing Jason Metzler off had been harder than Anders expected. He'd grown fond of the irreverent Eustan in spite of—or perhaps because of—his lack of proper military discipline. Their service on Grenwold had gotten off to a prickly start, but their shared travails had built a mutual respect and a genuine liking. For a vacuum-head, Metzler was surprisingly human, and spending off-duty time with the garrulous Eustan took Anders back to the days before he'd gone for a soldier, back when he'd had more to think about than weapons, and tactics, and fighting the enemy. Some might say that Metzler was a bad influence, and before Grenwold Anders would have agreed. Since Grenwold there were a lot of things of which Anders wasn't as sure as he had been. But Anders *was* sure that exposure to Metzler had woken him from a lethargy born of long years of war. Metzler had reminded Anders that just as the Eridani way was not the only way to be an effective soldier, the Eridani way was more than just being an effective soldier.

The tiny insystem shuttle carrying Anders between *Prince Rupert* and Tarsus Station was a civilian model with the frivolity of observation ports. Through one, Anders could see *Prince Rupert* and her sister ships accelerating for their designated jump point.

Envious, Anders watched as Metzler headed out for

duty. The Eustan hadn't been able to tell Anders where he and his task group were headed. It wasn't a question of security, as was so often the case. Metzler just didn't know and, if the shipboard rumors were true, neither did the task group's commander. The only thing for certain was that the group's orders had been changed as soon as they had established communications with Tarsus Station. Resupply was arranged as they crossed Tarsus System between jump points, as was Anders's departure. The task group, Metzler included, was headed out with no delay, suggesting that they were headed into action—unlike Anders, who was headed for staff duty. He should have been aboard *Prince Rupert*, outbound for action, or aboard *Santa Anna* with his troopers, wherever they were.

Watching the twinkling points of the drives receding sharply on a diverging vector, Anders was overcome with a feeling of foreboding. The galaxy had more than enough space to swallow forever such tiny ships as humankind built. Had he seen the last of his new friend? God and St. Michael willing, Metzler and his crewmates would be back to tell their tale.

In due time, the little shuttle was swallowed up by the enormous bulk of the station. When the docking procedures were complete, the pilot called "All Ashore" to his lone passenger and opened the inner hatch. Anders made his way across the chill dock, past busy tech crew in heavy coveralls, and into the lift tube. Weight slowly came back to him as he neared the hab ring. Sighing to a stop, the lift opened its door. He shouldered his stowbag and stepped onto Tarsus Station proper.

The docking officer who met him with a sloppy salute and a mechanical greeting was a Holsteader lieutenant. He took Anders's order chip with a pale white hand and a lackadaisical attitude that reinforced the stereotype of Holsteader slothfulness. The fact that the man carried the extra weight that was often a sign of steady behind-the-lines duty didn't do anything to dispel the image. A visible change came over the Holsteader after Anders thumbed the pad and blinked into the scanner, confirming his identity sufficiently for the machine to cough up an approval.

"You have immediate orders to report to the command center, Major," the Holsteader announced, handing over a newly cut ID card.

To hurry up and wait on the commander's convenience, no doubt. "Acknowledged," Anders said, accepting the card and slinging its thong around his neck. He looked about to see if there was a station layout map posted nearby. He didn't see one.

"Do you need any help with your stowbag, sir? I don't have a berth assignment showing for you, but I can hold it here and have it delivered."

"I'll keep it with me," Anders said, his voice sufficient to forestall the Holsteader's reaching hands. "I believe you said I was wanted in the command center."

"Aye, sir. That's right, sir. I can escort you."

"Directions will do."

"Aye, sir."

The Holsteader's directions proved good enough. Walking through the corridors of Tarsus Station, Anders noted that easily half of the personnel wore nationality bars that matched his own. By St. Michael, he hadn't seen so many Eridani since he'd shipped out of Eridani Station. Their presence gave the unfamiliar Tarsus Station an oddly homey feeling.

The last stretch of corridor leading to the command center Anders walked alone. Two ratings in hardsuits waited by the hatch at the far end. Contrary to his expectations, neither moved to bar his way. Only as the hatch slid aside did he realize that although there had been no visible or audible challenge, sensors must have interrogated his ID tag and accepted it.

The noise of the bustling command center flooded through the hatch. *Shaka's* command center, the largest to which Anders had previously had access, could have been dropped in a corner unnoticed. His eyes swept across the controlled chaos, taking it in. The commander's dais was empty; the door to his private office was closed and its "present" light dark. Anders started looking for the officer of the deck. The highest rank he spotted was that of a general. He headed in that direction, noting along the way that the general, an Eridani, was in conference with a tall, slender Holsteader colonel, and showing an unusual amount of deference to the lower-ranked officer, which could only mean one thing: the colonel would be the sector commander's executive officer.

Anders drew closer, and when a break presented itself, he saluted and announced himself. "Major Anders Seaborg reporting as ordered, sir."

"Hollister." The Holsteader colonel stuck out his hand without looking around. "Welcome aboard, Seaborg."

"Thank you, sir."

Hollister concluded his business with the general and turned to Anders. His eyes were piercing and nothing in his manner hinted of slovenliness. This was no stereotypical Holsteader.

"Do you have any baggage beyond that stowbag?" he asked brusquely.

Puzzled, Anders replied, "No, sir."

"Good. Swing it up and let's get moving. The commander wants you expedited through. I've saved you a seat on the last shuttle out."

Stunned, Anders was slow to start after Hollister. Hadn't

he been assigned to Sector Command? And wasn't he standing in the sector's command center? Hollister implied the commander was aboard a ship. What was going on?

When he caught up he tried to ask his questions, but the colonel didn't give him a chance; he seemed to have a word to say at every station they passed. Exiting the command center, they picked up an escort, a Lancastrian major with a logistics specialty with whom Hollister had a long involved exchange of requisition numbers, loading dates, destination designations, and arrival dates. It was only after they entered a lift to be lowered to a docking deck that Anders got the chance to say, "I don't understand, sir. My orders were a station assignment."

"You made it to the station, didn't you?"

"Aye, sir."

"Fine. Stop living in the past." The lift door slid open and Hollister pointed at the waiting shuttle. "There's your ride, Seaborg. Good luck."

Anders stepped from the lift and turned to ask Hollister another question, but the door slid shut and the colonel was gone. An eager pilot was waving at him from the shuttle's boarding hatch. Anders barely had his bag secured before the lift warning chimed. Within minutes he was back in space, headed who knew where.

God and St. Michael willing, he would be back to tell the tale.

## IDL DEFENSE SECTOR 31-ORANGE
## UNCLAIMED SPACE

Jason Metzler had thought he'd been sentenced to purgatory when he learned to whom Lieutenant General Schley's task group had been assigned: Marshal Randolph Ashton Pierce, late of Franconia and said by all honest men to have left his soul on the Remor-conquered world along with his family and heart. Pierce was known throughout MilForce as the hardest-assed, most demanding, least sympathetic commander this side of Old Stone Face. Some, such as those who survived serving under Pierce, said he was *worse* than Old Stone Face.

The run out to the Kansias System was full of drills and maneuvers, sims and briefings, inspections and training sessions. It was a brutal schedule. As an interface flight commander, Jason seemed to figure only lightly in the fleet commander's plans. But instead of lighter duty, he and his crews picked up cross-training assignments that worked them as hard as the rest. Each day at his off-watch he was drained, but he knew more than he had the watch before. Intellectually he understood what Pierce was about, but neither intellect nor emotion gave him what he needed to appreciate the frenzied pace of Pierce's demands.

The one saving grace Jason could see in his current life was that IDLS *Prince Rupert* was not IDLS *Retribution*, the fleet's flagship, for which he was duly grateful. Scuttlebutt said that Pierce ran the crew who shared a ship with him harder than anyone else. Being unable to conceive of working harder than he already was, Jason had a difficult time believing that, but he feared that it was true; he'd seen the growing piles of requests for transfer from Pierce's *Retribution* that sat on Commander Coleman's console.

But Coleman was as wise as any commander in the fleet, and he had approved none of them. He probably thought that it made his own crew grateful, as they would have been the source of replacements for anyone transferring to *Prince Rupert*. And in thinking that, Coleman was right.

Purgatory ended when the fleet left Kansias and crossed into hell. That was as good a description as any for travel through uncharted space where there were no beacons to ease the transition from jump space. Every time *Prince Rupert* rattled through the bumpy transition to an unbeaconed star system, Jason was sure they had crossed a hellish circle boundary.

Military ships could make such unaided jumps, but they weren't easy on the ship's systems or on the crew. Despite the best efforts of air filters, recycling systems, and cleanup crews, the air aboard ship began to take on a distinctly more solid aspect. After each jump, it got worse, Jason contributing to the effluvium as much as anyone. Pulmonary reconditioning aerosols were issued at each watch change, cutting the risk of ailments, but doing little for the discomfort and general unpleasantness.

And still Pierce drove them on.

Jason suspected he had drawn close to perdition's inner precincts when *Prince Rupert*'s general alarm rang before the all-clear on their seventh transition. Within a minute, the fleet commander addressed them.

"Attention the fleet. This is Marshal Pierce. An enemy hulk is lying athwart our course. Preliminary data suggests that this is the same enemy vessel that destroyed *Shaka*. If so, we have been blessed.

"Enemy screening forces are light, and at this time most of them are accelerating away from the hulk and from us. We have been given the opportunity to show our enemy the error of his ways. Our opponents have made a miscalculation in allowing this fleet to intercept them, and we shall make them pay for that mistake. We will give battle.

"It will not be easy. I could exhort you all to do your duty, but I don't think I have to do that. The enemy lies before us. You know your duty better than I. We will face the enemy, and we will defeat him! Decisively!

"You all have my fullest confidence. Together we can do what must be done. And do it, we will! Why? Because

Humanity is counting on us. We are the protectors, the defenders, and, by God's grace, we will become the saviors.

"Vessel commanders, stand by to receive battle orders.

"God be with us all.

"Pierce out."

Pierce sounded confident. Jason wondered about that. As far as he knew, Human forces had fought Remor hulks only four times before, and none of those encounters had yielded any Human survivors.

The wardroom aboard *Prince Rupert* had a luxury: a console slaved to the ship's general navigational systems. Its display of insystem traffic confirmed what Pierce had said about enemy deployment. Humans might never have come away from an engagement with a Remor hulk, but neither had they ever enjoyed meeting one with so little in the way of protective forces. And Pierce's fleet was as big or bigger than any force to face such an enemy. Perhaps there was some reason for confidence.

For hope, anyway.

*Prince Rupert* went to full battle stations as she closed. Since the posted battle orders did not require Jason to stand ready in the cockpit of his interface shuttle, for once he didn't have the comforting routine of preflight checks to fill his time. He was also isolated from watching the fleet's progress. He, his crews, and the landing force troopers were all supernumeraries in this battle. They waited in the ready rooms adjacent to the flight deck, all strapped down, with nothing to do until the ship commander decided he needed their services. Like his fellows, all Jason could do was listen as *Prince Rupert* fought her battle. Deprived of his link to the command systems, he had no data to place the sounds he heard and the jars he felt into a rational context. The ship's few and terse announcements and warnings didn't tell him nearly enough about what was going on. He didn't like it at all.

"Now you know what we feel like when you rocket-jocks take us planetside on a hot drop," joked the commander of *Prince Rupert*'s ground detachment.

Jason grimaced at the man, hating his "gotcha" grin.

Without warning *Prince Rupert* slewed sideways. Jason knew for certain that had he reached the heart of hell when fire exploded through the compartment.

# 22

## CHUGEN SYSTEM
## CHUGEN IV

The spotted ghost's lunge took it toward Ah'zzt. The agile hunter leapt from its path. The beast twisted to follow him, its secondary limbs raking wide. One clawed paw slammed into Langdorf. Blood sprayed as the hooked claws ripped through the man's clothes and flesh with equal, terrifying ease. Langdorf spun away, screaming.

Kurt, frozen in fear, could only watch as the spotted ghost took a step toward the fallen man.

Ah'zzt rushed the monster, jabbing with his spear. He struck the creature's side, just behind the last of its secondary limbs. Hissing, it reared again. Ah'zzt danced away, neatly avoiding the monster's retaliatory lunge.

The distraction turned the monster away from Langdorf. Ah'zzt shouted at him to run. Langdorf tried to get to his feet and failed. He started dragging himself away from his attacker.

The spotted ghost twisted around, looking for another victim. Its head bobbed as it sought new prey. All around Kurt, H'kimm dropped spears and bows and backed away, retreating toward the brush. Langdorf crawled along the sandbar, away from the covering vegetation, but away from the monster as well. Kurt backed a few stumbling steps, unable to take his eyes from the monster. Several of the H'kimm halted their retreat once they gained the cover of the brush at the river's edge. The monster showed no interest in them. In moments Kurt and Ah'zzt were the only two still standing, sharing the sandbar with the spotted ghost. The creature made its choice. With slow, deliberate steps, it advanced on Kurt.

At each step, it lifted the row of secondary limbs on the side of the advanced forelimb. Those paws spread, and the dark hooks tipping the digits glistened evilly. At the next step, those limbs swept down and the ones on the opposite side lifted and clawed the air. Step by sinuously twisting step, the creature came closer.

Step by tiny step, Kurt backed away from it. He stared at the wide, gaping jaws and watched saliva drip from the roof of the creature's mouth. His eyes followed the course of the viscous drool as it flowed around sharp, sharp teeth and dripped to the ground to stain the sand dark.

He was not fast enough to escape this monster. He knew that. The spotted ghost seemed to know it as well; it was in no hurry to make its final, fatal lunge. It took another step toward him, its tail swishing back and forth and erasing the tracks of its passage. Like a real ghost, it left no footprints as it stalked its prey.

Kurt's foot struck water. His back was to the river—there was no further retreat for him. The spotted ghost had him.

The beast reared up, flexing its secondary limbs as it had before striking Langdorf. It was Kurt's turn.

But the attack never came. The monster's hiss changed from threat to annoyance as Ah'zzt jabbed its hindquarters with his spear.

The spotted ghost abandoned Kurt. Its baleful gaze turned to Ah'zzt. Its body twisted. Secondary limbs swept out toward the hunter. Ah'zzt leapt high above the scything claws. His toes barely touched the sand again before he was scrambling away. The spotted ghost stalked him along the sandbar.

Kurt had been given a reprieve.

By Ah'zzt, who had replaced Kurt as the creature's next meal.

Ah'zzt, a good member of the pack, was defending his fellows while Kurt stood useless and shamed. If not for Kurt's request, the hunter wouldn't be here, wouldn't be facing this danger. Kurt had been grateful for the H'kimm's help in searching for the missing Shanholz. He had gratefully accepted the solidarity that the pack had offered.

Accepted.

Ah'zzt was proving just how accepted *Kurt* had been. Hunters like him were defenders of the pack, expected to safeguard the pack as a whole and its members as individuals.

He had come to Kurt's defense.

The H'kimm had accepted him, but he—hugging close his fear of his past indiscretion, of identifying too strongly with the Cassuells—had not accepted them. He'd been promised that the H'kimm would be a second chance for him, an opportunity to redeem his mistakes of the past. Since first contact with the H'kimm, he'd told himself he was working on that redemption by keeping himself aloof from them. Each day he denied the ever stronger pull the H'kimm had on his heart. Each day he felt more and more the hypocrite.

Others, Burke especially, could tell him that the H'kimm were not his kind. *They're not humans*, they would say. *Just look at them.* Kurt looked, and he saw that the H'kimm were not *Homo sapiens*, but deep down he knew that Burke's kind of *truth* was no truth at all. Humanity lay in more than genetic heritage.

The H'kimm had taken in the castaways and treated them as their own. Was that not *human* kindness?

They had shared all they had with the castaways. Was that not *human* generosity?

The H'kimm loved and hated, feared and laughed, sorrowed and were joyful. Were not all those things *human* traits?

And now Ah'zzt had drawn the spotted ghost away from Kurt, at the cost of turning its ravenous attention to himself. What more *human* trait was there than sacrifice of oneself for one's fellows?

Kurt could no longer doubt the kinship of spirit—the humanity—shared by the Human species and the H'kimm. The only doubt remaining was his commitment to accepting and embracing that kinship.

On a tiny spit of sand by the edge of a river with no name, one kindred spirit—one human—fought for his life and that of his fellows.

On that same small island, one human stood and did nothing, too afraid of himself to help another.

Lo'gnen had called Kurt *tuoyal*, naming him a respected member of the pack. Did he deserve it?

The pack did not abandon its own.

Could Kurt abandon the pack?

He had once before.

But not of his own will.

No one was dragging him away this time.

And no one would. Bending down, he snatched up one of the spears abandoned by the H'kimm who had fled. The rough, uneven shaft felt awkward in his hands. That didn't matter; it was a weapon. Unarmed, he could do nothing against the spotted ghost. Armed with a weapon he didn't know how to use, he might do little better; but he'd made his choice. Kurt couldn't let Ah'zzt face the monster alone.

Pointing the tip at the spotted ghost he took a small step forward. The shout of hostile defiance he'd intended came out like a bleat.

The monster swung its milky eyes toward him.

Ah'zzt seized the chance. He darted past the spotted ghost's head and struck the beast in its side. The monster squalled in pain, twisting back on itself to snap at the hunter. Its jaws closed on Ah'zzt's carry bag. The strap parted, freeing the hunter from his monstrous captor, but unbalancing him. The spotted ghost gulped down its catch and turned to Ah'zzt. The hunter's left forelimb was injured, preventing him from humping away in the H'kimm's speedy four-footed "run." The monster snapped at him, harrying him and preventing him from getting up on his hind feet. Ah'zzt scrambled as fast as he could, barely keeping himself ahead of the clashing jaws.

Yelling, Kurt rushed forward. He ran past where Langdorf had collapsed. The man looked dead. As if he could keep terror at bay, Kurt held the flaked stone point of his weapon well before him.

The shock of contact with the beast shook him. He hadn't expected the animal to be so *solid*.

But although the stone point had barely penetrated its skin and done it no great injury, the spotted ghost reacted. It hissed an indignant whistle at this new assault. Its lashing tail clipped Kurt and tumbled him to the sand.

But he had won Ah'zzt his chance. The hunter was on his feet again. Kurt, too, scrambled upright. Side by side, they presented their spears. The spotted ghost stared at them, apparently dumbfounded by their defiance.

"It is too strong," Ah'zzt stated. "We will both die here if we stay. You must go, *tuoyal*. Let the spotted ghost be satisfied with me."

"I was about to suggest that *you* go."

"That is not right."

"Too bad. I'm not leaving you here to fight it alone."

"Why do you do this?"

"A good man is loyal to his pack."

"But I am *grawr'tayo*."

"Aren't we all?"

Ah'zzt's eyes left the spotted ghost. He stared at Kurt with disbelief. "But you are *tuoyal*."

"That's what Lo'gnen says." Kurt shrugged. "I still think you should go."

"I cannot go."

"Then, as you said, we will both die here."

"I had not thought to join the spirit pack as anything other than *grawr'tayo*. We will join the pack as *daramak*, you and I, yes?"

Kurt's translator was silent concerning the new word. *That*, he realized, *is because I've lost it, probably when the spotted ghost sent me tumbling. Oh, well.* Not that it mattered. He would be beyond the need for translators soon. He didn't believe in Ah'zzt's spirit pack, but if the hunter found comfort in it . . . "Sure, friend Ah'zzt. *Daramak* we will be."

Grinning, the hunter returned his attention to the increasingly restive spotted ghost.

To Kurt, it seemed that the beast was working up its nerve. Any moment now, it would decide that it was willing to risk the pinpricks of their spears to take them down. He was sure that it knew there was soft, tasty meat to be had.

But the beast didn't attack. Its agitation grew. Head swinging from side to side, its attention seemed divided between him and Ah'zzt and something behind them.

Kurt risked taking his eyes from the monster. Turning his head slightly, he saw that he and Ah'zzt were no longer alone on the spit. Several of the H'kimm had returned. Most had recovered their spears and were holding them out, points aimed at the spotted ghost. Three had readied bows, setting arrows to string, but seemed unsure of the wisdom of using their weapons against the spotted ghost.

The rallied pack was too much for the spotted ghost. It backed away, hissing furiously. The black patches on its hide expanded and the rest of its hide darkened, becoming more nearly the color of the sand and the muddy water of the river toward which it backed.

Yet it was unwilling to take a total loss on its venture. Two of its left-side belly appendages whipped out and snagged Langdorf's body. The man never twitched. His body was dragged in close to the beast where all six secondary limbs hugged his corpse tight against the monster's belly.

Had Langdorf still been alive, Kurt would have thrown himself at the spotted ghost in a futile effort to rescue him. Defending the living was one thing, but with his companion dead, such a gesture was worse than futile. It was stupid and pointless.

Once its hindquarters reached the water, the spotted ghost reared. But instead of lunging forward, it twisted to one side, throwing itself into a sideways dive. The dark waters hid the monster as soon as it submerged. Within seconds even the ripples of its passage were lost in the river's ordinary movement.

Staring at the river, Ah'zzt spoke. "The spirits are angry with your folk, *daramak* Kurtellicot."

"Why do you say that?"

"They sent their brother, the spotted ghost, to our territory out of season. But he did not come to punish us. He came to punish your star-folk. He has taken not one, but two of your folk. What have you done to offend the spirits?"

"Nothing that I know of."

Ah'zzt tilted his snout, expressing dissatisfied acceptance. "The world is as it is, and the spirits know more than we do."

The hunter left Kurt to watch the river in case the ghost

decided to return, and began a long, loud argument with the other H'kimm about whether to leave Kr'ezt's body for the spotted ghost or to take it with them to the pack's spirit-ground to be properly exposed in the trees. Ah'zzt's desire to take the body with them seemed to be losing support when a sudden, solitary peal of thunder rumbled down through the canopy and stilled the argument.

The noise was not the herald of one of the forest's typical downpours, for the glimpses of sky seen through breaks in the canopy over the river showed a serene expanse of cerulean blue.

"This too is bad," Ah'zzt pronounced.

Ah'zzt was agitated. So were the other H'kimm. Their argument resumed and soon reached a conclusion. Kr'ezt, a victim of the spotted ghost, belonged now to the spotted ghost. His body would be left. There was, however, something else to be done.

"We must go speak to the spirits," Ah'zzt said.

"I'd rather just go back to the village."

Ah'zzt turned his snout aside in negation.

"Why not?"

"We cannot."

"Because the spirits are angry?"

"Angry, yes."

Ah'zzt led them back into the forest, away from the river, and away from the village as well for all that Kurt could tell. Though the hunter followed no path that Kurt could discern, Ah'zzt walked with confidence, speaking only to announce which direction they would take. The other H'kimm murmured worriedly among themselves. From listening to them, Kurt learned that none of them had ever been in this part of the forest before. In fact, they were agreed that Ah'zzt had never been here before either. They wouldn't tell Kurt how they knew that, and he suspected that they were only guessing. Ah'zzt certainly wasn't acting like a man in a strange land; he showed no hesitation when alternate paths presented themselves. Striding swiftly and surely, he seemed to know exactly where he was going.

The ground grew drier the further they went from the river. More rocks showed through the forest floor. Occasionally Kurt glimpsed naked rock faces and huge, moss-covered boulders through the trees. The path along which Ah'zzt led them began to drop away, taking them into what might have been an old river course or lake bed. The H'kimm's conversation faltered. When they spoke, they did so in hushed, reverential tones. Beyond their silence Kurt noticed the greater silence that enwrapped the area. Even the buzz and chatter of Chugen's bugs was muted, sounding as if it were coming from a distance, which it might well be. Try as he might, he could not spot any insects among the vegetation.

The vegetation itself was unusual in this quiet place. Leaves were a darker russet than normal. Their edges were yellowed and shriveled. As the party progressed, the air itself changed, becoming laden with the stench of decomposing organic matter and sulfur. The leaves grew more yellowed.

The H'kimm refused to answer Kurt's questions, other than to say that this was a sacred place, and not one to be visited casually.

They passed a pair of stones rising like sentinels from among the dead brush and sickly green moss that covered the ground. A little further on was another pair, these capped by a lintel stone. Kurt saw no marks of tools and couldn't tell if it was a natural or artificial arrangement. Beyond the lintel-capped stones the path led down into a narrow, twisting gorge of naked rock.

"The place of the spirits," Ah'zzt announced.

The hunter led them down into the shadows. Kurt shivered, as much from the drop in temperature as from the uncanny *feeling* of the place. He felt the awe that was reported by those who stood before a Yanellocyx megalith or in an Old Earth cathedral, the awe he'd felt every time he'd entered a Cassuell *quantaraden*. This *was*, as the H'kimm said it was, a sacred place.

Then he saw what was on the rocks. Everywhere the stone was covered in paintings executed in red and yellow ocher, soot, and an unfamiliar green pigment of surpassing vividness. There were geometric shapes, H'kimm handprints, and other renderings of varying degrees of representative accuracy. Kurt hadn't seen anything like them in the village, no indication at all that the H'kimm practiced painting—one of the things supporting the argument that the H'kimm culture was unrelated to the Cassuells', with their elaborate pictographic symbology.

Most of the likenesses decorating the rock were primitive, little more than stick figures. Upright walking and humped, hurrying H'kimm were easy to spot, but the rest of the simple pictographs were enigmatic. Kurt didn't recognize what they represented, but study and comparison with the more elaborately rendered images would rectify that. Many of those more intricate renderings made immediate sense. He identified spotted ghosts and a lot of the bugs he'd seen, many of them shown at sizes far larger than life. Of course, size was more often an indication of importance than of biological appearance in art such as this; and with bugs forming most of Chugen's fauna, they were certainly important in the H'kimms' lives.

Ah'zzt stopped in a dead end arm of the main gorge. There was just enough flat space for all of them to find a seat. When everyone was settled, Ah'zzt began to hum a

three-toned tune. One by one, the other H'kimm joined
him until only Kurt remained silent. Kurt resisted joining
the song for several minutes, but in the end the soothing
sound sucked him in. He began to hum along with his
pack-mates.

Time receded in importance. There were only the
sound and the images on the rock. And the pack. Closing
his eyes, Kurt rested in the comforting embrace. It seemed
to him that he still saw the rock paintings. He had no better
idea of their significance, but he knew them. Some hinted
at motion, moving when he was not paying attention to
them. Others glowed with importance, shifting in color as
the song went on.

The sound of thunder rolling over the forest canopy
brought the communing session to an abrupt end. Thunderstorms were a daily occurrence in the forest, but this one
was different. Kurt found the sound troubling somehow,
threatening in a way normal thunder was not. The H'kimm
seemed to share his dread, exchanging frightened looks.

Unspeaking, Ah'zzt left the place of the spirits. Since
none of the others rose and Ah'zzt didn't even look his way,
Kurt stayed, too. A few minutes later, the hunter appeared
at the top of the gorge. He stretched, standing tall as he
could, attentive to something. The other H'kimm watched
him silently. Kurt remained silent as well.

Ah'zzt did not rejoin them until after the distant storm
had spent its thunderous fury and moved on. When he did,
his head hung low. He exuded a forlorn air.

"We cannot return to the village," he said. "We must
travel to Rasseh."

The other H'kimm bobbed their heads in agreement,
accepting Ah'zzt's pronouncement. Kurt protested, wanting
to know what Ah'zzt was talking about, what Rasseh was,
and why they must go there, but Ah'zzt didn't answer him.

When the hunter led the H'kimm from the place of the spirits, Kurt had to follow or be left behind in the trackless forest.

Rafe wasn't stupid enough to go running out into the open when he heard the engines. The locals weren't as bright. Several were scattered across the village's open space, snouts high as they sought the source of the thunder they heard in the clear sky. Juli, guileless as the Chugeni, wandered out to join them. She shaded her eyes as she looked up.

Rafe had the angle to see it first: an aircraft, an armed one to judge by the pods slung under its belly. It flew low, nearly at treetop level. It overshot the clearing, flashing by dark and ominous. Its shadow trailed over the clearing like a hawk's. Hearing the engine sound change pitch, Rafe knew that it was coming back. He had no doubt it was looking for trouble.

The aircraft appeared again, with its snout tilted down. It was moving slower this time. Light sparkled from its nose as it spat fire. Gouts of blaster energy splattered several of the Chugeni into lifeless gobbets. Miraculously, not a single pulse touched Juli, who stood frozen, a shocked look on her pretty face, now smeared with Chugeni blood and pulverized organs.

Or maybe not so miraculously, he decided as he noted the markings on the aircraft's tail.

But even if the Humans weren't the targets of this attack, accidents happened when so much firepower was being tossed around. She needed to take cover.

Lockhart seemed to agree with him. From beneath the shade of the communal roof, she was shouting for everyone to run for the jungle.

Of course, Lockhart herself wasn't going anywhere fast.

Not without help anyway. Rafe was the only one strong enough to haul her ass out of there.

A line of pulsed fire raked the brush behind the cast-aways' hut. The screams told Rafe that two Chugeni hadn't made it to cover.

The aircraft hovered, working the clearing and selectively cutting down any Chugeni humping for the jungle's cover. One blast clipped the hut in which Rafe sheltered and ignited the debris that it blasted loose.

No doubt about it, staying put was unhealthy.

Juliana joined the H'kimm in the open space. She heard their questions, but was too busy looking to tell them that what they heard was an aircraft engine.

She barely glimpsed the aircraft as it screamed overhead. All she had was an impression of size and shape, but it was enough to allay her last fears that it might be Remor. She'd seen pictures of Remor aircraft in news footage and this ship didn't look at all like anything she'd seen.

The aircraft came back. She could see that it was marked with abstract graphical symbols, but no letters, numbers, or pictorial representations, nothing to tell her who was operating the craft.

Nose canted down, the aircraft moved slower on its second pass. It seemed to be inspecting them. She waved, hoping to attract the pilot's attention. You couldn't be rescued if your rescuers didn't know you were there.

The aircraft responded with fire.

Energy blasts ripped into the ground, into huts, into H'kimm. Dirt and something else warm and sticky spattered her. She raised her hands before her face, but she didn't dare look at what was sliming them. If she did, she was sure that she would start screaming hysterically.

She forced her hands down. *Don't look, girl,* she admonished herself. *Do. Not. Look.*

But if she didn't look at her hands, she had to look somewhere. Wherever she looked H'kimm were being killed as the aircraft's fire raked the village. One shot hit the castaways' hut, exploding a corner of it.

Rafe burst out of the steam and smoke. He looked at her and shouted something, but he didn't come for her. He ran for the communal roof under which Lockhart lay, disappearing into the smoky haze.

Engines howling, the aircraft set down atop the crater that was all that remained of the females' ceremonial hut, squatting over it like some obscene hen on a nest. Even before the craft had fully settled on its landing gear, hatches opened on its flank. A tumble of men in armored battlesuits spilled out. Pulse rifles whined. Grenades flew and exploded. All around, H'kimm died and the destruction grew.

The soldiers started to spread out through the village, burning and killing and destroying. The communal roof collapsed, burning. Two soldiers emerged from the castaways' hut. Between them they carried a net into which had been piled all of the Humans' computers and most of the rest of their belongings. A female H'kimm, one forelimb missing, crawled from the wreckage of a hut and started limping toward the jungle. A soldier saw her and shot her dead.

Juliana had no idea why *she* hadn't yet been shot and killed.

*Only a matter of time*, she told herself. *Run away, you stupid girl!*

She turned and ran. Right into one of the soldiers. She bounced from his solid battlesuited mass and landed flat on her butt. He reached for her, hand extended. She backcrawled away from him. Between his legs she could see a quartet of angry-looking H'kimm humping toward them.

Coming to her rescue?

Somehow the soldier knew they were coming. He raised his weapon. A burst of pulses tore the H'kimm apart.

Juliana screamed.

"Nothing to worry about now, ma'am. We're League MilForce." The soldier's voice coming through his battle-suit's speaker was cool and detached, even bright. "We're here to rescue you."

The smoke was the first visible sign that something was wrong. It disturbed the H'kimm, but no more than Kurt. He had been right to insist that they return to the village before heading for Rasseh.

Ah'zzt increased the pace, his objections to returning to the village apparently forgotten. Despite the frantic speed with which they covered the last few kilometers, they were too late to do any good. Kurt's first glimpse of the village made him wonder if Ah'zzt had been right all along.

The clearing where the H'kimm had lived was a scene from hell. Blackened craters pocked the ground and dead H'kimm littered the place. Little was left of the huts. Those that weren't smoldering piles of debris and charred wood were ravaged cavities where glassy specks sparkled among the clods of seared earth.

The castaways' hut was the least demolished of the village's structures. One wall still stood, a chunk of the roof leaning against it. The green leaves of that chunk marked it as part of the section that had just been repaired before Kurt left the village to hunt for Shanholz. Flames ate at the leaves, producing the smoke that they had seen from afar.

Against the ruddy glow of the fire, Kurt could see the silhouette of a charred Human corpse. It lay where the comatose Singh had lain for weeks. That was enough to identify it for Kurt. He had no desire to go closer.

He turned away. But he could not escape the horror.

Everywhere the dead surrounded him. Many of the bodies were unrecognizable smears of ash and scraps of burnt bone. Some were all too recognizable. At least none of the partial corpses belonged to his fellow castaways. He didn't know what he would do if he saw Juli's dead, cold face.

But she didn't have to be dead!

She could have escaped into the jungle. He shouted her name. When he got no answer, he ran to the forest edge and shouted again. And again. He shouted all their names, but no one answered. He kept calling to them until Ah'zzt put a hand on his arm.

"It is no good, *damarak* Kurtellicot. All are here."

"No." Did he really think that denying the evidence could change reality? Apparently, because he continued to do so. "We haven't seen their bodies. They must have run away."

"I see no sign of any fleeing the village. No star-folk spoor going from here is younger than the fire from the sky."

Fire from the sky?

*My god! The Remor!*

The Remor had finally come. They had done their devil's work and left. Kurt turned his eyes to the sky, but humankind's enemy no longer lurked there. The calm blue mocked him. It was a mask, hiding the stars where the enemy dwelt.

Kurt turned away from the sky. With humankind's enemy ruling the system, he was bound to Chugen now. This was where he would live out his life and, sooner or later, die. Sooner, if the Remor found him.

Twelve H'kimm and two Humans had left the village to hunt Shanholz. Eleven H'kimm and one Human had returned, a dozen lost souls wandering the desolated village. Some knelt by mangled corpses mourning the loved ones lying there. A few scratched at the rubble, searching for something or someone. Kurt didn't have the heart to search. Seeing the bodies of his dead companions would only make his isolation too real to bear.

He found himself standing at the edge of the cinder heap that had once been the village's shaded gathering place. G'riv knelt in the midst of the ash.

G'riv, a sub-adult female who had been old enough to run with the hunters and too young to have joined the other females, had gone with them on the hunt for Shanholz. That chance made her the last female of the pack. The fur on her cheeks was dark and starting to mat from her tears.

"Lo'gnen has joined the spirit pack," she wailed.

Lo'gnen, as pack leader, had been considered father to all of the pack's pups. Given the markings on G'riv's pelt, his paternity may have been literally true in her case.

"He will hunt with the spirit pack," he told her to comfort her. "The hunting will be good. He will be happy."

She burrowed against Kurt's side, still weeping.

The other H'kimm gathered around them. They were all that was left of the pack. Things weren't hopeless for them. There were other H'kimm out there somewhere. This pitiful remnant could be saved. But what about him?

"What do we do now, *tuoyal*?" they asked.

*We?*

They considered him part of the pack. Just now, though, he didn't feel part of anything.

What was there to do?

"Rasseh," Ah'zzt said.

The H'kimm heard him, but they looked to Kurt. "What do we do, *tuoyal*?"

Why him? Why were they asking him?

"*Tuoyal*?" G'riv looked up at him. She still gripped him

fiercely, as if afraid that he too would be lost to her. "What do we do?"

Sometimes second chances weren't quite what you expected them to be.

"We go on," he told her. His gaze took in the whole pack. "We go to Rasseh."

# Part 3

# Conjunction Anthesis

## 23

**CHUGEN SYSTEM**
**CHUGEN IV**

Two days huddled in the belly of the League transport aircraft raised doubts among the castaways about their "rescue." Juliana, Rafe, Zandowski, and Lockhart were jammed into the rear of the main compartment and walled off by a makeshift bulkhead. The furnishings were acceleration couches and a tiny head. There were no windows, no entertainment except a slim library of leisure sims and old news on one portable player, and, beyond the woman who brought their meals, no contact with their "rescuers." Their confinement was "for their safety," a justification that only Zandowski believed. The result was four cranky people who immediately noticed the changes in the sounds coming from outside their limited world.

Warrant Officer Sharon Vestler wore the uniform of an IDL MilForce medical specialist, but she was their jailer as well as their physician. For two days the laconic Vestler hadn't had any information for them other than the news of Singh's death, their own medical reports, and the menu for their meager meals of preserved foods. That made the polite but aloof woman the most communicative and human of the Leaguers with whom they'd had contact. When she came through the door in the makeshift bulkhead, Juliana pounced on her, demanding to know what the change was about.

"We're preparing to leave, Professor Tindal. Please go back and strap down."

Juliana didn't move. "Where are we going?"

"Back to base camp, ma'am." Vestler looked past her to the others and requested that everyone strap in. She put a tentative hand on Juliana's shoulder. "Please, ma'am. You don't want to be standing when we lift."

"So we go to your base camp." Juliana removed Vestler's hand. "And what happens then?"

Vestler gave her a frown. "You ask a lot of questions, Professor Tindal."

"I have an inquiring mind. Why now? If you've got a camp, why haven't we gone there before now?"

"We were waiting on the search parties, ma'am," Vestler replied as if the reason were perfectly obvious.

Were they hunting down villagers that they'd managed to miss in their massacre? "What search parties?"

"The ones who have been looking for Professors Ellicot and Langdorf, ma'am."

Until now Vestler had shrugged off her questions about Kurt and Langdorf. Now she was telling Juliana that the Leaguers had been looking for him all along. "You found them?"

Vestler hesitated, looking unhappy. At length she said, "The scouts found where they had gone."

"What do you mean?" The peculiar form of the response woke a small gnawing animal in Juliana's stomach. "Are you saying that you didn't *actually* find them?"

Vestler shrugged. "It appears that they and their native friends had a fatal encounter with local wildlife."

No! It wasn't fair! Kurt couldn't be dead. Not now!

"The teams reported a lot of blood," Vestler continued. "When we analyzed the samples this morning we got a match to Chugen Project medical records, confirming that both professors were present and injured. One Chugeni was killed—and partially eaten. There were Chugeni survivors, but they have disappeared into the jungle."

"You said Chugeni survivors. What about Human survivors? You didn't say anything about finding *their* bodies."

"I'm sorry. The scouts found a portion of Professor Langdorf downriver from the attack site. Whatever killed the Chugeni got him as well."

Juliana wasn't ready to give up. "But you didn't find Kurt's body, did you?"

"No, ma'am. But you shouldn't hold out any hope. The scouts cannot confirm any Humans leaving the attack site."

"No?" Everything went blurry as the tears welled up.

"I'm afraid not," Vestler said sympathetically.

Juliana leaned back against the wall. She was losing it, but she didn't care. Kurt was *gone*. They hadn't even had a chance to . . .

She felt a prick against her skin.

"It'll help you sleep," Vestler told her from very far away.

## PAN-STELLAR COMBINE
## CYGNUS

The audience in the briefing room sat quietly, listening to Sector Commander Stone deliver the staccato summation of his address. Had the meeting taken place in the public Guildhall Chamber, with the full Board of Directors for the Pan-Stellar Combine, Stone's voice would have been echoing off the walls; but here in the muffled confines of the ruling Governing Committee's most secret and private chamber, the soundproofing ate the sector commander's words almost as soon as he uttered them. Looking at the pinched faces of the Pan-Stellar Combine's highest officials, Anders Seaborg suspected that those worthies wouldn't have minded if the soundproofing were even more efficient. They didn't look as though they enjoyed at all what they were hearing.

To Anders, the secluded nature of the conference made it patently clear that the PSC leadership wanted to keep the current situation quiet. So far they had been doing a good job; as far as he could tell, not a word about the Chugen situation had reached ordinary Combine citizens. Combine media reported nothing untoward going on in Combine space—other than the usual celebrity scandals and the standard charges and countercharges of fiscal impropriety, price fixing, dumping, influence peddling, corporate espionage, and insider trading. But of reports that Humankind's alien enemy had infiltrated Combine space, there were none.

Commander Stone was supposed to be here to give the Combiners a wake-up call that they couldn't ignore, but the Board had managed to keep the League visit quiet. So far Commander Stone had not authorized any breach of the news blackout, claiming that anything the League tried to tell Combine citizens would just be put down to propaganda. Actually, he'd said, "They'll just call us liars."

From what Anders knew of the average Combiner's attitude to the League, the commander's expectations were not far out of line. Without the backing of the PSC's Committee and Board, there was little the League could do to mobilize popular sentiment in the Combine, thus the commander's mission to win the leaders' hearts and minds to the League's way of thinking.

So far, however, the commander's presentation had failed to erase Anders's own doubts. What hope did he have of winning over the even more skeptical Combiners? Nevertheless, he was giving the effort his best.

"The conclusion is obvious," Stone said. "To within all reasonable tolerances, the aliens whose bodies we recovered on Grenwold are a match to the aliens who had inhabited Cassuells Home. You have seen the pictures of the Grenwold aliens tending the enemy's harvester beasts while undeniably Remor machines herd the beasts. We were dealing with the enemy on Grenwold. On both Grenwold and Cassuells Home, we dealt with a single species, an enemy species. The evidence is clear that these beings are Remor. It follows that the Chugeni are Remor as well.

"The League made the right choice on Cassuells Home, striking before the spacefaring segment of the enemy could stop us. We hurt them there. We have been handed another opportunity to do the same. The enemy cannot be allowed to infest planets in Humankind's space. They can and should—hell, they *must*—be eliminated!"

Nervous silence greeted the commander's thunderous finish. The cheers or applause he would have heard from a League audience did not come. The board members just exchanged significant looks among themselves. Their unenthusiastic response did not sit well with the commander; Anders watched his brows draw together like storm clouds above the Garibaldi Mountains back home. Just before the storm broke, Monsieur Stephen Dillon, the cadaverously lean principal speaker of the Committee for Administration and executive chairman of the PSC Board, cleared his throat.

"Thank you for your presentation, Sector Commander Stone," he said with cold, formal politeness. "You leave us with no doubt about your personal position on the issue to hand. I must say that I find your, er, devotion to League ideals almost overpowering."

"This isn't about me personally," Stone growled.

"No, it isn't," Madame Adèle Hynes agreed quickly. Hynes, a woman whose pinched expression broadcast her case-hardened manner, was the seated chairman, second only to Dillon in power and influence and fiercely loyal to her superior. Intel had predicted that she would be a good second and act as Dillon's stalking horse; she fulfilled their expectations by adding, "But your reputation as the Casual Slaughterer precedes you."

"Twenty credits at three to two Old Stone Face is going to lose it," Captain Shaler whispered to Anders. The Lancastrian political specialist was a betting man, one of his less endearing characteristics.

"Quiet," Anders said, declining Shaler's proposition. Sector Commander Stone had been dubbed the Casual Slaughterer by the Combiner media for his part in commanding the Cassuells Home Affair. It was an appellation that had come into common usage far and wide, but one that Stone found undeserved and insulting. More than once, the use of the phrase in his hearing had gotten a Mil-Force soldier a full ration of unpleasant duty.

But here in the PSC Board's chamber, Stone was not the unquestioned commander. And he had a mission. He reddened but he didn't blow, and when he spoke his voice was icily cold. "My *reputation* is irrelevant."

"Some think otherwise, Sector Commander Stone," Hynes stated.

"Also irrelevant," he stated, continuing to refuse to be baited.

Hynes was persistent. "Who can deny that personalities color decisions?"

"We are not talking about anyone's personal conclusions, Madame Hynes." Stone fixed his gaze on Dillon. "I have presented you with Strategic Command's evaluation, and I am asking you to look at these facts and face their implications."

"Ah, yes. The implications. That is the issue, isn't it? The implications, I'm afraid, are what leave us in something of a quandary." Dillon sucked in his cheeks, making his gaunt face look almost skeletal. He smiled, increasing the resemblance to a skull. "Our scientific advisors assure us that your evidence is valid, as far as it goes. Yet evidence is nothing more than data, and—as we all know—data must be interpreted. It is, I think, in the *interpretation* that we find a sticking point. As should be obvious to your Strategic Command after all these years, not everyone shares the League's interpretation, Sector Commander Stone. Many people have alternative interpretations of this data. The Concordat ambassador, for example, holds a rather different view of your evidence. She calls it inconclusive and subject to *mis*interpretation."

Stone's expression hardened. "Is the ambassador denying that the Cassuells, the Grenwold aliens, and the Chugeni are all the same? The new evidence from Chugen is—"

"Is quite compelling," Dillon interrupted. "At least with regard to the *biological* sameness of the aliens in question. We will stipulate to that."

*How generous*, Anders thought.

The principal speaker continued. "Responsibility is the issue here. *Who* is responsible for the attacks on humankind? The Remor, yes, but *who* are the Remor? Your conclusion that this sameness of biology makes the aliens who dwell on our protected affiliate, perforce, the spacefaring Remor enemy who have brought so much tragedy to humankind is subject to question. Your evidence does not prove that the Chugeni are, in any way, responsible for humankind's woes. It does seem that these furred aliens are all of a species, and perhaps they are the same species as the Remor. Perhaps they are not. It is the Concordat ambassador's position that the alien species in question are servitors and nothing more. In short, they are an enslaved species."

"Ridiculous." Stone snorted. "Such a conclusion has no basis in fact. Where are the supporting data? Slaves need masters. Where are they? There is no evidence of any other intelligent species on Grenwold or Cassuells Home, and so far none from Chugen. The Chugeni *are* the enemy, which makes the planet Chugen an enemy base. It is an intolerable situation, and must be dealt with.

"If the Pan-Stellar Combine is not willing to deal with the problem, others are. As the representative of the Inter-stellar Defense League charged with defense of this sector of space, I formally call upon the Pan-Stellar Combine to relinquish all claim to the planet known as Chugen. The war must be carried to the enemy."

"Are you threatening us with Leaguer military action, Stone?" Hynes asked.

The commander ignored Hynes's impolite omission of his rank. "As I said, others are prepared to deal with the problem."

Hynes readied another volley, but Dillon forestalled her. "I think we have heard all that needs saying for today. Sector Commander Stone, gentlemen of the IDL Military Force, thank you for your advice. We will consider what has been said here today. I declare this session closed."

Dillon rapped his gavel and that was it. The meeting with the Combine leadership was over. The Committee members departed, and low-level functionaries replaced them. The flunkies announced their intention to escort the League visitors to their shuttle. Following the commander's example, Anders and the rest of the Leaguers bore the snub in silence.

When they reached their landing field and were left alone, Stone asked, "Well, Seaborg, where do you think it's going?"

Anders noted that the commander spoke to him and not

to Shaler, the putative expert on Combiner politics. Anders and Stone were both Eridani, the only ones in the landing party. Anders had always found a fellow Eridani's opinion valuable; perhaps Stone felt the same way. Unfortunately, Anders wasn't sure how the Combiners would react. "They seem reluctant to accept the League's position."

"Damn right. The Pansies will dither until a Remor fleet goes into orbit around Cygnus, and then scream that it's all our fault, that we didn't do enough to stop the enemy."

MilForce was doing all it could, with its limited resources stretched so badly. "We're fighting the Remor wherever they appear, sir. Isn't that enough?"

"It won't be enough until we've killed every damn specimen of the enemy we can find."

"Meaning the Chugeni?"

"They are the enemy. This isn't a limited conflict. This is as total as war gets, and it's them or us, son. Personally, I prefer that we be the ones to survive, don't you?"

"Yes, sir." In a war, you killed the enemy. Anders just wasn't completely sure that the aliens whom the troopers had dubbed "stink-weasels" were the enemy. Associated with the enemy, certainly, but the source of humankind's travails? Whatever the truth of it, there were additional concerns. "Action in the Chugen System could have repercussions."

"Understood. That's why we came here and did what we did. We've asked politely. Now it's up to the Pansies to make the right choice."

"And if they don't?"

"Son, we're in a war where the fate of Humanity is at stake. Petty jurisdictional disputes—as dear as they are to our species—cannot be allowed to hinder strategic necessity. God as my witness, we *will* deal with the enemy."

Stone raised his voice to include the other officers, who were of course discreetly listening anyway. "We will do what we have to do make sure Humanity survives. Isn't that right, gentlemen?"

"Sir! Aye, sir!" came the reply.

"The Pansies won't like interference in their protected affiliate. They could stage a confrontation," Shaler said.

Anders thought that very likely. StratCom must be very convinced of the importance of striking against the Chugeni to risk starting an intraspecies war among humankind.

Stone downplayed the danger. "Oh, they'll put on a show, sure enough, but when the line is drawn, they'll back down. They haven't got the will to block us."

How could he be so sure? Anders pointed out, "Action against an indigenous species on one of their affiliated planets strikes at their sovereignty. That could be enough to goad them into something stupid."

Stone smiled grimly. "As I said, it's up to them to make the right choice."

## CHUGEN SYSTEM
## CHUGEN IV

Lockhart was evacuated from the League aircraft in a medical stretcher, protesting all the while about being separated from the others. The League troopers ignored her. Juliana wondered if Lockhart was right to be suspicious of Vestler's assurances that she was just being taken to hospital.

Rafe picked up on Lockhart's complaints, blustering about *official* unhappiness at the treatment of Combiner civilians and demanding to see the officer in charge of what he called a "kidnapping and hostage taking." That last remark brought a smile to the League pilot's lips.

"We can arrange for you to see the officer, sir," he said. He glanced at his copilot and got a confirming nod. "We just got clearance for you to disembark."

The air outside was fresh and clean and the sunshine was glorious. Juliana was glad to be out of the aircraft, but her relief only lasted as long as it took her to tear her eyes away from the wonderful ochers and rusts of the surrounding trees and lower them to rest on the tall, slim figure in sharply creased League tropical khakis waiting for them at the foot of the ramp. Juliana sucked in her breath when she recognized him.

"But you're dead!" she exclaimed.

Major Ersch shrugged. "Clearly an inaccurate report."

## SERENTEN CONCORDAT
## SERENTEN

The projected image of Ambrose Alsion's doppelganger appeared in its usual spot. Danielle Wyss noted that there was no chair today, typically a sign that the construct had something on its electronic mind.

"Good morning, Premier Minister. How are you this morning?" the construct asked, its usual greeting. Without waiting for an answer, it continued, "I presume that your interest has been piqued by the new reports from the Combine."

"Yes, indeed." She had given up being surprised that the construct was as well informed as she. "Members of the Board are making quite a public show of concern over the League's reports of Remor activity very close to their periphery systems, and the minority proposing affiliation with the League appears to be growing. With the League reiterating its position that it cannot afford to detach forces to aid nonmembers, and given the climate of fear in the Combine, I'm afraid that full disclosure of the incident with the Remor raider in the Chugen System could have the unfortunate effect of pushing the Combine into the League's arms."

The construct nodded. "A possibility. Yet a disclosure, if it were truly a *full* disclosure, might be less beneficial to the League than one might expect."

"You've got information that you're not sharing."

"Of course." A disarming smile opened the construct's expression. "But my reason for frustrating you on this point is that I am dealing in speculation and prediction rather than fact. Introducing unwarranted speculation has a deleterious effect on prediction."

Danielle had heard this excuse before. It sprang from the principle of alinear sociodynamics that stated, "Interference invalidates information." Yet sociodynamicists seemed content to interfere indirectly. "But prompting others to speculate is acceptable?"

The construct smiled enigmatically. "I can control neither the physical nor mental actions of others. It is not my place to prompt anyone to anything."

Which didn't mean that he—it—didn't do just that. Alsion's interest in the Chugen System remained, despite the loss of his "nodal point." Why was that? Ellicot and the rest of the Concordat's representatives had been lost in the Remor raid. The pawn had been taken, the game ended. Or had it? What if the Ellicot business was but a gambit? What if Chugen itself was the significant piece in the game and Ellicot simply a pawn employed to bring Danielle and the Concordat into play? She knew that Alsion was a deep player. But how deep? And how friendly was he to her and the Concordat?

Alsion professed only the best of motives. Was this Chugen affair all an elaborate salutary lesson about what might happen to the Concordat? They were sheltering a branch of the same alien species from which the Chugeni came. Were the Combine's dealings with the League a foreshadowing of what the Concordat would face when the nature of the Uritans became known? Or was this all working to some obscure end that only Alsion foresaw?

"When you first contacted me, you said that this situation was going to revolve around Ellicot," she pointed out. "You said that he was your 'butterfly,' about to emerge from his cocoon and affect events far beyond himself."

"True."

"Only we've lost Ellicot. Your focal point is gone. What's happened to your alinear sociodynamic flow now that your butterfly is dead?"

"He is lost certainly, but are you so sure that he is dead?"

"Aren't you? The League ship *Henry Hull* reported him dead with the rest of the crew and passengers after the ship's number two shuttle was attacked by the Remor raider. You were the one who pointed out that all of the Chugen Mission representatives from both the Concordat and the Combine were aboard that shuttle. I seem to recall you dubbing it a 'less than coincidental sort of coincidence.'"

"A warranted description," the construct agreed affably.

And annoyingly. The construct was making her work very hard for very little result. She needed to pin down fact and prediction and understand the difference between the two. "And now you're telling me that it's not true?"

"I am—as your growing agitation shows you are aware—'telling' you very little. However, I will say that I am in possession of information which suggests that the League report is not entirely accurate."

"In what way?"

"Regarding the lack of survivors, at least. Most likely in other ways as well."

"You're saying that the League is running some kind of scam," Danielle concluded.

"I am saying no such thing, although such a thing is far from unlikely."

No, not unlikely at all. The IDL was expansionist. In ten years they had added far more worlds to their "protective alliance" than had been lost to the Remor. "Is this a League ploy to gain the Chugen System for themselves? Did they place the Chugeni there?"

"Oh, I believe that the Chugeni are present as legitimately on the planet as the Uritans are on theirs. I also believe that the League has a quite legitimate—by their lights—interest in the Chugeni presence."

"So the Chugeni are just an excuse to legitimize a League action against the Combine."

"A visitation by a high-level League official to the PSC leadership has most likely taken place by now," the construct surmised.

Correctly. The morning's diplomatic pouch had carried a note from a friend on the Combine's Board of Directors, telling her of just such a meeting. Her friend was worried and more than a little afraid. According to him, fear that the war was coming to Combine space was pervasive. Almost as common was the belief that the League was allowing the war to spread in an attempt to harness the Combiners' fear and drive the Combine into the League. Her friend's report was supposed to have been a private communication.

"The outcome of that meeting has yet to play out," the construct added.

"Do you want to tell me how *you* learned of the meeting?"

"Such a meeting was an almost inevitable bottleneck in the flow of the dynamic. I welcome your question, bringing as it does confirmation and exoneration. Clarity," the construct said with obvious satisfaction. "Clarity is coming. From the chaos, order and insight are gained."

Danielle was in no mood for mysticism. "I am growing a bit weary of your riddles," she snapped.

"Study alinear sociodynamics," the construct suggested.

"And I don't need advertisements for your product!"

"Alinear sociodynamics is not a product." It actually sounded indignant.

"My apologies to your prototype, but there is only so much obfuscation a person can stand. What is it you want me to do?"

"A very direct question." A holographic chair appeared behind the construct. It sat. "You must consider your position. Consider what you will do."

Danielle stared at the silent holographic image, wondering just how like its prototype it was and how much it could be relied upon to display its prototype's wisdom and insight.

As if the lull in the conversation was a cue, Pyanfel appeared bearing a tea service on a silver tray. Danielle didn't bother to treat the construct, an unfeeling electronic entity, with courtesy, but the Uritan maid followed a different standard of decorum; she poured a cup for the construct, treating it as she would a real guest, before serving Danielle.

Watching the faithful Uritan, Danielle thought about her species. Pyanfel was no ravening enemy of Humankind. In fact, every Uritan Danielle had ever met was deferential and unfailingly polite, and seemed more than a little awestricken by Humans. The League had to be wrong.

What would protect the Concordat when the League learned of the Uritans? Certainly not the Concordat military. Were she to order a full-scale buildup today, they could not hope to match the League's MilForce in less than a dozen years. And the cost! It didn't bear thinking on.

The government had elected to keep Uritan existence a secret, knowing from the start that such a secret could not be kept forever. Already they had held it for nearly a dozen years.

And when it came out? Oh Lord, what would happen then?

The Chugeni had been linked to the Cassuells and the Grenwold aliens. According to her researchers, all were linked to the Uritans. If the League-dominated research on Chugen conclusively linked the local aliens to the Remor, then the Uritans would be linked to the Remor. Concordat secrecy would turn around and bite them, making the Concordat look like collaborators, or at the very least enemy sympathizers. No one would listen to protests about cultural divergence among the aliens. Once a fear-dominated human mind saw the face of the enemy, anyone with a similar face was the enemy. And who was the friend of my enemy, but my enemy also?

But where did one look for friends?

She stared into the face of the construct. Was this a friend, or the agent of a manipulator, callously using her and the Concordat for his own purposes? Whatever Alsion's agenda, it seemed that for the moment his interests were allied to her own. The best way to ensure that they stayed that way for as long as possible was to convince him that the Concordat's health was in his best interest.

"So help me, if this Chugen affair turns out to be a dress rehearsal for us dealing with the League, I will drag you and your institute into it just like you dragged us," she told the construct. "If our protection of the Uritans leads the League to brand us as collaborators, your secret links to me will mark you as well. If the Concordat goes down, the Alsion Institute will go with it."

The construct looked unimpressed. "You must, of course, do what you think is right," it said and—to Wyss's chagrin—turned itself off.

Its teacup sat untouched. Danielle's own grew cold.

**CHUGEN SYSTEM**
**CHUGEN IV**

"Quarantine" was what Warrant Officer Sharon Vestler called their new confinement, and if she was telling the truth about Lockhart's medical misfortune, it might even have been justified and reasonable. But Juliana wasn't interested in being reasonable. She and Rafe and Zandowski had been exposed to the same environment as Lockhart. *They* hadn't had a reaction. She didn't see the need to keep them in separate quarters. The Leaguers thought otherwise, calling it "a standard precaution." She understood how daily physical examinations might be part of the "standard precautions," but she didn't understand how the equally routine visits from Major Ersch and his staff of interrogators fit into any medical program.

At first she'd answered the major's questions, but when she figured out that he had no intention of answering any of hers, she stopped. He didn't like that, but he didn't stop coming either.

Most of Ersch's questions dealt with the H'kimm, whom he never called anything but Chugeni or "reputedly indigenous aliens." Why he bothered asking about them, she wasn't sure. He had her computer and those of the others; every note and observation and hypothesis the scientists had logged was on those machines.

Sometimes she wondered if he had found the Alsion construct, but he never mentioned it. In most of the sessions the institute was never mentioned at all. She guessed that Ersch had no idea that she was Alsion's agent, a small victory that gave her a warm glow of satisfaction. She liked the idea that she had a secret, however small and unimportant, that the League intelligence officer didn't know.

Another area in which she had made some gains was in thawing relations with Sharon Vestler. Vestler remained as brisk and efficient in her examinations as she had been since day one, but she seemed a little less impersonal about it. Juliana intended to take advantage of the change.

As Vestler was packing the instruments back into her kit after finding nothing more than she had found in any of the previous weeks' examinations, Juliana asked, "Sharon, how is Lockhart doing?"

Vestler frowned at Juliana's use of her first name, but answered amicably nonetheless. "As well as can be expected. We believe that we've identified the antagonist as a local bacterium. Scans showed that you all picked it up, probably from eating local foods. It doesn't seem to be a danger to a healthy person, but Ms. Lockhart's system was overstressed by her injuries. We should be able to flush it out, but the damage it did to Ms. Lockhart has precluded any further work on her legs. I'm afraid she'll need a full medical facility, possibly even regeneration-transplant therapy, before she walks again."

"Why can't you do that here?"

Vestler chuckled ruefully. "*Henry Hull's* only a patroller, ma'am. She's but so big, and medical systems aren't her first priority. You won't find the necessary facilities aboard anything less than a *Warlord*-class cruiser."

"Why not transport her back to Midway Station?"

"When *Henry Hull* goes, she will go," Vestler assured her, then sighed. "The repairs aren't proceeding well."

"Why can't the station send a ship?"

"They could, if they wanted to. Unfortunately for your friend, your fellow Combiners aren't interested in risking one of their ships for an extranational as long as there might be Remor still in the system."

It was all the information Juliana was able to get out of the medical specialist, and it left her wondering if she would have been better off not knowing. She hadn't really wanted to be reminded that the Remor were still out there, haunting the dark.

# 24

"Drone Sixteen, sir. Yesterday oh-seven-thirty-two," said Lieutenant Yorke.

Major Ersch called the designated reconnaissance drone's feed onto his screen. He scanned at triple speed until he flashed past the sequence he wanted to see. Retracing, he viewed the video and telemetry again at normal speed. The technicians were right. There he was. A fleeting glimpse, to be sure, but enough to confirm his location. Now they could concentrate resources.

"Pull all of the drones in the northeast valleys and shift them to this region. I want complete information on the region, its inhabitants, and especially everything we can get on the whereabouts and habits of the target."

"A full workup will take two to three weeks." Yorke wasn't telling Ersch anything he didn't know. The reconnaissance specialist looked worried. "Do we have time for that, sir?"

"A good question."

The Remor were an unpredictable enemy. So far, despite ominous appearances of the enemy in other systems, Intel had no hint of imminent local attack. Also so far, the beacon in orbit around the moon had remained silent. No one could make predictions about how long that situation would obtain, save that it wouldn't last forever. *Did* they have enough time?

Ersch hoped so; he had a job to get done.

"If we move too quickly, we will have just been wasting our time here, Lieutenant. It is vitally important that the experiment have sufficient time to mature."

"Aye, sir." Yorke's response lacked full confidence. "But isn't it possible that he could be ready now, sir? He's been fully isolated for more than a month. That's more time than it took before, and he started further along here."

"You're not the one who will have to explain to Intel what went wrong if we pluck him out too soon," Ersch pointed out. "This experiment does not have the luxury of repeatability."

"And if it doesn't work, sir? If we're wrong about him?"

Ersch thought about the beacon, and about the enemy whom it would, sooner or later, call. "We don't have time to be wrong."

Juliana found the air around the Leaguers' base camp drier and cooler than that of the H'kimm village, unsurprising given that the Leaguers had chosen to camp in scattered meadows on a mountainside rather than in one of the jungle-choked river valleys. There weren't quite as many insects either, though much of the lack of wildlife could be credited to the vegetation lost due to the Leaguers' intruding presence and their sun-blocking camouflage screens and their antivermin generators. Juliana thought the electronics an unnecessary disruption to the local ecology, given the lack of truly annoying pests in the Chugeni fauna, but the Leaguers showed little concern for treading lightly on the land. Juliana was beached on an island of shrouded, lifeless gloom amid the exuberant sea of Chugeni life.

Gloomy was certainly how she felt.

Since arriving she had been mostly confined within the

isolated jail that her rescuers—captors, really—called the
"guest house." Armed guards—"for her protection"—followed her when she was let out—which wasn't often—and
then she was confined to the area beneath the enshrouding, tented camouflage screening that wrapped all beneath
it in shadow.

Her cabin, an odd mix of technic nano-restructured
materials and hand-hewn local woods and vegetable products, was as out of place on Chugen as the Leaguers. Its
style wasn't the least bit H'kimm; neither was it like the
squat huts of the S'kimm, the mountain-dwelling Chugeni.
The cabin's presence was as intrusive as everything else the
Leaguers had done, symbolic of their dominance and control fixations.

Dominance was what the League was all about. The
local S'kimm, like the local jungle, were under their control, forced into a subservient role by the technologically
superior intruders. Most of the time, Juliana felt sorrier for
the S'kimm than she did for herself.

*Most* of the time. Today her pity was reserved for herself
on her miserable first, full day of her period. Between the
bloating, cramps, and headache, she felt utterly wretched.
The castaways had recovered only the smallest supply of
cyclikeez after the crash, and that had soon run out. Since
then, she'd thought she'd gotten used to feeling the effects
of her period, but her current piteous state disabused her of
that idea.

*As if things weren't bad enough*, she moaned to herself.
*The overall unpleasantness of my captivity* has *to be enhancing the effect.*

The Leaguers said they didn't have any cyclikeez to give
her, but she was sure that they were lying. They had female
troopers, so they had to have *something*—the highly touted
MilForce efficiency wouldn't allow female troopers the

luxury of letting such elementary biology affect their performance. They *had* to have cyclikeez, or *something* equivalent. But not for her. The Leaguers just didn't want Juliana to have any. *Another notch tighter on the rack of coercion*, she supposed.

The outer door of Juliana's cabin opened. She didn't need to see or smell them to know at once that her visitors were S'kimm and not Leaguers. For all their disregard for the environment, the brutish Leaguers retained some human manners, always knocking before entering. Even Ersch knocked. But the locals, having no clear concept of privacy, were poor respecters of it.

The visitors were Kmo and her companions of the cleaning pack, one of the groups of S'kimm charged by the Leaguers with doing the necessary work that was beneath the Humans' martial dignity. They were unsupervised, as usual; beyond the initial assignment to work-packs, the Leaguers paid no more attention to their S'kimm servitors than conquerors had ever paid to servants pressed into service from the conquered people.

Kmo crossed the outer room and entered Juliana's bedroom.

"The *shedenky* are excited about something," she reported.

A *shedenky*—what the H'kimm called a *shadakey*—was a loathsome local bug that armored itself with the shells of its previously consumed prey. Juliana found herself agreeing with the suitability of the name for the League troopers since they were loathsome and their battlesuits armored them in hard shells. In fact, it was her initial chuckle over the term that had been the icebreaker between her and Kmo. They were both out of place here; Kmo was of a different lineage than the rest of her League-formed workpack. Despite the presence of other members of her own species, each was as alone as if she were stranded on an asteroid. The two estranged women, drawn to each other, shared what little they could. Juliana offered explanations of Human behavior and translations while Kmo, as she did today, brought news and rumors.

"Do you know why they are excited?" Juliana asked.

"They have found the one they call Target. They send the metal insects to watch him while they wait to take him up. Who is Target, friend Juliana, that the *shedenky* hunt him?"

Who the unfortunate Target might be, she couldn't say. All the Hos'kimm she'd known were scattered, and could be anywhere; or they were as dead as Kurt.

Juliana tried to put aside the pain that arose at the thought of Kurt. He was gone and she'd just have to get used to it. It was not as though that they had actually been lovers. In a way that made it worse, since her romantic thoughts of him were still unclouded by the tarnish of an everyday relationship.

Forcing other, more immediate concerns into the forefront of her thoughts dulled the pain a little, but her attempt at explaining her lack of omniscience was interrupted by the arrival of Major Ersch, lord and master of the League's imperialistic outpost on Chugen IV.

"The house is being kept to your satisfaction?" he asked with unctuous cordiality.

"The cleanliness is fine," she replied. "I can't say I care for the way the lock sticks at night. It's rather inconvenient."

"Is it? I honestly do regret any inconvenience, but with things as they are . . ." Ersch shrugged. "I understand from Mr. Decloux that the scientific studies are progressing well on all fronts. He reports confidentially that the socioxenology segment remains weak, but Professor Mowbray isn't exactly a hard-charger. I imagine he sees little need to stretch, since he is expecting to receive the report's sole credit in his field. I can see that the situation distresses you, Professor Tindal. You know that it doesn't have to be this way. You can still be a part of it, Professor. You need only sign the parole."

She'd read the so-called parole when he had first shoved it under her nose. One clause would have put her under the authority and discipline of the IDL MilForce for "the duration of the emergency on Chugen IV," a position she desired not in the least. That "authority" was likely to demand that she support the League's contention that the Hos'kimm were the enemy, and the "discipline" was there to deal with any recalcitrance. As long as she remained under Combine authority, Ersch and his stormtroopers had no legal right to hurt her. Of course they had no right to confine her, either. The last thing she wanted to do was to give them license to go further.

"I will *not* be a rubber stamp on the death warrant you're trying to write here. I won't be a part of the League's infamy."

Ersch's expression was a study in pained confusion. "I don't understand why you remain so stubbornly mistaken," he said. "The Chugen Project is not a League operation. Yes, we are participating, but only because we want to know the truth about the Chugeni, as much as anyone does."

"Which is why you have so much military force here."

"So much? A patroller and her complement? Hardly a planet crushing force, even were that our intent. We are here by accident, or rather by incident. Had we not been attacked by the Remor raider, we would have dropped you and the others off and left you all to your scientific studies. You puzzle me, Professor. Where does your malice come from? Why must you attribute villainy to our presence here?"

Ersch's innocent act didn't fool Juliana. "Yes, you've been perfect angels, all on the side of right. Is that why you're keeping me prisoner? Why you're isolating me from the others?"

"Once you've signed the parole, you can see them all if you'd like. Except for Ms. Lockhart, of course."

"Vestler said she was doing well."

"As well as can be expected, given our limited facilities. But, to be frank, her health is not the reason she is being kept isolated. She has been interned—yes, interned, we acknowledge our prisoners for what they are—because she is an agent of the Serenten Concordat's military intelligence apparatus. Ah, I see that you did not know. Indeed, her concealment of her true affiliation should demonstrate to you our need for caution. Lockhart's clandestine assignment betokens duplicity on the part of the Concordat's leadership, and without knowing how far that duplicity extends or what motivates it, we cannot allow her to view or have any access to our facilities. The IDL authorities take a dim view of spies. Accordingly she is being held under confinement."

And what about Juliana? Being an agent for the Alsion Institute didn't exactly make her a spy, but would the paranoid IDL authorities agree? The institute was avowedly apolitical, but did the League see them that way? Was an unannounced agent the same as a spy to them? And if it was, did they already know and had they already judged her? Was Ersch here to get her to admit to her affiliation so that he could change her designation from "protected guest" to "interred prisoner"?

"Why are you here? What is it you *really* want from me?" she asked.

"This morning I have something *for* you. News."

She doubted it could be good.

"There is news of Professor Ellicot. Like my own, his death appears to have been reported prematurely."

Juliana's heart leapt. Kurt *alive*! She wanted to believe it, but she feared that Ersch might just be playing with her, using her emotions to open her up to some interrogation ploy. But Ersch didn't seem inclined to strike while she was in obvious turmoil. Instead he waited patiently until she asked, "You're sure he's alive?"

"Alive and in apparent good health. We have ascertained that Professor Ellicot is at present traveling south in the company of a small band of Chugeni."

Suddenly Juliana understood just *who* Kmo's mysterious Target was. "Why are you hunting him?"

"Hunting him? You seem determined to see whatever we do in the worst possible light."

"Then you admit that you're tracking him."

"I admit that we are trying to. Professor Ellicot is only here on Chugen because of IDL insistence. We have an obligation to see that no harm comes to him. Hunting him?" Ersch shook his head sadly. "My dear Professor Tindal, we're trying to rescue him."

## CHUGEN SYSTEM
## MIDWAY STATION

Jane had left their cabin an hour before Ken Konoye had stirred forth. She had, as usual, used the time to brighten up her eyes and bush up her tail so that she was operating at full efficiency while he was still gathering steam. His arrival on the command deck was greeted with a wicked smile and, "The weekly report is in from Ersch and his squatters."

Jane ignored his groan and continued. "The major says his ship will be repaired in two weeks, three tops. He expects to ferry out the project scientists as soon as he can lift."

"He's got no authority to pull them off," Konoye said, stating the obvious.

She shrugged. "He *says* the crash of shuttle two destroyed too much vital equipment and too many supplies. He *says* the scientists can't get along without his ship there, and that whether they stay or not, *he's* leaving. He *says* it's pull them off or let them starve to death."

"As if we can't supply them."

"He *says* the Remor raider might still be hanging around."

Konoye frowned. It was entirely too possible that the Remor raider that had attacked during the landing operation *might* still be around. *If* it had ever existed. The lack of further attacks made him suspicious. What if the major had invented the attack to hide his shuttle pilot's incompetence? "If a Remor raider really did attack Ersch's ship, why didn't we spot the bastard?"

Jane, being no more of a spacefarer than he, didn't have an answer. "Mr. Hoppe?"

"The attack, she took place in the shadow of Chugen IV, out of our sight. But the weapons discharges, those we seen. Hard to be hiding high energy discharges."

"So why haven't we seen more of this raider?"

"We be keeping traffic away from Chugen IV, where the raider lay. The major, he be saying that the raider be a low-emissions lurker-type craft. Even military sensors be having trouble picking up lurkers. Out here, we be seeing nothing unless we happen to be looking in the exact right place at the exact right time."

Hoppe was the authority on matters to do with ships, but Konoye didn't like the answer. "So you think that the raider's real? That it might still be out there?"

"Can't be saying one way or other," Hoppe temporized. "But a Remor ship now, that be something no wise man be taking chances with. We not be seeing her arrive, could be we not be seeing her leave. Of one thing I be sure, Director, if she be out there, she be trouble."

"It seems like the sensible course is to go along with Ersch's plan," Jane said.

Konoye didn't like that either. "So we can look forward to his company around here again, I suppose."

"Only briefly, unless he doesn't get his look at this alleged Remor beacon."

Ersch's requests to investigate the object in orbit around Chugen's moon had stopped since his ship was grounded. With the ship flying again, Konoye could expect that the bombardment of requests for permission would start again. "I guess we'd better prepare for a siege then."

"The major already has a request," Jane reported.

Could it be starting already?

"The major requests that we transmit to him the coordinates and field strength for the secondary jump point. He claims the information is necessary for making proper defensive plans."

"Right he be about that," Hoppe said.

Konoye didn't care. "How the hell did he find out about the point? We only confirmed the point's existence and location yesterday."

Jane shrugged. "The day an operation run by the Combine doesn't have leaks will be the dawn of a new age. Shall I send him the information?"

"You'll get your new age when this place belongs to the League. Until then, I'm in charge, and I'm not about to hand out proprietary data, especially not before it's filed with the survey office. Ersch wants to know the coordinates, let him do the work himself!"

After that start, the rest of the morning's reports didn't register at all on Konoye's annoyance meter.

✳      ✳      ✳

## CHUGEN SYSTEM
## CHUGEN IV

The evening of Ersch's announcement about Kurt's survival, Juliana had a surprise visitor. Rafe showed up on her doorstep. The locked door kept them separated, but they were able to talk through one of the screened windows. They kept their voices low so that they disturbed neither the S'kimm whose hut sat nearby nor the more distant League sentries patrolling the clearings.

"You're not supposed to be here," she reminded him.

"Yeah, no kidding," he said agreeably.

Unlike her, he had made his peace with the Leaguers, signing the parole; but though he was free to come and go around the camp, that freedom didn't extend to visiting her.

When she pointed out that he was endangering his position with the Leaguers, violating his parole by talking to her, he said, "Sure I signed the parole. Why not? It's not like it's worth anything in the interstellar courts. Duress and all that. None of that matters now anyway."

"What's changed?"

"The whole Chugen Project is a sham." Rafe looked around, an uncharacteristic display of nervousness. "You know me, always sticking my nose where it doesn't belong. You used to tell me that someday I'd find out something I didn't want to know. So I came by to tell you that you were finally right."

"Then Ersch's line about the scientific research is just so much crap?"

"Oh, they're doing the research all right, but that's not why *they're* here. The marts are running a different scam, and it all revolves around your troublemaking boyfriend Ellicot. It's all about him."

"What do you mean?"

Rafe's voice dropped. "Our shuttle was *supposed* to crash. Actually it was supposed to *fake* a crash. It was all part of a crackpot plan to get Ellicot here and into the hands of the local aliens. Only something went wrong and the shuttle really did crash. Some people who weren't supposed to die did, and some who were supposed to die didn't."

Juliana stared at him.

"We were among the intended dead, Juli."

Stunned, she finally managed to stammer, "H-How did you find out about this?"

"I got Shanholz drunk. He's really not such a bad guy— for a mart."

"Didn't you just say that he was part of a plot to kill us?"

"It wasn't like it was personal or anything. To him we were just Pansies, and his bosses didn't want any Pansies around to interfere with Ellicot's assimilation by the locals. Obstacles to the plan had to be dealt with."

"So, your Mr. Shanholz is really not such a bad guy— for a heartless beast. That bas—"

"Look, it wasn't his plan, okay? He doesn't matter. What does matter is what he told me. I got tipped off when he let slip that the pilot and the rest of the shuttle crew weren't supposed to be dead. At first I took it for the usual too-bad-my-friends-are-dead riff, but after a bit I figured out that he really meant the crash *shouldn't* have happened, and that his friends *shouldn't* be dead, that something else was supposed to happen. He couldn't, or wouldn't, tell me anything else, but what he *did* say was plenty to get me suspicious. I started poking around. Remember that cylinder of tranq gas we found? That was supposed to knock the passengers out while *they* arranged things to their satisfaction."

"While they killed us all, you mean."

"All but Ellicot."

"So why aren't we dead now?"

"The major, for all his bloody-mindedness, isn't an indiscriminate killer. Once he lost the chance to blame our deaths on the crash, I think he decided that getting us out of Ellicot's life was enough. You know they dragged a goddamn spotted ghost up from the southern part of the continent just to keep Ellicot and the Chugeni busy while they rescued us? And it nearly backfired on them, too. I hear Ersch shat a brick when he heard that Ellicot might be dead. Went out to the attack site himself to be sure, and damned if he didn't find something his scouts had missed. Ellicot walked away from there." Rafe paused, looking perplexed. "You don't look surprised."

"They've found him. Ersch told me."

"We're not really important to them," Rafe said. "Don't you see? It's Ellicot, and *only* Ellicot, that they're interested in. This has all been a big plot to get him on-planet and alone so that he'd go native again."

"Why? What could they possibly gain from that?"

"I haven't a clue. But what I do know is that as far as anyone in the Combine or the Concordat or anywhere outside the IDL knows, the grieving survivors of the Chugen Project who came down in the other shuttle are steadfastly doing what they came here to do, and we, my dear, are dead. Whether we stay dead depends on whether we go along with them."

"Is that why you're here? Did he send you to frighten me into signing the parole?"

"He doesn't know I'm here," Rafe asserted.

Juliana doubted that, but she didn't contradict him.

Rafe's unveiling of the Leaguer's heartless plan had woken something cold in her. Her hatred for them and what they stood for had not been personal before. Now the matter was very, very personal.

"So if I don't sign the parole, I end up another crash victim. Is that why I'm being kept isolated, because if any of the others see me, they'll know I survived the crash? He said Lockhart was a spy, and the IDL doesn't like spies. Is he going to murder her and claim *she* died in the crash? Is he going to murder *me*?"

"If that's what you think, sign the parole. Let the others get to see you."

"That doesn't save Lockhart. He can't make me lie about her dying in the crash."

"Nobody is asking you to say anything about Lockhart, for God's sake. This is about *you*, Juli. It's about staying alive! You were nearly killed once so the League could implement their plan for Ellicot. Nothing we can do will change the League's plans for him. If we try, we'll get run over. He's not worth it."

"Shut up," she told him.

He didn't listen. "I've seen a couple of their tapes of him. He's gone native again. The man isn't fit company for any human being, and you're wasting your time worrying about him."

"You're wrong! Kurt's not like that! Kurt's—"

"Trouble, nothing but trouble. Forget him! He's only going to get you killed."

"Don't you care about anyone but yourself?"

"I care about you, Juli. I don't want to see you killed over him. He's caused enough deaths."

"It's not him!"

"Isn't it?"

She slammed her fist against the screening, not even denting the mesh. But Rafe jumped back anyway. "You think about what I told you," he said as he slipped around the corner of her cabin.

She locked her fingers in the screen and stared out at

the night. How could she *not* think about it? Kurt was out there, safe for the moment. But he wouldn't be safe for long. Neither would the Hos'kimm. *But*, she thought, *if Kurt could escape Ersch's dragnet . . .*

As long as the League wanted him and didn't have him, he was safe, and the Hos'kimm were safe because the League couldn't be sure that he wouldn't be killed by any general action they took against the Hos'kimm. Without Kurt in their grasp, the League couldn't start sterilizing the planet the way they did on Cassuells Home. If only there were some way she could warn him to hide, to go to ground where the Leaguers couldn't find him. But she was trapped, and unlike his hunters, she had no idea where he was.

She sagged against the window, forcing the mesh harshly against her cheek. Frustrated, angry, and afraid for herself, Kurt and the Hos'kimm, she couldn't hold back the tears. The mountain breeze chilled the runnels on her cheeks.

Kmo appeared from the darkness. Her fingerpads lightly touched Juliana's flesh where it was not warded by the mesh. "Why do you cry?"

"Kurt," she said, voicing the first thought in her mind. "Kurt is the one they're hunting."

"He is Target?"

"Yes," Juliana sobbed.

"He is also your pair-mate?"

"I wish."

Kmo nodded sympathetically. "I will keen for him. I will ask the others to keen with me."

Keening was a form of Chugeni prayer. Juliana didn't see how it would help, but she thought she might try some prayer herself.

✳        ✳        ✳

Ersch glared at the trooper on the other end of the link. He knew his fury was being communicated to the trooper by the way the man flinched.

"Repeat what you just said," Ersch ordered.

"The target is not here. There's no sign of him."

How could he not be there? The village had been going about its routine before the raid. Nothing out of the ordinary. No one had arrived. No one had left. Ellicot had been there last night; reconnaissance drones had recorded him going into the hole in the ground with the village's gray-furred Chugeni. Ersch had watched them go through their preentry ritual. Both by previous observation and by Professor Mowbray's testimony, that sort of ritual meant that the Chugeni were expecting to stay in their underground holy place for at least a day. Ellicot *should* have been safely mewed up. So where was he?

"You checked the holy hole?"

"Nothing down there but three old stink-weasels wailing their heads off. Visuals, thermographics, and sonics are all negative, sir. He's not down there and there's no way out."

Clearly that was wrong. There *had* to be a way out. It was a problem to be dealt with another time. "Return to base."

"What do you want us to do about the village, sir?"

The mission brief had called for minimal destruction, to allow Ellicot to believe that his refuge could be regained. That concern seemed to have gone by the board. "You're sure the target is not there."

"Positive, sir."

"Then you can burn that stinking collection of mud huts and everyone in them for all I care. Ersch out."

Somehow Ellicot had been warned. But by whom? Ersch's team was loyal and no one outside of it knew—no, wait, he had told someone: Tindal. He recalled how friendly she remained with the indigenes. Could she have slipped out a warning?

Of course, Ellicot might have just gotten lucky and put himself elsewhere. Warned or not, he was still out there, which was a serious problem. Ersch disliked problems.

Time was running short, and not just because the fictitious repairs to *Henry Hull* were supposedly nearly complete. New delays could be invented to drag out the supposed repairs. Unfortunately the universe didn't operate on Ersch's schedule and had just decided to remind him that it didn't operate to his liking either. Last night Captain Needa had reported a blip from the Remor beacon. If the beacon was active, Ersch's time on Chugen was running out.

Unfortunately his reason for being on Chugen had just pulled another vanishing act.

# 25

Kurt stopped keeping track of time as he traveled with Ah'zzt and the survivors of Lo'gnen's pack. There didn't seem much point in worrying about what hour of the day it was, or what day of the week. The prey they hunted in the morning was different from that found at midday or at evening, and to that rhythm he paid attention. One day followed another, little different from the one before or the one to follow. Only the slow procession of the seasons would change the Way of a day, and such changes came in the world's time without the urging or forbidding of an artificial calendar. Adrift in such timelessness, he grew closer to his pack-mates. Living within the rhythms of Chugen IV was the H'kimm Way, and it was his Way now.

Ah'zzt, normally a loner, stuck close. No longer did he disappear for days, only to return and sit on the fringes of the group. These days he sat with the others, like Kurt, huddling for comradeship and comfort. The rock of stability that had allowed the hunter to roam had been knocked from beneath him with the devastation of Lo'gnen's pack. He needed the reassurance of a pack, however small and shaky.

Like his *daramak* Ah'zzt, Kurt wanted to be reassured that he had a place where he belonged, a pack, a home, a family, friends. Like Ah'zzt he put aside anything that made access to such reassurance harder. He abandoned the marks of a pack no longer his: his clothes, boots, and all but a few tools which he stuffed into a H'kimm satchel of vine fiber and bark. Kurtellicot they called him, and Kurtellicot he became, just one of Lo'gnen's orphaned pack.

By coincidence or the whim of the spirits, they were not the only ones on the move. They met small groups of H'kimm who were also headed for Rasseh. Meetings were brief, always terminated while in the greeting stage as soon as Lo'gnen's orphaned children told their tale and revealed their plight.

"Why do these others travel to Rasseh?" he asked his pack-mates. "They are not orphaned as we are."

"It must be the Gathering time," Ah'zzt answered. "Is it the Gathering time, *tuoyal*?"

Kurtellicot, as *tuoyal*, was supposed to know, but he didn't. He supposed it must be so. Why else would so many Hos'kimm be on the move?

As they traveled it became obvious that the time had indeed come. Joined packs of R'kimm were trekking across the coastal plains. One by one, packs of S'kimm were coming down from the mountains. Packs of H'kimm were moving through the forest, gathering other packs and moving on, headed where Kurtellicot and his pack-mates were headed. For in Rasseh, among the hills of Teclananda, the Hos'kimm were Gathering.

Yet while this knowledge excited his pack-mates, especially G'riv who had never made the trek before, they did not increase their pace. Each day brought them closer, but not as close as they might have marched had they not followed the rhythms of the day with its hunts and rests and meals. And this was as it was supposed to be, the Way of traveling to the Gathering.

Ah'zzt's guidance brought them unerringly through the forest and out onto the delta plains. Away from the trees the fact of the Gathering could be seen in the clumps of Hos'kimm making their way across the plains toward the hills of Teclananda.

The hills themselves were not tall, but they were curious things: abrupt, irregular, serpentine mounds covered in sedge weed, no one much taller or shorter than another. They made a maze of this part of the plain and within their folds hid the shelters, gathering circles, and holy caves of Rasseh. Only a few R'kimm actually lived in Rasseh, but now the hills were overflowing with people. More could be seen crossing the delta in groups large and small, coming to swell the Gathering.

Kurtellicot and his pack-mates caused a stir when they entered Rasseh. People stared and pointed. Some, usually hunters like Ah'zzt, were bold enough to approach and sniff at Kurtellicot. Following his *daramak*'s advice, Kurtellicot ignored such rudeness. Lo'gnen's orphans wandered Rasseh, looking for a place to settle themselves before seeking out those who could settle the future of their pack.

After a solid morning of tramping the hills unsuccessfully, they paused before a beetle-seller. The seller's wares, strung up by their hind legs, whirred and clacked, making a strangely musical accompaniment to G'riv's haggling. Kurtellicot was anticipating the fresh lunch that would come from G'riv's efforts when Ah'zzt prodded him in the side. Kurtellicot looked where his *daramak* indicated. Coming toward them was a clump of gray-furred elders— mostly R'kimm, the short, wide, moderately furred folk of the plains, but there were H'kimm and heavily furred S'kimm among them.

"We are fortunate that the Gathering is the time of the elder pack," Ah'zzt whispered. "They are the wisest of the wise, *tuoyal* all, come together. Their wisdom is a bond stronger than blood, and they will have an answer for us when the time is come. They will know what the spirits want of us. Is it not a wonder to see such wisdom gathered, *daramak* Kurtellicot?"

"A wonder, yes."

This group could be none other than such a special pack. Their leader, shorter than the usual R'kimm, was so well fed that he looked as if his belly would drag on the ground if he tried to hump along on all fours. Fortunately for his belly fur, he was in no great hurry, but strolled, elaborately carved walking stick in each hand, at a sedate and dignified pace.

"*Zhent'ah-rhull,*" Hos'kimm around them whispered in awe.

Zhent'ah the seer? Zhent'ah-rhull must be a great seer indeed to have the word made part of his name. Such a one would be honored with leisure and the choicest catch from the hunt, which accounted for his prosperous appearance. What prompted the honored elders to stir forth?

His answer came as Zhent'ah-rhull led his distinguished pack right toward Lo'gnen's orphans. The crowd of Hos'kimm edged away. The beetle-seller and his noisy merchandise vanished into the throng. Lo'gnen's orphans were left in awkward and embarrassing isolation. Pointing with his stick, Zhent'ah-rhull singled out Kurtellicot.

"You are the one who came to Lo'gnen's pack." There was challenge in Zhent'ah-rhull's voice, and his bright eyes studied Kurtellicot like a hunter studied prey. "It has been said that you are come to end the age."

"I do not say that." He desired acceptance, not enmity. He wanted no association with the evil that had come from the heavens. "I am here because my pack gathers here, as all packs gather."

"Your pack?" Zhent'ah-rhull barked a laugh. "You are not like us."

"I do not *look* like you. Yet I walk upright as you do. I have hands as you do. I speak. I think. I was not born here, but then neither were the most honored ancestors, yes? If I am not Hos'kimm, what am I?"

Several of the elders murmured approvingly at his words, but Zhent'ah-rhull only wrinkled his nose and said, "That remains to be seen."

Zhent'ah-rhull pointedly looked past Kurtellicot. "Who stands first among you? Who, of Lo'gnen's children, speaks for Lo'gnen's orphans?"

After a glance at the silent Kurtellicot, Ah'zzt drew himself up. "Honored Zhent'ah-rhull, my *daramak* Kurtellicot speaks for Lo'gnen's orphans."

"*Daramak*?" Zhent'ah-rhull repeated in disbelief. Ah'zzt might as well have said that he and Kurtellicot were lovers, from Zhent'ah-rhull's shocked expression. "You have accepted this one as your *daramak*?"

"And he me," Ah'zzt replied.

The elders spoke softly among themselves, their words lost in the louder, and more confused gabble of the onlookers.

"We must beach the mother swordfin before we net the fry," Zhent'ah-rhull mumbled. Louder, he spoke to Kurtellicot. "Fast. Drink only water. Come to the *rass'arass* at the hour of testing."

The hour of testing was that in which the moon was highest in the sky, and the *rass'arass* was the holiest of the holy places in Rasseh, the place of holiness. And so, as the moon rose toward its zenith, he walked into the heart of the hills of Teclananda. Ah'zzt and G'riv and the others accompanied him, both to lend him their support and to partake of his own strength, for until the elders were satisfied, Lo'gnen's orphans were to the Hos'kimm as a *grawr'-tayo* individual was to his pack.

A thick press of Hos'kimm thronged the lanes among the hills and crowded up onto the steep slopes, but the orphans of Lo'gnen passed among them unjostled, even untouched, for as they walked a passage opened before them and closed again behind. No one came close or spoke a word to them, although many pointed or whispered to their pack-mates as the strangers moved past. Even Ah'zzt, *grawr'tayo* his whole adult life, bristled in discomfort at such isolation amidst so many Hos'kimm.

At last they reached the field where the entrance to the *rass'arass* lay. Three H'kimm elders met them. Two took Kurtellicot's arms while the third motioned for the rest of Lo'gnen's orphans to stay behind as the elders led Kurtellicot to the center of the field.

The moon was nearly dark in the sky, adding little to the light which the stars shed. Kurtellicot wished for a different balance, for he was sundered from the stars and he disliked their cold and foreign regard. Still, there was enough light for him to see the moving shapes of dancing Hos'kimm ringing the edge of the field, close against the flanks of the hills. He couldn't see the drummers but the sound of their playing echoed among the hills in a slow, steady beat that lulled and soothed.

The very center of the field was a deep darkness that was the entrance to the *rass'arass*. As dancing Hos'kimm ringed the field, so a solemn, sober pack of elders ringed the hole to the sacred place below. The elders shared among themselves a great bowl made from the iridescent carapace of an insect. Each took a sip and passed it on to the next. When Kurtellicot reached them, he was offered the bowl.

He sipped and felt the rich complex of flavors that was Hos'kimm ale spread across his tongue.

The bowl went round and round again until Kurtellicot's head started to pound slightly and in perfect synchrony with the drumming. The next time he held the bowl, the elders said their first words to him.

"Drain it."

He did his best, but he didn't have the physical control he'd had when he first arrived. He splashed quite a bit into his beard and onto his chest. Still, when he turned the bowl over to demonstrate that it was empty, only two drops fell to the ground.

The elders nodded solemnly.

The ring of elders parted slightly as Zhent'ah-rhull climbed falteringly from the darkness below, moving slowly without his sticks. In his hands he bore a small cup, this one of metal that gleamed in the starlight. Offering the cup to Kurtellicot, he said, "The testing. Will you drink or not?"

*Sure,* Kurtellicot thought. *Why not? What's another hit at this point?*

He took the cup, placed the chill rim against his lips, tilted his head back, and gulped down the testing draught.

It was not Hos'kimm ale. Whatever it *was*, it went to work in short order. He doubled over as a cramp hit his stomach with the force of a mule's kick. Behind his eyelids, stars—traitorous, treacherous stars—spun and danced. The stars laughed at him and he cursed them. They only gave back taunts and danced on. As the pain in his belly eased and he opened his eyes, the stars didn't go away. Their dance grew merrier as they metamorphosed into sinuous Hos'kimm shapes dancing to the beat of the drums. A pale shape danced with them, a human shape, a female shape. He knew her face.

"Juli!" he shouted.

His body responded to the provocative gyrations. His

member rose, straining hard and hot. His blood pulsed, beating, beating like the drums. The explosion from his loins echoed in his head as he fell to his knees, moaning.

From behind, someone pulled a musty bag over his head. Hands grabbed him and drew him to his feet. Strong arms spun him around. Again and again. When they released him, he staggered.

"Walk," Zhent'ah-rhull commanded. "Show us your path. Show us your self."

He took a step and almost fell. No one reached out a hand to steady him. He was on his own.

Regaining his balance, he tried another step, more successfully this time. Another step. He knew he was not walking in a straight line, but there was little he could do about that. Stones and gravel rocked under his soles, making him unsteady. The beer he'd downed didn't help. And that other drink! Struggling to keep his balance, he tried to do as Zhent'ah-rhull commanded.

He was walking, not well, but managing. He zigged and he zagged, but he kept moving. All around him he could hear excited talk among the Hos'kimm elders. His mind was too muddled to understand what they said. There were too many voices. He thought they sounded disappointed.

That wouldn't do. He needed to show them. He needed to walk like a man. Bracing himself up, he took a step forward and found the ground firm beneath his feet.

The voices stopped. The drums stopped. All sound might have vanished from the world, leaving him alone in the silent dark. He didn't want to be alone. His hands lifted, going to the thongs that snugged the hood against his neck. But much as he longed to tear off the hood and see if he were truly alone, he knew that he should not. He forced his hands down to his sides.

He told himself to remain calm. He didn't need to see

the Hos'kimm around him to know they were there. They *were* there. Perhaps it was the faintest stir of a breeze from their breathing. The echo of sound from their hearts hammering in their chests. They *were* all around him. The pack *was* present!

His pack.

They were waiting for him to do something.

*Oh, yes!* He was supposed to walk.

He took another step. The ground remained firm beneath him. He seemed to have found a path. With each step he tried to stay in that path, to stay on the firm ground. It was hard. He was light-headed. A part of his mind told him that he was suffering from oxygen deprivation as well as from whatever drug had been in the testing draught. He was not in full possession of his senses.

No, that was wrong. His senses were in full possession of him. He heard faint insect sounds buzzing through the air, creeping on and through the earth. He could smell the leather enfolding his head, a scent that said nothing but *Hos'kimm*. Against his skin he felt the faint stir of air moving through his fur. When he licked his lips, he tasted salt and the lingering, faint tang of the draught. And he saw—

He saw—

Wonders!

Stars beyond counting clustered in heavenly majesty, and walking among them were the gods, the founts of life, the nurturers of thought, the taskmasters, the caregivers, and the arbiters of death. He trembled before them, knowing he was insignificant to them while at the same time he owed all that he was to them. They had lifted him up, separated him from the creatures of the earth, and set him upon the path of light, scattering his brothers and sisters among the heavens. To them he was but a clever child.

And yet, he saw something else. For beyond the gods

there *was* something else, something greater, a power to whom even the gods bent low, which was to the gods what he and his brothers and sisters were to the powers that had lifted them up. And that power sang. A glorious, beautiful, haunting, sad song! It was a song with no words, but it touched his heart. As he trudged along, the song was now louder, now softer, but he knew that its strength was not touched by anything he did. The faceless singer was apart, even more apart from him than it was from the gods. He could command it in no way, no way at all. He could not even call and have it come, unless it willed to come. And that was as it should be.

Borne up by the song, he walked the path before him. His uncertainty was gone. All was as it should be.

His foot struck a stone and he stumbled to his knees, losing the vision.

"No!" he cried in the pain of his loss. "Do not leave me!"

Fingers fumbled at his throat, loosening the cords. Someone pulled the hood off and he saw Zhent'ah-rhull crouched before him. The seer put his hands to Kurtellicot's cheeks, his claws pricking the soft skin beneath the beard. Zhent'ah-rhull's eyes glittered in the starlight.

"*Daysha-lo'daramak*," he said. "The Star Walker is come. Speak, *Daysha-lo'daramak*. Are the Hos'kimm forgiven? Tell us if you are doom or salvation."

"I don't know," Kurtellicot moaned, tears washing across Zhent'ah-rhull's trembling hands.

# 26

CHUGEN SYSTEM
CHUGEN IV

"They're closing in on Ellicot again," Rafe whispered to her, confirming Kmo's report that the *shedenky* were excited again about finding their target. Juliana thought he sounded somewhat satisfied.

Since she had learned of Kurt's survival, she had done little but worry about him. "They know where he is?"

"They haven't got him pinned down exactly, but they're close. A whole lot of Chugeni are gathering in the hills by the mouth of the big river that dumps into the southern sea. You know, the one Singh dubbed New Ganges because it reminded him of a river in his ancestral homeland. A bunch of the locals want to go down there, too. *They* say they've been called to go, but I think they're making up an excuse to get away from the Leaguers. Not that anybody *needs* an excuse."

"Do you think they'll catch him this time?"

"After the way Ersch raked his people over the coals for failing last time, I don't think they dare come back without him."

She stared past Rafe, at the jungle and the star-filled sky above it. "What then?"

"I don't care and you shouldn't either. Ellicot's only going to get what he deserves." Rafe ignored Juliana's censuring frown. "He's why they're here, right? They were willing to kill people to get him here and isolated the way they want him. I've been thinking a lot about that."

So had she.

"The parole I signed binds me to the IDL's Emergency Secrecy Act. What do you want to bet that the shuttle's crash and everything surrounding it is a secret emergency? They don't want anything but their own official line getting out about what happened here."

"Their law has no force in the Combine. They can't shut us up," she said with brittle conviction.

"I'm not so sure," Rafe responded with less than his usual confidence. "With Combine law based on the sacredness of a contract, I think that the courts just might uphold the League's authority to enforce a gag clause."

"Weren't you the one who pointed out that a contract made under duress wasn't worth anything?"

"Yeah," he replied sullenly. "But *they* think it is. *I* signed their damn parole, but *you* didn't. So what are they going to do with *you* when they leave? They don't even have their legal fiction to keep *your* mouth shut."

She'd reached the same conclusion, but was still having difficulty putting it into words. "You don't think they would—"

"Yeah, I do. After all, they've already tried to kill us once. And when I started thinking about what they might do to you, I started to realize that, unlike the bunch from the other shuttle, I knew that you *didn't* die in the crash. And if they got rid of you, who might be next?"

"You."

"Yeah. Only I don't feel like sitting around until *they* find a convenient time to shut me up permanently. Much as I hate this planet and the damned stink-weasels, I figure living in the bush here is a damned sight better than living in a nice modern League facility for those who pose a risk to state security. Assuming they *let* me live. They do *seem* to prefer the dead-men-tell-no-tales modus operandi. All other things being equal, I think my chances are better in the bush. Yours, too."

"What about Zandowski?"

"Zan?" Rafe forced a laugh. "If she were a Combiner, I'd worry, but she's a loyal citizen of the Hanseatic Coalition. Her government will go along with what the marts want, and she'll go along with what the Coalition wants. She'll be fine."

"But you and she—"

"Are not exactly life-mates," he said quickly. "She won't cry if I vanish. The way she's been working lately, she might not even *notice*."

Having had personal experience with Rafe vanishing and having some idea of Zandowski's feelings for him, Juliana doubted he was right. But he seemed to believe it. He certainly seemed ready to act on it.

"Ersch will howl when he finds us gone," Rafe said with satisfaction.

To Juliana, locked in her cabin by night and guarded by day, the escape from the League compound seemed implausible.

"I've got it figured," Rafe assured her. "Look. The way I see it, Ersch is in a hurry. You can see it in the way they're all scurrying around. And if he's pressed, then time is on our side and not his. This whole thing is a clandestine operation, and they know they can't keep it hidden forever.

"I saw what happened when he didn't pull Ellicot in. If losing *one* guy is such a problem to Ersch, what happens when he loses us too? Trouble, that's what. His schedule will go out the window, and then time *really* starts working for us.

"If we can get out into the jungle and go to ground, he'll

have to hunt for us, too, which means he can't hunt for Ellicot as well as he has. It's a big planet, and Ersch hasn't got a lot of resources. If Ellicot can stay out of sight, so can we. We'll be better off than sitting here under the marts' control, just waiting for them to decide that they can dispose of us.

"And we won't be out in the bush forever. Pretty soon somebody upstairs will figure out that there's something wrong and the Combine will start an investigation. The League's shenanigans won't stand the light of scrutiny. We'll be rescued—for real this time—and we can laugh in Ersch's face.

"You just be ready tomorrow night," he told her. And then he was gone, spooked by a rustle in the brush that foretold the arrival of the patrolling sentry.

Juliana spent a sleepless night worrying over Rafe's dire hints and the vagueness of his plans for escape. She wanted to be free of the League's control, and if she were, she knew where she wanted to go—and it wasn't into the bush with Rafe. Kurt was out there, and she wanted to be with *him*.

*Whatever happens then*, she told herself, *I'll be able to handle it*.

The next morning she whispered her hopes and fears about Rafe's plan to Kmo. The S'kimm female had little understanding of the danger and difficulty of the plan, and Juliana's attempts to work out the flaws in Rafe's plan went nowhere. Still, Kmo was entirely sympathetic toward Juliana's desire to be free of the League camp, and her support did much to stiffen Juliana's resolve to make the attempt.

"I would take you if I could," Juliana told Kmo.

Kmo looked searchingly at her for a moment and said, "I understand."

In midafternoon the routine of the camp was suddenly

disturbed. Juliana began to hear the passage of troops in the other clearings. Two aircraft lifted off and headed west. She couldn't tell what was going on, but it was clear that *something* had stirred up the Leaguers. A soldier came and politely requested that she return to her cabin. Obeying the order—for that's what it was despite its veneer of civility— she entered the cabin and was locked in. Her warder had barely passed out of the clearing when Rafe arrived, brandishing the cabin's key.

"Come on," he said, opening the door. "It's now or never."

"What's going on?"

"I scheduled an exercise to keep the troops busy. Idle troops are troublesome troops, you know."

"How?"

"When Shanholz is drunk, he's not too careful about who accesses his computer. There are damned few computer systems I can't mess up *somehow* once I get inside." Rafe grinned in self-satisfaction. "I also arranged transportation to get us a good long distance from Ersch and his stormtroopers. It's ready and waiting, but it won't be for long. We've got to move."

Rafe tugged on her arm to get her moving. They ran for the cover of the trees and threaded their way through the brush, avoiding the places where Leaguers milled, marched, and hurried. Finally Rafe led her back into the sunlight and into a clearing occupied by an ungainly transport aircraft.

To Juliana's surprise, there were no Leaguers in sight. Rafe seemed to find all as he had expected, and headed straight for the open hatch near the transport's nose. Fearful that they would be stopped at any moment, Juliana followed.

"Can you really fly this?" Juliana asked as Rafe strapped himself into the pilot's seat.

"Not a problem. I've been practicing on a sim."

"A *sim*?"

He frowned at her disbelieving tone. "Ease off. It's not like this crate is a fighter. It's a lot like the Radisson *Safari* I flew on Shand. Don't worry, I can fly it."

Juliana couldn't help but worry. Rafe's mention of fighters didn't help. She couldn't imagine that the Leaguers didn't have at least one on-planet, and that one would be all it would take to shoot them out of the sky.

Motion on the landing field dragged her eyes down from the clouds. Instead of the dreaded IDL troopers, she saw Kmo humping lopsidedly across the dirt. The camp's S'kimm had been warned not to go near the League aircraft under pain of death, and Juliana had no doubt the troopers would enforce the rule. If any saw Kmo, she would be shot dead.

"Come on, come on," Rafe urged. "Shut the hatch. We've got to go!"

"Just a minute," she shouted back.

Panting, Kmo reached the hatch. She looked up into Juliana's eyes, and held out the burden that had hampered her rush across the landing field. It was the dark case of Juliana's computer.

"I bring you the lost," Kmo said, offering it up.

Juliana was stunned. She recognized the formal phrase, of course. One of the ways a Hos'kimm could gain acceptance into a pack was to restore something that had been lost, and here was Kmo, offering such a gift price. Juliana had no pack and was unable to fulfill all the obligations that acceptance of the gift would bring. Surely, Kmo knew that.

Rafe shouted at Juliana to shut the hatch.

She couldn't abandon Kmo. Reaching down, she took the computer. Grinning, Kmo swarmed aboard. Her furry pelt brushed against Juliana as she twisted within the hatchway, thrust her head back outside, and yipped, calling out her clan name.

Five sleek S'kimm burst from the brush around the clearing and humped with frantic haste toward the aircraft. The gift price bought one entry, not six, but Juliana couldn't bear to see anyone who wished to be free of the Leaguers left behind. Shouting Rafe down, she urged the S'kimm on, waiting until the last had tumbled aboard before sealing the hatch. The aircraft lurched. Rafe wasn't waiting for her to confirm the seal before lifting the aircraft.

Leaving the S'kimm to fend for themselves, she fought the mounting acceleration and struggled up the slanting deck, barely reaching the copilot's seat before Rafe opened the throttles. The rearward screen showed the Leaguer camp dwindling behind them. To her relief nothing rose to contest their flight from captivity.

How long could that last?

Rafe leveled their flight. A glance at the control boards told her that the craft was not moving at anything like its maximum velocity. Rafe assured her that it was the safest course. Still, it made her nervous knowing that they could be running faster, but weren't.

"How long till we fly off their radar screens?" she asked.

"Another twenty or thirty minutes."

"I can't believe they haven't challenged us."

"Oh, they have, but I've got an agent that sounds remarkably like our pal Shanholz talking to them. Our pseudo-Shanholz is keeping them busy until the comm unit has an unfortunate failure. It should be very convincing."

Apparently it was. Nothing launched to chase them before the camp fell below the horizon. They had made good their escape.

✻       ✻       ✻

The roar of the aircraft passing overhead thrummed through the command hut, rattling windows and doors and causing loose items to dance across the desks.

"That was an unscheduled lift," Ersch commented to the sergeant on duty at the operations console.

"I believe that you're right, sir. I'll check into it at once."

"Do that."

Ersch returned his attention to the operational plan for collecting the wayward Professor Ellicot. He'd been embarrassed by the failure of the previous attempt to scoop up the professor. He would not be so embarrassed again. Only a few details remained to be added, such as where his strike team would do the deed. Ellicot remained frustratingly hidden among his indigenous xeno-friends, but that would soon change.

He looked up with a smile as the operations sergeant requested his attention.

## CHUGEN SYSTEM
## MIDWAY STATION

The buzz of the intercom did nothing to hide the worry in Jane Van der Hoogt's voice as she reported the result of her inquiry into the burst of static they had picked up emanating from beyond the orbit of the Chugen System's outermost planet.

"I don't like it, Ken. I told you when we picked it up that something about it seemed odd to me, so I ran it through the main bank with a couple of filters," Jane said. "Among the correspondences that the computer gave me back was a fifty-two percent probability of a Remor emergence. The whole signature isn't there, but it's got me worried. I don't like it at all."

If she was right about the origin of the static, no human in the system would like it. "I'll be right up."

After stepping into the lift and ordering it to the command deck, Konoye decided he didn't like riding the car. Sure, it was faster than swimming up a tube in zero-G, but in the lift all he did was stand there. There was nothing physical for him to do to distract his mind. Normally that was not a problem, but right now *any* distraction would have been welcome, so long as it kept him from thinking about what Jane had found.

"Could it be a mistake?" was the first thing he asked as he reached the command center. "It's awfully far out. We could just be looking at sensor noise and letting our fears get the better of us."

They both knew it was unlikely, and Jane said as much.

He checked Jane's figures and made a few runs of his own, but he couldn't eliminate the Remor possibility. He got the probability down to forty-seven percent, but he couldn't make it go away.

It was three days before they got any more data. Astrogation picked up a dark object on a ballistic course that would take it past the station and straight into the center of the untested exit point to Ursa. Backtracking put the object in the vicinity of the static burst at the right time. Whatever was out there was large, dark, and silent—and headed right for them.

"It's got to be Remor," Konoye concluded. "They want the gate to Earth."

Jane's face was scrunched in frustrated uncertainty. "If so, why didn't they drop into normal space a lot closer in?"

"Aye," Hoppe agreed. "They could have overwhelmed us or have passed us by. Either way there be nothing we be doing to stop them."

Konoye threw up his hands. "Who knows why they do what they do? They *are* the unknowable aliens, after all."

Jane sighed. "I don't know, I don't know. It doesn't make

sense. If they want something here, why make the transit so far out and come in so slow? And if it's an attack, where are the warships? We haven't picked up a single ship's drive signature on scans."

"They could be ballistic and masked by the big object. We not likely to be seeing them that way. Unless they be making a change in velocity, they be reaching weapon range in a week. Then we be having trouble if they be Remor," Hoppe observed.

"*If* they're Remor," Jane said.

"How can we assume otherwise?" Konoye said, wishing that any other, more palatable possibility were likely. He just didn't believe that the universe was going to give him one of those. "Jane, send a message out to Cygnus and copy Canessa Control. Tell them we've got more than a raider this time. Tell them we need help."

"And if we're crying wolf?" she asked.

"At least we'll be alive to be embarrassed."

"I'm not being so sure of that, Director," Hoppe said. "Canessa, she be having at most a dozen craft of her own and maybe twice that in transitories currently insystem. Them transitory ship masters will be wanting to go running, and any Canessa can hold, she will be wanting to reserve for her own defense. Any help they be sending be too little against what comes."

"Should we start an evacuation?" Jane asked.

She knew as well as he did that there weren't enough ships to get everyone off the station at once. And where would they go? Ursa would be the strongest system within a single transit, but with the jump route untested, the attempt was likely to be as suicidal as facing a Remor fleet. Canessa? Even if they crammed every jump-capable craft to the airlocks, more than two-thirds of the people in Chugen would be left to face the oncoming enemy, because the evacuation ships couldn't get back in time to take another load. Chugen IV? A planet was harder to destroy than a station. People on a planetary body had a chance of surviving until the Combine could drive the Remor away. He made a rough calculation. They probably could manage to get two round-trip runs out of each of their transit-capable ships and one for the slower insystem craft, but that still wouldn't be enough to get *everyone* down. Still, Chugen IV gave the best chance for the most people. He started giving the necessary orders.

It took thirty-eight hours to get the last of the first load away and by then they had received bad news: the object had accelerated, increasing its velocity in a way no natural object could despite the lack of a drive signature. There could be no more denying that it was a vessel, and the only vessels of such size were Remor hulks. Konoye ordered another plea for help sent through the jump point to Cygnus, even though he knew that there was insufficient time for the Combine to respond. "Tell them the intruder's identity is confirmed as Remor."

Two days of agonized waiting passed before Jane, who against Konoye's advice had volunteered to stay with the station, announced:

"The jump point's radiating. We've got someone coming through." Jane's voice peaked with excitement. "Ken, it's a whole fleet!"

A grin burst forth on his face. "So much for Mr. Hoppe's pessimism."

But his relief withered when the IFF code board started lighting up with the identities of the inbound ships. Each and every last one belonged to the Interstellar Defense League.

With the inbound point in close proximity to the station, communication time lag was minimal. The visual link came up. Konoye's stomach tightened as he recognized the face of Christoph Stone, the Casual Slaughterer himself.

"This is Sector Commander Stone, in command of alpha-squadron, IDL Fleet Thirty-two. We are on an ambassadorial tour and were in the Canessa System when your message torp came through. Its broadcast message said that you had confirmed Remor presence here. Request you transmit all information on enemy dispositions at once."

*Who the* hell *did Stone think he was, giving orders* here?

A mart general with a fleet at his back, was who. The proverbial 500-kilo gorilla, with hundreds of missiles and dozens of energy weapons trained on a nearly defenseless station. A bully was what he was, a playground bully who knew he was bigger and stronger than anyone else around. Konoye had never liked being bullied. He'd learned to fight back on the playground, but the Chugen System was not a playground.

"This is not League space," he managed to stammer out, trying to assert the authority vested in him by the Board of Directors.

"But we are here nevertheless," Stone replied calmly. "And ready to fight the enemy."

"You have no jurisdiction here," Konoye insisted.

"The mandate of IDL MilForce is to fight the Remor enemy. Did you not call for help against them?"

"I didn't call for *you*."

"As may be. I repeat, we stand ready to defend this system. With your own ships inbound to Chugen IV, the station is open to the enemy. You appear to be defenseless."

Was that a threat? Weren't the Remor enough of a problem?

"I expect a relief force from Canessa," Konoye told him, trying to make his hopeful wish sound like cold expectation.

"Do you?" Stone's expression betrayed nothing; not surprise, incredulity, belief, or even amusement at Konoye's bald bluff. "Canessa control had no ships bound for the jump point when we made transit. Your expectations are some distance from becoming reality."

"This system is a protected affiliate of the Pan-Stellar Combine."

Stone frowned slightly, disapprovingly. "I am surprised at you, Mr. Director. Combiners have a reputation for humanitarian concerns, yet you seem more worried about legal technicalities than about the approaching enemy and what they will do to any Humans that they find in this system. I assure you, sir, that the Remor know little of Human boundaries and care even less for them. You, and all your people, will be slaughtered. Will you not accept my offer to defend this system?"

"So you can claim control of the system?" Konoye accused.

"So that innocent lives can be saved. I do not relish the thought of going against that hulk with the squadron I have at hand. We will be hurt, at the very least, and could quite possibly lose every ship we have here, but my troops understand their lot. We exist to defend Humanity, sir. However, we do not wish to extend our protection where it is not wanted. Do you want our protection, sir?"

Protection was *exactly* what he wanted, but he wasn't sure he was ready to pay the price. There was still a chance that the Remor hulk might just pass through Chugen. It *had* happened once before: in Gallentin, a Remor hulk had jumped in, frightened everyone half to death, and disappeared without firing a shot. *Once.* Far more often the appearance of a Remor hulk had meant death and destruction. He couldn't bet lives that a unique occurrence would be repeated, could he?

He had to find a way to get the help of the League fleet without letting them use the Centauri Accords to claim ownership through defense.

"No one here belongs to your League, nor does anyone wish to become a part of it," he told Stone, thinking furiously as he spoke. No brilliant solution offered itself to him. He kept talking, looking for a straw to grasp. "We are all sovereign citizens of the Combine and this system belongs to the Combine. However, if you would place your fleet under my command, we could use your help."

"I cannot relinquish my command, sir."

Konoye hadn't expected him to, but he'd had to ask. "And I cannot relinquish the Combine's sovereignty in this system."

Stone was silent for a moment, but Konoye didn't think for a moment that his rant had cowed the Casual Slaughterer. Stone's words surprised him. "Very well, sir. If sovereignty issues are more important to you than survival, I am not inclined to argue about jurisdiction. If we are not welcome, we can go home. It is your choice, Director Konoye."

The comm link went dead.

Was that it, then?

Konoye stared sullenly at his system display. The presumed Remor hulk was closing on the station. Had he just forced Stone to withdraw and leave them to the feeble hope that the Remor would ignore them?

"Ken?" Jane's voice quivered. "Look at the screen!"

His hopes soared as the track on the incoming hulk broke up in electromagnetic interference. All the scanners washed out. It could only mean one thing: the hulk had transited out of the system.

But as the static of its departure faded, tracking began reporting drive signatures. Marker lights winked on in the system display faster than Konoye could count them.

Konoye's throat clogged, He would have tasted dust had the station's filtration systems allowed any in the air.

The hulk had gone, but it had left its spawn behind. More than two dozen enemy warships were boring in on the station. The Remor were coming for him and his people, and he had no way to repel them. The station would be vaporized, and the second set of evacuees would be run down and destroyed as the Remor turned their attention to Chugen IV. The only hope lay with the League fleet.

Konoye opened a link to the IDL flagship. "Sector Commander Stone?"

"Yes, Mr. Director?"

"Would you be so kind as to deploy your fleet to fight the Remor invader?"

Stone nodded once. "Will do, Mr. Director. I will keep you informed as circumstances permit."

Before the Casual Slaughterer finished talking, his ships were moving toward the enemy.

## 27

**CHUGEN SYSTEM**
**IDLS *CONSTANTINE***

Given the position of his fleet and its outriders, and his superior military sensors, Commander Stone knew about the Remor hulk's departure almost thirty seconds before Midway Station. He used the time to assess the situation.

Telescopes aboard his flagship had been tracking the hulk since they had fixed its position and course. As the scan station reported and tallied warships by their drive signatures, the optical station reported more objects than drives. Most, though not all, were on the same path that the hulk had been on. What were they? Sleeper missiles? Ballistic projectiles? Mines? Or something as innocuous as garbage dumped by the hulk before making transit? Whatever they were, there was a more immediate problem: enemy warships.

"Report on active hostiles."

"We're still trying to resolve some of the more distant ones, sir," Colonel MacAndra reported.

"Confine yourself to those headed this way for now."

"Aye, sir." MacAndra snapped his crew to action. Data started feeding into the main tactical viewer. "Scanners make it fifteen interface strikers, seven cruisers, and two dreadnought mass ships. All are identifiable classes except for one of the dreadnoughts."

The plot showed that the enemy commander had split

his force into two approximately equal groups, with the unclassified dreadnought drawing the extra consorts. The lighter vessels were grouped by mass category, preceding the dreadnoughts in what looked to be screening planes. The formation bothered Stone; typically the enemy came in as a swarm. Still, organized dispositions were not unknown among the enemy, just unusual.

"I make both groups on converging vector for Midway Station," he mused aloud.

"Astrogation confirms, sir. That's likely to change when we light our drives," MacAndra observed.

But only if the enemy showed their usual pugnacity toward Human ships. Given the enemy commander's unusual approach, that couldn't be counted upon.

Stone had two *Emperor*-class heavy cruisers including his flagship *Constantine*, five *Honorable*-class cruisers, nine of the smaller *Warlord*-class cruisers, the carrier *Ardennes* with an understrength complement of attack craft, and twenty patrollers, two of which were kitted out with electronics rather than a normal weapon complement.

By mass, his force was substantially larger than the advancing enemy, but that was a false comparison given the enemy's technological superiority. Factoring that in, the book's Combat Equivalency Ratings still gave him a 1.5 to 1 advantage, but those CER ratings assumed a typical uncoordinated Remor fleet. That wasn't the case here. He guessed that he'd be lucky to pull even odds.

Unfortunately the battle wouldn't be over even if the advancing enemy were dealt with. There were more enemy ships out there, scattering across the system. However, that long-term problem just might be his short-term salvation. Had those ships remained with the main body of the enemy, Stone's fleet would not have stood a chance. As it was, he just might be able to show the Remor commander the error of his ways.

"Prepare Contingency Green, Captain."

"Aye, Commander."

"Signal from Midway," commo reported.

As Stone had been expecting. He spoke briefly with the System Director Konoye. Logging off, he gave the order, "Initiate Green," and his ships began to move.

The next move belonged to the enemy.

**CHUGEN SYSTEM**
**CHUGEN IV**

Two days of hiking across the delta scrub didn't improve Rafe's disposition. He'd exploded when Juliana announced her decision to follow Kmo out into the delta plains, to the great Gathering of Hos'kimm.

At least his ranting had subsided. Once he seemed to realize that Juliana—grateful though she was for his help in escaping from the Leaguers—was going whether he did or not, he quieted down, but his anger hadn't gone away completely. She could see it boil almost to the surface each time their S'kimm guides insisted that they make an effort to disguise their trail. It was there now, ready to break the surface.

"If you want to go where we're most likely to get caught, why waste time hiding the trail?" he grumbled.

Juliana knew better than to try to answer him. She sank down on a dry rock and took the opportunity to dump out some of the water that had leaked into her boots. Stripping off her socks, she felt the air warm and wonderfully dry against her skin. She wrung out her socks, laid them in the sun, and dug through the emergency kit she had salvaged from the League transport until she found a container of absorbent powder. Puffs of fragrant dust drifted as she dumped generous amounts into each of her boots. She sprinkled some on her socks before stowing the canister away.

Rafe must have realized that he wasn't going to get a rise from her, because he found his own rock and looked to his own boots. They waited in silence while the S'kimm did what they could to confuse the trail.

Juliana stared out across the delta. There was little to see in the direction they were headed: tall grass, brief sparkling stretches of open water, the occasional clump of scraggly bushes, and the even more occasional gnarled tree. Against the horizon was a low, purplish smudge that hadn't been there the previous day: *Teclanandahotay*, the Hills of Teclananda where the Hos'kimm gathered.

Juliana longed to be there. From what Kmo told her about the Gathering, she knew that Kurt would go there if he were able. No matter the danger, he would not be able to stay away from such a significant gathering of the species he had come to study. It was an unparalleled opportunity, but she had a more immediate interest than socioxenology: she would find Kurt there. She could warn him about the League hunters, and *then* they could slip away into the wilderness and disappear.

But first they had to get to *Teclanandahotey*.

She saw Kmo and her tribe-mates beckoning from a spit a short way downstream. Juliana tugged on her boots and hauled herself to her feet, calling to Rafe to come along, and started walking.

*Soon*, she promised herself. *Soon*.

## CHUGEN SYSTEM
## IDLS JAGUAR

*Jaguar* emerged along with the rest of Fleet 32's alpha squadron, but unlike her sister ships she neither decelerated nor altered course. At high intrinsic velocity she continued on, boring in for the inner system. No challenge came from Midway Station. Indeed, there wasn't the slightest sign that anyone aboard Midway knew that *Jaguar* was present, which was as it should be, for *Jaguar* was a Predator-class lurker craft. In full stealth mode she was supposed to be virtually undetectable. Only the most observant, competent, and lucky observer could pick her emissions out of the background. Such an observer was unlikely to be among the Combiner sensor technicians, and even were there such a marvel aboard the station, the fleet's arrival should have proven an unavoidable distraction.

As far as Anders Seaborg could see, *Jaguar*'s insertion into the Chugen System had been a success. As the hours passed, and the squadron and Midway Station dwindled behind them, his remaining concerns over detection dwindled, too. They vanished when Captain Laura Perry, the *Jaguar*'s master, asked, "Shall we shape for Chugen IV, Commander?"

"Best speed she'll make, Captain, consistent with stealth, of course."

"Will do," she responded, with just a hint of annoyance.

She knew the orders and she knew her job and she didn't like being told how to do it by a mere groundpounder. Had he been assigned to *Jaguar* on a permanent basis, he would have needed to pay attention to her attitude. But matters sat otherwise and they both knew it; he was aboard only for this mission, which was why she allowed her pique at his apparent pedantry to show, and why he let it go.

He had no quibble with her competence, he was just being cautious, and attempting to avoid any procedural misunderstanding. They were treading on dangerous ground here. Slipping a lurker into the sovereign space of another star nation was a violation of the Centauri Accords and could be considered a provocation toward war. Which was not to say that it was never done.

The IDL was involved in enough questionable operations in this system already. Anders had no desire to complicate the situation by having a ship under his command become a *causa belli* by being caught in such embarrassing circumstances. If Perry's disdain was the price of a bit of insurance against that event, so be it. Not every vacuumhead was as understanding as Jason Metzler had been.

Recalling his old comrade in arms, Anders wondered what Metzler would have to say about the current mission. Something caustic, he was sure. Something about the perversity of the universe, too. *Curious*, he could hear Metzler's voice saying. *You must have sinned pretty hard in a former life to bring down this kind of karma.*

Was it for his sins?

Over ten years ago, he'd been ramrodding a squad tasked with taking up a wayward socioxenologist while Commander Stone sat the high guard in his flagship and waited for the enemy to come. Then, Ersch had been sent to find out why Ellicot was still on the loose. Now, here on Chugen IV, Ersch was the one chasing Ellicot and Anders was the deputation sent from on high to expedite the situation.

Some of the parallels made sense, given Intel's plan to utilize Ellicot and the location of Chugen. But what of the others? Were they due to coincidence, destiny, or God's plan? Or was it as the Alsionites liked to say, simply a case of strange order emerging from chaos? Whatever it was, it made Anders uncomfortable.

But what was discomfort to an Eridani? An Eridani took the uncomfortable in stride, occasionally allowed the daunting to make him pause, and refused to let the impossible do more than slow him down.

He looked to the system plot. They would be overtaking the refugees from Midway Station soon. A chance of detection existed at that point. He started looking for anything that could be done to minimize that chance.

**CHUGEN SYSTEM**
**CHUGEN IV**

The food they brought Kurtellicot was a bland, hot gruel. It was studded with soft white nodules and black and brown specks. Small insects and grubs, no doubt. A tiny, faint voice whined about its peculiarity, but he ignored the voice. This was food, and he was grateful to have something with which to fill his cavern of a stomach. When he had emptied the bowl, Zhent'ah-rhull approached him.

"Do you feel better, *Daysha-lo'daramak?*"

From his relationship with Ah'zzt, Kurtellicot had come to understand that *daramak* meant something like a blood-brother, and the reverence in the seer's voice whenever he used the word *Daysha* suggested that he spoke of some powerful spirit. Kurtellicot didn't feel particularly well, but he was well enough to do what was necessary and correct the seer. "I am not a godling."

Zhent'ah-rhull barked a laugh. "No one said you were. But you are the Star Walker, and the Star Walker is kin of the Daysha. *Grawr'tayo*, perhaps, but kin even so."

"I do not understand the Daysha."

"Who does? Even being permitted to know the mystery of his use name does not bring understanding. We seers remember more than most, and we recall so very little. But you have walked a pattern and are one of us now. You must learn what we know."

*Did he just say that I am now a seer?* Kurtellicot dazedly asked himself.

"Know you that the Daysha is god," Zhent'ah-rhull said.

"In the long ago, our ancestors were chosen to be among his people. The Daysha lifted us up and made us the Hos'kimm. We were prized among the Daysha's people and carried across the sky ocean. The Daysha gave us a place. Here. This place.

"In this place the Daysha gave us stewardship over his *teclananda*. It was a great trust. It was a great honor. To our great shame, we did not prove worthy. We failed the Daysha. We failed to care for his *teclananda*, and the Daysha turned his face from us.

"But the Daysha is infinite in wisdom and we hold hope of receiving his mercy. Since the days of our sin, father has told pup that when we have paid for our sins, when we are worthy again, then the Daysha will return and take us again to his bosom.

"That is the tale that seer has told seer through the long ages. Some say that this is the end of the age. Some say that the time has come, and that the Daysha has come and is already watching us from the heavens. Some say that the Daysha is come to judge and punish us, others that he is come to forgive us. Do you have his word for us, Star Walker?"

"I have no word. I wish that I did, but I am only a man and have no extraordinary connection with the divine," Kurtellicot said. He expected an explosive response to his apparent blasphemy, but Zhent'ah-rhull did not seem perturbed.

"We are all only men," the seer said. "We do not always know what we know. Though I have felt a shiver in the heavens, I do not know if the Daysha is truly come. But this I do know: you faced your testing and you have walked the whole of the path of the star. This has not been done before. You are Hos'kimm but not Hos'kimm. We must learn why the Daysha has sent you."

Zhent'ah-rhull heaved himself to his feet. A younger seer handed him his walking sticks. Zhent'ah-rhull tapped one against Kurtellicot's leg.

"Come, Star Walker. We must go down into the *rass'arass*. There is turmoil in the heavens, and our prayers must join to the song of the sky ocean."

Kurtellicot rose and followed the seers into the sanctum.

# 28

Stone's orders flashed through the squadron on tight beams. The reordering of the battle groups was minimal, accomplished without disruption among the deploying ships. Very smooth, very professional. He was proud of the skill they displayed in the intricate maneuvering. But the greater test was yet to come.

With each minute, the groups diverged and he became more committed to his strategy. Stinson's command was to be his blocking group. Anyone relying on a scan of their drives would judge them to be the smaller of the two task groups. While Stinson's command moved slowly into position near the station, Stone and his attack group accelerated aggressively toward the trailing enemy force. His dispositions mimicked those of the enemy: patrollers out in front and the heavier cruisers behind, with his heaviest units, *Constantine* and her sister ship *Ketsuwayo*, at the core. His attached electronics-crammed patroller, IDLS *Bohrs*, was up front and running decoys and spoof strategies, working as hard as it could to make his dozen fighting patrollers look like twice their number.

The attack group was supposed to look as if they were spoiling for a fight, but not so tough that the enemy would throw everything at them. Stone's chosen approach vector was supposed to encourage the enemy commander to believe that Stone had miscalculated and split his forces inexpertly, committing them to dangerously diverging vectors. An enemy intent on maximum destruction should see an opportunity to defeat Stone's split squadron in detail.

It was a gamble that relied on the shrewdness of the enemy commander, a gamble made doubly dangerous by the unpredictability of the alien Remor.

He had begun to fear that he had miscalculated when MacAndra pointed out what Stone's view of the holotank had hidden from him.

"They're taking the bait," the colonel announced.

Stone shifted the tank's view and saw that MacAndra was right. The enemy group centered on the *Hydra* dreadnought was still bearing on direct vector toward the station and Stinson's command, but the unknown dreadnought's group had begun to angle toward Stone's force.

Stone had expected the enemy commander to use one of his groups as a screen to hold off Stone's force, skirmishing while the other group bore in and eliminated Stinson's command, but the commander aboard the unknown dreadnought was turning and coming straight for him.

The Remor were intent on maximum destruction, all right. They were matching force to force, letting hell pay the piper, and damn the odds. He smiled grimly. He'd gotten more than he'd asked for and now he'd have to deal with it. He could only hope that he had more surprises for the Remor than they had for him.

"Signal our screens to shift course to direct intercept," he ordered. "Case C, Colonel MacAndra."

The course change slowed the patrollers down relative to the cruiser screen and brought them closer in. When the cruisers responded, they also slowed and ended closer to *Constantine* and *Ketsuwayo*. Stone's whole attack group was now closer together, and getting closer still as they drew nearer the enemy.

"Any response from the enemy, Colonel MacAndra?"

"Negative, Commander. They're coming on steady."

"Very well. Signal the squadron *prepare to engage*."

Aboard *Constantine*, battle alert sounded, as it would aboard each of the squadron's ships as they received the order. There was a flurry of activity on the bridge as everyone sealed their helmets. The intercom crackled as all stations reported their divisions ready. In the main holotank, the ghostly spheres of missile envelopes appeared around ships as the display shifted to combat mode. The leading ships' envelopes were solidly overlapping; the leading surfaces of the larger enemy spheres had nearly reached Stone's patroller screen.

As soon as each Human ship was within the attack zone of at least one Remor ship, the enemy launched his first salvo from his interface strikers. Still out of range, the Human ships bore on of necessity; they would need to survive the first barrage before they could return fire. Evasive maneuvers and countermeasures began. Many missiles were destroyed or spoofed, but some continued to close on the ships. Interceptors came into play as the tenacious missiles flashed closer. Most of the enemy birds were caught, but not all, by no means all.

The ships of Stone's patroller screen were hit hard. Three of them vanished entirely from the holotank. The markers for another seven began to flash in signal that they had suffered drive failure or some other major malfunction. Nearly all of the ships were reporting at least minor damage.

"Break off, break off!" Stone broadcast.

He had expected his screen to go at least another round before sustaining so many casualties, but the enemy fleet commander had put both of his *Typhoon*-class strikers with this group, and those ships packed a missile throw weight almost thirty percent higher than the standard *Thunder*-class strikers. Having to face both *Typhoons* was an unpleasant surprise, and a reminder that he wasn't the only one who could spoof an enemy.

Fortunately for the League forces, barely half of the casualties were real. Two of the "dead" and five of the "seriously damaged" ships were decoys deployed by *Bohrs*. Still, a third of the screen had been taken out of the battle, and the "real" result was nearly as bad as the apparent one. The damage wrought, both real and apparent, made plausible the disintegration of the screen's coherence as the patrollers reversed course and fell back among the cruisers. A handful of missiles were launched at or beyond maximum effective range, further contributing to the impression that the Human advance formation had been broken.

The Remor launched again. Their targets remained primarily patrollers, but the smaller ships, now under the aegis of the cruisers, benefited from the larger ships' defenses. More League ships took damage, but the only total loss to that salvo was another of the *Bohrs*'s decoys.

By then the League ships had reached the necessary orientation relative to the enemy. The cruisers launched simultaneously with the patrollers. As planned, the massive salvo saturated the defenses of the enemy interface strikers. Not one survived. *Thunders* and deadlier *Typhoons* were no more than expanding clouds of gas and debris. Their last flight of missiles, launched before their destruction, was dealt with relatively easily, although the cruiser *Blucher* took several serious hits, knocking her drive off-line and forcing her out of the battle.

The devastating, simultaneous loss of all of a squadron's light units would almost certainly have spooked a Human fleet, but the Remor were not in the remotest way human. As each of their cruisers reached range, they opened up.

*Maybe they* are *rattled,* Stone thought. A concerted volley would have been far more dangerous to the Leaguers. As it was, they handled the incoming missiles with relative ease and took minimal damage.

"Ignore enemy cruisers designated Two and Three," he ordered. "Direct all fire at Cruisers One and Four."

It was a gamble, but not a big one. Concentrated fire could cripple, or with luck kill, the leading enemy units. That alone would tip the odds in the cruiser action in the Humans' favor, a necessary prelude to the impeding action with the enemy dreadnought. And given the vectors, *Constantine* and *Ketsuwayo* would be in range for the next salvo—a decisive advantage if at least one of the enemy cruisers was out of action by then.

His troops made him proud, destroying Cruiser Four and sending One scurrying away, leaking debris, organics, water, and oxygen. Half the enemy force's cruisers were out of action.

But the enemy commander understood the danger bearing down on his force. The remaining Remor ships concentrated their fire on the approaching League heavy cruisers. The enemy salvo struck *Constantine* several hard blows, but failed to stop her from launching a full spread. As the damage reports came in, Stone had the satisfaction of seeing the last two enemy cruiser markers go dark.

Just the dreadnought now, and he had her—by numbers, by mass, and probably by weight of missile throw. If the dreadnought fought, she would go down. The only question was the size of the butcher's bill.

He had a few minutes before the engagement's conclusive action began. He used it to look deeper insystem, to see how the enemy commander of the *Hydra* group was handling his own surprise. Like her sister ship *Bohrs*, the electronic warfare patroller *Tesla* had pretended to be a squadron unto herself, drawing the enemy commander into misreading the dispositions of the blocking group. The *Hydra* group had closed on the phantom ships and ignored *Ardennes*'s attack craft, insystem boats whose drives didn't register easily on scanners searching for warships. *Tesla* was lost, but the enemy commander had made his mistake. While he was concentrating on attacking *Tesla* and her phantom sisters, Stinson's command sideswiped the Remor force. The attack craft took a toll out of proportion to their strength, and avenged *Tesla* and the other patrollers that had died with her.

But the *Hydra* commander was sharper than whoever commanded the unknown dreadnought. He didn't allow himself to be drawn deeper in what was obviously a trap. He couldn't know that Stone had already played all his cards, but he could see that *Ardennes*'s attack craft had mauled his strikers and were starting to tear into his cruisers. He showed caution, slowing his force's advance on Midway Station and keeping his own ship at maximum engagement range. Doubtless he looked over his figurative shoulder and saw that Stone's group would soon finish off the other dreadnought and be free to come down on him.

The *Hydra* launched a last spread of missiles and turned tail. The enemy's two surviving cruisers and a handful of strikers limped after him.

**CHUGEN SYSTEM**
**CHUGEN IV**

A hardsuited trooper emerged from beneath the camouflage net that had been draped haphazardly across the ditched aircraft.

"There were stink-weasels aboard, sir," he announced.

Ersch nodded. "The ones from the camp?"

"Must have been. The fugitives sealed the craft when they left her. No chance a weasel would figure a way in."

"Good." He activated the circuit to his commo chief. "Call in the flight crew. I want this aircraft serviced and ready for our new arrival by sunset."

The commo chief relayed Ersch's order and was back on the line two minutes later. "Relay from the fleet, sir. They've engaged the enemy space forces."

If the news had just gotten here, the battle was well under way. Ersch looked up at the sky. There was nothing to be seen, of course, but he had to look. Fates were being decided up there.

Ersch lowered his eyes and glared at the snarled yellow and brown jungle. Whatever way the battle went, there were fates to be decided here as well. He had a job to do, and he wanted it done before there were any more complications.

"Fire her up," he commed his driver. "Let's roll."

**CHUGEN SYSTEM**
**CHUGEN IV**

The *rass'arass* was unlike any other Hos'kimm sanctum Kurtellicot had visited. For one thing, it had a ramp cut into the earthen walls rather than the usual ladder to take the communicant into the darkness. For another, its floor was two or three times deeper, possibly six times the height of an erect R'kimm. And that floor held the most different feature of all. The typical sanctum had a fire pit, only kindled when the prayerful Hos'kimm reached the appropriate point in whatever ceremony they were performing. There was no fire pit in the *rass'arass*. Instead, in the center was a hole that flickered with a fiery glow but gave off no heat. The hole was covered with a woven mat and only stray spears of ruddy light escaped to paint irregular rusty splotches on the dirt walls of the *rass'arass*.

Zhent'ah-rhull walked to the edge of the mat, pointed to the floor, and told Kurtellicot to sit. Skirting the mat, the seer directed his fellow seers to their places. They formed a ring around the mat and Zhent'ah-rhull sat in the last open space, directly across from Kurtellicot. With everyone settled, the R'kimm seer conducted a union ceremony. Kurtellicot was pleased and proud to see how easily the others accepted him. He was quite comfortable by the time individual prayer began.

Unfortunately the warm glow of peacefulness did not last long.

"There is a wrongness," Zhent'ah-rhull announced.

The other seers murmured agreement before falling back to their individual prayers.

"What is wrong, Zhent'ah-rhull?" Kurtellicot asked.

"In the air, Star Walker. Can you not smell it?"

Kurt could smell gathered Hos'kimm and musty earth and little else. When he concentrated, he also thought that he detected the sharp tang of rising fear.

The light from beneath the mat flickered. The color of the radiating beams began to change, shifting along the spectrum. In reaction, the susurrus of prayer surrounding Kurtellicot grew more fervent, almost frenzied. One by one, the seers abandoned their prayers and fell into a wordless, moaning chant. Soon they were swaying back and forth. Kurtellicot tried to imitate their sound. Unable to feel whatever it was that his fellows felt, he was always a little off, a little behind. He was more successful in matching their rhythmic sway.

The chant went on and on. Sometimes it was so soft that he thought the singers had stopped. At other times the pace grew frantic and the tone strident. From time to time there was a lull, and with each lull came a shift in the character of the light from below. It was obvious that the timing of the shifts was related to the chant, but the meaning of it all escaped him.

Zhent'ah-rhull was the first to break the circle of the prayer chant. He rolled over onto his back, gasping. One of the S'kimm seers started to howl, a strange mix of pain and fear. Soon they all were rolling on the floor of the *rass'arass*, howling. Horrified, Kurtellicot stared at his violently distressed fellows. Though he didn't feel what so obviously tormented the others, Kurtellicot howled, too.

Whimpering, Zhent'ah-rhull forced himself to his feet. "We must flee."

He stumbled from seer to seer, urging them to their feet and repeating his exhortation. Trembling, Hos'kimm rose to their feet and wobbled to the ramp, bumping and jostling each other in their rush to leave. Propelled by Zhent'ah-rhull's firm push, Kurtellicot joined the chaotic exodus. He stumbled at the lip of the entrance, twisting his ankle, and fell. Hos'kimm seers humped heedlessly over him. They scattered toward the hills of Teclananda. Zhent'ah-rhull, humped, too, his proud belly dragging on the ground.

Kurtellicot didn't know what to do. Where were the others going? He wanted to follow them. He tried, only to collapse as pain shot through his leg. He could not run. He could not escape. Terrified, he howled his fear and frustration to the stars.

## CHUGEN SYSTEM
## IDLS *CONSTANTINE*

There was cheering aboard *Constantine*, as there would be aboard all of the squadron's ships. They had done something that was rarely achieved: defeated the enemy in space. The cost, as Stone had expected, had been high, but they had succeeded.

The shattered remnants of the enemy invasion fleet had re-formed on the *Hydra* dreadnought. Stone's force had picked off one more cruiser and another interface striker before the enemy fled out of range.

"No pursuit," Stone ordered.

No Human ship could catch a Remor ship that didn't want to be caught. Besides, his people needed time to lick their wounds. And there were other matters to attend to.

Stone ordered a display of the inner system brought up on the holotank.

# 29

The panic that had swept through Rasseh in the night had subsided by the time morning's light touched the hills of Teclananda. Many Hos'kimm had fled the gathering place, as Kmo had wanted to do, but many had remained or returned. The lanes among the steep-sided hills were again thronged by furred bodies.

"See, things are fine," Juliana told Kmo.

"Perhaps," the S'kimm replied, sounding unconvinced.

After visiting a merchant for bowls of taronna grubs to break their fast—Rafe stubbornly insisting on eating a League ration bar—they set out again, moving through the resurgent crowds in search of Kurt. Rafe spotted him first.

"God, will you look at him?" Rafe sounded disgusted.

Juliana looked where Rafe pointed, heart leaping to her throat. Yes! There he was, safe and sound! Kurt stood head and shoulders taller than any of the Hos'kimm, making him easy to spot.

His height also meant that he could see over Hos'kimm heads to her and Rafe, but he showed no sign of recognizing them, even when Juliana waved and called his name.

Kurt stood amid a group of gray-furred Hos'kimm made up of all three of the racial variants. All of them, Kurt included, wore the necklaces and bracelets of tribal elders. Kurt's were those of a H'kimm chief. Although they were less elaborate than those worn by poor dead Lo'gnen, they were no less fine; the Hos'kimm artisans did their best work to honor their elders.

The trinkets and bangles were all he wore. His skin was darkened by Chugen's sun, and even from across the plaza Juliana could see dirt and grime. His hair and beard were scraggly and unkempt, and there were dark, oily smears on either side of his throat where the Hos'kimm had scent glands. Despite all that he looked healthy, and that was what was important. He was limping, though, and that worried her.

She called to him again, but like the Hos'kimm at his side, he just ogled at her. His lack of recognition cut her but, remembering what had happened to him on Cassuells Home, she found hope. *He's having another identification crisis. That's all it is,* she told herself. *He'll be fine once he's back among Humans.*

Calling and waving, she tried to get closer. Hos'kimm bunched together between them, keeping her from passing simply by the density of their bodies. She saw him exchange a low-voiced comment with one of the Hos'kimm elders at his side. She didn't hear the words, but by the rhythms he was speaking a local dialect. The S'kimm to whom he spoke barked a laugh at his comment.

"Let me through," she cried in both Anglic and the H'kimm dialect as she ineffectually tried to squirm her way through the blocking Hos'kimm. When she finally managed to reach him, she understood why he limped: his lower right leg was splinted and he leaned on a carved walking stick.

"Are you all right?" she asked.

"I am well," he answered, smiling pleasantly at her. The smile, though reassuring, held none of the warmth she'd hoped to find.

"It's me, Kurt. It's Juliana."

The pleasant smile didn't change. "Have you come for the Gathering, friend Juliana?"

"I came to find you."

"I am not lost."

"Delusional," Rafe commented, having come up behind her. "Whacked out again."

"You hush," Juliana snapped at him. She turned back to Kurt, staring him in the eyes and willing him to want to return to himself as much as she wanted him back. "Kurt, you're confused. You're having an identification crisis."

"I am touched by the concern I hear in you, friend Juliana, but I fear that it is you who are confused. The one you knew no longer dwells as an outsider among the Hos'kimm. He is gone. My name, though similar, is not Kurt. I am Kurtellicot, elder of the Star Walker H'kimm, *tuoyal* and *Daysha-lo'daramak*."

"You are Professor Kurt Ellicot, socioxenologist, citizen of the Serenten Concordat," she insisted.

"It is our custom that when a man changes clans, we Hos'kimm no longer remember what he was, only what he is."

"You're not Hos'kimm," she cried. "You're Human!"

"We Hos'kimm are very human," her told her in a lecturing tone. "To think otherwise insults the pack and diminishes the thinker. Do you not have the wit and the heart to see this?"

"Of course I do. You know I do. But I also have eyes to see who stands before me. You know as well as I do that when I say Human, I am speaking of species, not spirit. Kurt, please. Listen to me. Think. Remember who you are. Kurt?"

He touched her cheek with a finger, temporarily damming a tear.

"Is this sadness for me?" he asked.

"Yes." *And for us*, she wanted to add.

"Then let it go. In his wisdom, Lo'gnen saw my path. He was my first guide among the Hos'kimm. He recognized my true self before I did. And he was right, you see. Now I have been honored by the seers. They have let me walk the pattern and find my way. I have talked to the spirits, and they have whispered their secrets to me. My path has brought me to where I belong. I walk the pack's Way and am content."

Juliana could find no more words to throw into the face of his conviction.

"Looks like the League got what it wanted," Rafe commented to Ellicot's departing back.

If he had harbored any lingering doubts about his course they had gone up in smoke. Ellicot had gone native, just like on Cassuells Home. Rafe was glad that Juli had gotten the chance to see the demented bastard for herself. She obviously needed the shock to understand how warped her idol was. Now she would understand just how right he had been about Ellicot all along.

"Look at him," he exhorted her. "Buck naked and smearing himself with goo so he'll smell like them. If that's not turning your back on Humanity, I don't know what is."

"He's just confused."

God in heaven, she was still defending him! "Confused, eh? His kind of confusion gets people killed. He got confused on Cassuells Home, too, and people died. The bastard doesn't like people trying to unconfuse him."

"What are you talking about?"

"Isn't it obvious?" Her expression said it wasn't. She was still blinded by her puppy love for the bastard. "Ellicot's not right in the head. He doesn't just identify with the aliens, he thinks he *is* one. He *likes* being an alien. And he *doesn't* like being told he's not one. He *doesn't* like people who disturb his delusion. Try to take his delusion away from him, and he *does* things about it. There were people on Cassuells Home who tried to tell him he wasn't an alien. They had *accidents*. That's what the official reports called them, anyway. Expert flyers with years of flight time don't have *accidents* in perfectly functional aircraft. Someone has to arrange those kinds of *accidents*. The sort of person who doesn't like people disturbing his delusion. Ellicot's that person, Juli. He's been that way since he went crazy on Cassuells Home. He murdered people there. He'll do the same here if given the chance."

"Don't be ridiculous. Kurt's no killer."

"Don't be *stupid*!" For an intelligent woman she could be so damfool simple. "What about Langdorf, eh? He went off into the woods with Ellicot and his furry friends. He didn't come back; the one other Human in the party and he didn't come back. I guess he just had an *accident*, eh? Ellicot's a killer, I tell you. And now you've challenged his delusion. He's marked you. You get in his way and you'll be finding yourself having an accident."

"That's not going to happen."

Her expression told him that she had fallen so far under the bastard's sway that nothing he said would convince her of the truth. Ellicot would kill her the way he'd killed Franchesca. Only this time something was different; this time Rafe was here, and Rafe wasn't the sort of guy to stand aside and let the bastard kill again. "You're right. I'm not going to let it happen."

He slung off his backpack and started rummaging through it for what he needed.

"What are you doing?"

"Making sure that the bastard isn't going to kill anyone.

Gonna burst his little 'me *tuoyal,* me holier than thou' bubble."

He found what he sought.

"What's that?" she asked as he drew it forth. "It's not a weapon, is it?"

"It's justice," he told her. It wasn't the justice that Ellicot deserved, but it was the justice he was going to get. In some ways it might even be better than anything Rafe himself could have done to the bastard. Wishing Ellicot a long and painful new life, Rafe activated the locator.

The Mark 8 combat car lurched forward as its driver responded to the signal. Ersch didn't even have to give the order. He swayed and bounced as they careened through the narrow lanes of the miserable shantytown that the natives called Rasseh.

A town? *What a laugh*, Ersch thought. *Just more job-inflating hyperbole from the researchers. A town needs real buildings.*

The only structures they encountered were flimsy market stalls that disintegrated when the Mk. 8 rammed them while bulling its way through the tighter sections. Some of the rickety things simply blew down from the wind of the combat car's passage as the vehicle blasted down the wider avenues. Everywhere Chugeni scrambled from his path. Most of them made it, but none impeded the passage of the armored vehicle.

The Mk. 8 screamed into the central plaza ten minutes behind the advance teams. Hardsuited troopers had already located and formed a protective cordon around Tindal and Burke. Some Chugeni were taking exception to their isolation.

He heard Tindal scream "Kmo!" as one of the troopers backfisted a female that was rushing his buddy. The

Chugeni fell back, slumping to the ground. Ersch lost track of it in the press of bodies stampeding back and forth across the plaza.

The sound of engines confirmed what he could see in the panic of the scurrying indigenes. The hulking shapes of Mk. 3 Universal Carriers bulked large in the wide entrances to the plaza. As the armored vehicles swept into the plaza, troopers disembarked from them, spreading out with brisk precision to take up defensive positions. Fast-moving teams double-timed to the smaller exits and cut off the trickle of escaping Chugeni. The squalling natives assaulted the troopers, but they had no weapons that could significantly affect the hardsuited soldiers. Butt strokes and armored fists soon convinced the Chugeni that the troopers meant to stay where they stood and had no intentions of letting the natives past them. The turreted support weapons on board the Mk. 3s traversed slowly, waiting to deal with any organized attempt to overwhelm the troopers.

Inside of five minutes the company commander signaled *all secure*. Ersch scanned the dispositions and found nothing to complain about. The troops had every entrance to the plaza blocked. No one would be departing without his permission.

Major Ersch emerged from one of the vehicles. Unlike his troops', the major's visor was not polarized and Juliana could see the satisfaction on his face as a squad of troopers dragged Kurt to one of the big hovercraft and stuffed him inside. Ersch waited until the armored door slammed closed, then sauntered in her direction.

"Another rescue?" she asked sarcastically, recalling what she had been told the last time she was held at gun point by armored League troopers.

"You can call it that if you wish," he replied pleasantly.

"For my part, I prefer to think of it as the successful conclusion of a mission."

They both knew that the League wasn't done on Chugen IV. "When do you start the slaughter?"

He sighed theatrically. "You are inclined to the pejorative view, aren't you, Professor?"

"I see nothing worthwhile about genocide."

"The Remor seem to hold a countervailing view. They set the parameters of this war, Professor. We didn't start the killing."

She wasn't interested in his biased history lesson. "But you're going to start the killing here, aren't you?"

"No, not really," he said, adding, "my little command couldn't begin the job you expect of us."

Was she hearing correctly? Could she have misunderstood the situation? "Are you saying that you're *not* going to exterminate the Hos'kimm?"

"They are the enemy, Professor, death is what they deserve. However, I do congratulate you on finally figuring out that my mission isn't about extermination."

He paused, watching her. She knew he had another shoe to drop. She glared at him, daring him to continue. He did so, telling her, "That's what Commander Stone and the fleet are here for."

# 30

Kurtellicot shivered alone in the swaying, lurching, bouncing box into which the *shadakey* had shoved him. He didn't shiver from the cold, for the box was hotter and stuffier by far than the delta plain in full sunlight. He didn't shiver from fear of injury, for the *shadakey* did not threaten him. He shivered because he was alone, despite the black-carapaced *shadakey* seated to either side of him and the others seated on the bench across from him.

The *shadakey* had not taken up any of the others, not even Zhent'ah-rhull. It was almost as if they had come specifically to seek out Kurtellicot. Why him? There were others wiser and more knowledgeable. It was not because of the *shadakeys'* causeless war against Lo'gnen's pack, for they had ignored Ah'zzt and G'riv and the others. The *shadakey* had only been interested in Kurtellicot.

It could only be that he had walked the star pattern. Such a feat could be nothing other than a portentous sign.

Zhent'ah-rhull had said he was the Star Walker, naming him *Daysha-lo'daramak*. The Daysha was at work. The Daysha's return meant trial and, ultimately, either forgiveness or punishment. Was this the Daysha's trial, his testing of the one who stood between him and the Hos'kimm? If so, Kurtellicot could do nothing but endure, hoping and praying that he would prove worthy.

It would not be easy.

He had been ripped from among his pack—had he not once dreamed this terrible fate?—but they could not tear his pack-mates from his heart. He clung to their memory. Hugging himself close, he tilted his head down and sniffed. The odor of his clan was there, comforting and reassuring.

He was not *really* alone, for in his mind he was still with the pack and always would be.

He would endure.

## CHUGEN SYSTEM
## MIDWAY STATION

The SSC *Agincourt* and her escorts hung motionless relative to Midway Station as a small fleet of shuttles plied between them and the station. The arrival of the squadron from the Serenten Concordat had caused quite a stir among the inhabitants, raising Konoye's hopes that all was not lost to the League marts. The Leaguers made no response to the new arrivals beyond a perfunctory statement of Remor activity insystem and a warning to avoid interfering in League affairs. The commander of the Concordat squadron was nearly as taciturn, keeping communications short and confined to navigational exchanges, although he had requested a meeting with Chugen's civilian and military authorities "at the earliest convenient time."

"Welcome aboard, Captain Vess," Konoye said, greeting the squadron commander as the stern-faced captain came through the airlock and onto the station proper. "We are so very glad you're here. So *very* glad. I can't tell you how happy I am that the Concordat has seen fit to support us in this time of crisis."

The Concordat officer shook Konoye's hand, but didn't

return his smile. "Let's not jump to any unwarranted conclusions, Managing Director Konoye. The Concordat is not interested in unnecessary entanglements at this time. As I am sure you can guess, we set forth with a less than perfect understanding of the situation here in Chugen. That being the case, I am obliged to inform you that any support offered will depend on how the gaps in our understanding are filled. Is that clear to you, Managing Director?"

"Perfectly, Captain Vess. Perfectly. And very reasonable, I must say. But given the Concordat's public condemnation of League adventurism, I feel sure that, once you are fully apprised of what has been happening here, any reservations you may hold will be swept away. The threat *we* face today could well be on the *Concordat's* doorstep tomorrow."

There was a round of formal introductions as Konoye acquainted the Concordat captains with his staff still aboard the station, and with the commanders and masters of the two small PSC warships and the handful of Survey Service ships and armed merchantmen that had come through from Canessa. The group retired to the command deck where, with the help of the archives and Mr. Hoppe's prerecorded commentary, Konoye did his best to review the events before, during, and after what was being called the Battle of Midway Station. "Right now," Konoye concluded, "the League forces seem to be hunting down the *Hydra* and its escorts."

"So she's not just running?"

"No, Captain Vess, she's not. The Remor commander seems determined to make it to the moon of Chugen IV."

"What makes you say that?"

Konoye reactivated the main display, bringing up a schematic of the inner system. "Each track represents an attempt by the remnant of the Remor fleet to get deeper into the system. Watch as I extend the vectors past where they were turned back by League ships. As you can see, each closing vector would have taken the Remor into the orbit of Chugen IV's moon."

Captain Vess nodded in understanding. "So there is something they want there."

"Or something they need to do."

"What makes you say that?"

Konoye explained the League's theory about the beacon in orbit there. "They may be attempting to call reinforcements."

"I would certainly want reinforcements were I in their position," Captain Vess commented. "Assuming I couldn't just run. Is there any reason they can't just run?"

"I have no idea," Konoye admitted. "They're Remor."

"Too true." A Concordat captain shifted and whispered into Vess's ear. The squadron commander nodded. "Managing Director, is the League still claiming that the Chugeni indigenes are the remnant population of an abandoned colony?"

"That or shipwreck survivors."

"And they continue to update reports from the scientific team on Chugen IV?"

"Regularly."

"May I review those reports and anything else the League has sent you regarding the on-planet outpost?"

The meeting adjourned to allow Captain Vess to absorb the reports. A few minutes before the meeting was to resume, Captain Vess requested a private moment with Konoye. When they were alone, Vess held up a chip.

"This contains a code for accessing a certain circuit in your communications array."

"How did you get such a thing?" Konoye asked suspiciously, taking the offering.

"I am afraid that the source is confidential. Don't look so put out, Director Konoye. I am as in the dark about this as you. However, I am given to understand that it is *your* people who are being protected by our mutual ignorance. Yet this information has been placed into our hands, presumably with the expectation that it will offer some insight to the present situation. I suggest we see what is to be seen."

It turned out that the circuit, supposedly dedicated to secondary telemetry, had been handling occasional transmissions from Chugen IV and piggybacking encoded versions of them out on the station's outgoing transmissions. Konoye recognized the nature of the decoded versions at once.

"This is scientific data."

"Curious. Does it contradict that coming out of the League-controlled transmissions?"

"I don't know. That will take time to determine."

Vess harrumphed. "Time may be in short supply. What about the source of these clandestine transmissions? Can we learn anything from that?"

Konoye ran an identification program on the signature blocks. "They all appear to originate from Juliana Tindal's personal computer."

"Tindal? Wasn't she among those reported killed in the shuttle crash?"

"Yes. And her equipment lost."

"Perhaps someone recovered the equipment and failed to report it."

"That would have been my guess, but some of the reports have Tindal's personal cipher on the data. The problem is that *all* of these transmissions deal with Chugen IV and its inhabitants—and all of them date from *after* the crash."

"Suggesting that the crash never took place." Vess's

expression grew harsh. "It would seem that your friendly League saviors were engaged in some kind of duplicity well before Stone and his defenders arrived. Perhaps you were right when you spoke of League adventurism."

"Could they have faked the Remor attack?"

"The first one, possibly. As to the hulk and its warships, no. Sometimes when the boy cries wolf, the wolf is really there. But wolf or no, it would be improper to let them profit from this affair."

"What can we do?"

"That, I think, we need to discuss in council."

Following Captain Vess's advice, Konoye didn't mention the probability of the lost shuttle's survival when he reconvened the captains and masters. He stuck with the plan he had earlier developed with Jane, to play up the more obvious faults in the League's power grab.

"I launched a message drone for Canessa to explain what happened here," he told the assembled officers. "I wanted them to know how the League put pressure on us by threatening to abandon us in the face of the Remor enemy. I did so to establish my claim that the Pan-Stellar Combine has not relinquished this system to the League despite allowing them to aid in its defense."

"So you formally contested the League's claim," Vess observed. "Curious. The League ship that hailed my squadron as we entered the system stated that the system was under the League's martial jurisdiction by right of sole defense. They didn't mention your opposition to that claim." Vess shared a wry grin shared with the captains. "When do you expect a response from Canessa?"

"I don't. One of the League ships destroyed the drone. They apologized afterwards, said they thought it was a Remor object."

"Criminal," Vess said over the sputtering outrage of the

Combine officers to whom Konoye's announcement was news. "So it is clear that they plan on keeping the station isolated from PSC authorities until they have consolidated here."

Vess frowned in thought for a moment. "This is Sector 32 by League reckoning. That would put it under Christoph Stone's jurisdiction. Who did he send in command of the fleet?"

"He didn't *send* anyone. He's here himself."

Captain Vess's frown deepened. "That's not a good sign at all. It suggests that the League has every intention of adding this system to their sphere of influence."

"How be we supposed to stop them?" asked the master of a merchantman.

"Yeah," echoed another. "We can't be matching them ship to ship."

"And there's *still* the Remor to worry about," a PSC war-ship captain added. "We fight the marts, and the Remor will be biting us in the butt before the debris clouds disperse. I say we *let* Stone do what we all know he came here to do. *Let* the old Casual Slaughterer have his gallons of alien blood. Then we can combine all the ships and kick some serious Remor butt. If we kick the aliens out, Stone'll go home once he gets his mound of corpses."

"This is bigger than one man's monomaniacal impulse to genocide," Konoye warned. "Even if it wasn't, we would have to take a stand. The Combine has staked a claim to this system and extended its protection to the natives. We can't allow a dependent population to be exterminated."

"Can't we?" the outspoken captain challenged.

"No, we can't," Konoye replied, finding his voice steadier than he thought it would be.

"The marts won't like us telling them to stuff it."

"He's right, Director Konoye." said Captain Vess. "We

are facing a difficult situation. There is no certainty that the League is bluffing here. We cannot assume that they are. Thus we are left facing a single basic question that must be answered before we take another step. That question is a simple one, gentlefolk, but a far-reaching and perhaps irrevocable one. Are we prepared to start a war here?"

## CHUGEN SYSTEM
## CHUGEN IV

Anders suspected that had he been Sector Commander Stone rather than only the commander's representative, Major Ersch would have reported directly rather than first seeing to the safe interment of the extranationals. The extraction mission wouldn't be complete until everyone the troops had gone after was settled safely back in the camp, and from the way Professor Tindal was yelling as she exited the transport craft, he suspected that she would take no small bit of calming on the major's part. Part of Ersch's mission on Chugen was to see that there were as few repercussions as possible, and upset extranationals were prime sources of repercussions. While Ersch attended to his duty, Anders took the time to interview Ellicot. The professor's condition made for a short, one-sided conversation that left Anders more disturbed than he had been when first briefed on this clandestine mission. He was still sorting through his feelings when Ersch finally reported.

"You have seen him?"

"Yes, I've seen him." Anders declined to express how appalled he had been at Ellicot's state. The man's physical condition Anders understood; living in the bush was often easier when you lived as the bushmen did. But Ellicot's mental state! "The man was in virtual denial of his Humanity."

"He has assimilated rather thoroughly, wouldn't you

say? Why, if he were furry and a little shorter, you could mistake him for one of them."

Anders doubted he would do that. Still, there could be little doubt that Ellicot was thoroughly identifying with the Chugeni. "Do you really think that this will work?"

"Intel has high expectations."

Intel believed that Ellicot, properly interrogated and debriefed, could supply insight into the enemy's way of thinking. But what gave them the right to use Ellicot that way? And why did they believe that any information gained would help them battle the Remor out among the stars? "These Chugeni are hunters and gatherers, for God's sake. They wouldn't know which end of a pulse rifle to hold, let alone know how to pilot a starship."

"I've heard that speech from Tindal. Don't make the same fundamental mistake that she's making. The aliens' technical abilities are irrelevant. It's their psychology we need to understand. How much of Humankind's psychology was formed when we were hunter-gatherers, eh? Most of it, I'd say, possibly all of it, and technology, like civilization, springs from a species' psychological base. Ellicot is going to provide us with a window into that psychology, one that we'll be able to open far faster than by studying the indigenes in place."

"Wouldn't it be surer to study the aliens themselves?"

"It would surely be slower. Ellicot's is a Human mind that has adapted to the aliens' way of thinking. That's what we need. With him, we'll save time and we'll save lives. Imagine how many lives can be saved by eliminating even a little of the enemy's unpredictability."

*Many*, Anders was sure. But how many lives—and whose—was it worth to achieve that goal? Ellicot hadn't volunteered for this. If he had—

"So, Captain Seaborg, speaking as the sector commander's representative, do you find Ellicot sufficiently acculturated to warrant our moving on to the next phase of the operation?"

"He does appear to have acculturated," Anders said reluctantly. "I wish we had more concrete evidence of a connection between the Chugeni and the Remor. Everything we have seems so coincidental, and coincidence is insufficient to justify genocide."

"Wiser heads than ours have made the decision. What's to worry about? Everything we have points to the connection."

"Everything?"

Ersch looked at Anders out of the corner of his eye. "Everything reliable."

"So you discount the data that Burke correlated?"

"The man is a sensation-seeker. Headlines are more important to him than truth, and his assertion that the Chugeni have genetic correlation with Earth-descended life-forms would get him the attention he is so sure that he deserves. His data—or rather his supposition—is unsupported by any of the other Chugen Project scientists."

Given that Anders had found the data file buried in Ersch's report, he doubted any of the other scientists had even heard about Burke's discovery. "I think you're trying to conceal this data."

Ersch surprised him by chuckling. "Of course. It has been a test that has proven its worth, too. Once I uncovered Burke's hidden data in the computers we took from our Combine guests, I erased his copy. Had it been real data, a conscientious scientist would have tried to replicate it, or talked to someone about it, or at the very least complained about our 'tampering' with his computer. Burke has done nothing. He is no wronged innocent, Seaborg, if that's what you're thinking. His spurious data is not worth the space it takes up in the files. If you want to worry about correlation, you should worry about what correlates to the blips we've detected from the lunar beacon. Do you really think it was coincidence that the first one was recorded just before the Remor hulk entered the system?"

"Not every blip coincides with Remor activity in the system."

"Space-borne activity, I'll grant you," Ersch said. "But I find the simultaneity of the long burst from the beacon and the turmoil at the Chugeni gathering at the Ganges delta suggestive, don't you? Especially coming so soon after our battle with the Remor fleet."

"I don't know what to make of that," Anders admitted.

"And that is why we need to understand Remor psychology. You wouldn't want to delay the use of the intelligence resource we have in Ellicot, would you?"

There was an implied threat in Ersch's remark. Delaying the transmission of intelligence data was nearly sinful to an Eridani. Still, dubious intelligence could be worse than none. "I would like to have a clearer idea of what we're dealing with here."

"As would we all, Seaborg. That's why Intel wants Ellicot, remember? We get nothing from him while you and I debate, and I believe that Commander Stone expressed a desire for an expeditious close to this operation, did he not?"

"He did." And getting this operation finished was what he had sent Anders here to do. "All right, I'll sign off on his acculturation."

"Very well," Ersch said with a firm nod. "I shall see that the debriefing is begun. You know, it's too bad that we didn't realize Ellicot's susceptibility to alien cultures when we had our hands on him after Cassuells Home. We could be years ahead of where we are now."

*And where,* Anders wondered, *would that put us exactly?*

# 31

**CHUGEN SYSTEM**
**CHUGEN IV**

The soldier who opened the door of her cell was bigger than most. Juliana guessed that he was one of the Eridani super-soldiers even before she saw the patch on his uniform that declared his planetary allegiance. Strange, then, given the Eridani reputation, that he seemed nervous.

"Anders Seaborg, ma'am. I can take you to see Professor Ellicot."

Of course he could, being one of their mutual captors. "And why would you do that?"

"I think the two of you need to talk."

No doubt he hoped that they would commit some sort of indiscretion that his masters could capitalize on. Jailers did that sort of thing. "I don't care to be your stalking horse."

"You won't be monitored. I've arranged that as well. Well, except by me."

"And from your mouth to Stone's ears."

"No, ma'am. You have my word of honor that anything either you or Professor Ellicot says will go no further without your explicit permission."

Eridani were as renowned for their devotion to honor as they were for their martial abilities. This one sounded earnest enough. Did she dare believe him? "Why are you doing this?"

He hesitated, apparently still unsure himself. "For the moment let's just say that I want to know the truth. I'm not a biologist, but even I can see that the Cassuells and the Chugeni and the Grenwold aliens are no more different, physically, than Combiners and Leaguers. But even though a bunch of trees look alike, that doesn't make them all part of the same forest. For the moment, let's just say it makes me a little uneasy knowing that the fleet is making preparations to do to Chugen IV what was done to Cassuells Home."

"Oh my God! You can't do that!"

"The fleet can, and will, unless presented with good, solid reasons not to. I hope you can convince Professor Ellicot to give us those reasons."

If there was something that she could do to stop this genocide, she would, but— "What makes you think he knows anything that would stop your masters' plan?"

"I don't know that he does, ma'am. But when you spoke to him in the plaza, he talked about learning secrets. What are those secrets, ma'am? Are they something that can save the Chugeni? I may be just grasping at straws, but I've got to do something. I have a feeling that we might be making a serious mistake here. If we are, and there is some way to stop it, I'd like to know."

It was a plea with which she wholeheartedly agreed. And she wanted to see Kurt again.

"And what if he *does* know what you want?" she asked.

"Then, by St. Michael, we must find a way to use it."

"You'll go against your own people?"

"No honorable man knowingly obeys criminal orders."

"You didn't say you *would* go against your own."

"I don't know yet if we are dealing with criminal orders."

*That* was an honest answer, quite different from what she would have expected from Ersch. Seaborg gave her no easy reassurance that her convincing Kurt to share his secrets *would* save the Hos'kimm. *She* didn't have much to lose whether or not he proved trustworthy, but the Hos'kimm stood to lose much if he *was* trustworthy and she *didn't* trust him. She told him that she would do what she could.

Kurt's cell was next to hers. Seaborg palmed the lock to admit her and closed the door behind her. Like hers, Kurt's cell was an office converted to a prison by sealing its lone window and providing a reinforced lock on the door. It was adequate for the short-term confinement of such mild prisoners as they.

He sat on the floor in one corner, arms folded around himself, singing a H'kimm children's song about the dangers of roving away from the pack. As he had in the plaza at Rasseh, he only acknowledged that she was speaking when she used the H'kimm dialect.

"Are you all right?" she asked.

"As well as one can be, kept alone in a box. Why have they done this?"

She told him about the League plan to use him to understand the Remor. He barked a Hos'kimm-like laugh, and said, "They waste their time. I am useless to them."

"Why is that? Have you learned something that will prove the Remor and the Hos'kimm are unconnected?"

"What I have learned I could not tell you, even were you Hos'kimm. You walked among us. You know that some knowledge is reserved for the elders and some for the seers. What I have learned is not for you." He raised his eyes to the ceiling. "Or for any profane listeners."

As frustrating as his remarks were, his last comment struck a spark in Juliana, showing as it did an appreciation of his situation that would have been unthinkable to a Hos'kimm. Something of the old Kurt still survived. There was still hope that he could be brought back to himself. And to her.

"Kurt, this is not the time to protect the indigenes' mystery religion. There won't *be* any religion, or any *indigenes*, if we don't find something to show that the Hos'kimm are *not* the Remor."

She had spoken in Anglic, and so he had ignored her. She tried again in the H'kimm dialect, adding, "Keeping secrets now won't help anyone. When the League specialists get hold of you, they take what they want."

"I will confound them. I tell you that the soldiers will not get what they want from me."

"It's not the soldiers you will be dealing with."

"Who riddles with me doesn't matter. Soldiers, specialists, it is all as one. Better than they have tried. Ask Nellis."

Where did that come from? "Nellis? Who is Nellis?"

"She thought she saw the heart," he said dreamily. "All she saw was another wall. They'll do no better. Worse, even. I am stronger now. Kurtellicot has a strength that Grammanhatay never knew. I will confound them."

His words sounded confident, but there was an edge to them. Nellis. Grammanhatay. Where did they come from? What relevance did they have for him? Could they be part of his past? If so, was his mention of them a sign that he hadn't completely left his old self behind?

"They wanted this to happen to you, Kurt. They wanted you to lose yourself. Don't let them win. Don't be part of their plan."

"The only plan in which I play a part is that of the gods. I live by the Hos'kimm Way."

"You are *not* of the Hos'kimm!" she shouted at him.

He replied with a pitying smile.

"You are not Kurtellicot. You are Kurt Ellicot. Kurt. Ellicot."

He looked away from her and started to sing the children's song again.

"Talk to me, Kurt!" But he would not. "So you have nothing to say. You think that you're safe from whatever the League can do to you. What about the Hos'kimm? What about your pack? Do you think that by fooling the League you'll save the Hos'kimm? If you do, the only one you're fooling is yourself. And they say you are *tuoyal*.

"The League is coming for your precious pack, Kurt. They are coming for the Hos'kimm, the way they came for the Cassuells. Are you going to let them destroy the Hos'kimm? Are you just going to turn your back, wise one?

"Ha! You are not fit to wear the tokens of an elder. Not when you close your eyes and try to wish the problem away like a barely weaned pup."

Kurtellicot huddled in the corner. He heard all that Juliananatindal said, and though he pretended indifference, indifferent he was not. Troubled, he was.

*She's right.*

The voice came from deep within him, whispering from the corners of his mind. It was a familiar voice. It had cried so often in loneliness, wailed so many times of how his life was not what it should be. When his life had changed here on Chugen, he had recognized the voice's words for the lies they were. He had thought the voice stilled, buried in his oneness with the pack. But now it had come back; he had not buried it deep enough.

Could he ever still it?

Did he dare?

*Juliana Tindal is right*, it whispered. *You are a fool. You endanger the pack.*

Did the voice lie now, as it had in the past? Could he let the safety of the pack rest on his belief that the voice lied?

*If they take you away, the pack will die.*

No. That was the nightmare, the dream that must not be.

*It is the truth. It is the past. You will make it the future.*

No!

*Do nothing. Let them take you away, and it will happen.*

He would tell them what they wanted to hear. He would use them to escape. Then he could warn the packs. He could tell the Hos'kimm to flee. He would flee himself. He had to have faith. He had to believe. The Daysha was come. The Daysha would save them.

*A lie.*

It's not a lie, it's a belief.

*The Daysha is the Remor.*

Now you lie.

*No. Now I state a belief. Your belief.*

Say rather, my fear.

*You fear that if the children cannot be separated from the father, they will die.*

You are right.

*You also fear that father and children are truly one.*

Yes.

*You must face your fears. You must face the truth. You know where the answer lies. What will you do?*

He hung his head between his knees and folded his arms across the back of his neck. Juli had stopped speaking. She was watching him now, waiting to see what effect her words had. He groped for long minutes, searching for his voice, until at last he was able to say, "There is a place where the secrets lie buried."

She said nothing. Was she waiting for him to speak again? Or did she wait to see who looked at her from behind his eyes?

*Who does look at her from behind our eyes?*

My eyes, he corrected with feeble conviction.

He lifted his head and saw that a man had joined her. The man was dressed in the clothing that the *shadakey* wore when they laid aside their shells. Kurtellicot had never seen the man before, but Kurt recognized him from the terrible dream of separation—no, this man came from the past. He was as real as stone, sky, and water.

As real as life, and as real as death.

The nightmare was real, his unavoidable past.

Kurt shivered, seeing Cassuells falling and burning and dying in a glade under the sun of Chugen IV. Lo'gnen called out to him in the voice of Shessone the Bright-eyed. The pups of the H'kimm ran to the *quantaraden*, seeking safety that was not there. The fire was falling again from the sky, falling forever, and burning away all he had known. Kurtellicot was a ghost, adrift and alone, as past, present, and nightmare crashed together.

"Will you take us there?" Juli asked amid the din.

"Zhent'ah-rhull knows."

"What does Zhent'ah-rhull know?" Juli knelt at his side, her arms around him, comforting, welcome. Her face was anxious. "Does he know the truth?"

"The truth," he sobbed. "Yes, the truth."

*The truth will set you free.*

"We need to know the truth," said the shell-less *shadakey*.

*We all need to know the truth*, said the voice. And, oh, it was true. Who could deny? "We all need to know the truth."

Ellicot's agreement to share his secrets committed Anders to the course. He had hoped to simply gather the information from Ellicot, but he'd known from the start that such an attractive, simple solution was also an unlikely one. Fortunately he'd anticipated the socioxenologist's insistence on traveling to where the secrets were learned, and had made the necessary preparations. While Tindal and Ellicot donned the MilForce coveralls he'd brought for them, he accessed the camp's net and reassured himself that his preparations remained undisturbed and ready.

Taking a route through lightly trafficked parts of the camp, they made it to the hangar revetment unchallenged. The Intruder R-LAV sat ready and waiting for them, freshly serviced. The tech crew, their job done, were nowhere in sight. There was no one to see Anders hustle his escapees aboard.

"Professor Tindal, you'll find your gear in the crew locker. Professor Ellicot, I wasn't able to get your computer, since it's already been shipped aboard *Henry Hull*. I brought a GP portable for you. I don't know if you'll need it, but I loaded it with the latest updates from the research group. I hope it'll help."

Tindal dived on the locker at once. Pulling out her computer, she opened the top and tapped in a short sequence. Anders guessed she was testing to see whether her security wall had been breached. Her flash of a smile suggested that she was satisfied that it hadn't.

Ellicot just sat in the crew chief's couch and tugged at the cuffs of his coveralls as though they chafed him.

"I'm going to the arsenal now," Anders told them, nodding at the bunker across the clearing. "I'll be putting on my hardsuit. It'll take me a few minutes."

"What do you want us to do?" Tindal asked tensely.

"Sit tight. Nobody should bother you. If you want to help get us out of here a little faster, ask the computer to run the preflight checks."

"I'm not a pilot," Tindal protested.

"You don't have to be. Everything should come up green. If anything doesn't, have the computer open a prelaunch review file. That's prelaunch review, got it?"

Tindal nodded, still looking nervous.

"You'll be fine," he said with what he hoped was an encouraging smile. "One more thing. I know hardsuits look alike to civilians, so don't panic when you see one heading this way. It's just going to be me, okay? You see more than one trooper, or somebody with a suit set to camouflage, then you can panic."

"What do we do then?" Tindal asked.

"Give up," he said matter-of-factly. "They'll kill you if you try to resist."

Anders stepped out from under the revetment's camouflage awning, feeling naked and vulnerable and wishing he were as confident as he tried to sound. If he was wrong about this, he would be lucky to survive his mistake, and even if he was right, his career was most likely dead. But if he was right and didn't act, a lot of innocent beings would be dead. In the abstract the equation was easy. It didn't feel easy, but God, in His wisdom, had put him in this spot. It was up to Anders, with a little bit of luck and the help of St. Michael, to pull through.

Fortunately the guard inside the arsenal didn't object when he requested his hardsuit and a recon kit; command rank had privileges.

"Taking a look-see at the locals for yourself, sir?" the sergeant asked. "Or are you shopping for dinner?"

"Just need to stretch the muscles a little, sergeant. Too much desk work lately."

The sergeant nodded understandingly as he keyed the access to the suit lockers. It looked as though Anders's harebrained scheme had a chance of succeeding.

It wasn't until he closed the locker room door behind him that he realized that all might not be going as smoothly as it seemed. The sergeant's status screen had said that the suit area was unoccupied, but Anders's senses told him otherwise. A slight stir in the air. A whiff of fresh sweat amid the stale, old odors. He was not alone.

# 32

Despite Seaborg's warning, Juliana's heart leapt into her throat when, looking through the Intruder's cockpit canopy, she saw a figure in black armor emerge from the arsenal bunker. Just one. Just him.

But something *was* wrong. He wasn't walking very smoothly, and his left arm hung down at his side, shifting limply at each step.

Her toe snagged in Kurt's discarded coverall as she moved past him. She kicked it free of her foot, sending it sailing to the back of the cabin. She was at the hatch when Seaborg reached it.

"What happened? Are you hurt?"

"I ran into someone," he said. "We had a scuffle."

His speech rhythms were off, jagged in the way of a man clamping down on pain, but if any of his suffering was creeping into his voice, the mechanical distortion of the suit's speaker hid it.

"You *are* hurt. There's a medkit in the locker. I don't have any real training but—"

He seized her arm. The gauntlet's fingers gouged into her flesh with the armor's augmented strength. She squeaked. He released her at once.

"Sorry," he said. "There's no time for that. The 'suit has paramedical systems. They'll do. We need to go."

He squeezed past her and moved into the nose of the aircraft. Settling his armored bulk into the pilot's couch, he acknowledged the positive preflight check and started hooking into the controls. As she followed him forward, a throaty dragon's cough came from the rear and the craft began to vibrate as the engines came alive.

"We can't just fly out of here, can we? When Rafe took out the transport he needed to subvert—"

He cut her off again, but this time only verbally. "The Intruder's a good design and, with the IFF shut down—" he touched a control, prompting the aircraft's computer to announce that the IFF transponder was off—"it's well enough stealthed to avoid most of our sensors. If we stay in the ground clutter, we won't be picked up on scanners. You just tell me where we're going and I'll get us there."

Where *were* they going? "Kurt?"

"Zhent'ah-rhull knows," he said in reply.

"Rasseh, then?" she asked him. When he didn't object or offer an alternative, she turned to Seaborg. "Rasseh, on the Ganges delta."

"Will do." His augmented voice was nearly drowned out as the engines began to howl. "Strap in. We're lifting."

He barely gave her and Kurt time to get back to the cabin and pick couches. She was fastening the first restraint when the Intruder's gear left the ground. As it moved forward, the craft wallowed like a drunken seaman freshly ashore. Juliana hastened with the restraining harness. Clearing the revetment, the Intruder nosed up and started crossing the clearing, rising in lurches. As she snapped home the last fastening, she heard tree branches scratch and claw at the Intruder's belly as they made their wobbly escape from the clearing. The Intruder's engines roared in earnest as it shot away across the jungle, shearing through the flimsier vegetation and barely slaloming around the more substantial.

Once it was clear that they were not being pursued, she tried to talk to Seaborg. He didn't respond. His slumped form worried her. Was he unconscious? Maybe he just hadn't heard her over the howling of the Intruder's engines? She searched for and found a connection to the intraship intercom, but her words continued to go unheeded.

Had he put the ship on autopilot? If not, was he still controlling their flight? If his armor's medical systems were attending to his needs, he might be pumped full of chemicals and drugs that affected his concentration, narrowing his focus to the task at hand. He *might* be coping quite well. Unfortunately, his lack of movement did *suggest* that he could be unconscious.

The idea that they might be careening across Chugen at treetop level with only an automated control disturbed her. She knew that computers were supposed to be better than humans at such things, but it was hard to ignore the visceral surge occasioned by the scenery streaming past, especially when the sudden jerks and rolls of the aircraft had such an uncontrolled feeling, a feeling that could conceivably *be* due to an uncontrolled flight.

She started unfastening her safety harness, unsure *what* she could do but decided that *something* needed to be done.

"Manual override of safety harness is inadvisable at this time," the Intruder's computer warned her. The synthetic voice sounded calm and assured.

Aircraft had all sorts of safety features and watchdog programs. *Wouldn't the computer have noticed and issued a warning if the pilot wasn't responding properly or within safety parameters?* she wondered.

A civilian aircraft should have, but this wasn't a civilian aircraft. She looked again toward the cockpit and her worries were reduced when Seaborg lifted his right arm and reached out with a finger to touch a control.

Their hurtling speed slowed. The roar of the engines abated. They had reached the delta region. Seaborg took the Intruder lower and pointed its nose toward the Teclananda hills. Twenty minutes later they were on the ground, nestled in a cleft between two of the rounded mounds that was barely big enough to fit the aircraft.

Disembarking, she helped Seaborg spread a camouflage tarp over the Intruder. He needed the help, for although he was walking better, he still only had the use of one arm. Kurt did nothing to help, squatting on the ground and drawing lines in the dirt.

"We are alone no longer," he announced, while Juliana was helping Seaborg gingerly guide the cover over the hot engine nacelles. A dozen or so Hos'kimm were approaching cautiously. They didn't look actively hostile, so she went back to helping Seaborg.

By the time they finished hiding the aircraft, quite a crowd had grown around the landing site. There had to be a hundred or more. The gathered Hos'kimm didn't look pleased to see them at all. A fair number held spears and bows and only a few were shy about pointing them toward the Humans.

"Kurt?"

"It's all right, Juli."

In point of fact, it was not. He could hear the muttering of this mostly R'kimm crowd. Their dialect was different enough that their low-pitched words were probably not very understandable to anyone less accustomed than he to working without a translator. They reminded him of the young Cassuells who had set themselves to keep the Nightskyers away from Grammanhatay, ready to give and receive violence in defense of their own. Juli was nervous, but not as frightened as she should be. He had no desire to increase her apprehension, so he lied to her. "It's going to be all right."

The lies were getting easier, which was good. He would be telling more of them. *Soon*, he thought.

These people were not very happy to have visitors, and the presence of a *shadakey* only made matters worse.

"What trouble do you bring us, Star Walker?" challenged a burly R'kimm hunter.

"I bring no trouble." Easier and easier. "I come to speak with the elders and with Zhent'ah-rhull."

"With a *shadakey*?"

"He is why I am back among you. This *shadakey* is not like the others. He defied the others and freed us. He seeks to know the truth of the Hos'kimm and to understand the heart of our Way. He comes, respectfully, to listen to the elders."

"He looks and smells like the others," the spokesman said with obvious distaste. "*Shadakeys* are no respecters of the elders. When the shelled ones took you away, they injured many of the elders. Two elders and one of the seers have gone to join with the ancestors. We will not let that happen again."

"Of course you won't." So very easy to lie. For all their numbers and resolve, these brave Hos'kimm couldn't stop Seaborg if he chose to unleash the might of his battlesuit upon them. A gesture of good faith was needed, or the appearance of one. He spoke in Anglic. "Put up your rifle, Seaborg, or they will not let us proceed further. We must demonstrate trust in them, so that they will trust in us."

"Is this necessary?" asked the soldier.

"I think so."

For a moment Seaborg did nothing. The battlesuit might have been merely an eccentric sculpture glorifying violence. Then with obvious effort the soldier brought his injured arm up to take a two-handed grip on his weapon. Juli flinched and appeared to be looking for a place to duck away. Kurt resisted the urge to do the same. The moment of threat passed as Seaborg thrust his weapon out, sideways, to the spokesman.

It did not escape Kurt's notice that when the rifle went into Hos'kimm hands, its power pack remained in Seaborg's. He doubted the Hos'kimm understood the significance of that. The pulse rifle was little more than a club now, but the battlesuit retained its integral weapons. Kurt did not intend to alleviate Hos'kimm ignorance of the situation, because he had not yet figured out a way short of violence to shed Seaborg's unwelcome presence. For the moment he was still bound by the unspoken condition of their release: that Seaborg accompany them and learn the secrets Kurt had promised to reveal. As long as the soldier's injuries required that he wear the battlesuit, he would not voluntarily put it aside, and who could blame him? Hos'kimm adapted to the way of the world around them. Kurt could adapt, too. The time had not yet come to try and alter the terms of his arrangement with Seaborg.

The gesture was successful. The Hos'kimm seemed satisfied that the *shadakey*'s teeth were pulled. Another lie had been accepted. It was time to move on.

"You will take us to speak with the elders and the seers," he said confidently.

And they did. The escort grew as they marched through the hills, and not just with hostile and suspicious Hos'kimm. Seaborg walked alone and isolated. Ah'zzt and the others rejoined Kurt, as glad to see him as he was to see them. Kmo and her S'kimm pack-mates appeared as well. They clustered around Juli, offering her the customary joy accorded the return of one involuntarily separated from the pack. Her face lit with happiness at the reunion, and he was pleased for her; she was what she wanted to be: a bridge between Human and Hos'kimm.

*Like me?* No. She knew who *she* was, knew her place and embraced it. He couldn't say the same about himself. The others thought that they knew who he was. Juli saw Kurt Ellicot the socioxenologist; his pack-mates saw Kurtellicot, *tuoyal* and chief; the other Hos'kimm saw Kurtellicot the Star Walker; and Ersch and his ilk saw Kurt Ellicot, tool and dupe. Who was right? Any of them? All of them? In one thing, at least, they were all wrong. He did not belong to any of them. There was something that he *did* know about himself, that none of them understood. He was, at last, fully and completely, *grawr'tayo*.

Still, it was good to be among the pack again, though he thought that their scent seemed a little strange. *No*, he admonished himself. *They smell as they always have. It's me. I am the one who is strange.*

"What will happen, Kurtellicot?" whispered G'riv as they drew nearer the center of Rasseh.

"I must save my words for the elders," he told her, using a small lie to save himself from using a larger one—or worse, from telling a truth whose time had not come. If any deserved to know what he feared and hoped, it was his pack-mates, but the *grawr'tayo*, despite their other sins, protected their pack-mates when they could. He would spare them as long as he could.

The elders and seers were gathered and waiting at the *rass'arass* when the parade arrived. The spokesman R'kimm, now identified as one Krahz, offered Seaborg's rifle to the seers, who declined it. Their eyes rested on Kurt and bored into him, but they said no word of greeting. He searched among them for a friendly expression, but he found none. No invitation was issued, but he spoke anyway.

"Venerable elders, and honored seers, I am come back to the Hos'kimm from the place of the *shadakey*. Among them I learned things that my heart had no longing to learn. But these things needed to be learned. To my sorrow, I was chosen to be the one to learn them. But they are not for me alone to know. You must know what I have learned. All Hos'kimm must know.

"You say to me that I am *Daysha-lo'daramak*. You call me *tuoyal*, he who sees what others do not. I listen to your words, venerable elders, and take them into my heart. You cannot say that I have not listened and heeded.

"Now I ask you to listen to *my* words. Open your hearts to my plea. Listen when I say to you that *you* must believe what you say to me and what you want me to believe. If I am *Daysha-lo'daramak*, then my words are the words of the *Daysha-lo'daramak*. Listen to them! Take them into *your* hearts!"

"We listen, Kurtellicot," Zhent'ah-rhull said. The other elders nodded and drew closer.

Could he convince them to show him the truth? And if he did, was he ready to hear it? Could he take the truth— whatever it might be—into *his* heart? He would not know unless he convinced them.

"This may not be the time of forgiveness," he said, embarrassed by the shakiness of his voice. "But it is a time when the star folk walk the skies. We do not know if the Daysha is among them, but we must know.

"Your wise eyes have not seen a single vision. What does this mean? Is your wisdom at fault? No, I do not think so. You are Hos'kimm. R'kimm, S'kimm and H'kimm, but still only Hos'kimm. But I—I am something else. I am of two minds and two hearts. My eyes see doubly: as Hos'kimm and as Human. That, my pack-mates, is what I believe the Hos'kimm need in this time of danger. But I cannot see all that I might. There are secrets that only the wisest of the elders know. Those secrets have meaning that must be understood. Now. Today. Before it is too late. Every moment that passes brings unstoppable danger closer to the Hos'kimm."

Silence followed his words.

The brittle moment was broken when Zhent'ah-rhull stepped up to him. "You ask for trust. Will you give trust?"

"Yes, honored Zhent'ah-rhull." Kurt replied. "I would trust you with my life."

"Your life is nothing. It is your soul I would take into my hands."

"You are the wisest of the wise, honored Zhent'ah-rhull. In whose hands would my soul be better placed?"

"Those who would know the greatest secrets must be fully of the Hos'kimm. The fire must blaze within. There is no choice in the matter. If one will give up his place among the Hos'kimm, you can be opened to the inner fire."

"If there is such a one, then let me be opened."

"You may be burned away to nothing," Zhent'ah-rhull said warningly.

"If I do not touch the inner fire, all Hos'kimm will be burned by a fire from without."

"You are brave," Zhent'ah-rhull observed.

*More desperate than brave*, Kurt countered, but only to himself. He needed the Hos'kimm secrets, and this was the only path open to him.

I am not being selfish, he assured himself. Certainly he wanted the knowledge for his own peace of mind. Yes, he needed to know that the Hos'kimm were as innocent as he believed them to be. Yes, he needed to banish all doubt that they might be otherwise. But there was more. Kurt needed a bargaining position with Seaborg and with his League masters. He needed some way to save the Hos'kimm from annihilation.

"I must do what I can to help the pack," he told the seer.

"Then let me see those of the Star Walker H'kimm who have gathered," Zhent'ah-rhull commanded.

Ah'zzt, G'riv, and the others came forward. One by one the old R'kimm seer stared in each H'kimm's eyes. He stared the longest into Ah'zzt's. He turned away, shaking his head.

"Too weak. All too weak."

"No," Ah'zzt protested.

"Do you doubt me?" Zhent'ah-rhull snapped, rounding on him.

"No, honored one," Ah'zzt replied, contrite, yet bitter.

"The will without the way is insufficient." Zhent'ah-rhull turned to Kurt. "All that must be, is not. What you ask cannot be granted."

"You have not looked far enough, honored Zhent'ah-rhull." It was Kmo speaking and stepping out from the crowd.

Zhent'ah-rhull's bright eyes fell upon her. "You I know. You are Kmo of Za'lo'frez's pack. At the last gathering you were promised to seer Gr'kezz's tutelage."

"Kmo I am, but no longer of Za'lo'frez's pack. I am of Julianatindal's pack and my elder is bonded with the Star Walker. Through her, so am I. Look into my heart, honored Zhent'ah-rhull. Take my strength if you find it great enough. The pack must endure."

Zhent'ah-rhull beckoned her forward. As she stood trembling before him, the seer searched her eyes as he had those of Kurt's kin. Minutes dragged on. With a grunt of satisfaction, Zhent'ah-rhull concluded, "Sufficient."

"Prepare them," he ordered.

An elder to either side of him, Kurt was led to a flat spot of bare dirt within the patterns encircling the entrance to the *rass'arass*. In a similar fashion Kmo was led to join him there. Braided cords of leather, dark and damp, were tied to their wrists and ankles.

"Lie down," Zhent'ah-rhull told him. "On your belly."

He did so. Kmo lay down as well, her face but a hand-breadth from his and their bodies aligned along a line that connected the Star Pattern and the *rass'arass*. Resting on their elbows, they looked into each other's eyes, and he was surprised to find fear in hers, but her voice was steady as she whispered, "Julianatindal believes you to be her true pair-mate. I tell you now, while I can. If you will not have her, tell her so that she may free herself for another. She is my elder and I would have her happy."

"Silence," Zhent'ah-rhull commanded.

Obeying the command, Kurt could make a virtue out of his loss for words. Fuddled he might be, but the Hos'kimm were not. The ritual proceeded.

Elders approached with mallets and stakes. The stakes were driven into the ground and each of Kurt's and Kmo's limbs was stretched out and bound to one so that they were spread-eagled. In such an exposed and vulnerable position, he could not help but apprehend some of Kmo's fear.

But what was she afraid of? Zhent'ah-rhull had spoken in dire seriousness, but no one had stopped long enough to explain exactly what was going to happen. Ideas—unwelcome and shuddersome—began to form in his head as he twisted his head around to watch three of the eldest seers approach, each holding a wicked, curved knife of star metal.

They stopped in front of Zhent'ah-rhull. In turn, the R'kimm seer touched the clasped hands of one of the other seers. Having done this, he clasped his own hands together and raised his snout to the sky, eyes closed. After a moment he reached out and touched the hands of the second seer. She offered her knife to him. Taking it, he turned to Kurt and Kmo, looked down at the restrained bodies, and spoke.

"In the times when nature fails the Hos'kimm as the Hos'kimm have failed the gods, we do what we can do. We do what we must do. The pack endures."

He crouched beside Kmo. Straining against her bonds, she looked up at him, fear and resignation shivering in her eyes. He whispered something in her ear, too softly for Kurt to hear. Tenderly the seer stroked her head while his right arm encircled her neck. The blade gleamed darkly from beneath her chin. The fingers of Zhent'ah-rhull's left hand buried themselves in the fur of her ruff just behind her ears.

"We shall be as we are," he said. "The pack endures."

"The pack endures," she echoed.

In a single deft motion he drew the knife around Kmo's throat. The blade bit deeply, penetrating through skin and muscle down to bone, severing every shred of tissue in Kmo's neck. Zhent'ah-rhull removed her head with a tug. The spinal cord came slithering after it, making a grisly sucking sound. As the R'kimm seer straightened and lifted head and dangling cord aloft like a gruesome trophy, Kmo's torso slumped to the ground, blood spurting from the stump of her neck and pulsing hot into Kurt's face.

Juli was screaming. He twisted his head. Blinking away the blood, he could just see her struggling in Seaborg's encircling arm. Her fists beat ineffectually against the battlesuit's armor.

Kmo's blood stopped spurting. Kurt was appalled by how much of it had flooded the ground. More blood and other fluids dripped from her excised spinal cord. As Kurt watched, something more substantial slipped free from the cord and fell writhing to the ground. It looked like some sort of sea-going worm, with tendrils that waved from each segment and the fronds like gills that undulated at each end. It writhed and coiled upon itself like any worm forced into an unpleasant environment.

Zhent'ah-rhull scooped up the squirming thing with a stick and stepped from Kurt's sight. "The pack endures," the seer said from somewhere behind Kurt's head.

"The pack endures," Kurt said as something wet and slimy dropped on his back. Feeling it twist, he knew it for the worm thing.

He felt a sharp prick above his spine, and cold numbness began to spread from that point. In seconds he could no longer feel the worm-thing wriggling on him.

*Has it crawled away?*

Pain blew curiosity out of his head. Screaming, he arched backwards, straining at the thongs that held him in place. Agonized, he thrashed. One strand holding his right wrist parted with a crack, but the rest held. They dug into his flesh, cutting, drawing blood. He barely felt the wounds for the fire pouring through his spine.

The flames etched into his brain and burned his mind away. Pain, white hot pain, was all he knew. A star exploded in blazing incandescence within him and made his universe a searing inferno of light. Zhent'ah-rhull's voice rumbled through the whiteness like distant thunder. It might have been the voice of god.

"Thus was the pack raised up. Heed the laws by which the pack was raised up.

"Tend the *teclananda*. Remember the signs. Build so that the spirits in the heavens can see. Teach your children to do as you were taught. Await the return."

Blackness swallowed Kurt Ellicot and he sighed in its blessed, cool embrace.

When the Hos'kimm seers cut Kurt's limp body free from the bindings, Seaborg released Juliana. She ran to the

prone form. The hole where the thing that Zhent'ah-rhull
had put on Kurt's back was raw and red and glistened with
fluids and slime. Was he dead?

*No, thank god. He breathed!*

His eyes fluttered open. He smiled.

"Hello, Juli."

She actually found herself shocked to hear him speak in
Anglic. "Kurt?"

"As much of him as is left."

Shakily he got to his knees and embraced her, careless
of the filth still besmirching her from the last meal she'd
given back upon Kmo's sudden death. She wasn't fastidi-
ous herself, ignoring the stickiness of Kmo's blood upon
him.

They were still alive! Right now, that was all that mattered. She repeated his name over and over, a prayer of
thanks for his survival and his return to himself. To her
hair, he said, "I never knew, I mean, I never thought, I
mean, I—"

"Never mind," she hushed him.

Zhent'ah-rhull loomed over them. She wished the
butcher dead and gone, and hugged Kurt closer.

"Haven't you done enough?" she snarled at the seer.

The R'kimm ignored her. "Kurtellicot?"

"Yes, my brother Zhent'ah-rhull?"

His answer to the seer was in the Hos'kimm tongue. His
tone was friendly.

"What do you hear?" the seer asked.

"I hear the song," Kurt replied. "The fire burns in me."

What Kurt told Zhent'ah-rhull was true, as far as it went.
He used the words that seemed to be the right words, but
he didn't know why they were right. Certainly he heard
*something* echoing in his mind.

He was sure that it was not the argumentative voice of his own confusion: he'd felt his sundered self die in the cleansing flames. His torn, conflicted self had merged into a new whole. He had been forged. As metals flowed together in a crucible to become an alloy, so had he; he was no longer truly *any* of the constituent parts, but something wholly different, that partook of the natures of its parts but *was* none of them.

And he was more than he had been. There was something else that was a part of him now: a distant murmur of true *otherness*. Strangely, or perhaps not so strangely, this new voice whispering in his head sounded a little like Kmo. He understood no words that the new presence spoke, but he felt its strength. Somehow he understood that though it spoke for the *other*, it spoke for *him* as well. He also sensed a promise that he would understand this word-less communication more fully with time.

The *otherness* had come to him out of the blazing inferno that had cleansed and scoured his mind. He knew that its fire burned in him, that he was no longer alone and never would be again. He was now joined with his pack-mates in a way he could never have been without the *other-ness* in him.

And yet he knew more clearly than ever before that he was not like them. He was a Human, a different sort of alien entirely.

But neither was he only Human anymore either. He was changed, irrevocably. He had become something new, but what the change portended, he knew not.

"Now you are fit to learn the mysteries," said Zhent'ah-rhull gravely. "Now you truly stand between two worlds, Star Walker."

"I am of the pack," he said to reassure the seer. "The pack endures."

"You are Human," Juli said, clearly fearful that he had forgotten.

*Not exactly*, he wanted to tell her. *Not anymore.* But he said nothing. If he told her the truth, it would sound like a lie.

And there was so very little time.

To Zhent'ah-rhull he said, "I am ready," hoping that he spoke truth.

**33**

CHUGEN SYSTEM
CHUGEN IV

When Kurt took Juliana's hand and motioned to
Seaborg to follow them, Zhent'ah-rhull barked a protest. It
seemed that the R'kimm seer had reservations about anyone other than Kurt entering the *rass'arass*.

"They must come with me," Kurt insisted. "If the pack is
to be saved, they must see."

They argued, speaking so quickly and heatedly that
Juliana had difficulty following what they said. Zhent'ah-
rhull cited tradition, precedent, and seemliness, while Kurt
countered with urgency, uniqueness of circumstances, and
necessity.

"Yet there must be symmetry," the seer complained, as
he finally conceded Kurt's points.

Kurt's told the seer to create that symmetry. Zhent'ah-
rhull elected to add only a single Hos'kimm to the group
that was to go below: Krahz, the R'kimm spokesman to
whom Seaborg had surrendered his rifle. A trembling
Krahz, still carrying the rifle, joined them at the entrance to
the *rass'arass*. The R'kimm shot looks of awe and dread not
just at the Humans but at Zhent'ah-rhull as well, and he
shivered harder whenever he glanced toward the dark hole
at their feet. Grumbling, Zhent'ah-rhull led the way down
the packed-earth ramp into the darkness.

"Watch your step here," Kurt cautioned Juli at one particularly treacherous point in the descent. "I nearly broke my neck before."

Lo'gnen had spoken to her once about the underground places where his species conducted special rituals. The village had not boasted such a place, so this was the first she had seen. Lo'gnen's description had made the place sound a little like the *quantaradens* of the Cassuells, and now she saw that they were indeed eerily like the Cassuell holy places she had seen in archival records.

She began to fear that any secrets they uncovered here would damn rather than save. With Seaborg present there would be no hiding anything that they uncovered from the League. *If only we find something to show the Hos'kimm innocent. If we can do that, there is still hope,* she told herself. The fulfillment of that hope was the only chance for the Hos'kimm.

The shaft of daylight pouring in through the opening was their only illumination, blinding against the underground blackness. Kurt's eyes adjusted quickly and he soon found that if he did not stare at or near the sunbeam, he could see the walls and floor of the *rass'arass* reasonably well. Only one thing seemed changed since he had last been there: no strange lights played from below against the reed mat in the center of the chamber.

Zhent'ah-rhull pointed one of his walking sticks at the mat and told Krahz to pull it aside. Though it would have made his task easier, Krahz refused to put down or even sling the rifle. Gripping the mat with one hand, he nearly lost it to the dark pit it concealed. Once he had cleared the way, again Zhent'ah-rhull led the way downwards.

This time, however, the ramp was made not of packed earth but of some hard, slightly yielding material that reminded Kurt of a drumhead, save that their footfalls made no sound. They wound their way down, deeper into the dark, to at least twice the depth of the upper chamber. From the bottom of the ramp, Kurt could just see an arch formed of dully gleaming metal or ceramic. Beyond that heavily framed opening there was a great vast open space. Zhent'ah-rhull spoke a word that Kurt didn't recognize, and a shaft of light appeared before them, spearing down from the top of the vault to impale a waist-high column of crystal. After its initial flash of brilliance, the beam subsided into a flickering, fitful spotlight that bathed the pedestal-like object in light tinged ever so slightly with green. Reflections of that wan viridity winked from the surrounding darkness, hinting at unseen objects within the chamber.

"The oracle," Zhent'ah-rhull announced, motioning to them to enter the chamber.

Breath held in awe, Kurt crossed the threshold. Lambent glimmers of pale jade came from the walls of the vault and from low consoles or high benches that lined the chamber. The walls were gorgeous, veined like a Sommerset marble with deep reds and blues and purples, though no stone he'd ever seen boasted traceries of yellow and green as these did. The spot-lit crystal column was the only freestanding thing on the floor, but it was not the only furnishing. Several oddly shaped slabs of unknown function hung suspended from the ceiling; they might have been bizarre chandeliers, save that they were low enough that a person lying upon one could reach out and touch the surface of a console; and, of course, they had no provision for lighting elements. The strangeness of the place made Kurt's spine tingle.

"No primitives made this," Seaborg said, stating the obvious as he wandered the open space inspecting the place. "It's all alloys and composites."

While he would not dispute the first of the soldier's observations, Kurt had some doubts as to the second. Certainly this place had been constructed, but it was not like anything he'd seen that Humans or even the Mimaks had built. Some of the materials in the walls and consoles that he touched felt warm, some cool, and some sent tiny shocks into his fingers, which he dismissed as static electricity. The warmer places felt unlike any synthetics he knew; their heat almost pulsed. Could it be that they were warmed by induction heating from power conduits below?

The suspended slabs were curious, and not just for their curving shapes or surface undulations. Their outer edges and lower surfaces were hard and cool, while their upper surfaces yielded to the pressure of his fingers and grew cooler as they did. The segmented cables supporting them looked as though they might collapse into themselves like an extendable antenna. What might they be?

"What do you call this place?" he asked Zhent'ah-rhull.

"This is the *rass'arass*."

"I thought the *rass'arass* was above us."

"That, too, is the *rass'arass*."

Examining the arch through which they had entered, Seaborg had his own idea. "This looks remarkably like a pressure frame. Could this be the ship that brought the Chugeni ancestors here?"

"We're under uncounted tons of dirt," Juli pointed out. "Why go to such effort to bury a spaceship?"

"*Maskirovka*," Seaborg replied.

"What?"

"Deception and camouflage. It is effective *maskirovka*, too. Our orbital surveys failed to detect the ship."

"What makes you so sure it's a ship? It could be any kind of structure. A temple, say."

Seaborg didn't reply at once. "You're right, Professor

Tindal, it *could* be. But whatever it is, building it is beyond the skills of the current generation of Chugeni."

Juliana agreed with Seaborg's assessment, as far as it went. Civilizations fell; it was a fact of history. Why, even Humans had been known to slip back from the technological edge and revert to more primitive lifestyles. Not so primitive as the Hos'kimm, perhaps, but perhaps the Hos'kimm had been forgetting their past for far longer. Certainly the generations recounted in H'kimm stories suggested a history on Chugen far longer than that of any Human colony's isolation.

Still, the more she looked around the chamber, the more sure she was that the Hos'kimm that she knew had no part in the making of this place. Something about it didn't *feel* right. There was nothing she could point to, no scientific deduction she could explain, but she felt a sinking, worrisome apprehension that the League might be right about the nature of the Hos'kimm.

*The* ancient Hos'kimm, she told herself. *The Hos'kimm alive now on the face of Chugen had and have nothing to do with the Remor war.*

But what of their past? Could this chamber be some sort of remnant of a time when the Hos'kimm traveled among the stars? And if it was, had Kurt uncovered the final, conclusive evidence the League was seeking to justify their actions toward the aliens?

Zhent'ah-rhull called them to gather around the oracle. As they did, the beam seemed to steady. A featureless silver octahedron appeared in the air above the crystal column and all around them the air filled with song.

It was *song*, not just music—of that she was sure—but she had no idea of what the words were or even what language was being sung. She had never heard its like before.

It was beautiful, like crystal bells ringing in delicate harmony. When it stopped, she longed for more.

Zhent'ah-rhull looked expectantly at Kurt, but his eyes were fixed on the argent shape and he didn't notice. The column sang a new phrase, then repeated its first song.

"It's an interrogative, I think," said Kurt.

"What do we tell it?" she asked.

"I don't think it matters. We can't understand it; why should it be able to understand us?"

"Let the Chugeni talk to it," Seaborg suggested.

Kurt translated the soldier's suggestion and Zhent'ah-rhull spoke to the octahedron, begging forgiveness for the intrusion and asking for attention. The seer addressed his words to the Daysha, which didn't surprise Juliana. Whom else would one address in the holiest of holy places, if not the greatest of one's guardian deities? But for the first time she began to wonder whether the gods and spirits of the Hos'kimm might be something more than psychological constructs.

Whoever the Daysha might be, he, she, or they did not respond to the seer's plea. The argent shape spun slowly, serenely, silently.

Without warning the light winked out. The sudden darkness was disorienting. She fought against the feeling that she had suddenly been disembodied. Krahz barked out fearfully, and she nearly joined him, feeling icy hands closing on her heart. Only the hardness of her computer case against her hip and the dig of its strap against her shoulder kept her anchored. Barely. Just as her own scream was about to rip free, the light was back.

The beam was paler now, tinted with blue rather than green, and the silver octahedron no longer floated in its light. She saw her own wonder and puzzlement reflected in Kurt's face. Krahz shivered, ears back and down, clearly unhappy. Zhent'ah-rhull was as dispassionate as Seaborg's blanked visor.

The seer pointed to the crystal column. "The offering stage is ready."

"For what?" Kurt asked.

"To lay bare the secret heart of that which is presented."

"I don't understand."

"I will show you."

The seer stepped forward and placed his hand on the crystal's upper surface. At once the beam expanded until Zhent'ah-rhull stood fully within it.

A meter-tall image of a Hos'kimm male in the prime of life appeared where the octahedron had floated. This Hos'kimm was neither R'kimm, H'kimm, nor S'kimm, but something of all three races.

Like the geometric solid, the miniature alien rotated. Planes of solidified darkness blossomed to flank the image. Three columns of brilliant yellow symbols appeared on the planes, crawling sinuously downward to disappear into nothingness as more incomprehensible symbols snaked on from the emptiness above.

The hologram continued turning, picking up speed, and suddenly the Hos'kimm's fur was gone and its naked skin shone ruddy, every muscle sharply defined. Another rotation and the skin itself vanished, followed by the muscles. The internal organs thus revealed also evaporated, and only a skeleton remained. All the while the squiggly symbols squirmed faster and faster.

The Hos'kimm skeleton dissolved, replaced by a succession of strange images comprising graphical shapes and colors. The garish symbols were succeeded by a representation of a solar system. Juliana knew at once that it was not Chugen. But where? When the third planet from the sun was highlighted, she was struck by the familiarity of the

planetary configuration: the represented system looked like
that of Old Earth.

It *couldn't* be the Terran System!

*Could* it?

"My god, it's Earth," Kurt gasped.

A new skeleton appeared, similar to a Hos'kimm but not
the same. Before she could be sure of the differences, it was
clothed in muscle, skin, and fur. New images cascaded
past: scenes of forests and plains—very Earth-like forests
and plains. Unknown but strangely familiar animals flickered across those ghostly landscapes, moving in unnatural
pixilation. Before she could make sense of the scenes, they
were gone. An image flashed by that looked remarkably
like the worm-thing Zhent'ah-rhull had transferred from
Kmo to Kurt, then the dazzling, colorful shapes were back,
moving faster than ever. More scenes blurred by, of what
she could not tell; many of them featured the Hos'kimm-
like creature. The geometric symbols appeared again, then
were gone again, leaving just the panels of darkness and
their writhing squiggles, for a second or three; then nothing.

A soft chime sounded from the computer slung over her
shoulder. Opening it, she found that her screen read: USE
THE EARPIECE SO THAT I MAY TALK TO YOU
FREELY—ALSION. A panel on the side of the case oblig-
ingly opened, offering her the suggested peripheral. As
soon as she had the earpiece snugged home, the Alsion
construct spoke to her.

"Good morning, Professor Tindal," it said. "I would like
to thank you for finding this surprise."

Dumbstruck by what he had seen, Kurt looked across to
Juli to see what she made of the display. Her head was down
and she was whispering excitedly to her computer, no

doubt recording her impressions while they were fresh. She was an admirably capable and dedicated researcher, far more detached from this wonder than he.

He found Zhent'ah-rhull standing by his side. "Now you," the seer said, taking Kurt's arm and pulling him forward. Trusting his friend's wisdom, he let himself be led to the crystal column. At Zhent'ah-rhull's nod, he placed his hand where the seer had placed his. The *other* within him belled a single, clear note that shocked him with joy. Juli started forward when he moaned with the sudden, heady intensity of the sensation.

Zhent'ah-rhull waved her back. "This is for him alone."

Gathering back his scattered wits, Kurt tried to smile reassurance at her. She looked dubious, but she didn't come any closer. As Zhent'ah-rhull stepped away, the beam widened and enveloped Kurt. He became aware that the crystal was chill, almost as cold as water ice.

An image of himself appeared above his hand. No generalized image this, but a detailed and faithful portrait, as fine as any holographic studio back on Serenten might produce. The black panels winked into existence, but instead of scrolling symbols a single glyph blazed from their darkness. But only for a moment before the panels disappeared, leaving his image to rotate alone in the air.

"The oracle has no secrets for you," Zhent'ah-rhull said with obvious distress.

"I'm not so sure," Kurt said. His image still spun slowly in the air. It seemed a sign that the device was not yet finished. "Let's give it a few more—"

His words were interrupted by the return of the panels. But they were not the same color as before; this time they were a royal blue and the symbols they bore a stark white. His image was replaced by a brief flash of the multicolored shapes that he was beginning to suspect were graphical representations of data; some he'd seen the last time. A few quick, obviously computer-generated landscapes flashed by, to be supplanted by another psychedelic swirl of graphs and charts, then another solar system with pale, iconic planets adrift in a sea of blue rather than space's midnight. He barely had time to note that the depiction included a yellow sun—a Sol-type sun—before the hypothetical system was replaced by equally hypothetical animals—at least they seemed to be conjectural types, judged by their cartoonish appearance. Then with a last kaleidoscopic flash, it was over.

"Quite the light show," Seaborg said. "But what is it supposed to mean?"

There was meaning in the images, Kurt felt sure, even for those who could not comprehend the accompanying language. The device had followed the same pattern in dealing with Kurt as it had with Zhent'ah-rhull, but the results were different, and in a qualitative way more significant than the difference in species should account for. The change in colors of the (probably) explanatory panels and their symbols suggested that the oracle was dealing differently with the two sets of information. Why?

The device had displayed detailed anatomical knowledge of Hos'kimm but not of Humans, suggesting that it knew the one well and the other not very well, perhaps not at all. Might the change in color signify that the first data set was recorded information and the second merely speculation? And if so, what was the significance of the graphical symbols that had appeared in both displays?

There was a connection somewhere.

The *other* sang to him a wordless song of belonging.

Struggling with bafflement, Kurt sensed that the answer was just beyond his understanding, but he couldn't get his addled wits organized.

\*          \*          \*

"Let me try something," Juliana told Kurt, tugging him away from the crystal pedestal.

He nodded, lost in thought, and stepped away from the light. No one else objected, so she gave the Alsion construct permission to try its experiment. She saw Kurt look up at the first strains of the playback of the oracle's first song. Together they stared at what the machine had projected onto the offering stage: another octahedron. But this one was not featureless silver; the image had the surface patterns of one of the infamous octahedrons that the IDL insisted were some sort of Remor monitor.

The image just sat there. Nothing happened.

She tapped a key, giving the construct permission to try variants. The construct complied, producing mellifluous variations and pausing briefly after each one. On the fifth try, the oracle responded. A schematic matching the projected octahedron appeared, flanked by black panels filled with squirming symbols.

*The answer's there, if only we could read it,* she thought.

They didn't have to read. The answer came in pictures as the image of the octahedron shrank and shrank, almost to invisibility, and a planet's image folded into the display area from somewhere out of sight. A dashed orbital path grew from the octahedron and ringed the planetary icon as the joined images shrank. More planets joined the first in the display area. Something else appeared in the display, a dot that had a long, flickering tail. It might have been a comet, but it followed a course that no comet could. Stopping briefly at each planet like a visiting starship, the dot approached the planet with the orbiting octahedron. As it did, a sphere of diffuse green light came into being, centered on the orbiting octahedron. The ship-dot's course intersected the sphere, and immediately spheres of intense green expanded from the octahedron's position in orbit.

Her hope of dispelling the Remor connection was dashed. "They *are* sentinels for the Remor."

"And the first sphere is supposed to indicate the distance at which they detect a star drive, is it?" Seaborg asked.

"Yes, I think so," she replied.

"And what are we supposed to conclude from this little display?"

"It gives us an idea of how closely a ship can approach one of the sentinels." *If* the scale could be determined. Perhaps the beacons could be avoided . . .

"Does it really?" Even the suit's speaker couldn't disguise the sarcasm in the soldier's voice. "Why should I believe this, Professor Tindal?"

"Why? Because it's almost certainly true! Why would this machine lie to—" She stopped, suddenly registering what he had said. "What did you call me?"

"Professor Tindal. Your name, remember? Or are *you* now having an episode of total identification with the aliens? Do I have to use a Chugeni name for you, too?"

"Seaborg always addresses me as 'ma'am.' You're not Seaborg," she accused.

"No, I'm not." The battlesuit's faceplate depolarized, revealing the sneering countenance of Major Ersch. "I am also not impressed by your carefully prepared evidence. The radius of detection for the beacons was a nice touch. Was that the hard data that was supposed to convince us to accept the business of the Chugeni being plucked from Earth? Really! That was where you overplayed it. Still, it was a well-orchestrated show, I must say, and the two of you played your parts well. It would have fooled that idiot Seaborg, no doubt. But you are not dealing with him anymore."

\*       \*       \*

Shocked as he had been to see Major Ersch's face appear, Kurt was more overwhelmed at the man's delusions. What kind of paranoia led him to think that this had all been arranged just to fool him and his masters?

"You think we're making this up?" he asked incredulously. "Look around you. How could we possibly have built this structure?"

"I know you didn't build it. And you can drop the 'structure' crap. I can see that it's a starship, Ellicot. Or what's left of one. And now that I've seen it, nothing you can say or do will divorce it from your alien friends. StratCom is going to be very pleased to get their hands on this Remor ship. We've never recovered a fragment anywhere near the size of this compartment before. " Ersch's tone shifted to the conspiratorial. "How long have you known their secret? Did you learn the truth on Cassuells Home?"

The *other* stirred at Kurt's memories of the Cassuells, sending him a pleasant lassitude that was as comforting as a huddle with the pack. The feeling dulled Kurt's enduring pang of loss.

*What do you know of them?* he asked the *other*, but it had no words to answer him.

"I still don't know the truth," he said aloud, as much to himself as in rebuttal to Ersch. His words brought him back outside himself, and he added, "Nor do you. Your *truth* is a self-deluding lie."

"As I believe you said: look around you." Ersch chuckled disparagingly. "How long have you known this ship was here?"

A yawning chasm of time threatened to engulf Kurt, but he fought back, asserting himself against the *other*. He told Ersch a truth. "I saw it when you did."

"I'm no fool, Ellicot. Did you think I didn't notice when you let slip that you had been down here before?"

"The upper chamber only," he protested.

"I told you to stop trying to play me for a fool," Ersch snapped.

The man was unshakable in his delusion. But deluded or not, Ersch wore an armored battlesuit. Kurt could not oppose him physically.

*How do I deal with a wild* grawr'tayo? *How do I deal with a crazy man?*

With compassion. With reason. With truth.

"Don't you comprehend what we have seen here?" he asked, pleading for understanding. "Can't you see what the oracle's riddle means? All of us are victims of the Remor. We because of the war, and they because of being taken into bondage. Humans. Hos'kimm. The Cassuells, too. We have all been shaped by the Remor." The *other* sang the joy of the pack. "The Hos'kimm are not the enemy. They are our brothers."

"Concordat propaganda garbage," Ersch said. "I have seen the enemy. They are here."

"Listen to him," Juli demanded. "He's trying to make you see the truth."

"I've heard and seen enough," Ersch announced. "This little jaunt is over. Your *maskirovka* has failed. Now it's time for you to go back into custody."

His good left arm reaching out, Ersch advanced on Kurt.

Krahz pointed the surrendered pulse rifle at Ersch, showing a clear grasp of how it should be handled. Juliana guessed that the R'kimm hunter had observed astutely during the raid that had taken Kurt and killed so many Hos'kimm. Krahz triggered the rifle, but only a low-energy targeting beam emerged.

Ersch stopped, looking down at the red dot on his

armored chest, and gave a contemptuous laugh. "So they don't understand modern technology, eh?"

He raised his right arm and pointed his wavering, gauntleted fist at Krahz. The air cracked as his wrist-mounted blaser discharged.

The side of Krahz's head exploded as fluid and tissue superheated. Mere flesh could not contain the high-energy pulse, and it went on to blow a small hole in the wall behind the R'kimm.

Kurt screeched, sounding simultaneously outraged and physically injured. Shocked by the sudden violence, no one moved, save for Ersch. He continued on his way around the oracle's pedestal, moving toward Kurt.

A moan, too loud and deep to be from the dying Hos'kimm, reverberated through the chamber as the oracle's light was extinguished.

The sudden darkness left Juliana blind, but Krahz's murder had taken away her fear of the Stygian blackness. What had terrified her before she now saw as an opportunity. Sliding around the hanging slab between them, she moved toward where she remembered Kurt standing, and found him still there. He started when she touched him, but fortunately he remained quiet. Trusting him to realize that her hands were not Ersch's gauntleted ones, she tugged him back the way she had come.

"Don't think you're safe, hiding in the dark," Ersch's voice boomed out, his speaker's projection seemingly amplified by the inky blackness. "I can still see you."

*Damn!* Of course Ersch could see them. His helmet was fitted with all sorts of sensory amplification.

But she, too, could see, she realized. Faintly, but more easily by the second, and far faster than she would have expected her eyes to adapt to the dark. Light was coming from somewhere. A way out? She looked for the source.

A sullen red glow emanated from the wall near where Ersch's laser pulse had hit. Dark-veined sacs had appeared there, growing on the wall like blisters on burned skin. They were the source of the ruddy light, and it was increasing: already she could see as well as on a starry but moonless night.

She didn't like what she saw: Zhent'ah-rhull hurrying to join her and Kurt, Ersch confidently approaching them, Krahz's lifeless form sprawling near the wall, but what commanded her attention was the chamber itself. Somehow, in the brief interval of blackness, the walls and ceiling of the vault had changed. They looked diseased.

Scabrous pustules bulged from the ceiling, dripping a nacreous, syrupy liquid. The fluid made puddles on the floor that bubbled and roiled and spread. The fluid dripping down the walls carved runnels. Wherever the liquid touched it effervesced, bubbling up a variegated foam of metals and synthetics.

The acidic goo was capable of wreaking its havoc on more than synthetics. Zhent'ah-rhull stepped in a puddle of the stuff and fell to the floor, howling in agony.

Kurt whimpered at her side.

"My foot! My foot! It burns!" Zhent'ah-rhull bayed.

But he was wrong—horribly, horribly wrong. His foot was *gone*! It had dissolved away, leaving the white bone of his ankle poking through the raw tissue at the end of his mutilated leg. Blood and other fluids seeped from the ravaged stump.

Juliana vomited.

Wide-eyed with horror, Kurt stared as a runnel of sludgy goo touched the tip of one of the seer's dropped walking sticks and began to flow along its length. The wood lost coherency and slumped into the puddle as fast as the destructive ichor advanced along it, until only a dark stain on the surface suggested that anything had ever lain there. Had the seer fallen forward, he too would have been no more than a oily smear on the spreading puddle.

Another puddle was spreading toward the seer. Intent on helping his friend, Kurt disentangled himself from the sobbing and retching Juli. There were no pools of destruction nearby; she would be safe for a moment.

But he was not. Hard fingers ground into his arm.

"You're coming with me," Ersch said, half-lifting Kurt from his feet.

"We've got to get the others out," Kurt protested.

"You're my only concern here," Ersch countered, starting to drag Kurt toward the antechamber and the ramp to the surface.

Kurt struggled, to no avail. His strength was as nothing to the powered battlesuit. His blows only hurt his hands.

Juli entered the affray, throwing herself bodily into the back of Ersch's knees. Her mere flesh and bone, like his, were insufficient to breach Ersch's armor, but mass remained mass. Striking against the back of the suit's knee joint, she forced Ersch's knees to bend.

In an instinctive effort to maintain his balance, Ersch released Kurt. As Kurt fell to the floor, something rolled under his flailing arm: Zhent'ah-rhull's second walking stick. It was a poor weapon, but better than his fist. He seized it, happy to have anything to aid his fight to be free of Ersch.

Ersch meanwhile had recovered and turned on Juli. She was on her hands and knees, dazed and helpless. Raising his good arm to slam her, he snarled, "I don't need you delaying me!"

His armored fist would smash flesh and bone, possibly kill her with a blow.

"No!" Kurt shouted. He flung the walking stick at the

soldier. Ersch ducked. As he did, his shoulder brushed one of the ulcerations pulsing on the wall. It burst. Thick drops spattered.

One landed on Kurt's necklace of bangles. With desperate haste, spurred by the acrid stench in his nostrils and the sudden fearful wail of the *other*, he wrenched the honor signs free before the acid could touch his skin.

A spray of droplets caught Ersch's armor. Pockmarks appeared where they fell and streamers of black smoke rose from them. One must have landed on the inside of his right elbow joint where the armor was thinner, for the soldier swatted at that point, yelling angrily. He staggered back, caroming off the wall. To halt his stagger he thrust a hand out to a nearby console. But no true surface was there to aid him.

Like a plate laid on the surface of a pot of molten metal, the console's surface had lain, as near dissolved as it could be and only a moment from oblivion. When Ersch's palm touched the surface, it parted, dissolving away to become one with the ravenous fluid that had claimed it. The soldier's arm plunged deep. Screaming, high and hysterical, he wrenched the stump free.

But Kurt's concern was not for the soldier. Through the thickening clouds of smoke, he caught sight of Juli. She had collapsed where he had last seen her. Thankfully, he saw that the area was clear of acid pools and the pustules above her were small, not yet swollen enough to burst. They wouldn't stay that way long. He got her up and pointed toward the exit. "Go," he told her.

With her on her way out, he went back for Zhent'ahrhull. There was no way the seer could escape without help. As he got a grip on his friend's shoulder, he heard Juli call his name and saw her start to turn back.

"No, keep going," he shouted to her.

She ignored him

For Zhent'ah-rhull's sake, it was good that she did. The raving seer was a dead weight, past Kurt's strength to move easily. Together they dragged him past the thrashing mass of raw flesh, melted armor plate, garish white bone, and smoking blood that would not be Major Jonas Ersch much longer.

The antechamber was less choked with the stench and smoke of destruction than the oracle vault, but here too the acid-filled pustules were growing. They hurried up the ramp, anxious to be away from the excrescences before they ripened and burst.

Emerging from the *rass'arass*, Kurt and Juli dragged their burden a meter or two before slumping under the weight of exhaustion. Juli crumpled to a cross-legged seat, her head hung low. Kurt let himself fall, first to his knees, then face-forward against the ground. The cool dirt felt wonderful. It smelled clean and rich and alive.

Alive!

"We have been vomited forth from the mouth of hell," he said.

"And received into the arms of the earth," Juli said, completing the quote from Weller's *Paradise Squandered*.

But the earth, it seemed, was not happy to have them. All through his body he felt the ground begin to tremble. Terrified, he forced himself up. He dragged the protesting Juli to her feet. Her objections stopped as she too began to feel the tremors.

"The ship below is collapsing, which means—"

He didn't have to say more. She bent at once to help him with Zhent'ah-rhull.

The tremors grew until the ground was heaving. Pits yawned open, swallowing dusty slides of dirt and rocks. The deep groaning rumble of shifting earth burst forth in a surf roar of rushing stone and soil.

Breathless, Kurt found strength where he thought he had none. The reason was simple: if he didn't move, he would die.

He helped Juli and together they scrambled over the bucking ground, pulling the helpless Zhent'ah-rhull along with them. Kurt didn't know where they were going, but he did know that they had to be somewhere, anywhere other than the collapsing ground.

They could have run far faster without Zhent'ah-rhull, but Kurt wouldn't abandon him—they were of the pack!

Juli wouldn't abandon the seer either. Grunting and heaving, she and Kurt struggled, barely managing to stay ahead of the slumping ground. The noise abated and the heaving lessened, but still they moved as fast as they could, until they reached one of the hills and hauled Zhent'ah-rhull a few meters up the slope.

The eternity of their struggle was over.

Together they stood and stared at the irregular crater that had appeared where the buried ship had been, swallowing the *rass'arass* and the Patterns that had surrounded it. The holiest place of the Hos'kimm was gone and in its place was a hollow filled with a low-lying and deadly cloud of greasy smoke, a hell that they had survived.

"The oracle?" Zhent'ah-rhull rasped.

"Gone," Kurt told him.

They had survived, but the ship and its oracle had not. And with the passing of that precious data store had gone the evidence that the Hos'kimm were not themselves the Remor, but pawns of the star-ranging enemy.

Exhausted and stinking of blood and smoke, he put his arm around her. She came into his embrace willingly. She felt warm and alive, comforting. He pulled her close and she laid her head against his shoulder.

"At least we're alive," he said to her.

"And very glad of it, I am," said a stranger's voice from behind them.

They turned to find seven battlesuited troopers standing there. The foremost one showed an officer's rank markings, bright against the dull red and ocher camouflage. "Lieutenant Horne, B Company, Thirty-fifth battalion, Third Regiment of Infantry, Free Franconian Forces, currently serving aboard IDLS *Constantine*. You would be Professors Ellicot and Tindal, correct?"

"God, not another rescue," Juli moaned.

"Ma'am?"

"A bad joke, Lieutenant," Kurt said. "Do you have a medic with you?"

"Are you injured, sir?"

"Nothing serious, but my friend needs real help." Kurt nodded toward where Zhent'ah-rhull lay on the ground.

Horne nodded. "Corporal Zatti, take care of the indigene."

Corporal Zatti stepped forward, adjusting a ring at the base of the wide-barreled weapon he carried. Before Kurt could protest, the corporal raised his weapon and fired. No devouring blast came forth, only a chuff of sound. Zhent'ah-rhull moaned once, loudly, and went slack.

"Don't worry, sir. It's not lethal," Horne assured them. "The sleeper is one of the first fruits of recent research. Hanson, get a med pack on the indigene's leg. He looks important."

Kurt and the *other* worried about Zhent'ah-rhull, but this *shadakey* didn't even know the seer's name. "What do you care whether he's important or not?"

"I have been tasked with collecting interrogation subjects, and in my experience the local higher-ups are generally the ones who know what our own higher-ups want to know. Speaking of higher-ups, where is Major Ersch?"

Juli pointed to the crater. "Down there."

"Unfortunate."

"I disagree," Kurt and Juli said in unison.

Their eyes met in understanding. Horne harrumphed, clearly not appreciating their attitude.

"You have an appointment with the commander, and I'd really rather that you not make a big fuss about refusing." The lieutenant turned slightly. "Corporal Zatti."

Zatti adjusted his weapon again and pointed it at Juli and Kurt. Two closely spaced chuffing sounds were the last things Kurt heard.

# 34

When he woke up, he was alone again, in a box again. Sundered from the pack, he moaned his grief and loneliness.

But the pack was not all that he had lost. While he had been unconscious, they had taken her from him. He cried.

No companion, no pack-mates, just the *shadakey* and their cold, hard boxes. They had taken him, made him theirs. But he did not want to belong to them. He *would* not belong to them.

And the song of the *other* told him that he need not.

He was a part of the pack and, through the *other*, the pack was a part of him. The pack was his refuge.

The tactical operations room of *Constantine* was crowded with the masters of the squadron's ships and their staffs. The press of humanity taxed the climate control and there was nothing to be done about it; *Constantine* lacked individual controls for the command section's compartments and Colonel MacAndra, her master, was unwilling to chill down his crew for the comfort of his guests.

Captain Shaler, Stone's Lancastrian political specialist, was conducting his briefing, a necessary complement to the tactical overview that MacAndra's executive officer had just concluded. Shaler had given Stone a précis earlier;

Stone found his attention drifting back to the holotank's display of the deployment of the forces active in the Chugen System. It was a troubling picture.

The balance was extremely fragile. Though League forces had mauled the enemy in the last hot, harsh encounter, they had not been able to finish them, foiled by the enemy's superior speed and maneuverability. Despite having lost the *Hydra* dreadnought in the last attempt to reach the beacon, the Remor were still a threat; they had hurt the League squadron and escaped with a force still capable of inflicting serious damage. And now there was the linked threat of the Combine–Concordat ships. Though neither opponent was strong enough to eliminate the League forces, conflict with either would likely weaken the squadron past the point of resisting the other.

The Combine and Concordat ships were the most urgent problem. They were moving slowly insystem toward the League squadron gathered near Chugen IV. It was an aggressive posture that aimed at the League and paid insufficient attention to the remaining Remor threat. Stone didn't understand. What were those people over there thinking? Couldn't they understand that the enemies of Humanity were out there, waiting like vultures? If Human ship fought Human ship, who would be left to deal with the real enemy?

Shaler was concluding his briefing. "The arrival of the Concordat squadron has altered the political balance far more than the military balance. Managing Director Konoye is not a bluffer, or rather not a competent one. His increasingly hostile attitude and belligerent language must have a basis; something assures him of a stronger position than he appears to have. I believe his saber-rattling can only be attributed to a commitment of Concordat support, and that he is expecting reinforcements in short order. Still,

I believe he is as yet unready to commit. For the moment, a moment that may pass soon, we hold the initiative."

"Time has always been the bane of this operation." Stone scanned his assembled officers' faces. He found concern, even worry, but also determination. He wished that he could offer them a better, cleaner problem on which they could exercise their professionalism. "Gentlefolk, Operation Chameleon has foundered. Intercepts of Combine and Concordat transmissions indicate that they are aware of the survivors from the crash of *Henry Hull*'s number 2 interface shuttle.

"We believe them still unaware that it was our lurker *Falsefox* that played the part of the Remor raider. *Falsefox* remains insystem, as does *Jaguar*, and there has been no mention made of their provocative existence. Even so, Konoye is disputing our claim to the system, and Concordat presence has put an unwelcome spotlight on our operations here. The military situation remains viable, but the political situation has become precarious." Stone schooled his expression to one of hard, detached professionalism. "We are looking at Cassuells Home all over again. StratCom will not welcome a repeat of the public relations debacle which followed that action.

"Suggestions?"

"We can't let the enemy reestablish contact with their colonials on Chugen IV," said Farmer, commander of *Montcalm*.

"I asked for suggestions, not a restatement of the problem," Stone growled.

Colonel MacAndra spoke up. "Our first priority must be dealing with the enemy. At present the Chugeni offer no threat. I recommend we let the Combine occupy Chugen IV orbit while we deal with the enemy space forces. It will strengthen our claim to sole defense of the system, and put us in a better tactical position should we be forced to engage Combine forces."

Stone nodded. "Take that as a starting point, but I want every contingency examined and planned for. Give me operational plans for every option consistent with our orders, gentlefolk. I want something that will work, and I want it soon. I will be in my quarters until thirteen hundred."

He left his officers to deliberate without the stifling presence of the senior commander. With luck, one of them would have the inspiration that had so far eluded him.

He hadn't been brooding on the problem for half an hour before MacAndra reported, "Ship's surgeon calling for you, commander."

"Pass it through," Stone told him.

"Ellicot and Tindal are awake," reported the surgeon without preamble.

"No aftereffects from the sleepers?" Stone asked, equally brusque.

"Very mild on the whole. Ellicot seems depressed and withdrawn, but I think most of that stems from a reversion to his Chugeni persona. He has also refused the clothing we offered. Shall we force him to dress, sir?" The surgeon looked unhappy when Stone told him not to bother, but he mastered his offended propriety and continued. "Tindal, on the other hand, is fine. Active, alert, and very interested in where she is and what's going to happen next. In fact, she has been asking to see you—vociferously and, if I may say, with some rather uncomplimentary references."

"Eager, is she? And she has been given access to her computer?"

"As you ordered. Watched discreetly, of course."

"Good." That she wanted to speak to him, rather than using the illicit transmitter in her computer, suggested that the squadron's jamming field was effective. She must not have had a chance to send her final report, which meant that her masters had no knowledge of the final act of the debacle on Chugen IV. He'd have to compliment the commo teams. "Have them escorted to my quarters, and ask Colonel MacAndra to join me. Stone, out."

The *shadakey* came for him. He stood tall, unafraid of what they could do to him. Although he did shiver when they said they were taking him to their commander.

They wanted him to wear their clothes, but he refused. He understood that even a small thing as dressing like them could lead to greater concessions. He was not like them, and he would not dress like them.

He belonged to the pack.

The pack was his refuge.

"You have no legal right to hold us," Tindal asserted furiously as she entered.

"Please sit down, Professor Tindal," Stone said amiably. "Your colleague has already made himself comfortable. No reason you should stand."

Ellicot had, in fact, plopped cross-legged on the floor just inside the hatch as soon as his escort's guiding arm was removed. Tindal seemed determined to ignore Stone's hospitality. She crossed her arms and scowled at him.

"Suit yourself. As to legalities, what have you to say about the theft of a transport aircraft, in which you participated with Professor Burke?"

"We were escaping illegal confinement."

"You'd make a good barracks-room lawyer, Professor. Was League law part of your training for this mission?"

"Mission? I don't know what you're talking about."

Stone tapped a signal button on his desk. An orderly

entered, bearing Tindal's confiscated computer, placed it on the desk and left. Smiling, Stone tapped the case lid. "Quite a sophisticated piece of work. I am afraid that the transmitter was damaged when my computer specialists examined it. They are impressed. They also advise me that the operating system displayed by the machine is a sham, a cover for a very powerful agent-based system." He dropped the smile. "This is a spy's machine, Professor, and we have every legal right to detain spies."

Her shoulders slumped in defeat. A quick concession, and hardly credible.

"Let Kurt go," she said. "He has nothing to do with this."

"Really?"

"Really."

"I am afraid I must disagree. I believe the two of you are very deeply involved in affairs on Chugen IV."

"I meant the spying stuff."

"So did I. Perhaps you think that we do not know about Professor Ellicot's condition, the only League witness being dead." He played for her the recording, taken by and trans-mitted from Major Ersch's hardsuit, of the ceremony in which Ellicot was implanted with the alien organism. "League law does not hold a person culpable for the forced implantation of spying devices, but consent to the implant, which the professor so clearly gave, changes the situation. Two months ago an espionage case against him would have been shaky; but now the directors of the Combine have agreed that the Chugeni are genetically indistinguishable from the Cassuells and the Grenwold aliens. And since League StratCom classified the Cassuells as the enemy over ten years ago, I find that I am dealing with another spy."

"He's not a spy!" she protested.

"I would like to believe that, Professor, but the law is very clear on collusion with the enemy. I'm afraid Professor

Ellicot is in an even worse situation than yourself. The Combine and the League are not at war, saving you from the death penalty, but Professor Ellicot has chosen to side with the enemy in a zone of active conflict. I could have him shot right now."

"You're wrong about me," Ellicot said, muffled voice coming from within the cradle of his arms.

And how could they not be wrong about him? He had been wrong about himself.

Yes, he was of the pack, and the pack sang in him, but the pack, while his refuge, was not his all. There was more to him than being a member of the pack. Seeing Juli had brought him back to himself. His real self, his Human self.

His only self?

No. He was not just Human anymore. He was not sure he understood what he had become, but he knew he was not the species traitor Stone made him out to be. Stone did not understand. None of them understood.

*And was he any different from them?*

Oh, *very* different! Physically, at least. He needed to understand about that.

Perhaps the pack would have answers for him, but they could give those answers only if they survived. So before a greater understanding could be achieved, a smaller one was necessary. Stone must come to understand, to see that his Way was wrong.

Kurt stood in the middle, but as little as he comprehended his new state, he knew more than the others. The truth was seeping into his mind, crawling up his spinal cord and whispering in his brain.

The *other* was not born of Old Earth, but it was bred to it by the gods—by the Daysha. The *other* had been made to make the Hos'kimm what they became when they were taken from Old Earth. He *knew* this truth, but he had no evidence, no scientific evidence to convince the Humans. He had only the murky churnings of his mind, and the song of the *other* that no Human but he could hear.

Looking at the huddled Ellicot sitting naked on his deck, Stone doubted that he was wrong about the man. "Really?"

"I stand between the jungle and the stars. I am brother to the Hos'kimm, and to you."

"Brother to the Hos'kimm? Would that be by virtue of the organism with which the Chugeni infested you? The ship's surgeon says that it has thoroughly insinuated itself into your spinal column, but declines to speculate on its nature without testing you. What do you have to say of its nature, Professor Ellicot? What do you think it is? Is it a parasite or a symbiont?"

Ellicot raised his head, the light of a fanatic in his eye. "It is the gift of the Daysha."

"Would that be Daysha the god or Daysha the Remor?"

Hanging his head again, Ellicot gave no answer. Though that didn't surprise Stone at all, he still couldn't be sure whether Ellicot's sullenness arose from embarrassment at being caught out in his collusion with the enemy, or honest indignation at Stone's presuming such collusion. Despite his own accusations, and despite the evidence of spying, Stone found neither of the academics plausible in the role.

"I invited the two of you here for a reason," he began, but Tindal interrupted him.

"I suppose you want us to watch while you destroy the Hos'kimm."

"When that action is undertaken, you may watch if you wish, Professor Tindal, but Professor Ellicot may not. Intel's program for him requires that he not see what is to come."

"You can't annihilate the Hos'kimm!" Tindal shouted with unfeigned passion.

"I most certainly can, Professor," he countered quietly. "And I have orders to do so."

"Your orders are wrong! The Hos'kimm aren't your enemy. They are victims of the Remor. Don't make them your victims, too. Don't make the same mistake you made at Cassuells Home."

Stone's eyes narrowed. "Some of us, like the late Major Ersch, believe that obeying orders is never a mistake."

"Just the sort of response I'd expect from a dyed-in-the-wool mart like the Casual Slaughterer, you bloody-handed bastard!"

"You will address the commander with respect," MacAndra snapped.

"I'll address him any way I please. I'm not one of your stormtroopers, nor am I a member of your deluded population. I am a free citizen of the Combine! I'm free to speak my mind."

"And free to answer for that speech," Stone reminded her. "I started to say that I invited you here for a reason, and believe it or not, I wanted you to talk to me. I was hoping you'd tell me what you found in the Chugeni holy hole."

"Don't you have Ersch's tapes of that?"

"Humor me. Pretend that we don't." Actually they didn't. Ersch's last transmitted image was of the Remor airlock. At least that's what his Intel staff interpreted the archway to be. Once Ersch walked through that underground arch, his transmissions had ceased. Now that the Remor disassemblers and acids had done their work, nothing remained of the Remor artifact, or of Major Ersch.

"Why do you care what happened?" Tindal asked defiantly. "You'll just call me a liar, like Ersch did."

"Are you a liar, Professor?"

"No!"

"Then tell me something that I'll believe."

She looked to Ellicot, who, absorbed in his own world, ignored her. Nervously she looked back to Stone and said, "The ship that was beneath the *rass'arass* may or may not be Remor, I don't know. I don't even know if it really was a starship, but I do know that it's not Hos'kimm."

"How do you know this starship did not belong to the Chugeni?"

"Why should I bother? You're not going to believe anything I tell you."

"You assured me that you are not a liar. I am willing to accept that." *At least I am willing to believe that you will be telling what* you *believe.* "But I must point out that hard evidence is far better than words. Anyone's words, Professor. Hard evidence does not have a political agenda."

He could see that she very much wanted to believe that he was sympathetic, but she seemed to be having trouble reconciling his attitude with his reputation. Would her need to defend her aboriginal friends overcome her reservations? He watched her eyes dart momentarily to her computer. She said, "There is a recording of the oracle and its chamber. If you see what we saw, you will know."

He slid the machine toward her. "Show me."

She opened the lid and ordered the computer to life. A holographic of a disembodied male head appeared, to Tindal's apparent surprise. *Not what she expected, eh?*

The computer introduced itself. "I am the agent which your technicians sought, Commander Stone. I am forbidden to identify myself or my source, but I will answer what questions I may. I assure you that any information I present will be honest and unadulterated."

Stone had much less faith in the machine's honesty than he did in Tindal's. "But not necessarily the whole truth."

"Who knows the whole truth, Commander? May I have a hard link to your display peripheral? My access hardware is dysfunctional; damage due to rough handling, I believe."

At Stone's nod MacAndra made the connection. The display came to life with a virtual replica of what Tindal told him was the "oracle vault."

"The image is a synthetic reconstruction based on my recordings. It is ninety-two percent accurate. I draw your attention to this console," the agent said, adjusting the image to show the surface of the console and the displays thereon.

"Mac?" Stone asked, knowing what he thought he was seeing and wanting the colonel's opinion.

"That looks like a stellar spectrum for Chugen's sun," said MacAndra.

"And this?" The agent highlighted another section of the console display.

"That looks like a map of local space. The positions of the stars are a little off, though."

"The effect of the passage of time," the agent explained.

"What do you make of it, Mac?" Stone asked.

"If I had to hazard a guess, sir, I'd say we were looking at an astrogation station."

Tindal jumped on the colonel's conclusion. "If that's a control panel, look what's in front of it. That hanging slab would be a chair or an acceleration couch. See the four indentations along the edge of the fore part, and note the undulating curvature of the slab. This thing is not made for a Hos'kimm. It should be obvious even to you that this was not a Hos'kimm ship. It belonged to someone else. Another species. The Remor."

"It does look as though those couches would be a damnably uncomfortable fit for a Chugeni," Stone admitted. "But even if another species flew the ship, that doesn't make that other species the Remor. The Concordat pundits like to prattle about your alien friends being slaves to the Remor. Who is to say that it isn't your friends who were the masters, with slaves to ferry them about? After all, we have seen no living example of this other species. History teaches us that the weak are oppressed by the strong, and that the strong survive. The Chugeni are the survivors here. Would that not make them better candidates for masters than slaves?"

Ellicot's muffled voice answered him.

"Thus was the pack raised up.

"Heed the laws by which the pack was raised up:

"Tend the *teclananda*. Remember the signs. Build so that the spirits in the heavens can see. Teach your children to do as you were taught. Await the return."

Ellicot raised his head, his eyes bleak. "These are the laws by which the Hos'kimm live. These are laws given by masters to slaves."

From what he saw with his eyes, from what he heard with his ears, and from the deep, silent song of the *other*, Kurt understood that the Daysha and the Remor were one. Daysha, a noun both plural and singular to the Hos'kimm. Who could say if their legends and beliefs referred to an individual Remor or to the species?

Did it matter? The Hos'kimm were what they were because of the Remor. They had been spread across space in the wake of the Remor, uprooted, changed, and abandoned. But not all of their kind had been abandoned, as the Grenwold pack showed. Some still traveled with their masters and makers.

The Hos'kimm's association with the Remor doomed them in League eyes, but the League did not see all that there was to be seen. They needed to see all of the story.

They needed to see the truth that was the Hos'kimm's only hope of salvation.

He had not known that Juli's computer had recorded the oracle chamber, but what he knew then didn't matter. What mattered was what he knew now. If the computer had a record of the chamber, it must also have a record of what the oracle showed them.

"Juli, show Stone Zhent'ah-rhull's secret heart. Show him the truth of the Hos'kimm."

Tindal looked perplexed by Ellicot's demand. He bypassed her and spoke directly to the machine. "Computer, do you have a record of what the oracle showed when Zhent'ah-rhull placed his hand on the pedestal?"

"Yes."

"Display it for Commander Stone. Let him see what his enemy knows of the Hos'kimm."

Stone could make little sense of what was displayed. He guessed that most of it was some sort of biological report; he'd have the medical staff look at the recording later. There was one thing, though, one thing that hit him like a taser on full charge: the star map. A yellow sun. Ten planets, the third a blue gem orbited by an overlarge moon.

This was not at all what he had expected.

"Get an analysis team on this recording, Mac," he ordered, his voice a little unsteady.

"You already know what you need to know," Ellicot said. "They are our brothers, born of the same mother and stolen away to the stars."

"Speculation," said Stone.

"Truth," said Ellicot.

But was it? If the images were true Remor data, they went a long way toward exonerating the Chugeni and their kind. One thing was clear: the Chugeni and the Remor were not the same species. Or was even *that* clear? Might this recording be false? Was this whole presentation a clever manipulation? Had he misjudged Tindal and Ellicot?

"You and your computer can hardly be considered a disinterested source. Your data are unreliable. Your hard evidence is gone and you've nothing to verify what you say. I'm afraid that your case is based on insufficient evidence to convince StratCom."

"So you *are* going to bomb Chugen. The Casual Slaughterer is going to live up to his name. You *bastard*! You are *such* a double-dealing, prejudiced, murdering—"

Stone cut her off. "Your opinion of me doesn't signify, Professor. Colonel MacAndra, have these people removed to their quarters."

After Ellicot and Tindal were taken away, MacAndra asked quietly, "Are we going to bomb or not?"

"Not."

"But our orders . . ."

"*My* orders, Colonel. My orders are my problem, just as yours are your problem. I am ordering you to contact Director Konoye. You are to tell him that we estimate our force is insufficient to deal with Remor forces insystem, and arrange a combined operation to eliminate all said forces in this system. We are here to fight the enemy, and that's what we'll do, by God."

"Aye, sir!" MacAndra snapped a salute and departed, leaving Stone to ponder whether he'd made the right choice.

Juliana was surprised when she heard the warning klaxon signaling that the ship was leaving orbit, without hearing the battle stations warning that would have preceded a bombardment. She got a second surprise when a warrant officer appeared at the door of her cabin and handed her the computer she'd last seen on Stone's desk.

"The transmitter is still disabled, ma'am," was all the soldier said before sealing her back in.

She didn't understand what was going on, but she intended to take advantage of it if she could. The Alsion construct had demonstrated its ability to remain aware of its surroundings even when the computer was supposedly shut down. If it had spent time in Stone's office, it could well know far more than Stone would want it to.

*If they haven't stripped it bare*, she reminded herself.

At her call, an image appeared: the cowled monk, not the stranger's head that it had used in Stone's quarters.

"Good afternoon, Professor Tindal," it said cheerily. "I hope you weren't too surprised by my disguise earlier. I thought it best that they not know exactly with whom they were dealing."

"Well, you've blown that. They bug a spy's quarters."

The construct seemed unconcerned. "Normally, yes, but Commander Stone ordered such surveillance ended. He is, I believe, finished with you."

What? "Then why am I still locked up?"

"Technicalities, Professor Tindal," the construct said airily. "Your freedom will come in due and reasonably expeditious course. I believe that you will find that the commander intends to put you aboard Midway Station before leading his squadron to engage the remaining Remor warships in this system. It would not do to have a foreign national aboard when going into action, even with ships of that nation in the combined fleet."

Combined fleet? If he was going into battle with Combine ships, he was acknowledging that Chugen was Combine space and that he did not have absolute power here. There was no way that he would be bombarding Chugen

IV now. Their arguments must have swayed him. They saved the Hos'kimm! And with the Combine and the League working together in this system, she wouldn't be facing imprisonment as a spy; she would be going home. But— "What about Kurt?"

"Commander Stone is under strict orders to see him brought to a League facility for a full and thorough debriefing by his nation's intelligence experts. Thus Professor Ellicot is scheduled to escape onto the station, from which the commander lacks the authority to extradite him."

*This is incredible.* "It's got to be some kind of joke."

"Perhaps. But if it is, it is the universe's joke." The construct chuckled. "We must enjoy it as best we can, while we wait for the rain to come thundering down in Kansas."

"What?"

"Study your alinear sociodynamics."

It was an insufferably smug remark, but Juliana was too buoyed by relief to be argumentative.

"Out of complexity, order," the construct continued. "The ripple spreads and becomes a wave. The Hos'kimm and their like shall be free of accusation in the war, and though the war with the Remor remains, we are closer to knowing the enemy's true face. It is a turning point of history, in which you have played your part and played it well. You have my thanks; and my appreciation, like your freedom, will come in due course. Nearly all is well. Can you see the bright sun sparkling on the crest of the wave? The conjunction has reached anthesis, blooming in its full glory. Only a few more pieces need to fall into place for the new equilibrium to be established." The construct's face lost its rapt expression, and a sly smile crept across it. "Ah, another rivulet joins the stream."

The construct's image vanished as someone rapped on the hatch. The door opened before Juliana could respond,

making the warning the most minimal of courtesies. A soldier stood in the hall, her hand on Kurt's elbow.

"He asked the commander if he could see you, ma'am."

"Alone," Kurt said.

The soldier eyed Kurt as if he were some kind of bug. "I
can stay if you'd like."

"It's all right," Juliana heard herself say, but she wondered if it really *was* all right.

Kurt stepped into her cabin, one step, no more. The dis-
approving soldier shut the door. Disturbed by his reserve,
she waited for him to speak.

"Stone told me that he will not sterilize the Hos'kimm's
world," he finally said. "The pack is safe."

"Yes, isn't it wonderful? We convinced him. We saved
the Hos'kimm."

"Yes," he said tonelessly.

His joylessness puzzled her. Maybe he was still worried
about what would happen to the two of them. "Didn't he
tell you he's setting us free?"

"Yes."

Now she *really* didn't understand and told him so. "Why
are you looking like he gave you a death sentence?"

He took a long time to answer. Ghosts of conflicting
expressions chased each other across his face. "They will
want me to go back to Chugen."

"But isn't that the best thing that could happen? This
time you can do what you set out to do. There won't be any
intrigue this time, just the Hos'kimm. They are a mar-
velous species and there is so much more to learn."

"I can't go back," Kurt said, body shaking his voice to a
stammer. "If I do I'll become one of them. It happened
before. I don't want to lose my self."

"But you didn't."

"I came so close. The call of the Other has always been

strong in me. I never really was Grammanhatay, but Kurtellicot was . . . stronger." He swallowed and, head hanging, gave a hopeless sigh. "I have a Hos'kimm symbiont living in me, and it changes everything. Now the Other has a real voice. How can I not listen? The pack whispers in my mind. If I go back there, I will fall into the Hos'kimm nature."

"Maybe. If you went alone." The symbiont was a big unknown, and it worried her, but she refused to let him see that concern. He needed to see her concern for *him*. She lifted his head. "But you won't be alone. You'll have an anchor."

He looked at her questioningly.

"I'll be your anchor," she promised, stepping close to him. "And I *won't* let you go."

"I can't ask you to."

She put a finger to his lips. "I want to."

He placed his hands to either side of her head, tilted her face up, and stared deeply into her eyes. He must have found what he sought, for he smiled. And kissed her.

She kissed back, wrapping him in an embrace. His arms were strong around her. As she backed her way to the bed, Juliana heard the soft click of the Alsion construct shutting down.

The battlesuited trooper who appeared at the cabin door said nothing, merely motioned Kurt to accompany him. Still floating in the memory of Juli, Kurt felt no fear, only anticipation. Juli had gone aboard Midway Station shortly after the *Constantine* docked. She was waiting there for him.

The future awaited him too, far brighter than he'd known for years.

The corridors through which they passed were empty. During the entire trip to the airlock, they encountered no one, an occurrence foreign to Kurt's limited experience aboard the warship. *Constantine* seemed a strange, hollowed-out place, empty of its life.

On entering the airlock, the trooper pointed to the pants and shirt neatly folded and tethered to the floor, then at Kurt's nakedness.

Kurt looked down at himself. As was his right, around his neck and waist he wore his few remaining signs and symbols of a Hos'kimm elder and seer. He was no more naked than any member of the pack, but most of those waiting aboard the station would lack understanding. They knew only their own Way. One would understand, but she was wiser than many, a seer of sorts herself. She would understand, but then, she was exceptional.

Kurt bent and released the garments. Tumbling awkwardly in the airlock's zero-G, he managed to tug on the pants and shrug into the shirt. He would look more Human now. It was fitting.

The trooper offered a hand to steady him and orient him to the station's airlock.

Kurt wanted to thank the man and, having recently gained a newfound hold on his own identity, to thank him by name, but the suit's insignia was blank. No name was to be seen, not even rank marking or national flash appeared on the dark surface of the armor. Kurt had to content himself with a simple "Thank you."

The soldier said nothing. He just stepped back on board the *Constantine* and cycled the airlock closed.

The hatch to Midway Station started to slide open. Kurt pushed himself forward happily, eager to get on with his life. There was going to be a lot to do for a man with his feet in two worlds.